PAK   MIYAZAWA   HERRING

MECH CADETS™

COMMAND AND CONTROL

Published by

MECH CADETS

COMMAND AND CONTROL

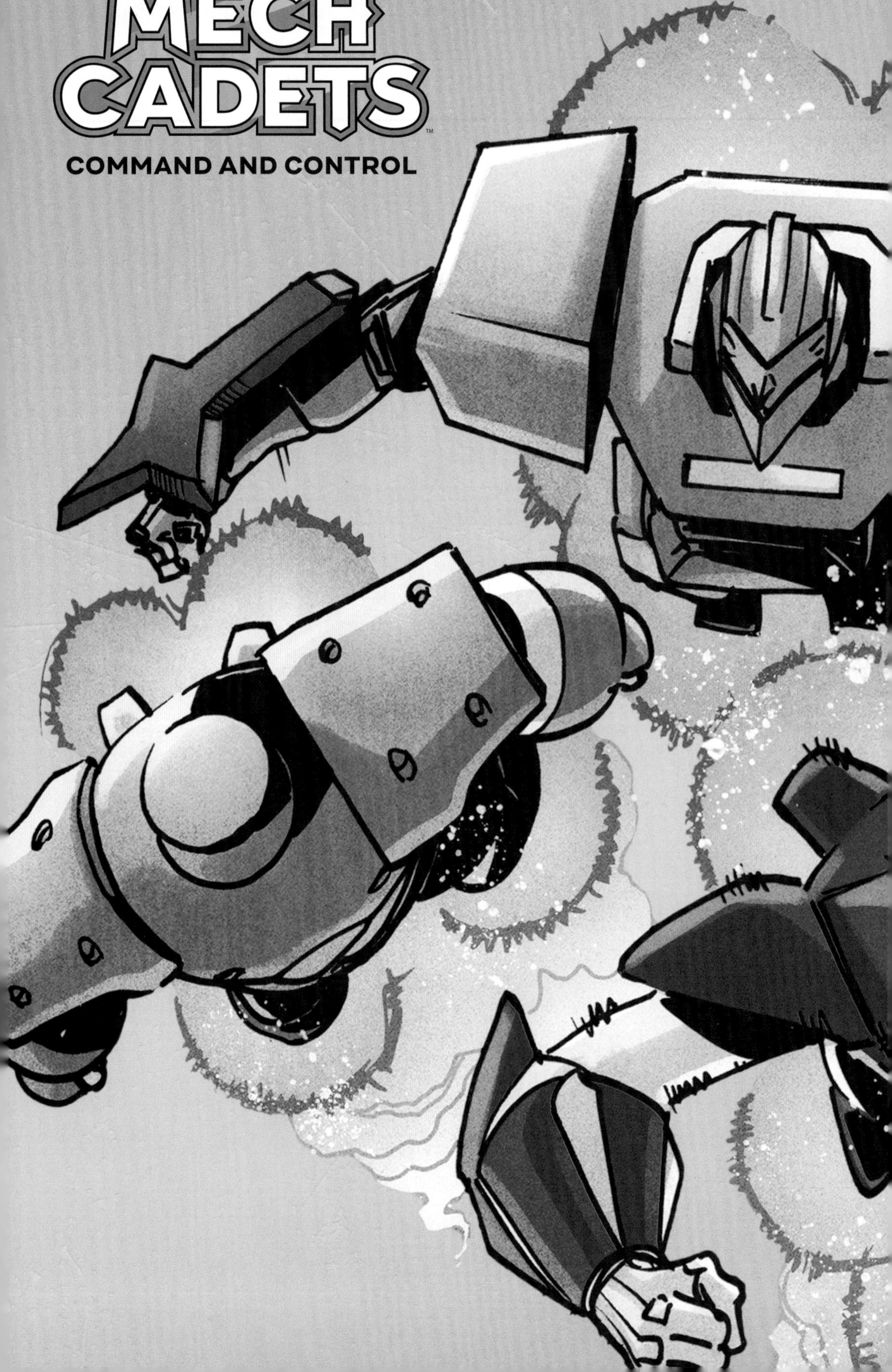

Written by
GREG PAK

Illustrated by
TAKESHI MIYAZAWA

Colored by
IAN HERRING

Lettered by
SIMON BOWLAND

Cover and Chapter Art by
TAKESHI MIYAZAWA
with **IAN HERRING**

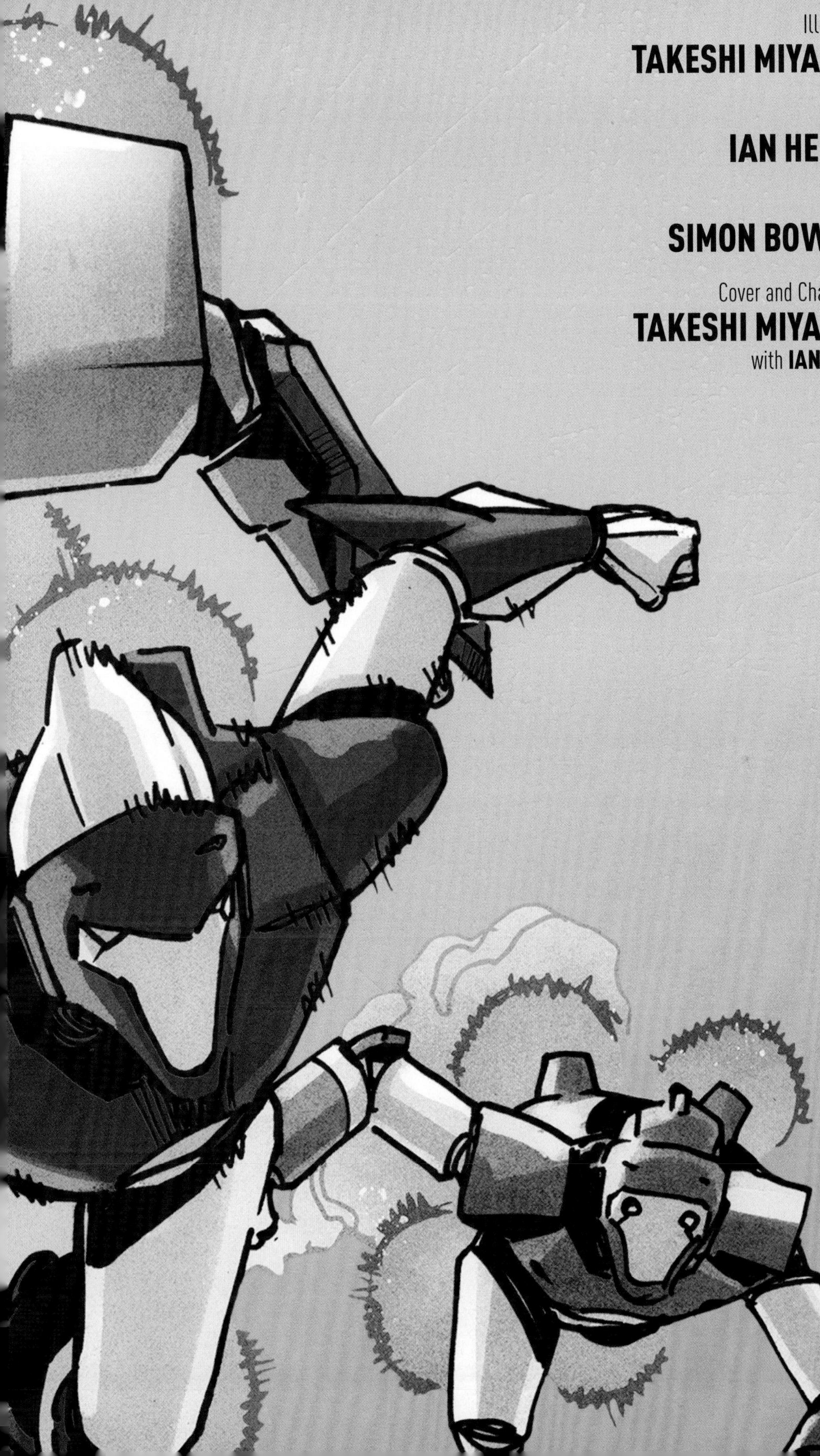

Series Designer
NANCY MOJIA

Collection Designer
ARMANDO ELIZONDO

Editor
SHANTEL LaROCQUE

kaboom!™   **MECH CADET: COMMAND AND CONTROL,** July 2024. Published by KaBOOM!, a division of Boom Entertainment, Inc. Mech Cadets™ & © 2024 Pak Man Productions, Ltd. & Takeshi Miyazawa. All rights reserved. Originally published in single magazine form as MECH CADETS No. 1–6™ & © 2023, 2024 Pak Man Productions, Ltd. & Takeshi Miyazawa. All rights reserved. KaBOOM!™ and the KaBOOM! logo are trademarks of Boom Entertainment, Inc., registered in various countries and categories. All characters, events, and institutions depicted herein are fictional. Any similarity between any of the names, characters, persons, events, and/or institutions in this publication to actual names, characters, and persons, whether living or dead, events, and/or institutions is unintended and purely coincidental. KaBOOM! does not read or accept unsolicited submissions of ideas, stories, or artwork.

KaBOOM!, 6920 Melrose Avenue, Los Angeles, CA 90038-3306. Printed in Canada. First Printing.

ISBN: 978-1-60886-239-9, eISBN: 978-1-60886-244-3

CHAPTER ONE

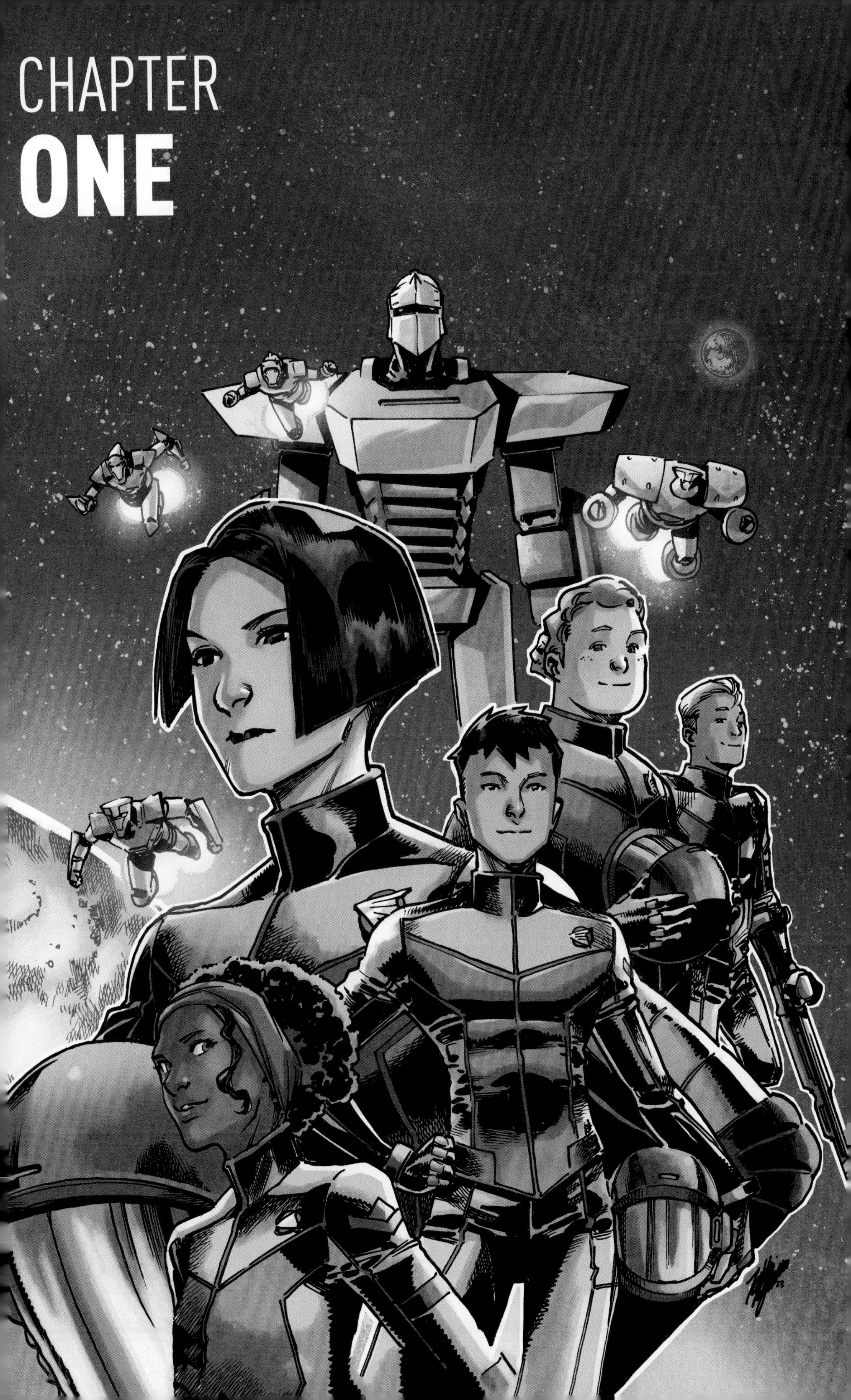

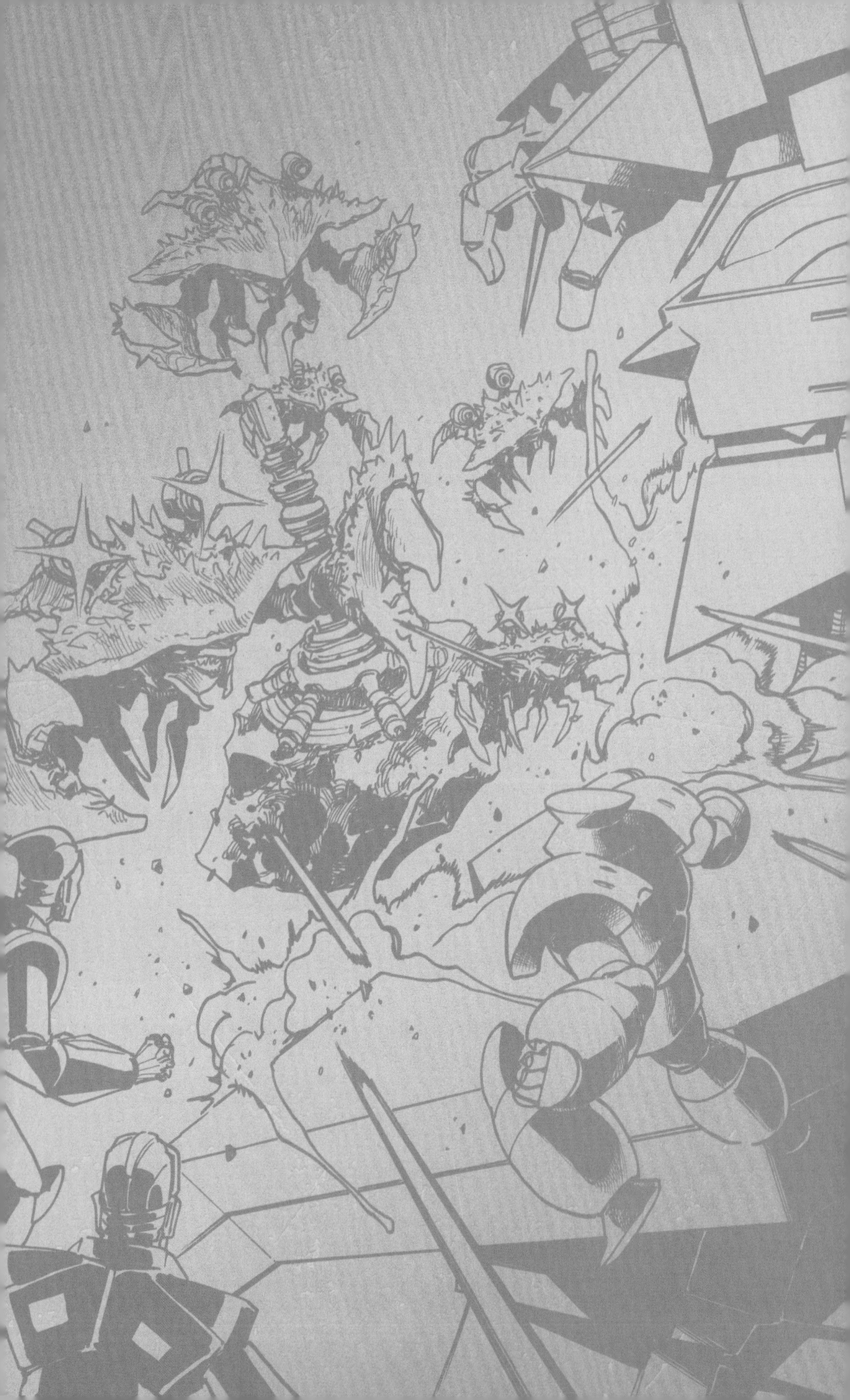

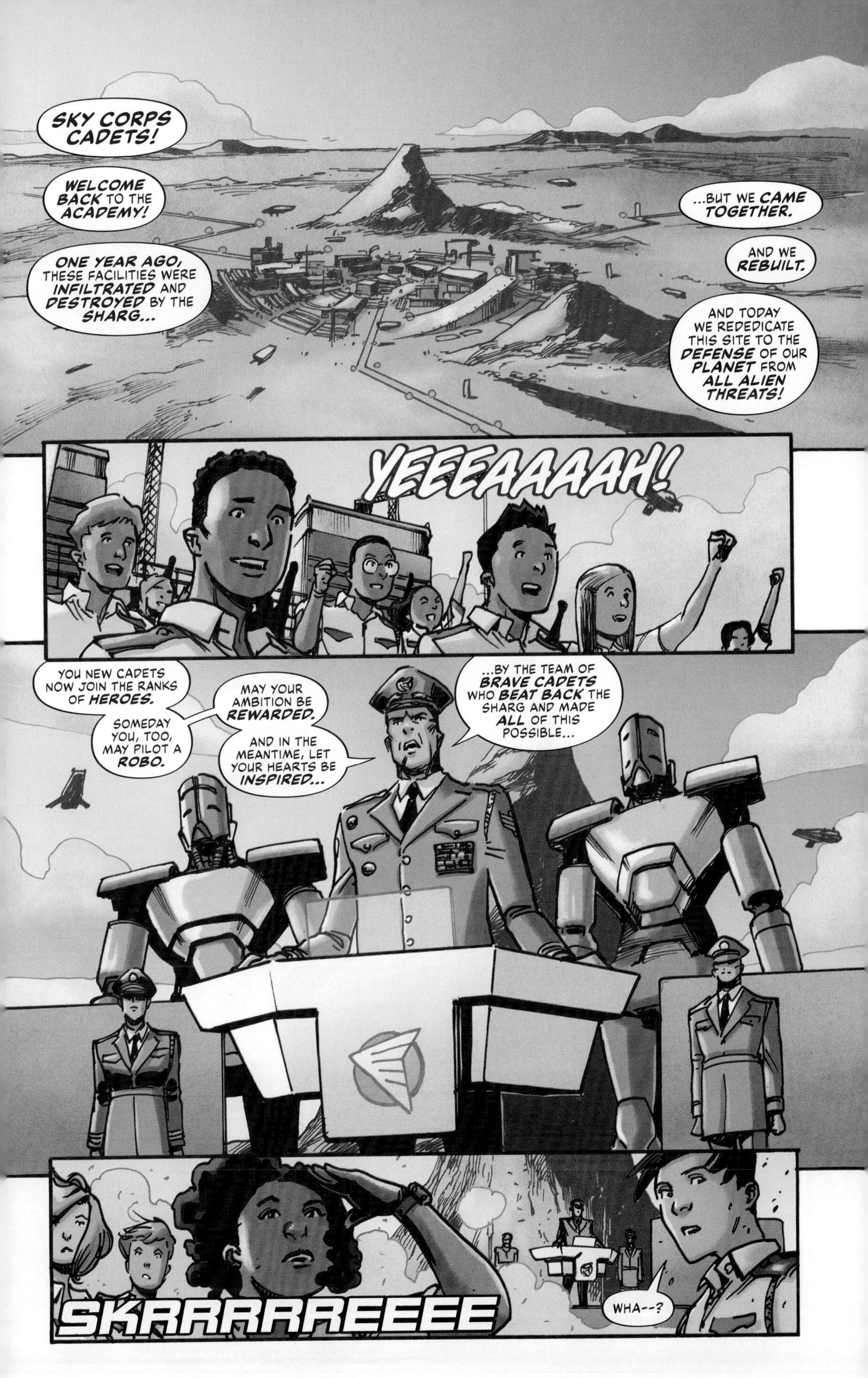

SKY CORPS CADETS!
WELCOME BACK TO THE ACADEMY!
ONE YEAR AGO, THESE FACILITIES WERE INFILTRATED AND DESTROYED BY THE SHARG...
...BUT WE CAME TOGETHER.
AND WE REBUILT.
AND TODAY WE REDEDICATE THIS SITE TO THE DEFENSE OF OUR PLANET FROM ALL ALIEN THREATS!
YEEEAAAAAH!
YOU NEW CADETS NOW JOIN THE RANKS OF HEROES.
SOMEDAY YOU, TOO, MAY PILOT A ROBO.
MAY YOUR AMBITION BE REWARDED.
AND IN THE MEANTIME, LET YOUR HEARTS BE INSPIRED...
...BY THE TEAM OF BRAVE CADETS WHO BEAT BACK THE SHARG AND MADE ALL OF THIS POSSIBLE...
SKRRRRRREEEE
WHA--?

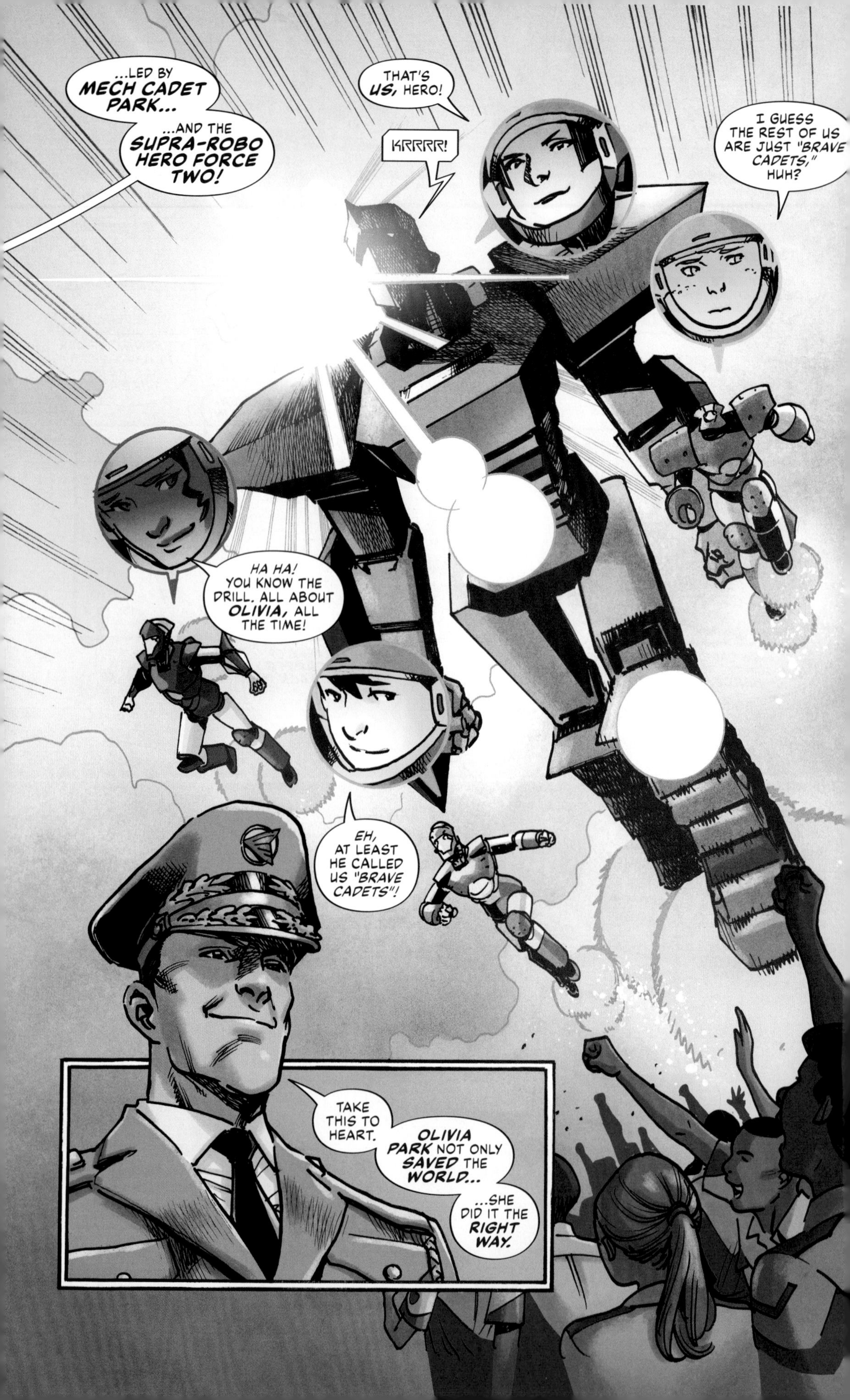
...LED BY MECH CADET PARK...
...AND THE SUPRA-ROBO HERO FORCE TWO!
THAT'S US, HERO!
KRRRR!
I GUESS THE REST OF US ARE JUST "BRAVE CADETS," HUH?
HA HA! YOU KNOW THE DRILL. ALL ABOUT OLIVIA, ALL THE TIME!
EH, AT LEAST HE CALLED US "BRAVE CADETS"!
TAKE THIS TO HEART.
OLIVIA PARK NOT ONLY SAVED THE WORLD...
...SHE DID IT THE RIGHT WAY.

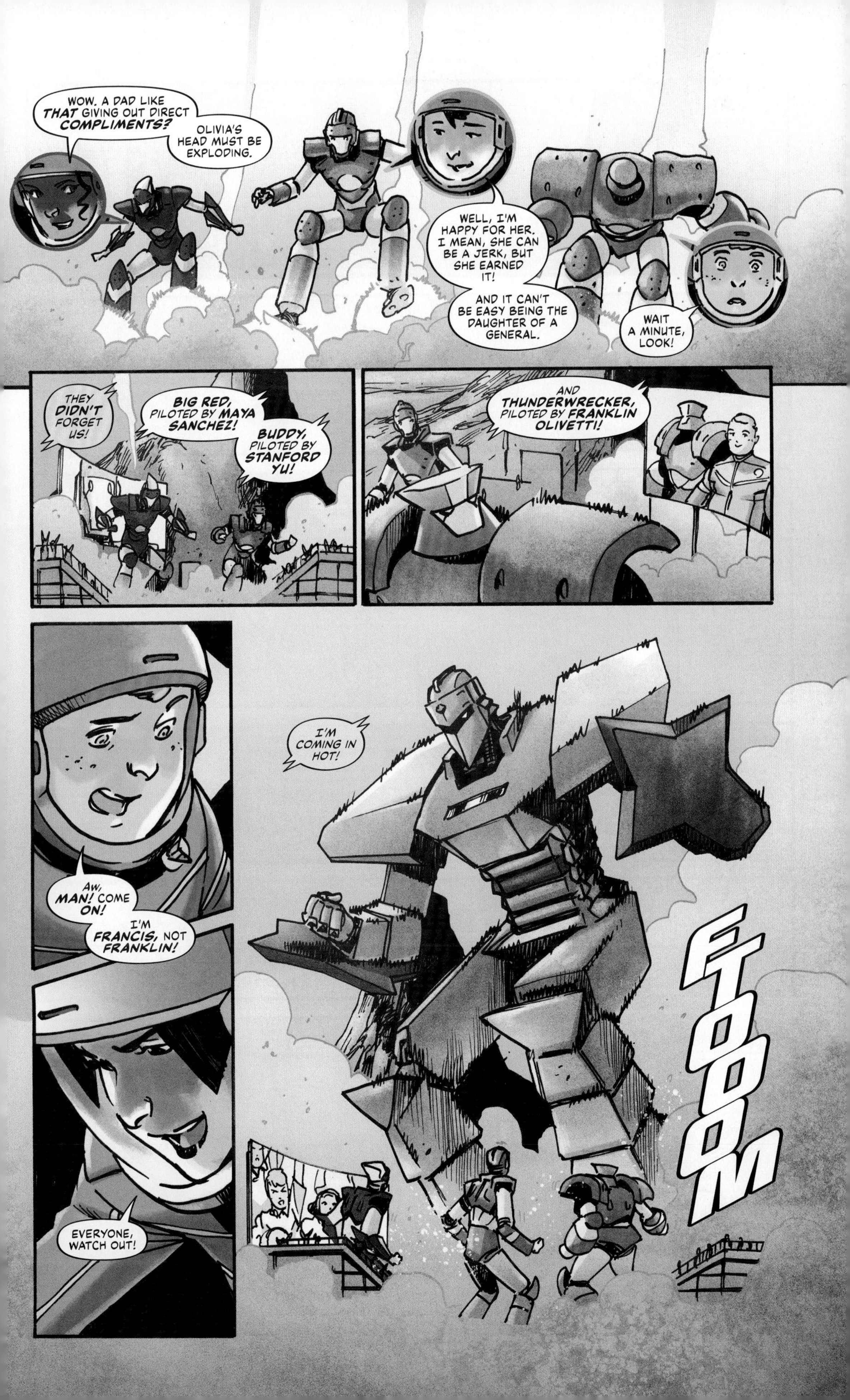
WOW. A DAD LIKE **THAT** GIVING OUT DIRECT **COMPLIMENTS?**
OLIVIA'S HEAD MUST BE EXPLODING.
WELL, I'M HAPPY FOR HER. I MEAN, SHE CAN BE A JERK, BUT SHE EARNED IT!
AND IT CAN'T BE EASY BEING THE DAUGHTER OF A GENERAL.
WAIT A MINUTE, LOOK!
THEY **DIDN'T** FORGET US!
BIG RED, PILOTED BY **MAYA SANCHEZ!**
BUDDY, PILOTED BY **STANFORD YU!**
AND **THUNDERWRECKER,** PILOTED BY **FRANKLIN OLIVETTI!**
AW, **MAN!** COME **ON!**
I'M **FRANCIS,** NOT **FRANKLIN!**
I'M COMING IN HOT!
EVERYONE, WATCH OUT!
FTOOOM

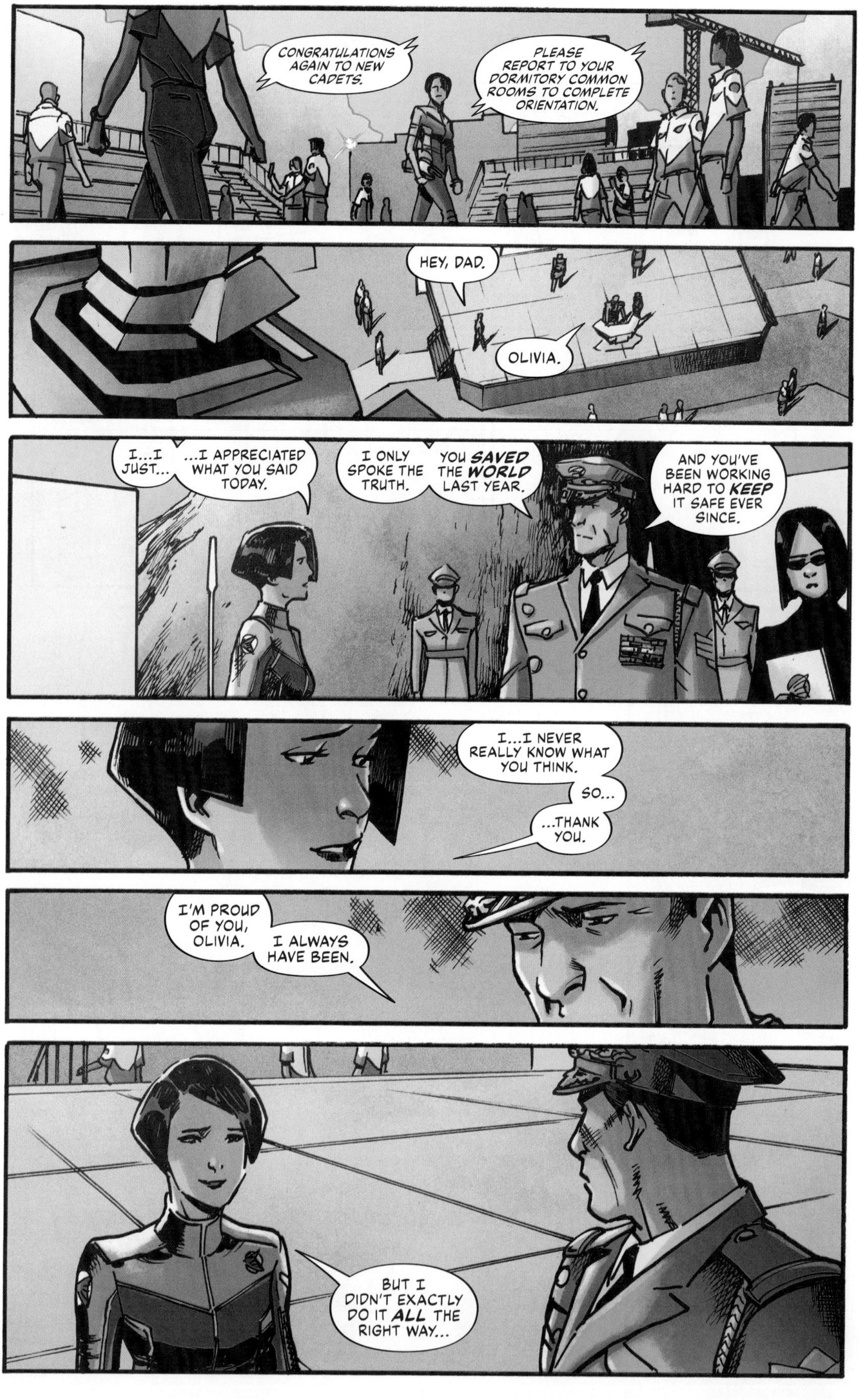
CONGRATULATIONS AGAIN TO NEW CADETS.
PLEASE REPORT TO YOUR DORMITORY COMMON ROOMS TO COMPLETE ORIENTATION.
HEY, DAD.
OLIVIA.
I...I JUST...
...I APPRECIATED WHAT YOU SAID TODAY.
I ONLY SPOKE THE TRUTH.
YOU SAVED THE WORLD LAST YEAR.
AND YOU'VE BEEN WORKING HARD TO KEEP IT SAFE EVER SINCE.
I...I NEVER REALLY KNOW WHAT YOU THINK.
SO...
...THANK YOU.
I'M PROUD OF YOU, OLIVIA.
I ALWAYS HAVE BEEN.
BUT I DIDN'T EXACTLY DO IT ALL THE RIGHT WAY...

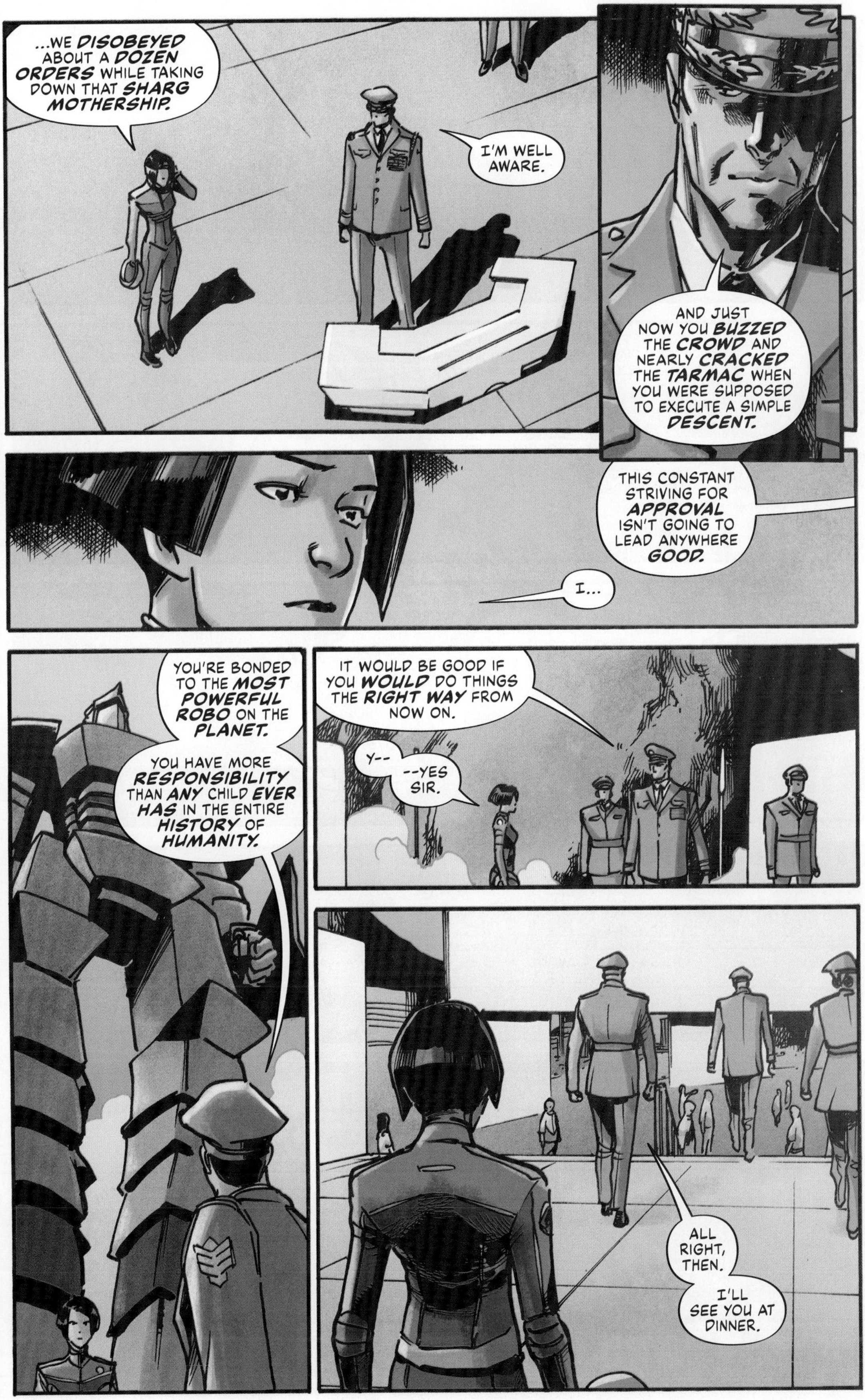
...WE DISOBEYED ABOUT A DOZEN ORDERS WHILE TAKING DOWN THAT SHARG MOTHERSHIP.
I'M WELL AWARE.
AND JUST NOW YOU BUZZED THE CROWD AND NEARLY CRACKED THE TARMAC WHEN YOU WERE SUPPOSED TO EXECUTE A SIMPLE DESCENT.
THIS CONSTANT STRIVING FOR APPROVAL ISN'T GOING TO LEAD ANYWHERE GOOD.
I...
YOU'RE BONDED TO THE MOST POWERFUL ROBO ON THE PLANET.
YOU HAVE MORE RESPONSIBILITY THAN ANY CHILD EVER HAS IN THE ENTIRE HISTORY OF HUMANITY.
IT WOULD BE GOOD IF YOU WOULD DO THINGS THE RIGHT WAY FROM NOW ON.
Y--
--YES SIR.
ALL RIGHT, THEN.
I'LL SEE YOU AT DINNER.

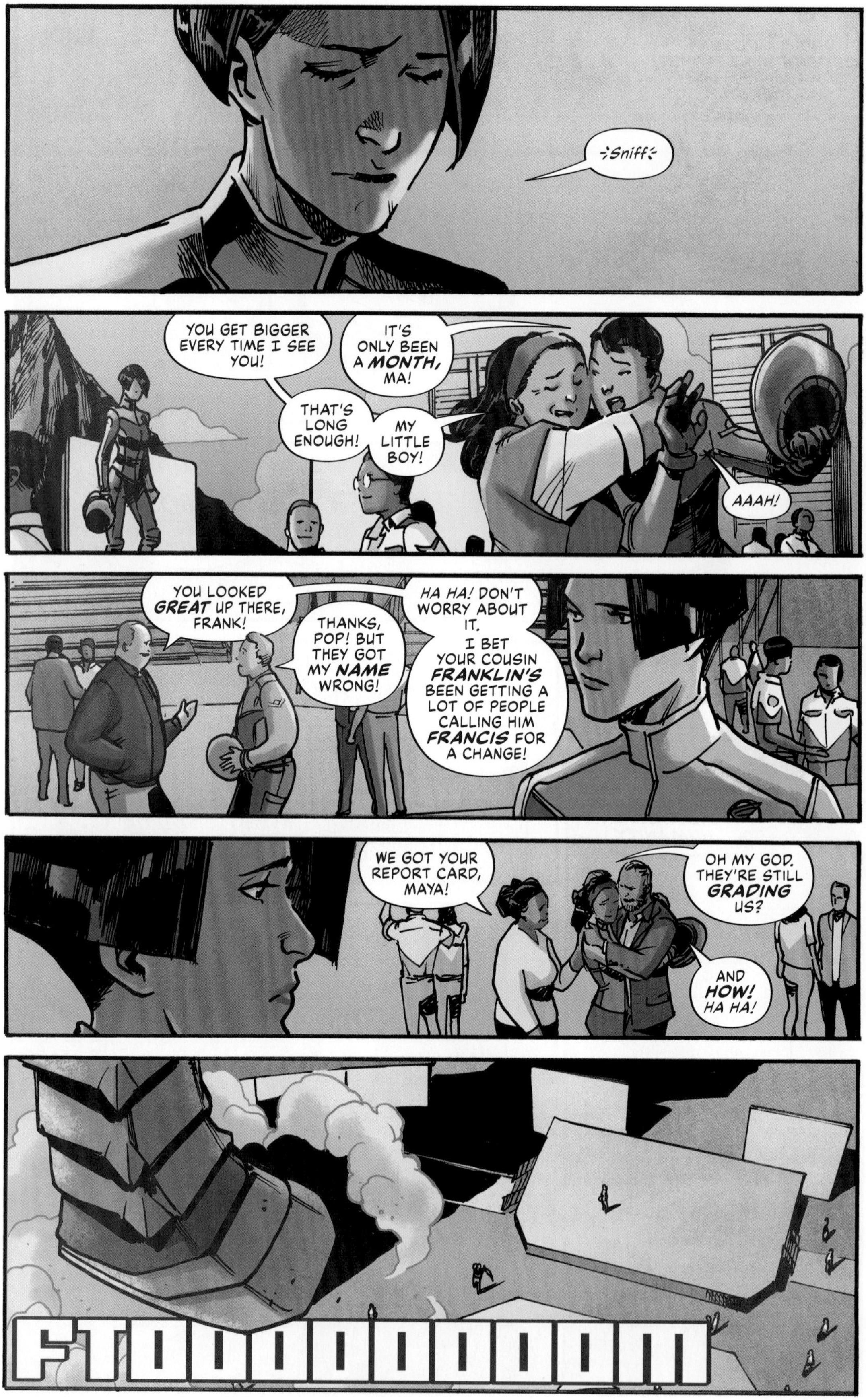

Sniff
YOU GET BIGGER EVERY TIME I SEE YOU!
IT'S ONLY BEEN A **MONTH,** MA!
THAT'S LONG ENOUGH!
MY LITTLE BOY!
AAAH!
YOU LOOKED **GREAT** UP THERE, FRANK!
THANKS, POP! BUT THEY GOT MY **NAME** WRONG!
HA HA! DON'T WORRY ABOUT IT.
I BET YOUR COUSIN **FRANKLIN'S** BEEN GETTING A LOT OF PEOPLE CALLING HIM **FRANCIS** FOR A CHANGE!
WE GOT YOUR REPORT CARD, MAYA!
OH MY GOD. THEY'RE STILL **GRADING** US?
AND **HOW!** HA HA!
FTOOOOOOOOM

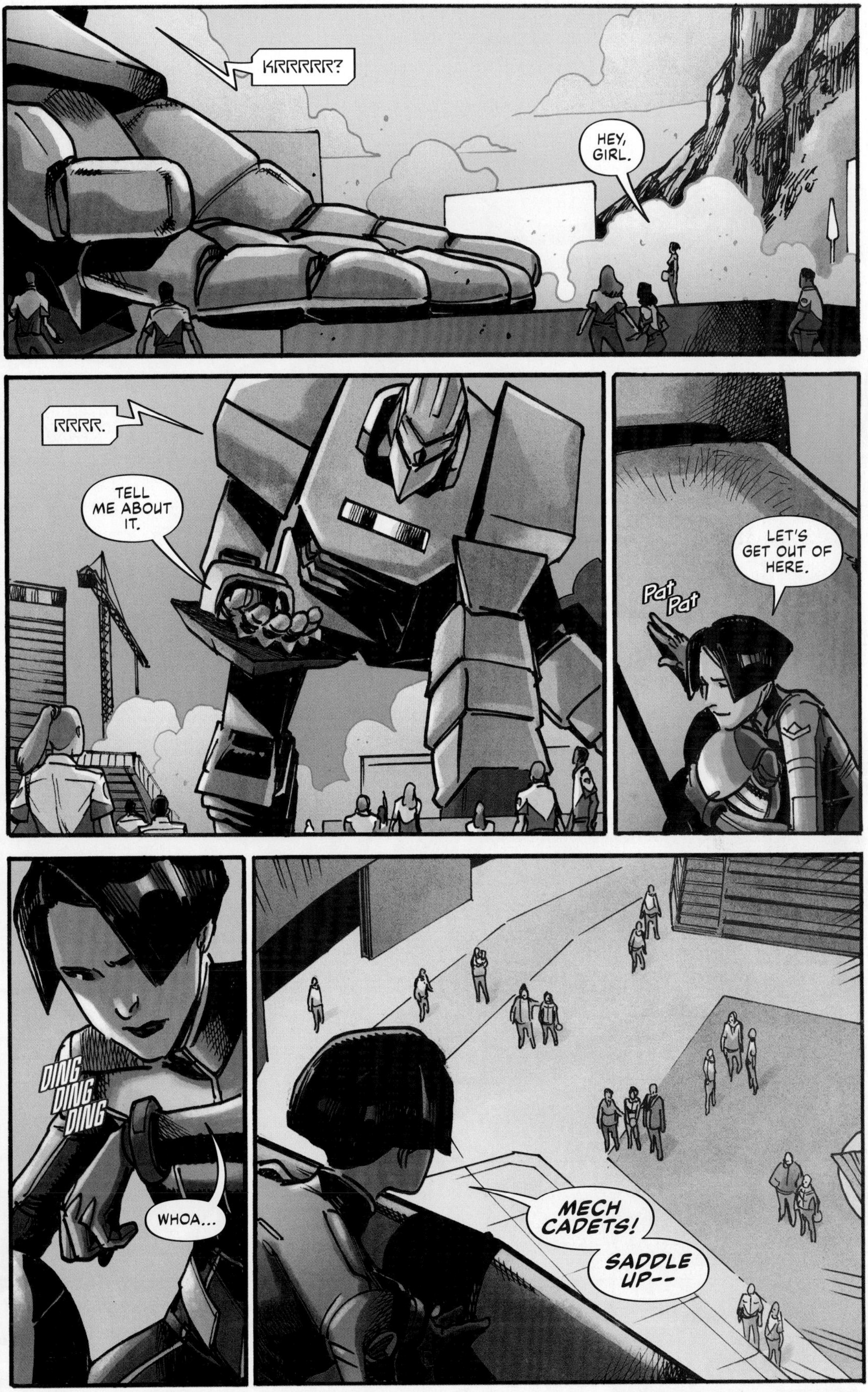
KRRRRRR?
HEY, GIRL.
RRRR.
TELL ME ABOUT IT.
LET'S GET OUT OF HERE.
Pat Pat
DING DING DING
WHOA...
MECH CADETS!
SADDLE UP--

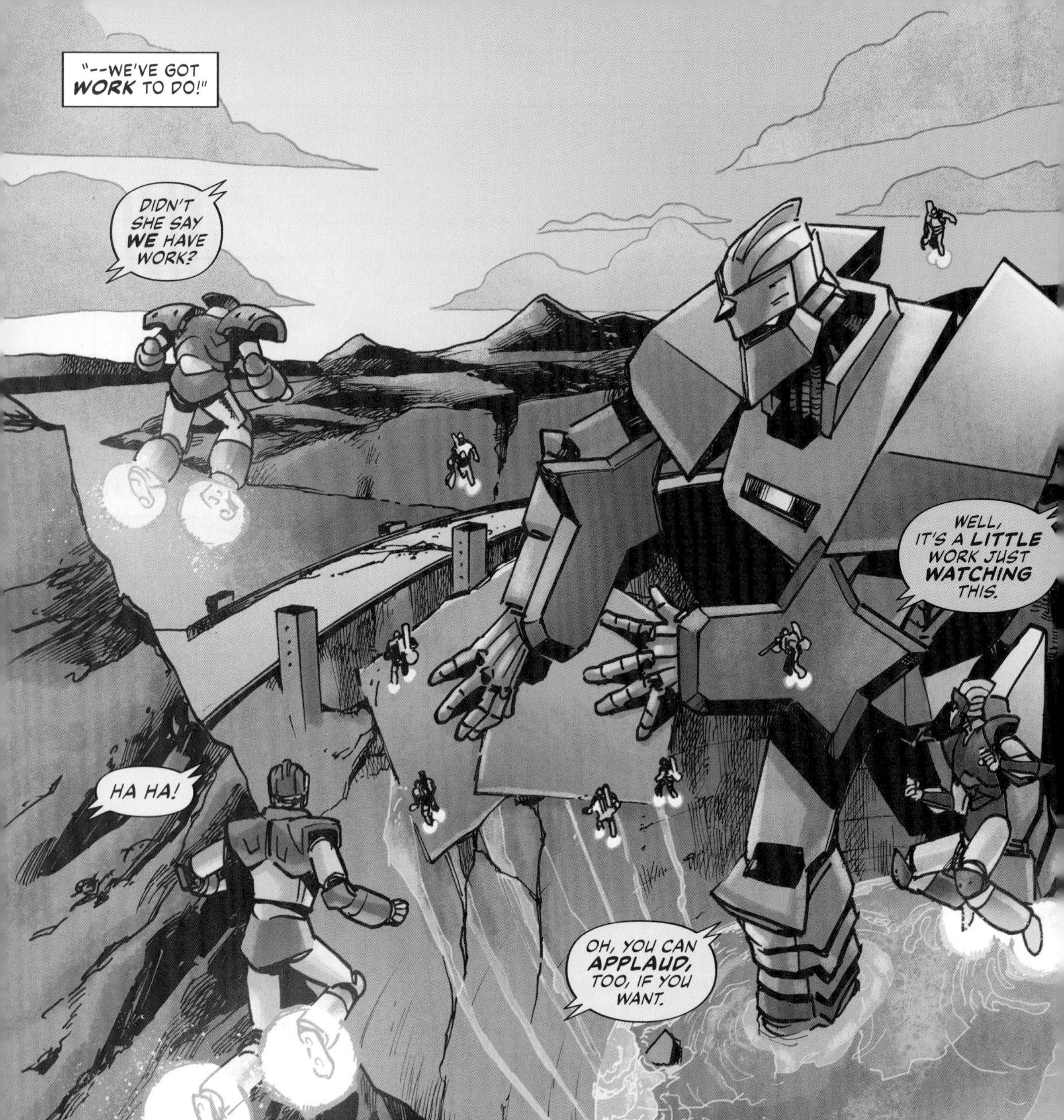
"--WE'VE GOT WORK TO DO!"
DIDN'T SHE SAY WE HAVE WORK?
WELL, IT'S A LITTLE WORK JUST WATCHING THIS.
HA HA!
OH, YOU CAN APPLAUD, TOO, IF YOU WANT.
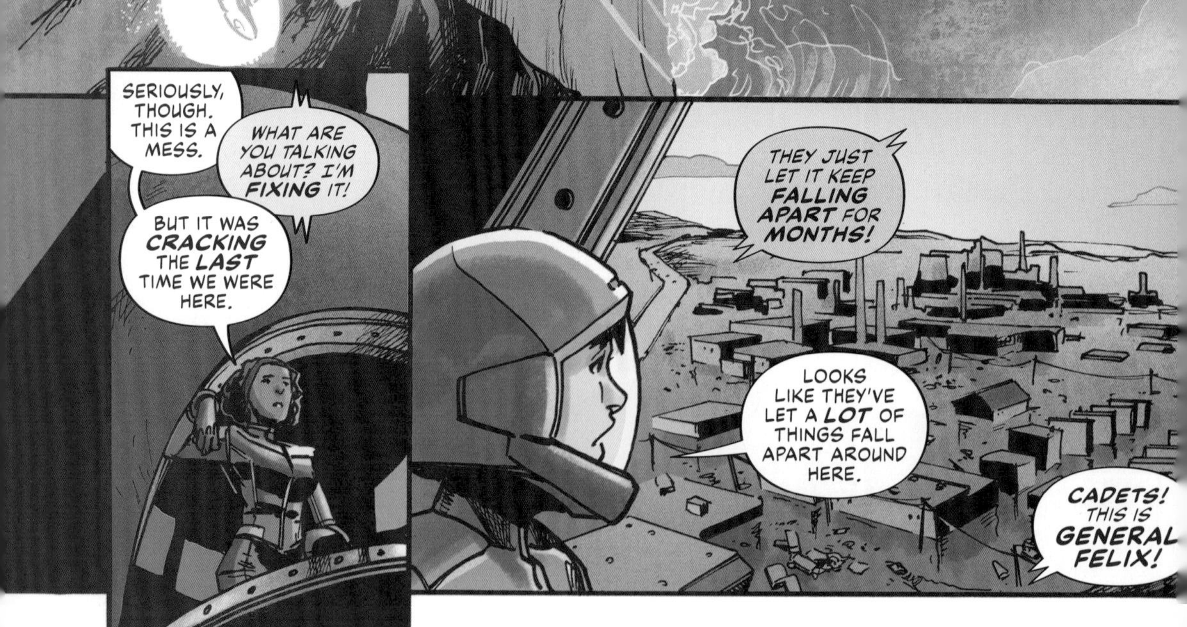
SERIOUSLY, THOUGH. THIS IS A MESS.
WHAT ARE YOU TALKING ABOUT? I'M FIXING IT!
BUT IT WAS CRACKING THE LAST TIME WE WERE HERE.
THEY JUST LET IT KEEP FALLING APART FOR MONTHS!
LOOKS LIKE THEY'VE LET A LOT OF THINGS FALL APART AROUND HERE.
CADETS! THIS IS GENERAL FELIX!

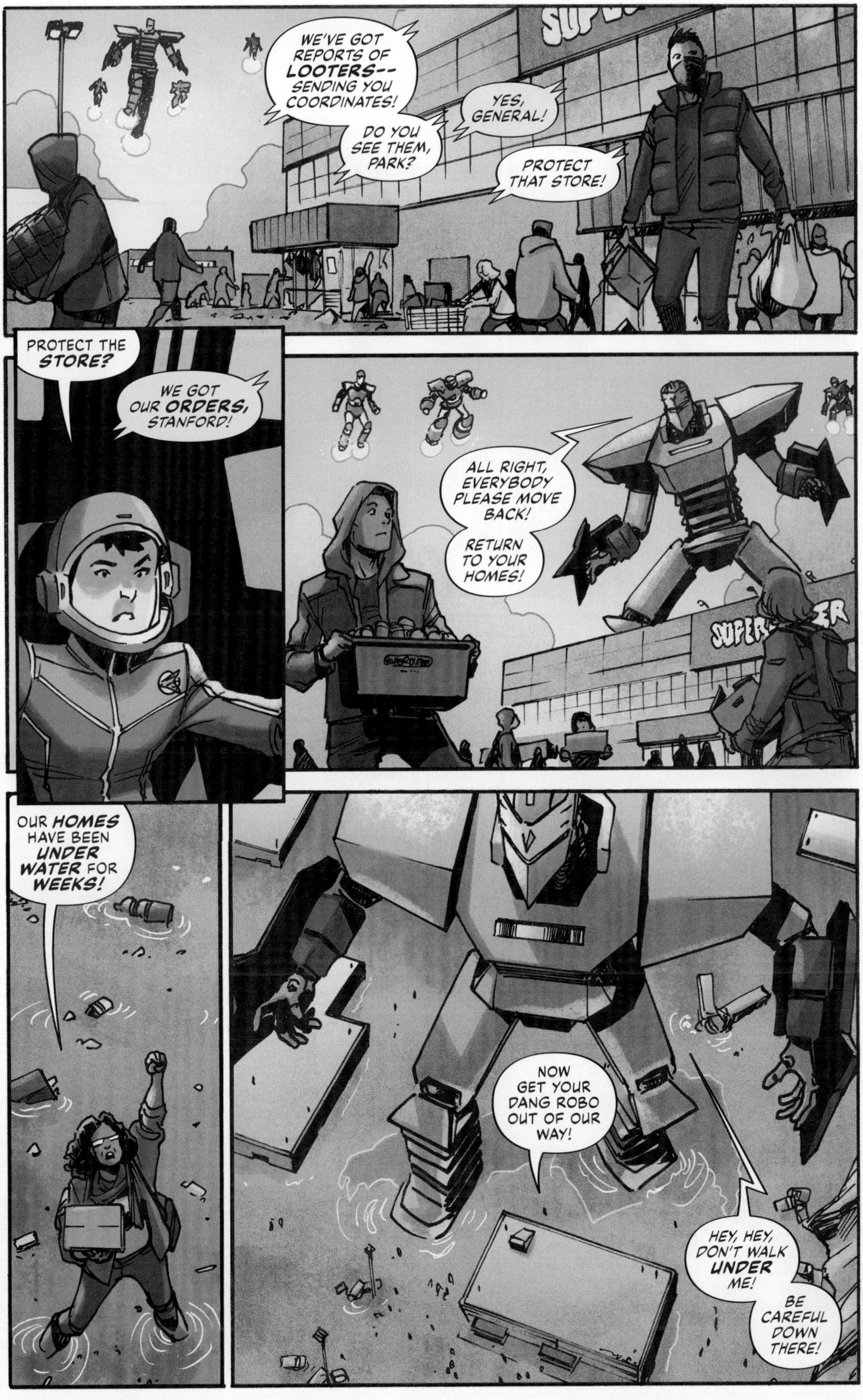
WE'VE GOT REPORTS OF LOOTERS-- SENDING YOU COORDINATES!
DO YOU SEE THEM, PARK?
YES, GENERAL!
PROTECT THAT STORE!
PROTECT THE STORE?
WE GOT OUR ORDERS, STANFORD!
ALL RIGHT, EVERYBODY PLEASE MOVE BACK!
RETURN TO YOUR HOMES!
OUR HOMES HAVE BEEN UNDER WATER FOR WEEKS!
NOW GET YOUR DANG ROBO OUT OF OUR WAY!
HEY, HEY, DON'T WALK UNDER ME!
BE CAREFUL DOWN THERE!

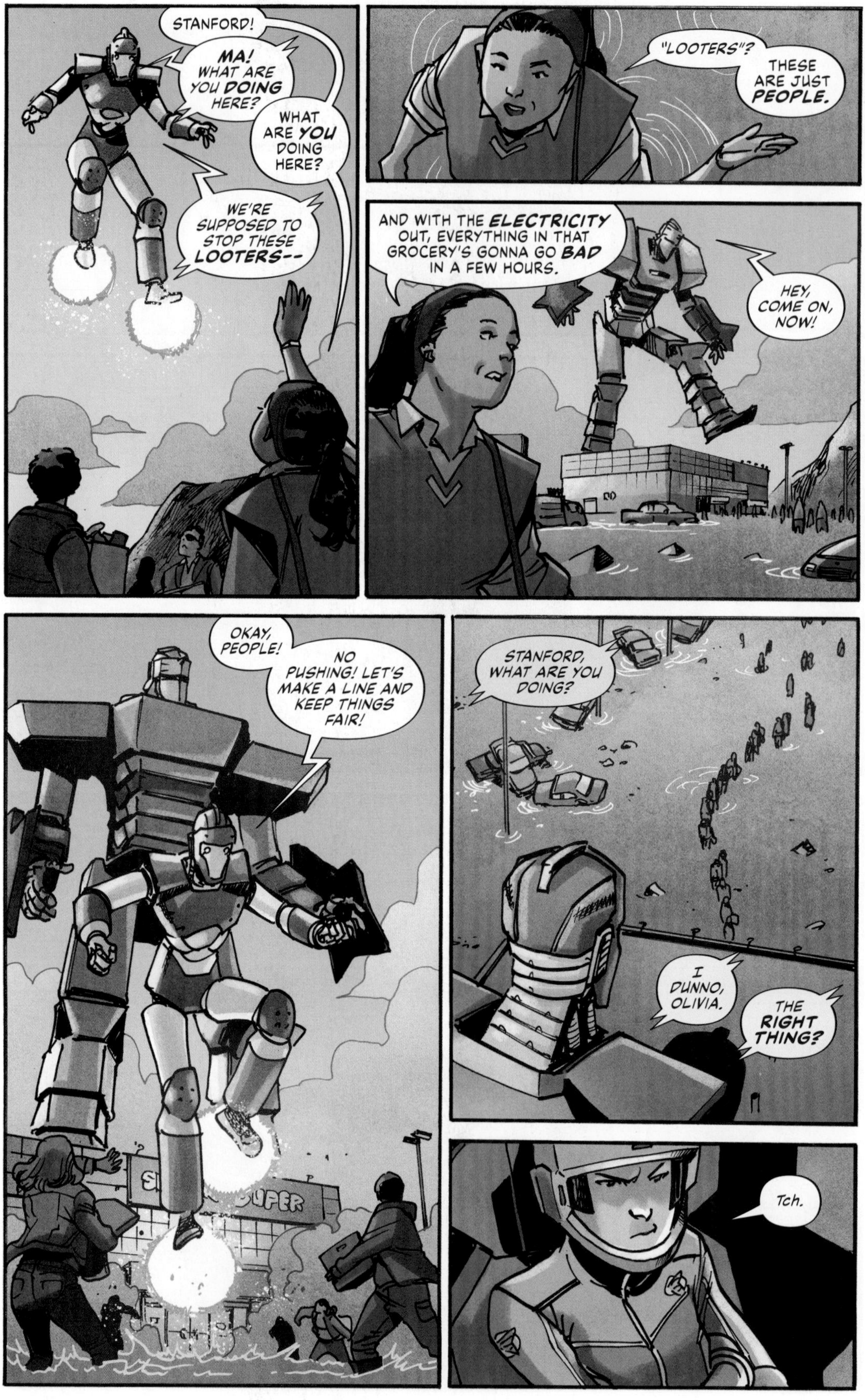
STANFORD!
MA! WHAT ARE YOU DOING HERE?
WHAT ARE YOU DOING HERE?
WE'RE SUPPOSED TO STOP THESE LOOTERS--
"LOOTERS"?
THESE ARE JUST PEOPLE.
AND WITH THE ELECTRICITY OUT, EVERYTHING IN THAT GROCERY'S GONNA GO BAD IN A FEW HOURS.
HEY, COME ON, NOW!
OKAY, PEOPLE!
NO PUSHING! LET'S MAKE A LINE AND KEEP THINGS FAIR!
STANFORD, WHAT ARE YOU DOING?
I DUNNO, OLIVIA.
THE RIGHT THING?
Tch.

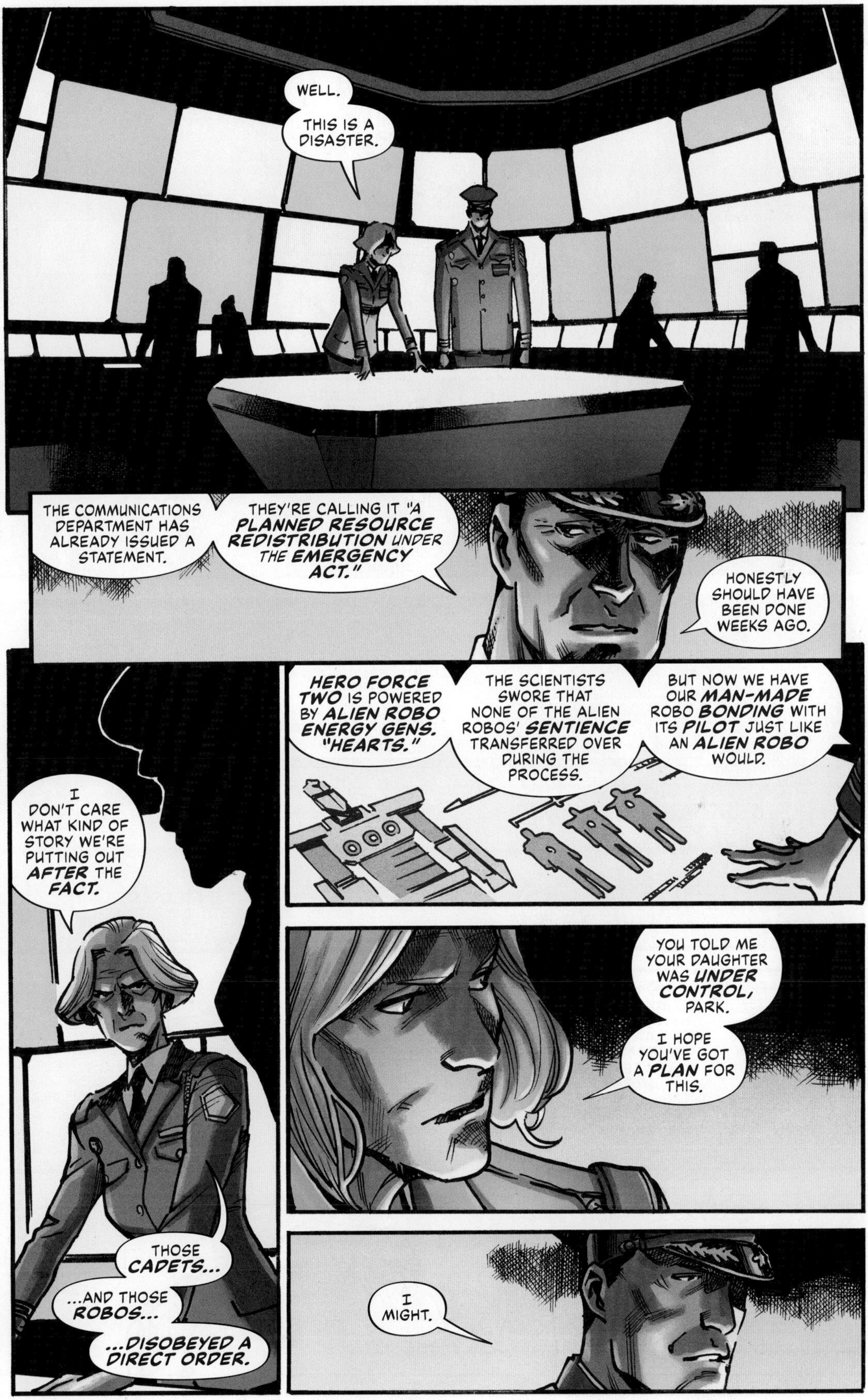
WELL.
THIS IS A DISASTER.
THE COMMUNICATIONS DEPARTMENT HAS ALREADY ISSUED A STATEMENT.
THEY'RE CALLING IT "A PLANNED RESOURCE REDISTRIBUTION UNDER THE EMERGENCY ACT."
HONESTLY SHOULD HAVE BEEN DONE WEEKS AGO.
I DON'T CARE WHAT KIND OF STORY WE'RE PUTTING OUT AFTER THE FACT.
THOSE CADETS...
...AND THOSE ROBOS...
...DISOBEYED A DIRECT ORDER.
HERO FORCE TWO IS POWERED BY ALIEN ROBO ENERGY GENS. "HEARTS."
THE SCIENTISTS SWORE THAT NONE OF THE ALIEN ROBOS' SENTIENCE TRANSFERRED OVER DURING THE PROCESS.
BUT NOW WE HAVE OUR MAN-MADE ROBO BONDING WITH ITS PILOT JUST LIKE AN ALIEN ROBO WOULD.
YOU TOLD ME YOUR DAUGHTER WAS UNDER CONTROL, PARK.
I HOPE YOU'VE GOT A PLAN FOR THIS.
I MIGHT.

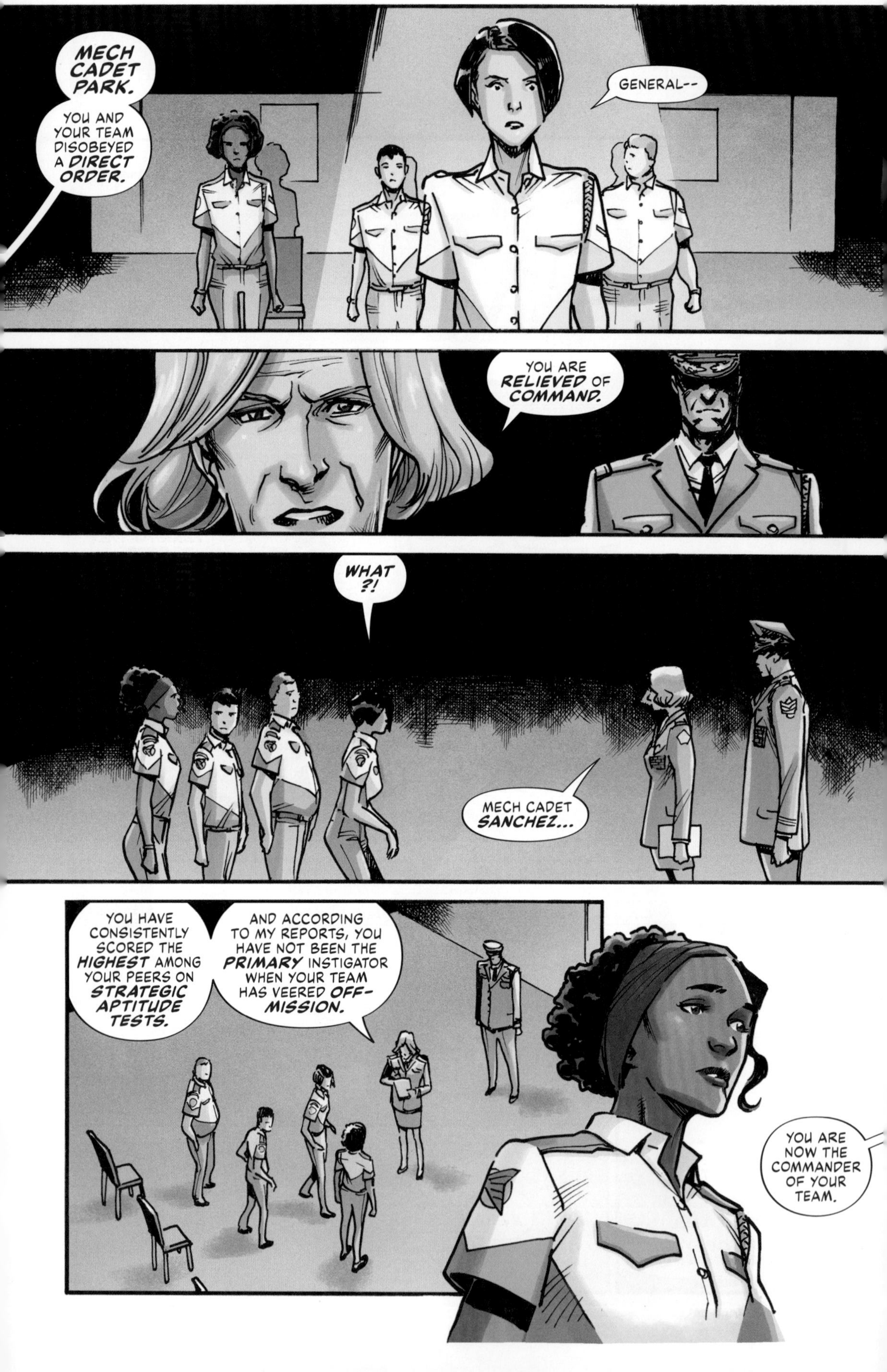

MECH CADET PARK.
YOU AND YOUR TEAM DISOBEYED A DIRECT ORDER.
GENERAL--
YOU ARE RELIEVED OF COMMAND.
WHAT ?!
MECH CADET SANCHEZ...
YOU HAVE CONSISTENTLY SCORED THE HIGHEST AMONG YOUR PEERS ON STRATEGIC APTITUDE TESTS.
AND ACCORDING TO MY REPORTS, YOU HAVE NOT BEEN THE PRIMARY INSTIGATOR WHEN YOUR TEAM HAS VEERED OFF-MISSION.
YOU ARE NOW THE COMMANDER OF YOUR TEAM.

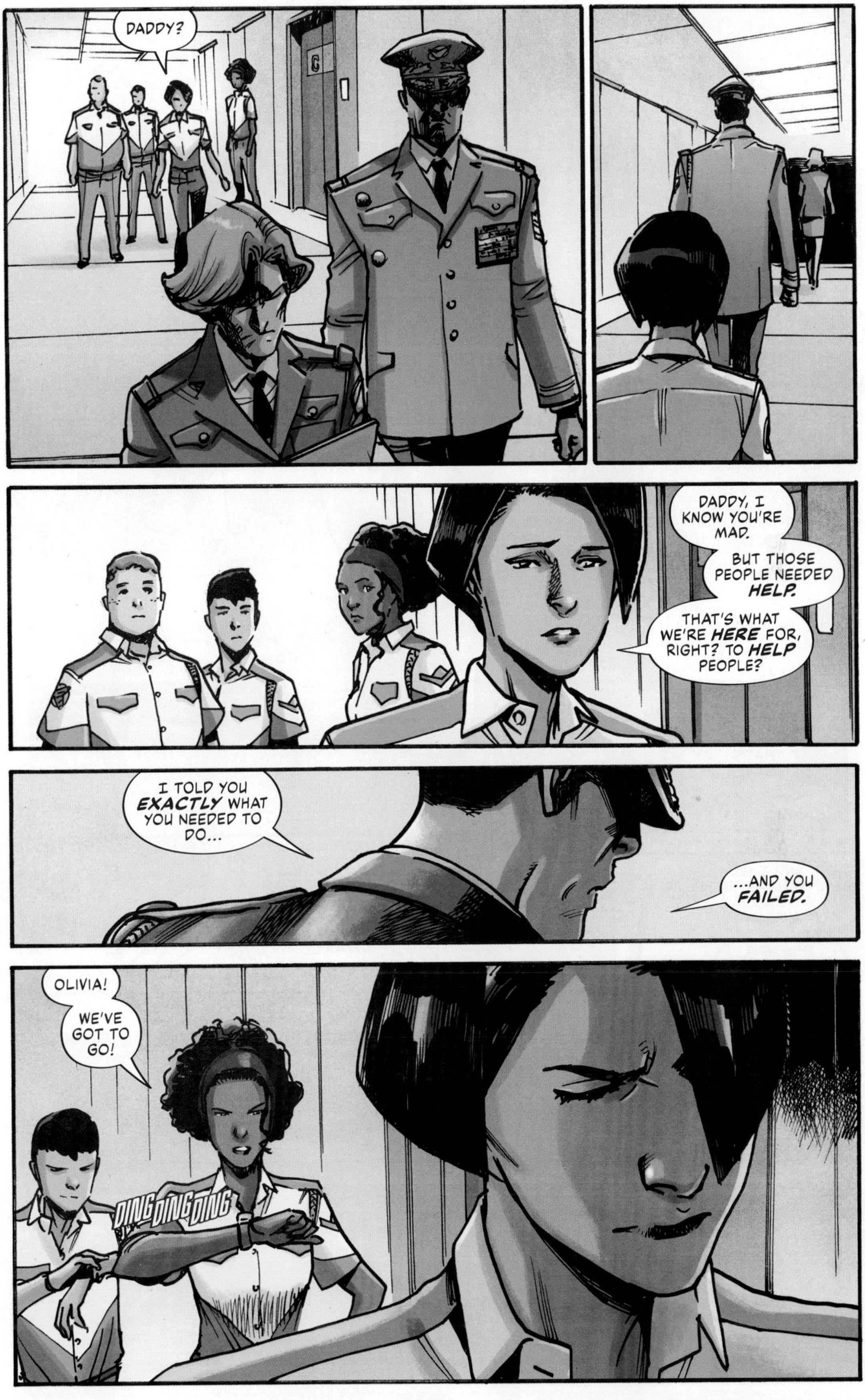

DADDY?
DADDY, I KNOW YOU'RE MAD.
BUT THOSE PEOPLE NEEDED HELP.
THAT'S WHAT WE'RE HERE FOR, RIGHT? TO HELP PEOPLE?
I TOLD YOU EXACTLY WHAT YOU NEEDED TO DO...
...AND YOU FAILED.
OLIVIA!
WE'VE GOT TO GO!
DING DING DING

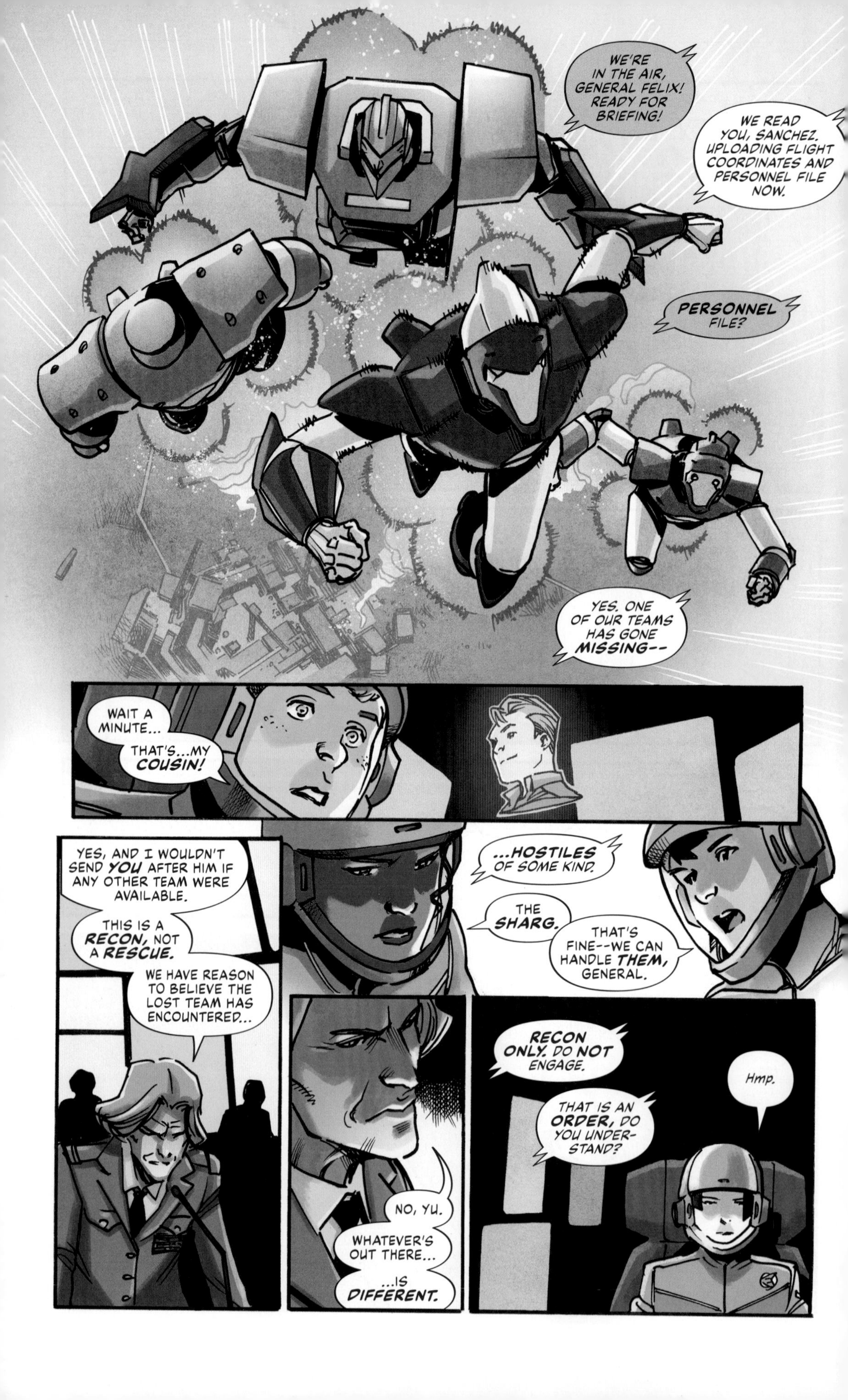
WE'RE IN THE AIR, GENERAL FELIX! READY FOR BRIEFING!
WE READ YOU, SANCHEZ. UPLOADING FLIGHT COORDINATES AND PERSONNEL FILE NOW.
PERSONNEL FILE?
YES. ONE OF OUR TEAMS HAS GONE MISSING--
WAIT A MINUTE...
THAT'S...MY COUSIN!
YES, AND I WOULDN'T SEND YOU AFTER HIM IF ANY OTHER TEAM WERE AVAILABLE.
THIS IS A RECON, NOT A RESCUE.
WE HAVE REASON TO BELIEVE THE LOST TEAM HAS ENCOUNTERED...
...HOSTILES OF SOME KIND.
THE SHARG.
THAT'S FINE--WE CAN HANDLE THEM, GENERAL.
NO, YU.
WHATEVER'S OUT THERE...
...IS DIFFERENT.
RECON ONLY. DO NOT ENGAGE.
THAT IS AN ORDER, DO YOU UNDER-STAND?
Hmp.

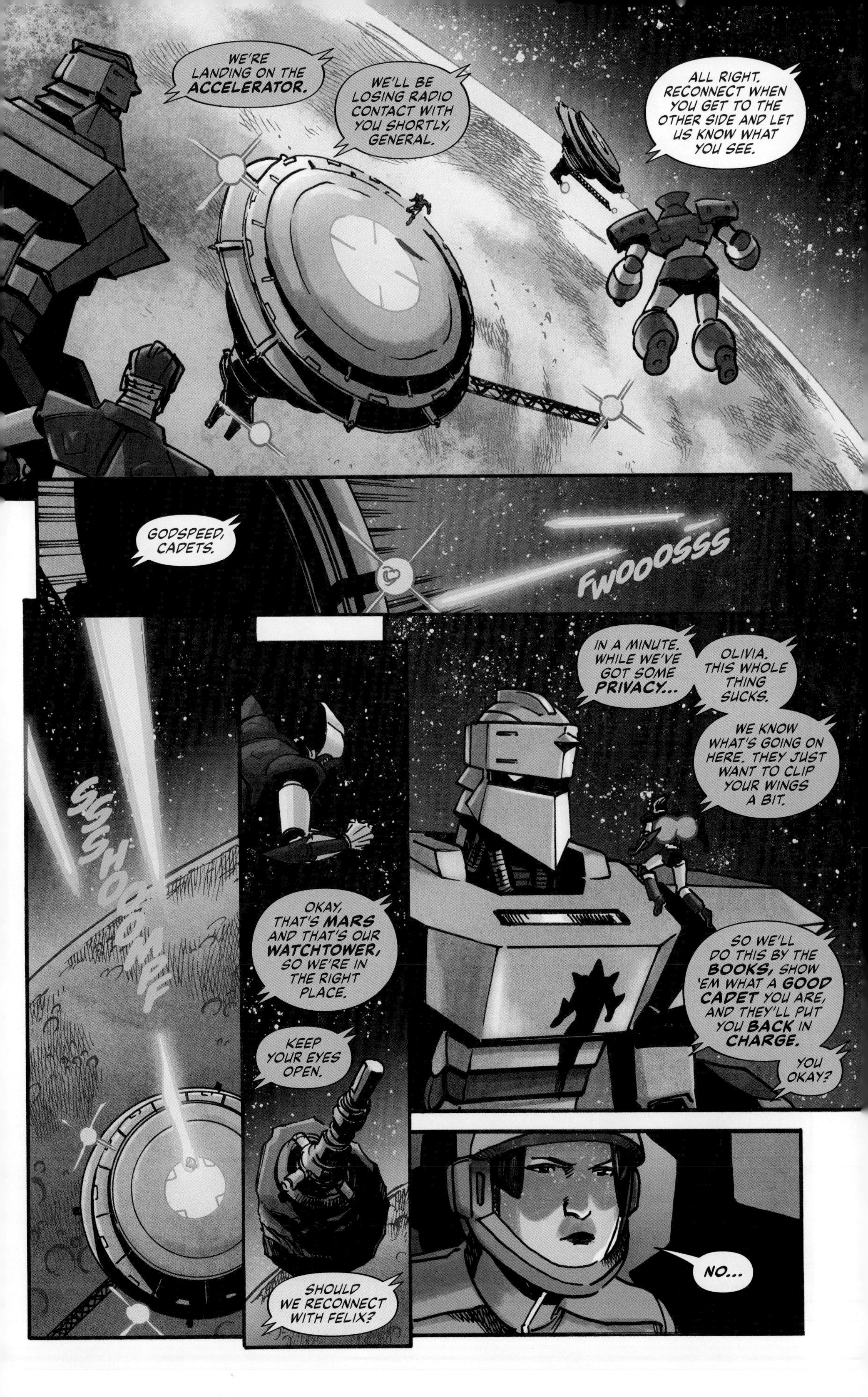
WE'RE LANDING ON THE ACCELERATOR.
WE'LL BE LOSING RADIO CONTACT WITH YOU SHORTLY, GENERAL.
ALL RIGHT. RECONNECT WHEN YOU GET TO THE OTHER SIDE AND LET US KNOW WHAT YOU SEE.
GODSPEED, CADETS.
FWOOOSSS
SSSHOOOMPF
OKAY, THAT'S MARS AND THAT'S OUR WATCHTOWER, SO WE'RE IN THE RIGHT PLACE.
KEEP YOUR EYES OPEN.
SHOULD WE RECONNECT WITH FELIX?
IN A MINUTE. WHILE WE'VE GOT SOME PRIVACY...
OLIVIA. THIS WHOLE THING SUCKS.
WE KNOW WHAT'S GOING ON HERE. THEY JUST WANT TO CLIP YOUR WINGS A BIT.
SO WE'LL DO THIS BY THE BOOKS, SHOW 'EM WHAT A GOOD CADET YOU ARE, AND THEY'LL PUT YOU BACK IN CHARGE.
YOU OKAY?
NO...

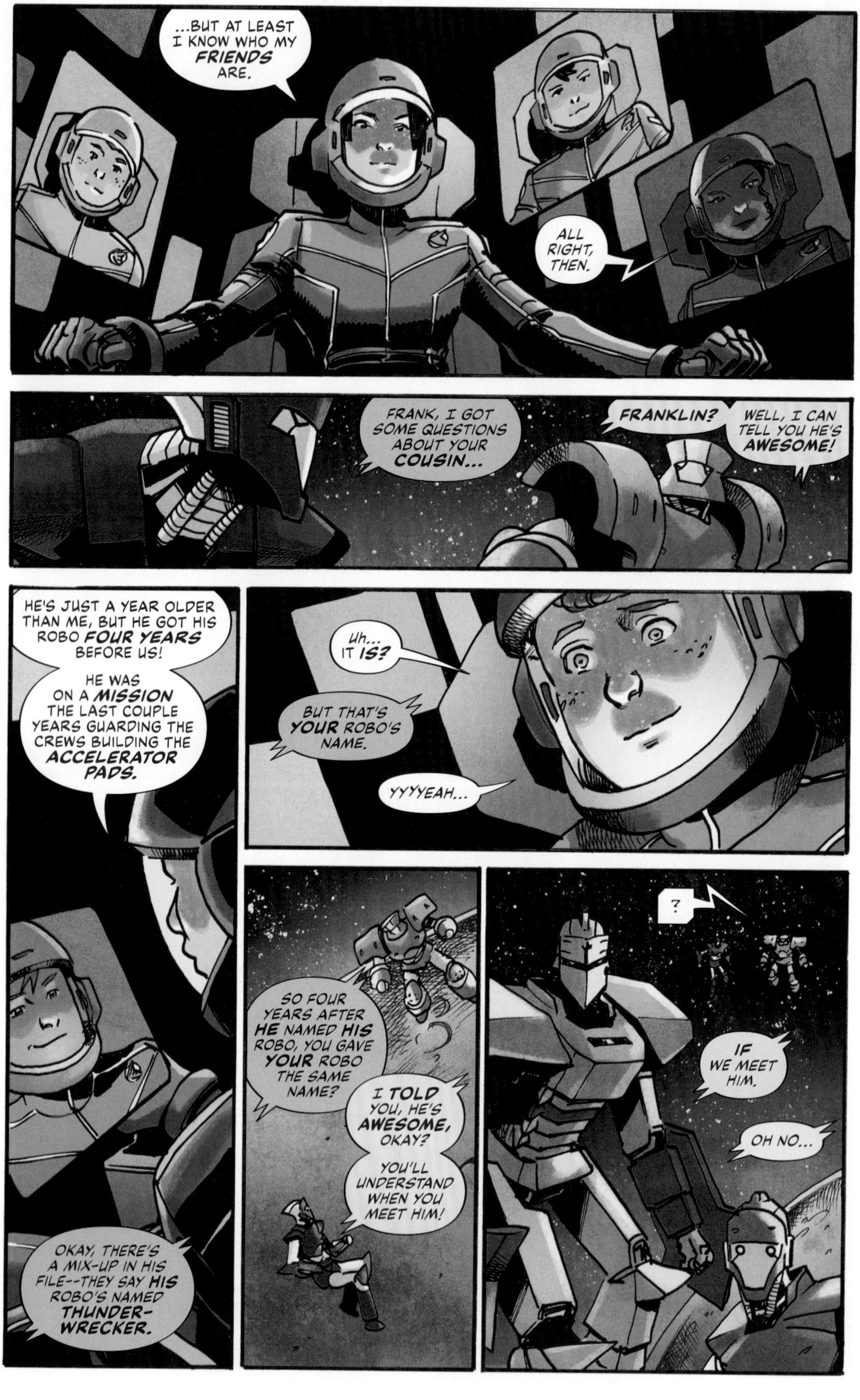

...BUT AT LEAST I KNOW WHO MY FRIENDS ARE.
ALL RIGHT, THEN.
FRANK, I GOT SOME QUESTIONS ABOUT YOUR COUSIN...
FRANKLIN?
WELL, I CAN TELL YOU HE'S AWESOME!
HE'S JUST A YEAR OLDER THAN ME, BUT HE GOT HIS ROBO FOUR YEARS BEFORE US!
HE WAS ON A MISSION THE LAST COUPLE YEARS GUARDING THE CREWS BUILDING THE ACCELERATOR PADS.
OKAY, THERE'S A MIX-UP IN HIS FILE--THEY SAY HIS ROBO'S NAMED THUNDER-WRECKER.
UH... IT IS?
BUT THAT'S YOUR ROBO'S NAME.
YYYYEAH...
SO FOUR YEARS AFTER HE NAMED HIS ROBO, YOU GAVE YOUR ROBO THE SAME NAME?
I TOLD YOU, HE'S AWESOME, OKAY?
YOU'LL UNDERSTAND WHEN YOU MEET HIM!
?
IF WE MEET HIM.
OH NO...

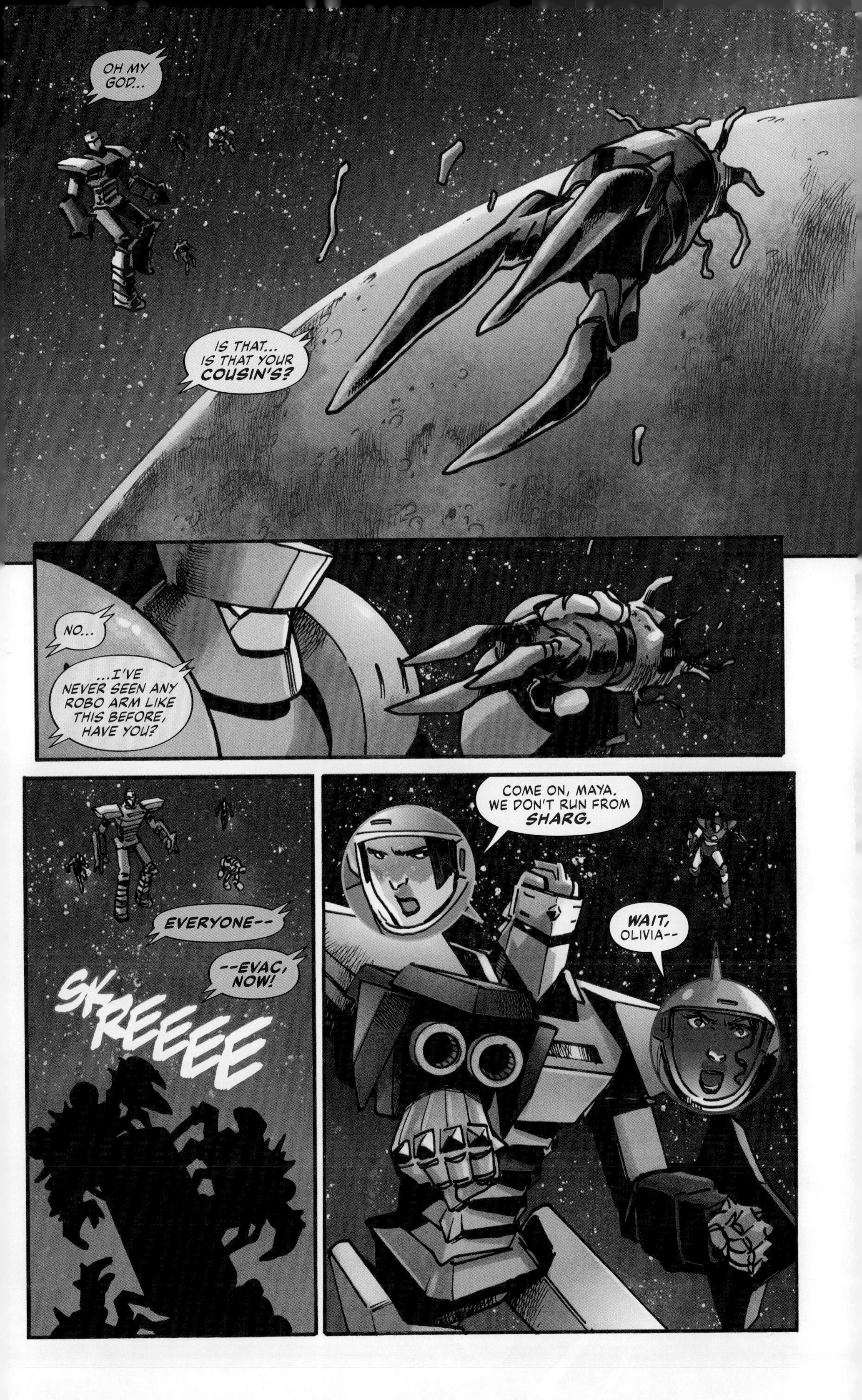
OH MY GOD...
IS THAT... IS THAT YOUR COUSIN'S?
NO...
...I'VE NEVER SEEN ANY ROBO ARM LIKE THIS BEFORE, HAVE YOU?
EVERYONE--
--EVAC, NOW!
SKREEEEE
COME ON, MAYA. WE DON'T RUN FROM SHARG.
WAIT, OLIVIA--

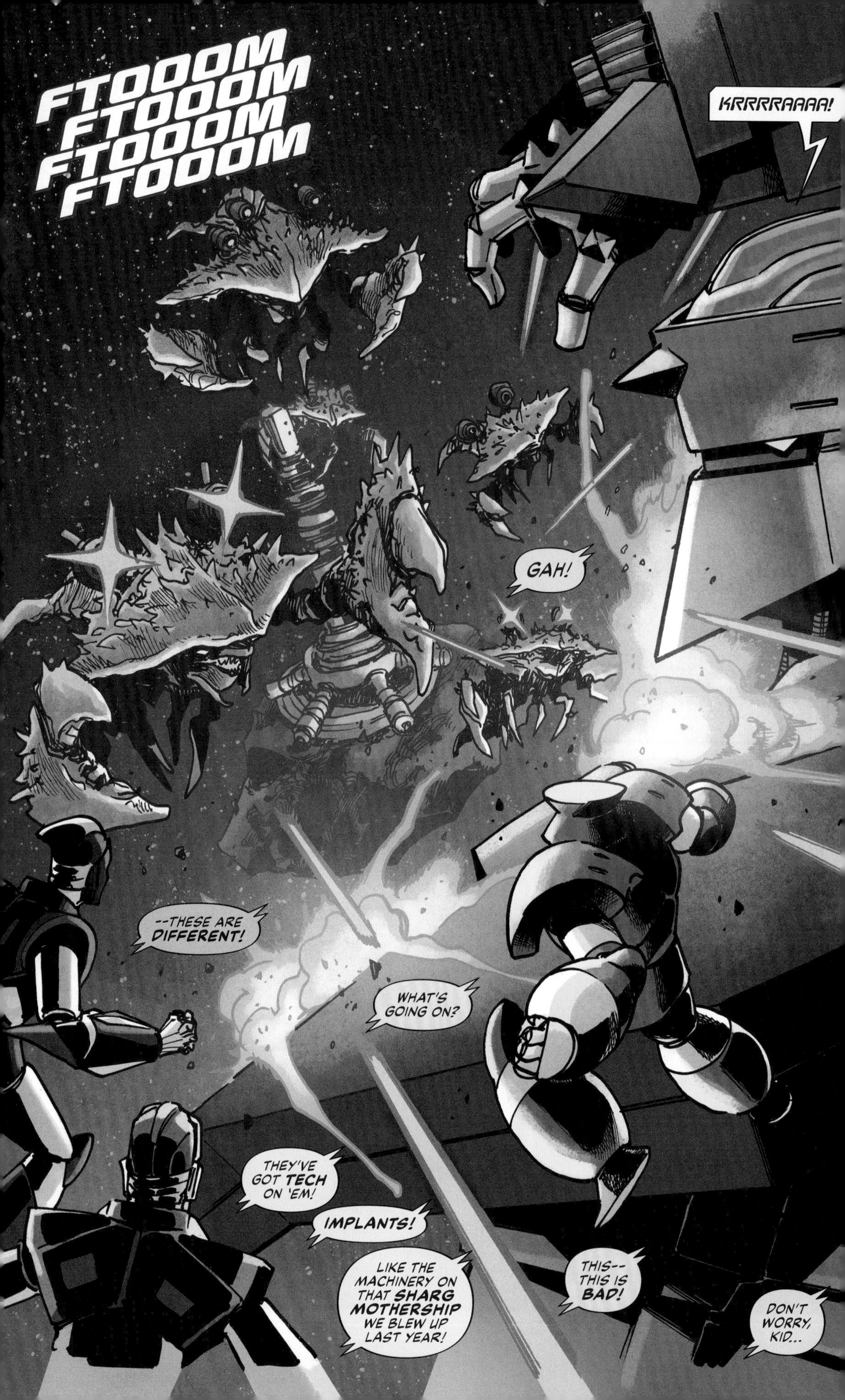
FTOOOM FTOOOM FTOOOM FTOOOM
KRRRRAAAA!
GAH!
--THESE ARE DIFFERENT!
WHAT'S GOING ON?
THEY'VE GOT TECH ON 'EM!
IMPLANTS!
LIKE THE MACHINERY ON THAT SHARG MOTHERSHIP WE BLEW UP LAST YEAR!
THIS-- THIS IS BAD!
DON'T WORRY, KID...

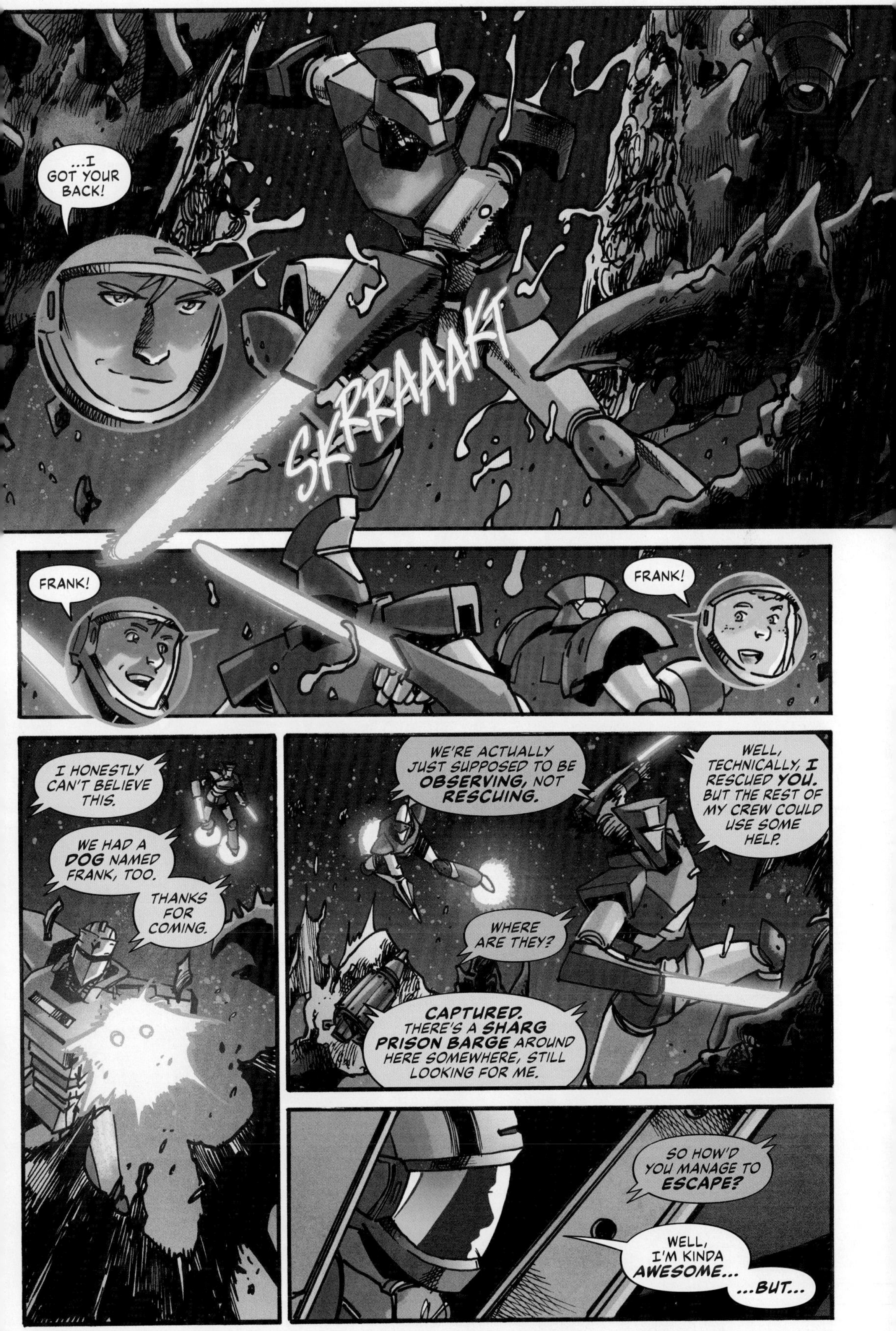
...I GOT YOUR BACK!
SKRRAAAKT
FRANK!
FRANK!
I HONESTLY CAN'T BELIEVE THIS.
WE HAD A **DOG** NAMED FRANK, TOO.
THANKS FOR COMING.
WE'RE ACTUALLY JUST SUPPOSED TO BE **OBSERVING,** NOT **RESCUING.**
WELL, TECHNICALLY, **I** RESCUED **YOU.** BUT THE REST OF MY CREW COULD USE SOME HELP.
WHERE ARE THEY?
CAPTURED. THERE'S A **SHARG PRISON BARGE** AROUND HERE SOMEWHERE, STILL LOOKING FOR ME.
SO HOW'D YOU MANAGE TO **ESCAPE?**
WELL, I'M KINDA **AWESOME...**
...BUT...

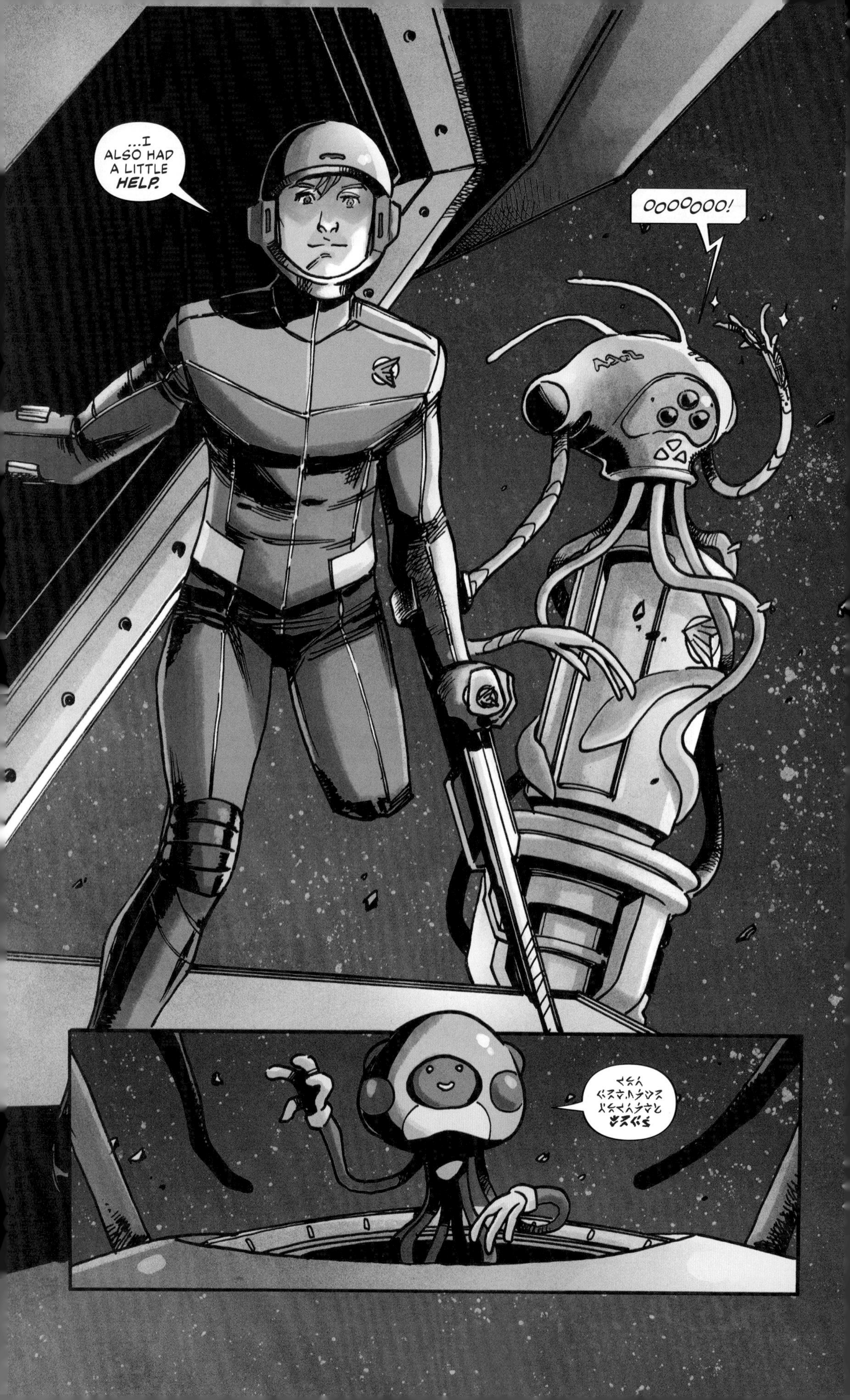
...I ALSO HAD A LITTLE HELP.
OOOOOOO!

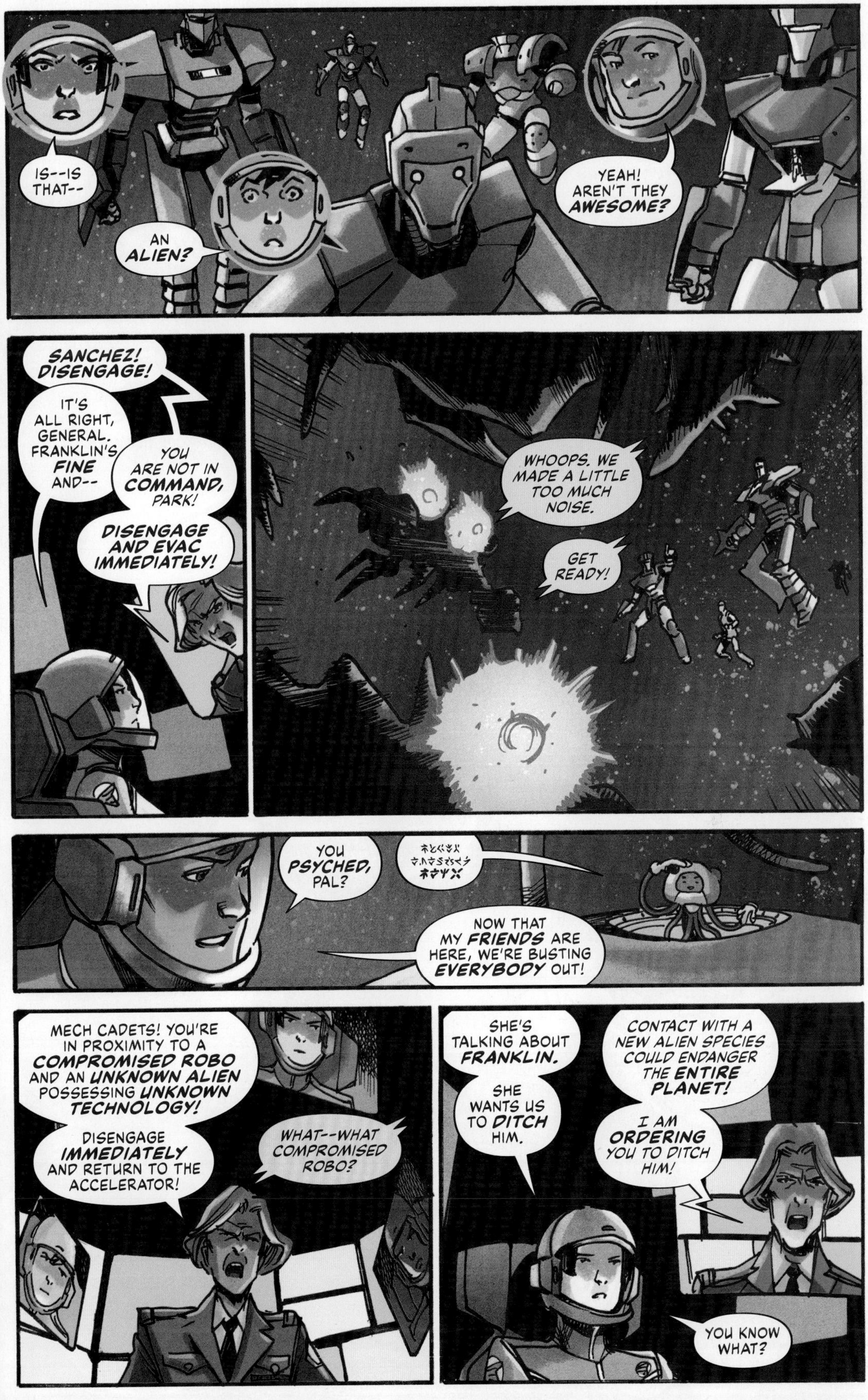
IS--IS THAT--
AN ALIEN?
YEAH! AREN'T THEY AWESOME?
SANCHEZ! DISENGAGE!
IT'S ALL RIGHT, GENERAL. FRANKLIN'S FINE AND--
YOU ARE NOT IN COMMAND, PARK!
DISENGAGE AND EVAC IMMEDIATELY!
WHOOPS. WE MADE A LITTLE TOO MUCH NOISE.
GET READY!
YOU PSYCHED, PAL?
NOW THAT MY FRIENDS ARE HERE, WE'RE BUSTING EVERYBODY OUT!
MECH CADETS! YOU'RE IN PROXIMITY TO A COMPROMISED ROBO AND AN UNKNOWN ALIEN POSSESSING UNKNOWN TECHNOLOGY!
DISENGAGE IMMEDIATELY AND RETURN TO THE ACCELERATOR!
WHAT--WHAT COMPROMISED ROBO?
SHE'S TALKING ABOUT FRANKLIN.
SHE WANTS US TO DITCH HIM.
CONTACT WITH A NEW ALIEN SPECIES COULD ENDANGER THE ENTIRE PLANET!
I AM ORDERING YOU TO DITCH HIM!
YOU KNOW WHAT?

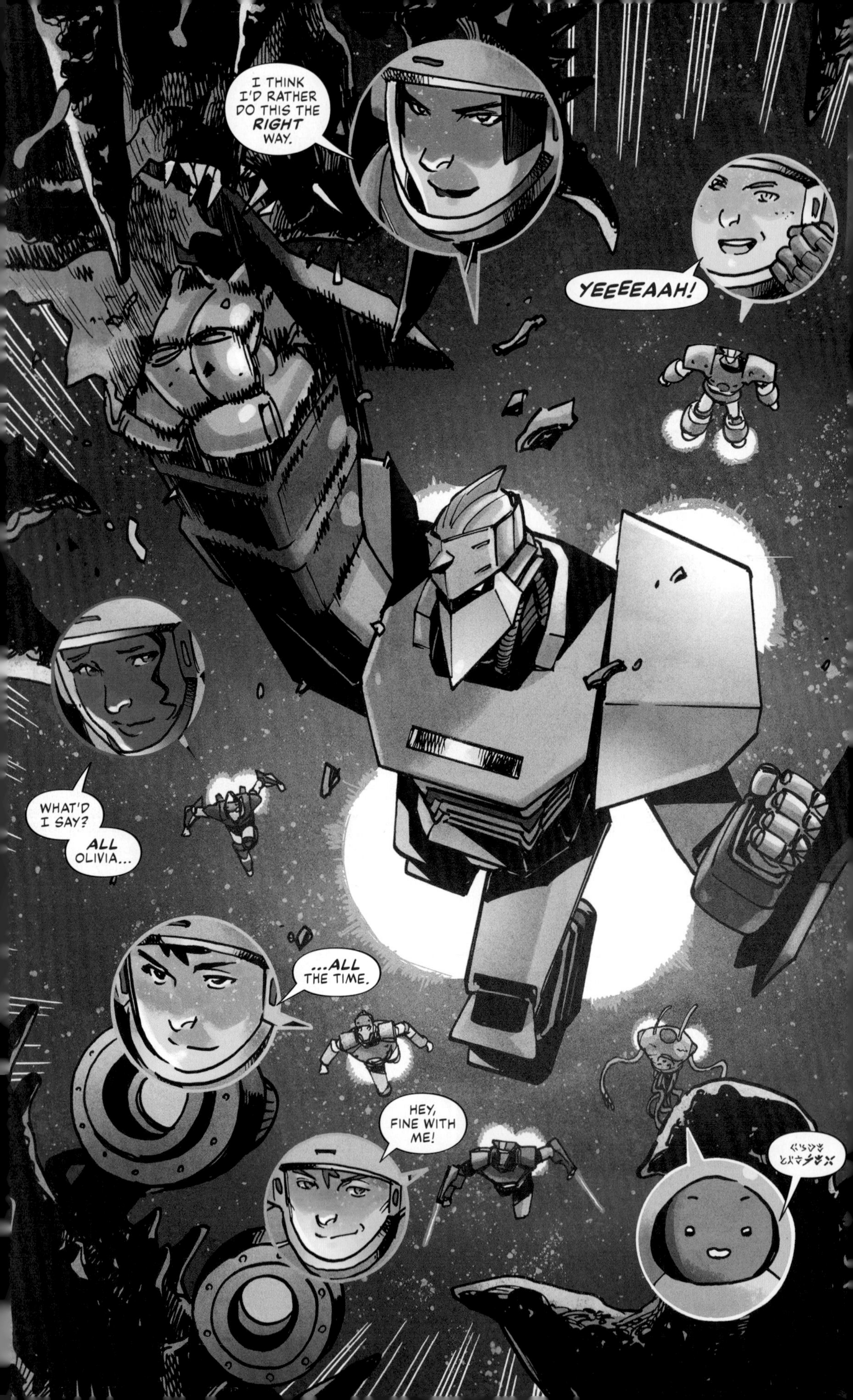
I THINK I'D RATHER DO THIS THE **RIGHT** WAY.
YEEEEAAH!
WHAT'D I SAY? **ALL** OLIVIA...
...ALL THE TIME.
HEY, FINE WITH ME!

CHAPTER TWO

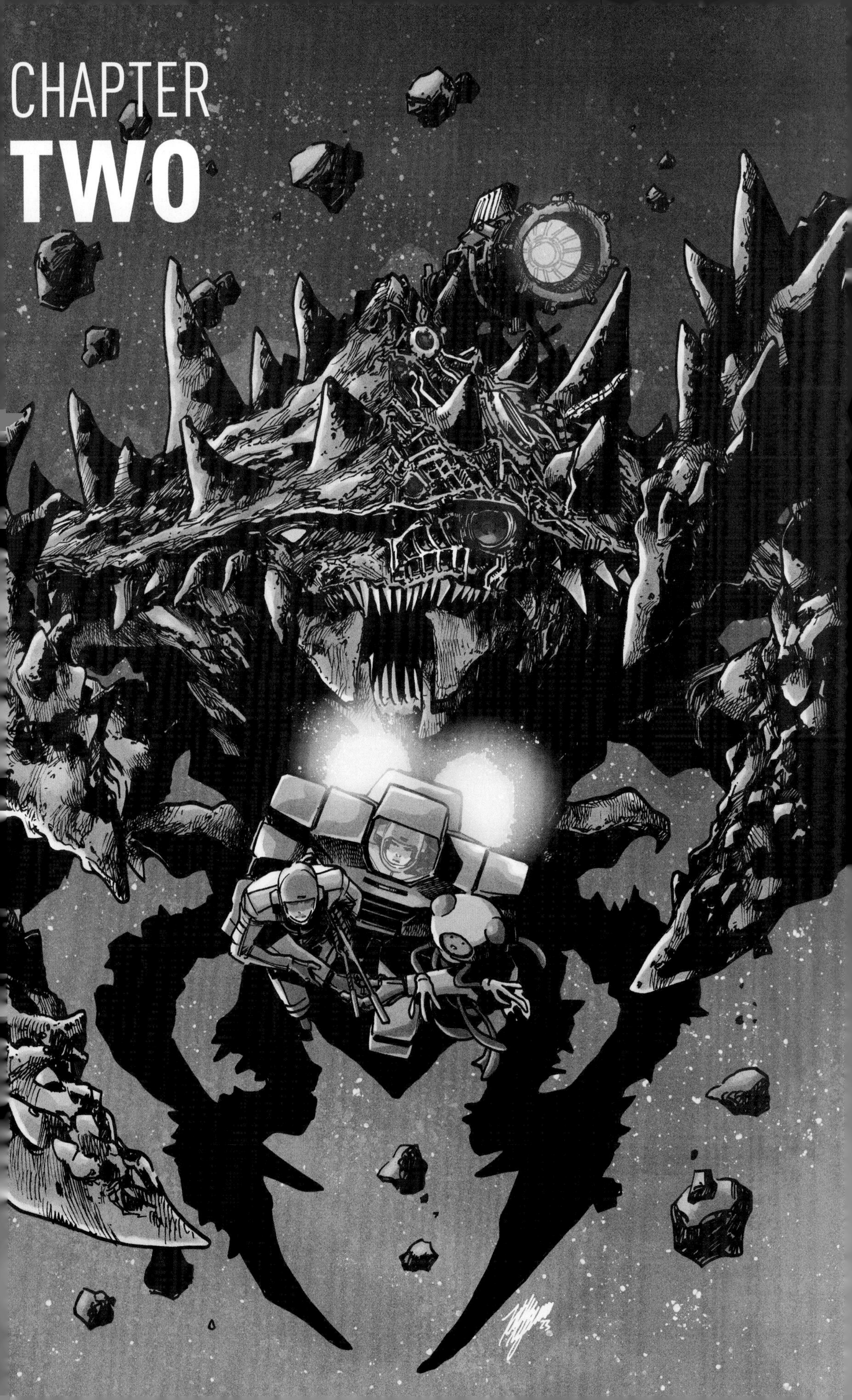

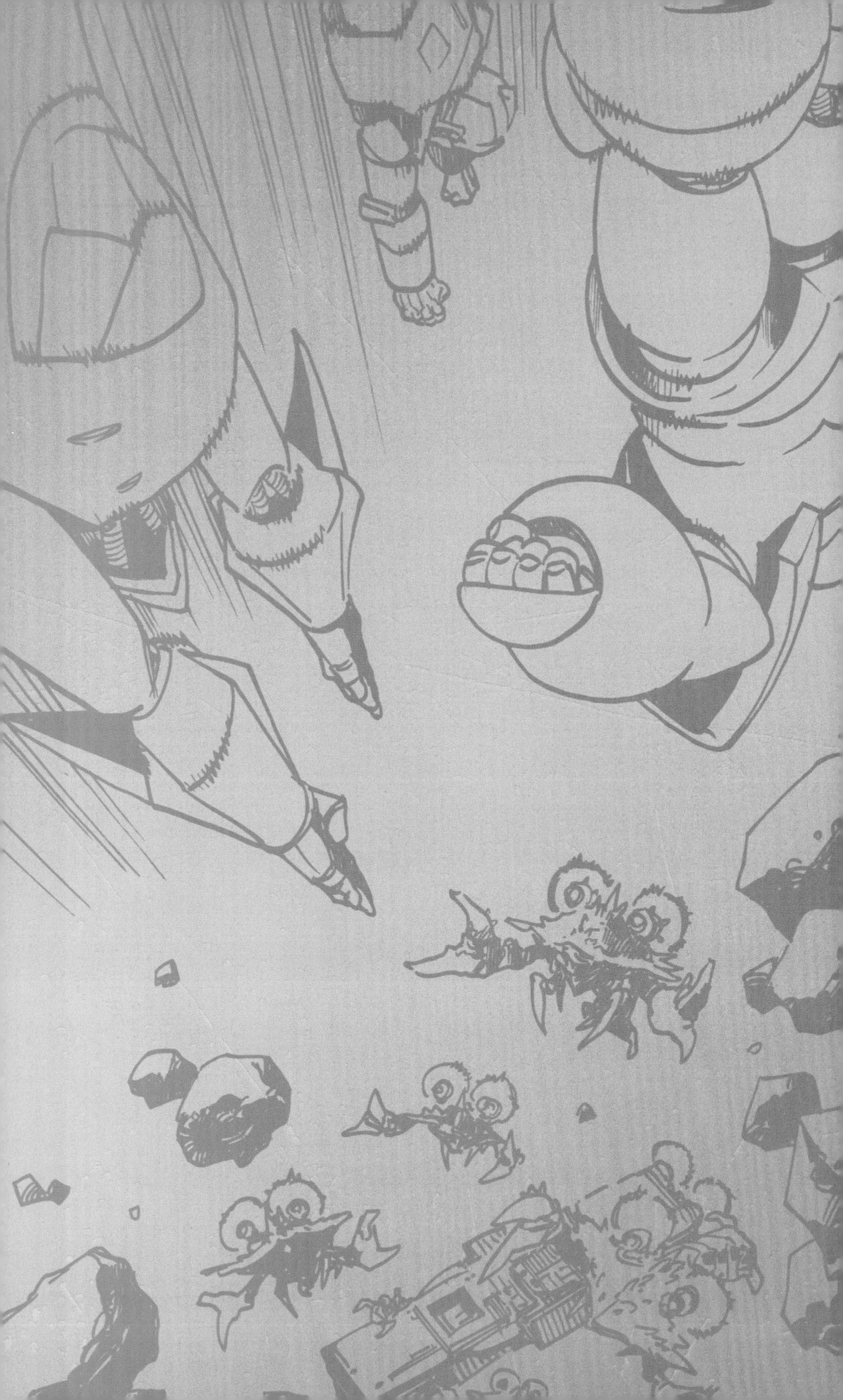

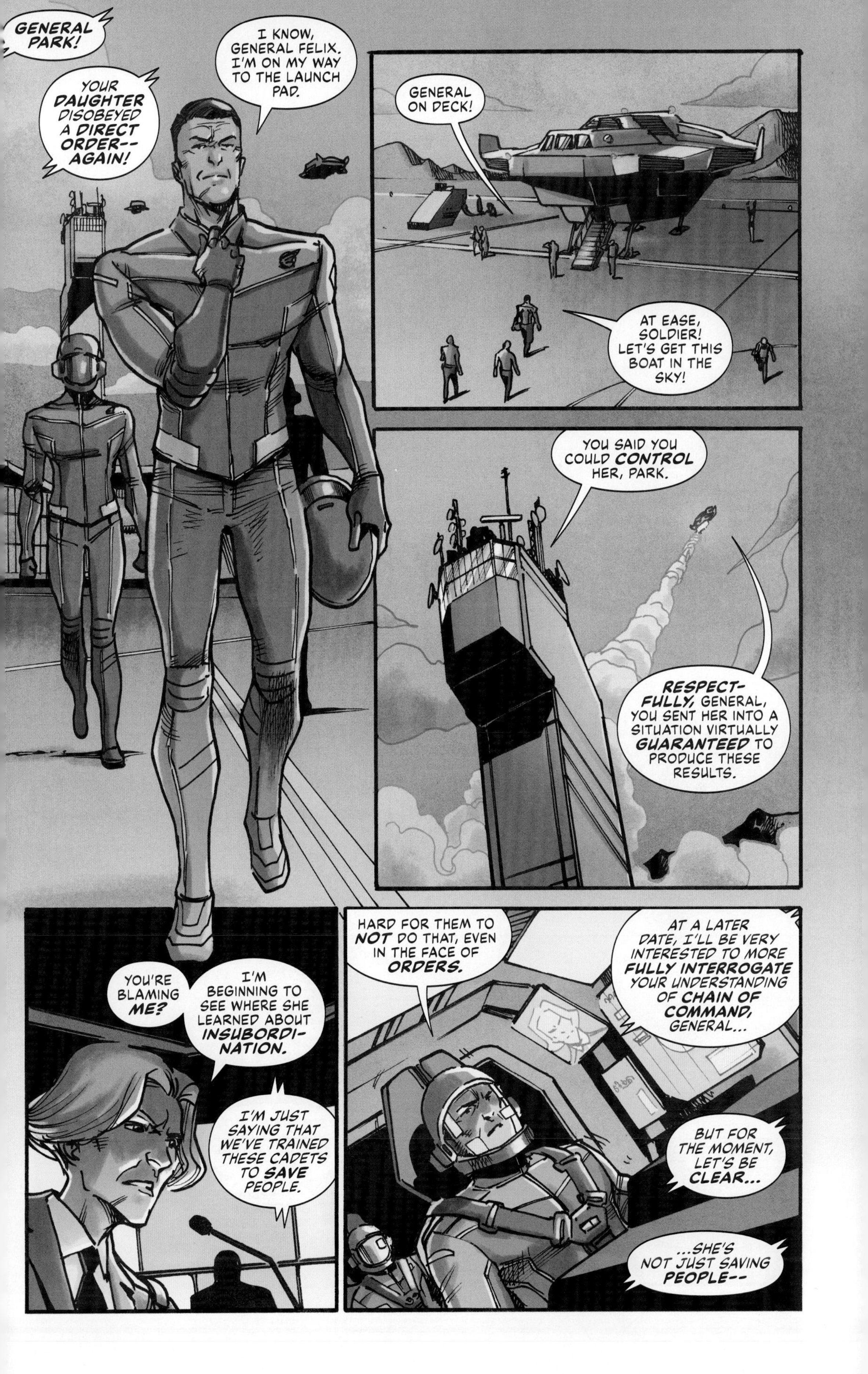
GENERAL PARK!
YOUR DAUGHTER DISOBEYED A DIRECT ORDER--AGAIN!
I KNOW, GENERAL FELIX. I'M ON MY WAY TO THE LAUNCH PAD.
GENERAL ON DECK!
AT EASE, SOLDIER! LET'S GET THIS BOAT IN THE SKY!
YOU SAID YOU COULD CONTROL HER, PARK.
RESPECTFULLY, GENERAL, YOU SENT HER INTO A SITUATION VIRTUALLY GUARANTEED TO PRODUCE THESE RESULTS.
YOU'RE BLAMING ME?
I'M BEGINNING TO SEE WHERE SHE LEARNED ABOUT INSUBORDINATION.
I'M JUST SAYING THAT WE'VE TRAINED THESE CADETS TO SAVE PEOPLE.
HARD FOR THEM TO NOT DO THAT, EVEN IN THE FACE OF ORDERS.
AT A LATER DATE, I'LL BE VERY INTERESTED TO MORE FULLY INTERROGATE YOUR UNDERSTANDING OF CHAIN OF COMMAND, GENERAL...
BUT FOR THE MOMENT, LET'S BE CLEAR...
...SHE'S NOT JUST SAVING PEOPLE--

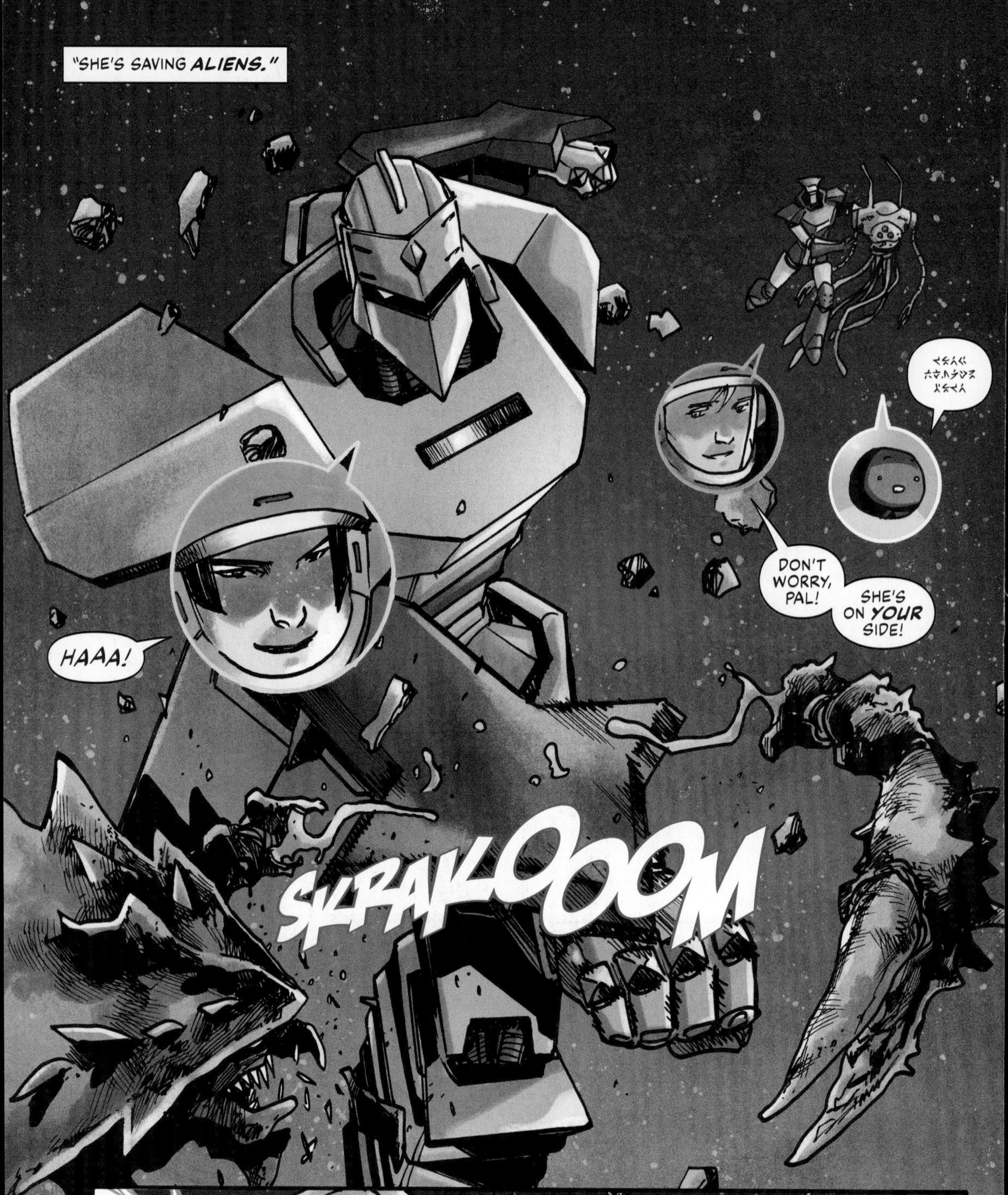
"SHE'S SAVING ALIENS."
DON'T WORRY, PAL!
SHE'S ON YOUR SIDE!
HAAA!
SKRAKOOOM

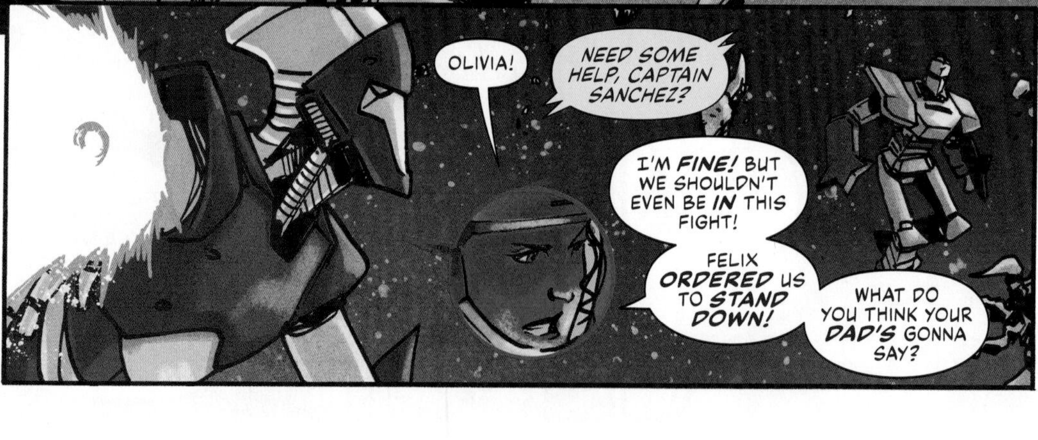
OLIVIA!
NEED SOME HELP, CAPTAIN SANCHEZ?
I'M FINE! BUT WE SHOULDN'T EVEN BE IN THIS FIGHT!
FELIX ORDERED US TO STAND DOWN!
WHAT DO YOU THINK YOUR DAD'S GONNA SAY?

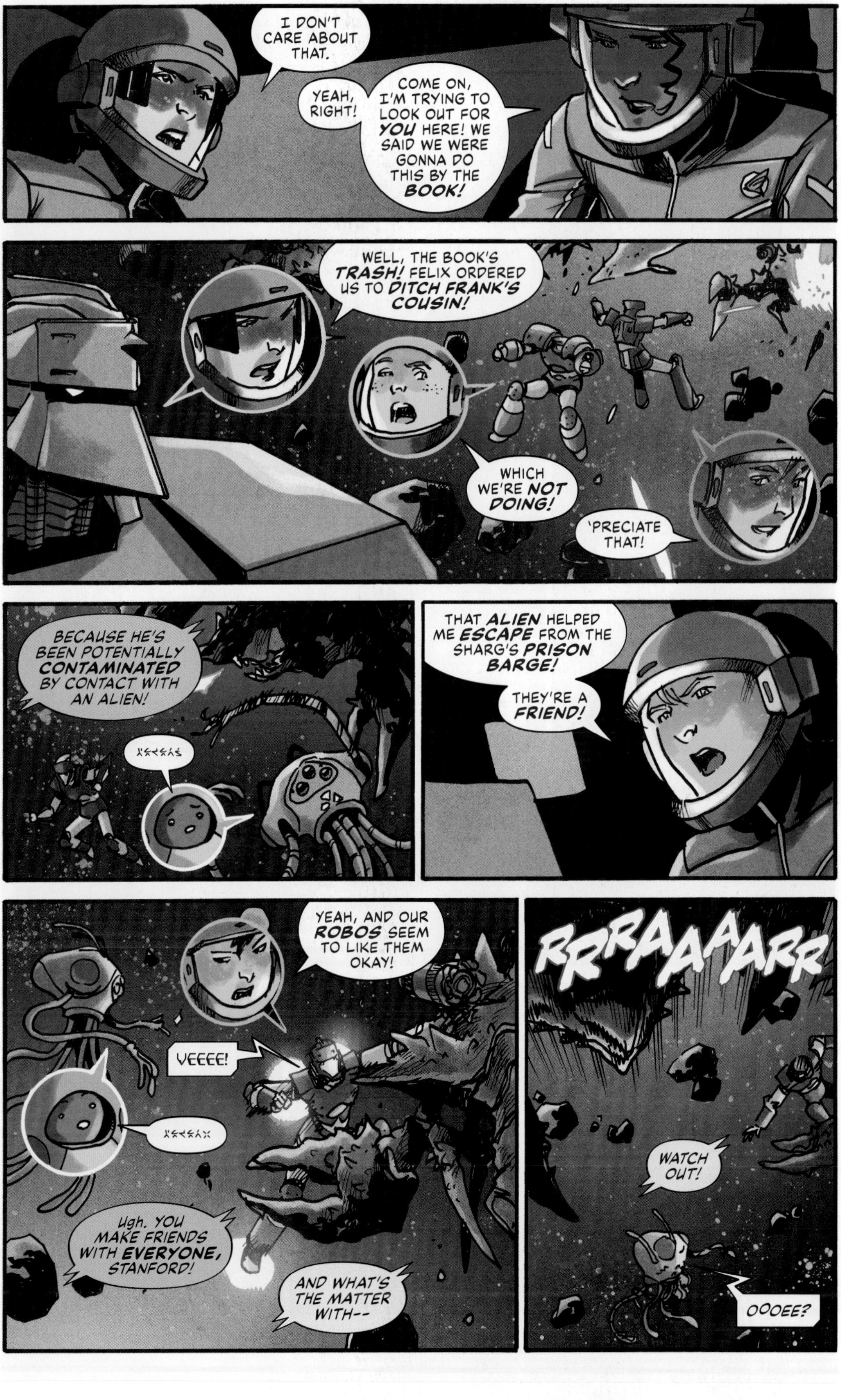

I DON'T CARE ABOUT THAT.
COME ON, I'M TRYING TO LOOK OUT FOR *YOU* HERE! WE SAID WE WERE GONNA DO THIS BY THE *BOOK!*
YEAH, RIGHT!
WELL, THE BOOK'S *TRASH!* FELIX ORDERED US TO *DITCH FRANK'S COUSIN!*
WHICH WE'RE *NOT DOING!*
'PRECIATE THAT!
BECAUSE HE'S BEEN POTENTIALLY *CONTAMINATED* BY CONTACT WITH AN ALIEN!
THAT *ALIEN* HELPED ME *ESCAPE* FROM THE SHARG'S *PRISON BARGE!*
THEY'RE A *FRIEND!*
YEAH, AND OUR *ROBOS* SEEM TO LIKE THEM OKAY!
VEEEE!
Ugh. YOU MAKE FRIENDS WITH *EVERYONE*, STANFORD!
AND WHAT'S THE MATTER WITH--
RRRAAAARR
WATCH OUT!
OOOEE?

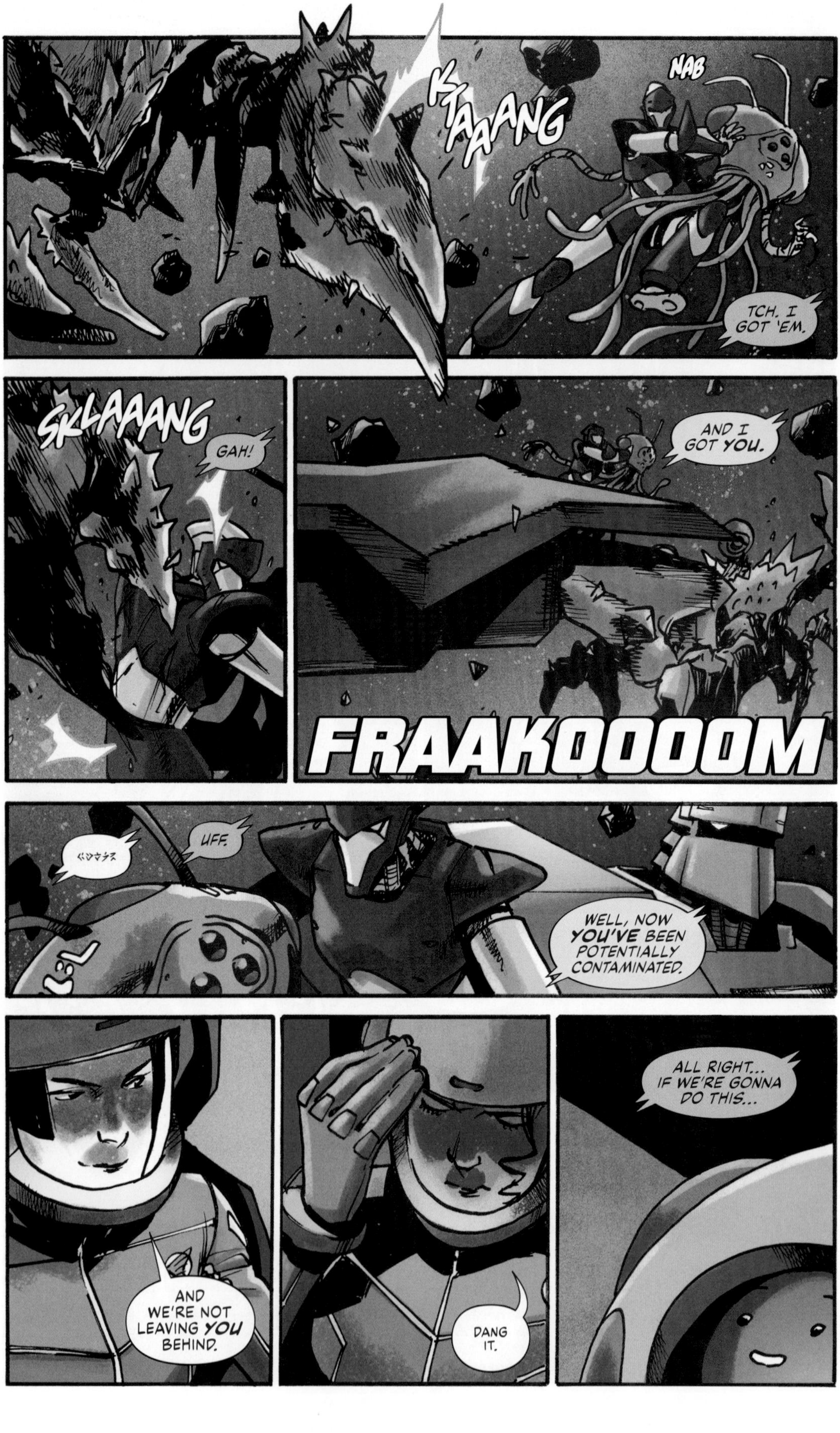
KTAAANG
NAB
TCH. I GOT 'EM.
SKLAAANG
GAH!
AND I GOT YOU.
FRAAKOOOOM
UFF.
WELL, NOW YOU'VE BEEN POTENTIALLY CONTAMINATED.
AND WE'RE NOT LEAVING YOU BEHIND.
DANG IT.
ALL RIGHT... IF WE'RE GONNA DO THIS...

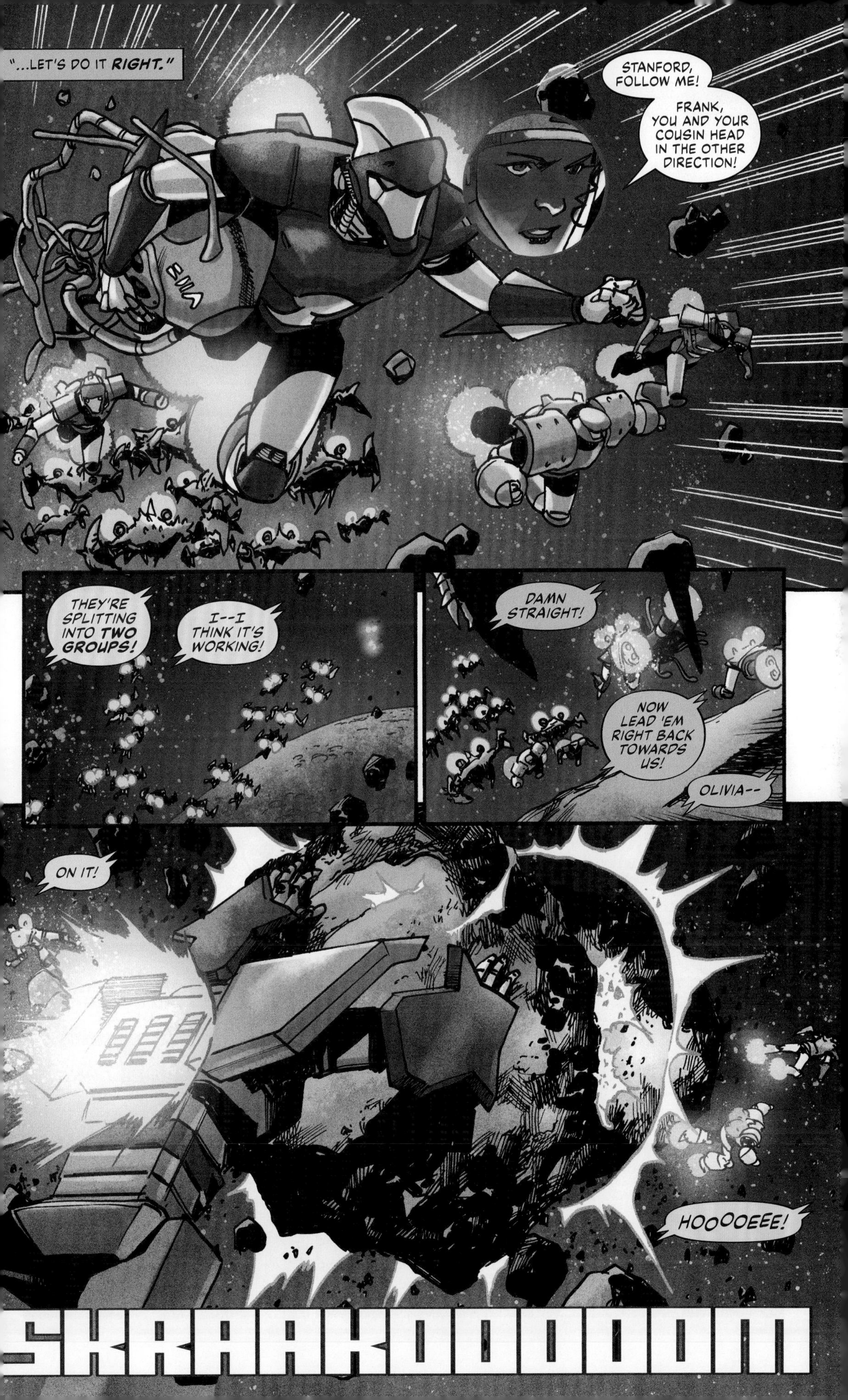
"...LET'S DO IT RIGHT."
STANFORD, FOLLOW ME!
FRANK, YOU AND YOUR COUSIN HEAD IN THE OTHER DIRECTION!
THEY'RE SPLITTING INTO TWO GROUPS!
I--I THINK IT'S WORKING!
DAMN STRAIGHT!
NOW LEAD 'EM RIGHT BACK TOWARDS US!
OLIVIA--
ON IT!
HOOOOEEE!
SKRAAKOOOOOM

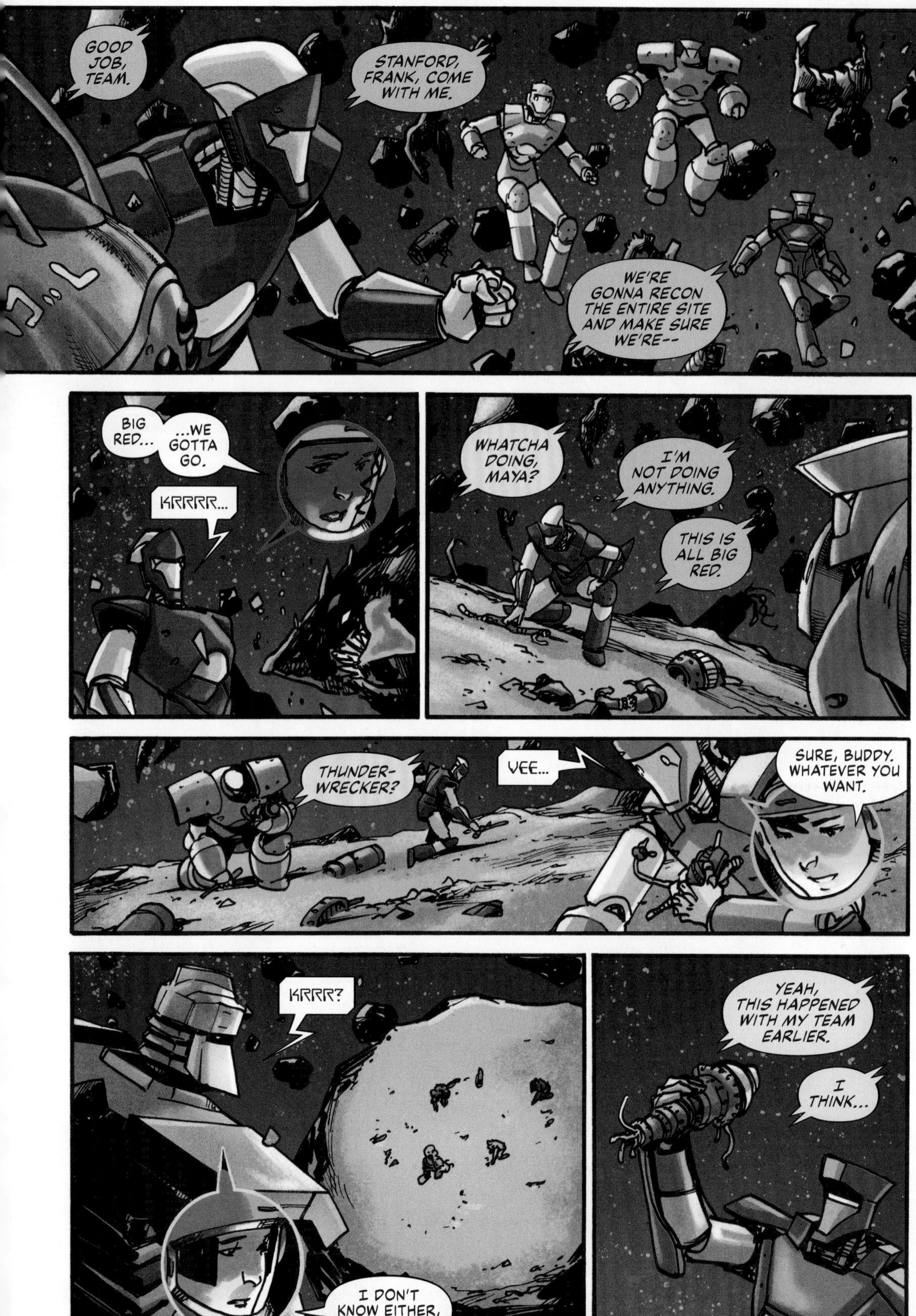

GOOD JOB, TEAM.
STANFORD, FRANK, COME WITH ME.
WE'RE GONNA RECON THE ENTIRE SITE AND MAKE SURE WE'RE--
BIG RED...
...WE GOTTA GO.
KRRRR...
WHATCHA DOING, MAYA?
I'M NOT DOING ANYTHING.
THIS IS ALL BIG RED.
THUNDER-WRECKER?
VEE...
SURE, BUDDY. WHATEVER YOU WANT.
KRRR?
I DON'T KNOW EITHER, HERO.
YEAH, THIS HAPPENED WITH MY TEAM EARLIER.
I THINK...

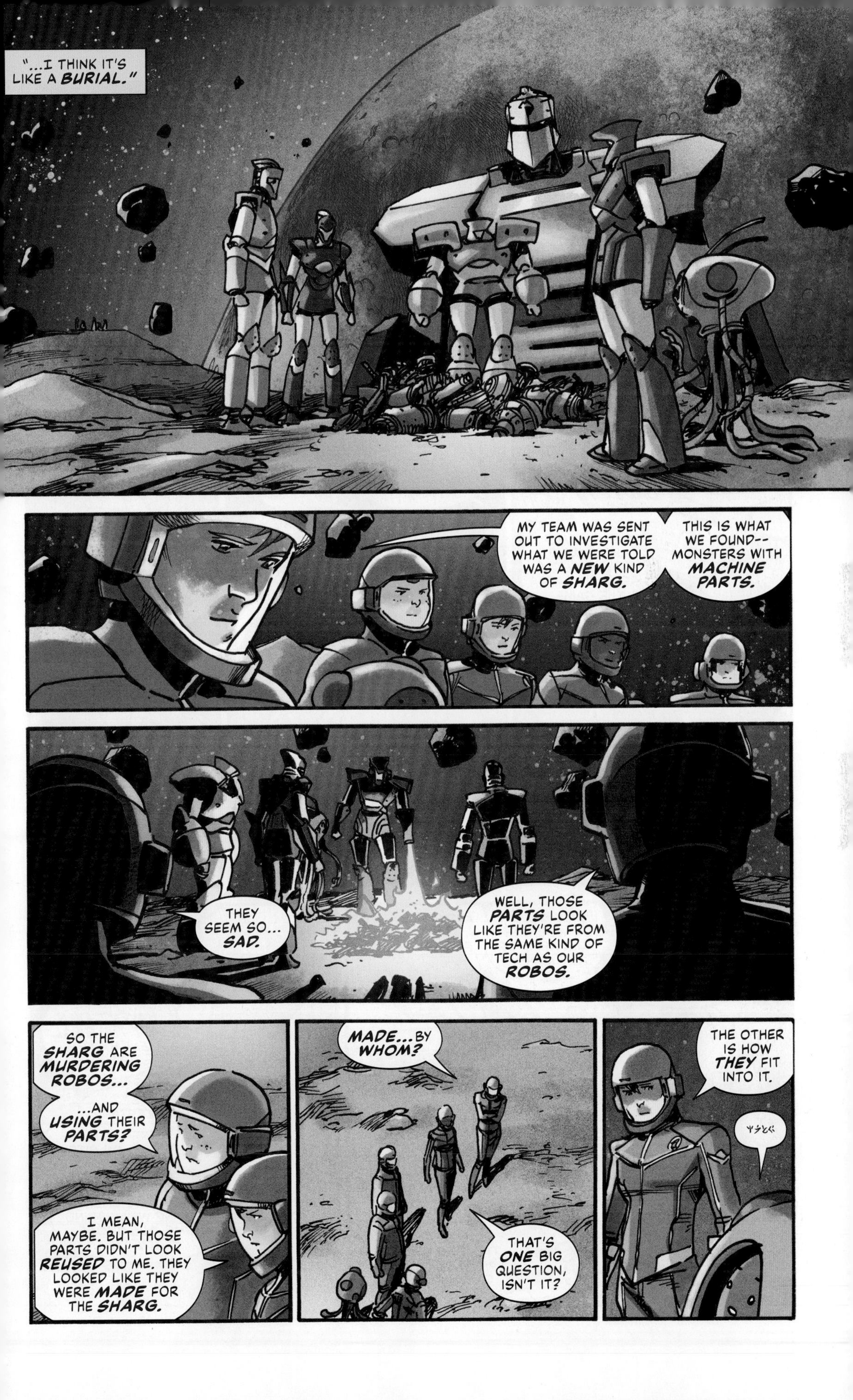
"...I THINK IT'S LIKE A BURIAL."
MY TEAM WAS SENT OUT TO INVESTIGATE WHAT WE WERE TOLD WAS A NEW KIND OF SHARG.
THIS IS WHAT WE FOUND--MONSTERS WITH MACHINE PARTS.
THEY SEEM SO... SAD.
WELL, THOSE PARTS LOOK LIKE THEY'RE FROM THE SAME KIND OF TECH AS OUR ROBOS.
SO THE SHARG ARE MURDERING ROBOS...
...AND USING THEIR PARTS?
I MEAN, MAYBE. BUT THOSE PARTS DIDN'T LOOK REUSED TO ME. THEY LOOKED LIKE THEY WERE MADE FOR THE SHARG.
MADE... BY WHOM?
THAT'S ONE BIG QUESTION, ISN'T IT?
THE OTHER IS HOW THEY FIT INTO IT.

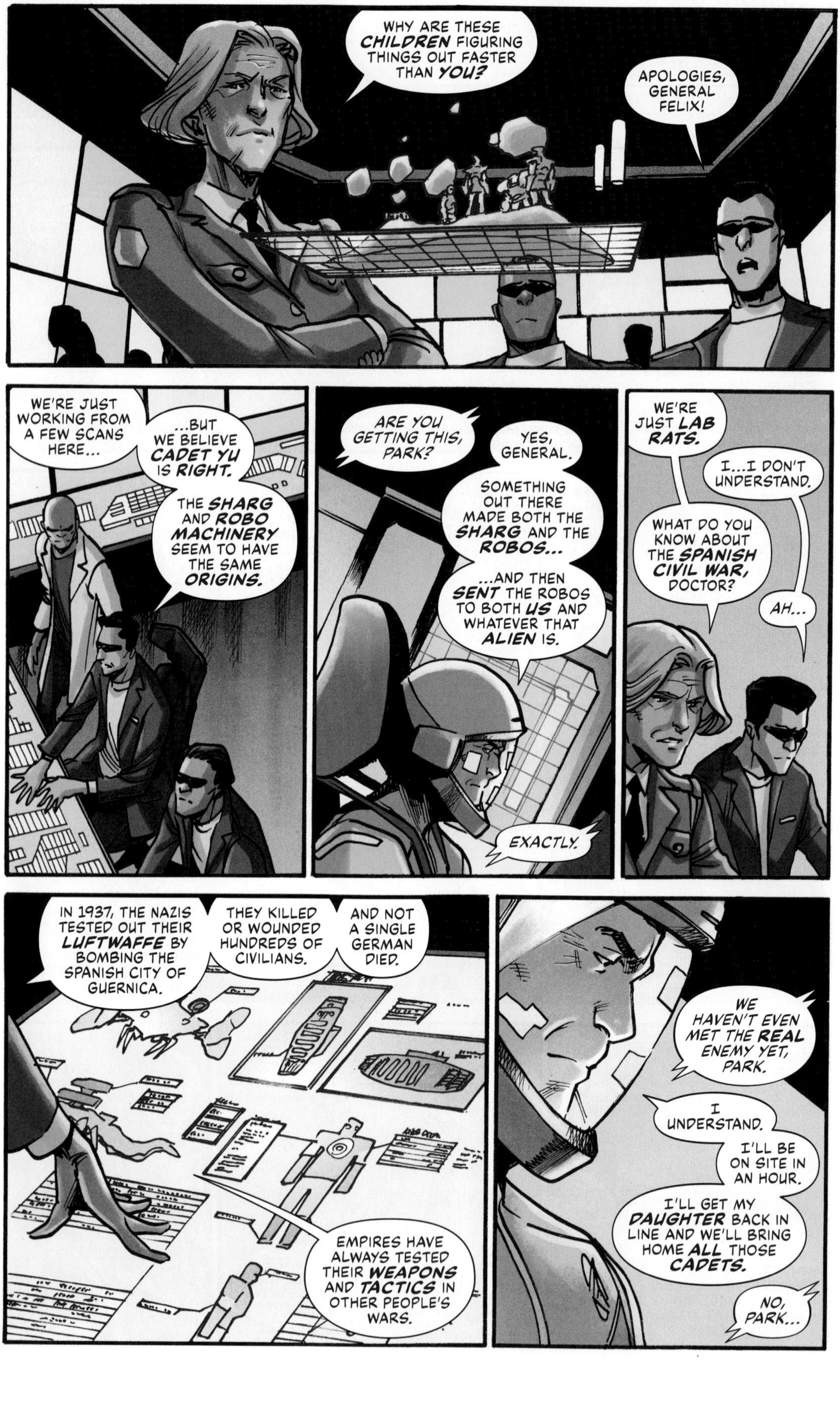
WHY ARE THESE CHILDREN FIGURING THINGS OUT FASTER THAN YOU?
APOLOGIES, GENERAL FELIX!
WE'RE JUST WORKING FROM A FEW SCANS HERE...
...BUT WE BELIEVE CADET YU IS RIGHT.
THE SHARG AND ROBO MACHINERY SEEM TO HAVE THE SAME ORIGINS.
ARE YOU GETTING THIS, PARK?
YES, GENERAL.
SOMETHING OUT THERE MADE BOTH THE SHARG AND THE ROBOS...
...AND THEN SENT THE ROBOS TO BOTH US AND WHATEVER THAT ALIEN IS.
EXACTLY.
WE'RE JUST LAB RATS.
I...I DON'T UNDERSTAND.
WHAT DO YOU KNOW ABOUT THE SPANISH CIVIL WAR, DOCTOR?
AH...
IN 1937, THE NAZIS TESTED OUT THEIR LUFTWAFFE BY BOMBING THE SPANISH CITY OF GUERNICA.
THEY KILLED OR WOUNDED HUNDREDS OF CIVILIANS.
AND NOT A SINGLE GERMAN DIED.
EMPIRES HAVE ALWAYS TESTED THEIR WEAPONS AND TACTICS IN OTHER PEOPLE'S WARS.
WE HAVEN'T EVEN MET THE REAL ENEMY YET, PARK.
I UNDERSTAND.
I'LL BE ON SITE IN AN HOUR.
I'LL GET MY DAUGHTER BACK IN LINE AND WE'LL BRING HOME ALL THOSE CADETS.
NO, PARK...

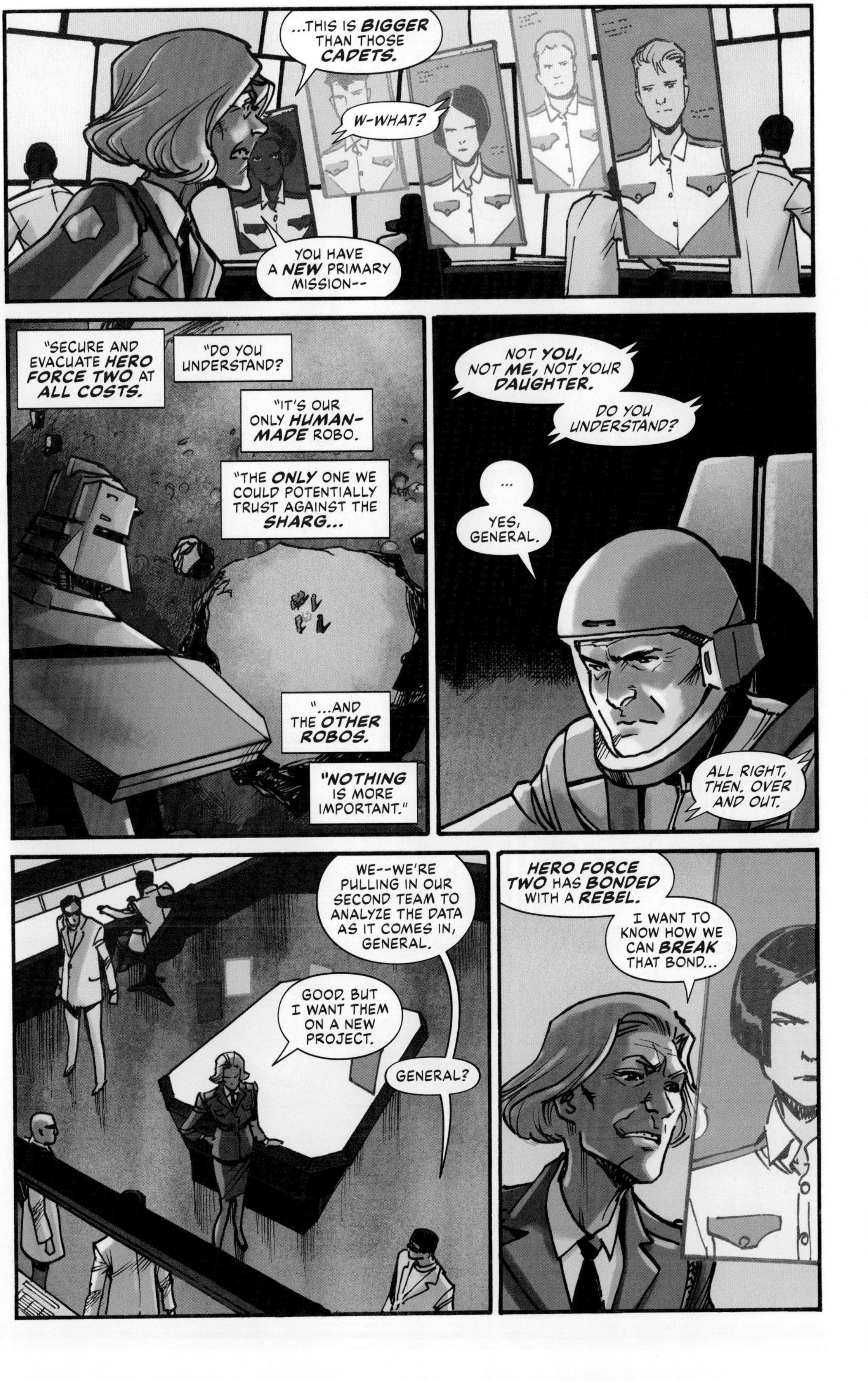
...THIS IS BIGGER THAN THOSE CADETS.
W-WHAT?
YOU HAVE A NEW PRIMARY MISSION--
"SECURE AND EVACUATE HERO FORCE TWO AT ALL COSTS.
"DO YOU UNDERSTAND?
"IT'S OUR ONLY HUMAN-MADE ROBO.
"THE ONLY ONE WE COULD POTENTIALLY TRUST AGAINST THE SHARG...
"...AND THE OTHER ROBOS.
"NOTHING IS MORE IMPORTANT."
NOT YOU, NOT ME, NOT YOUR DAUGHTER.
DO YOU UNDERSTAND?
...
YES, GENERAL.
ALL RIGHT, THEN. OVER AND OUT.
WE--WE'RE PULLING IN OUR SECOND TEAM TO ANALYZE THE DATA AS IT COMES IN, GENERAL.
GOOD. BUT I WANT THEM ON A NEW PROJECT.
GENERAL?
HERO FORCE TWO HAS BONDED WITH A REBEL.
I WANT TO KNOW HOW WE CAN BREAK THAT BOND...

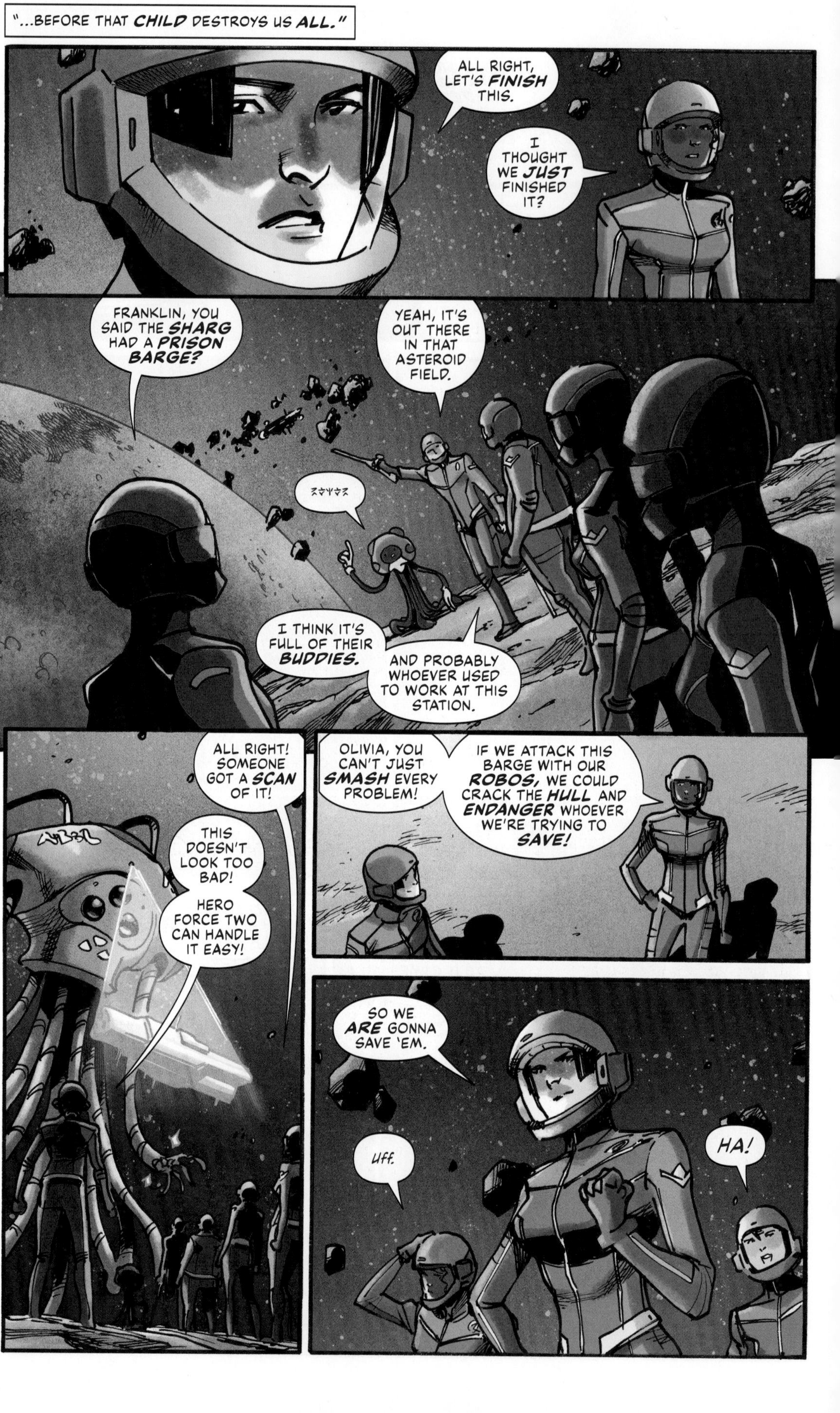
"...BEFORE THAT CHILD DESTROYS US ALL."
ALL RIGHT, LET'S FINISH THIS.
I THOUGHT WE JUST FINISHED IT?
FRANKLIN, YOU SAID THE SHARG HAD A PRISON BARGE?
YEAH, IT'S OUT THERE IN THAT ASTEROID FIELD.
I THINK IT'S FULL OF THEIR BUDDIES.
AND PROBABLY WHOEVER USED TO WORK AT THIS STATION.
ALL RIGHT! SOMEONE GOT A SCAN OF IT!
THIS DOESN'T LOOK TOO BAD!
HERO FORCE TWO CAN HANDLE IT EASY!
OLIVIA, YOU CAN'T JUST SMASH EVERY PROBLEM!
IF WE ATTACK THIS BARGE WITH OUR ROBOS, WE COULD CRACK THE HULL AND ENDANGER WHOEVER WE'RE TRYING TO SAVE!
SO WE ARE GONNA SAVE 'EM.
Uff.
HA!

ALL RIGHT. TWO TEAMS.

FRANK, STANFORD, THE THREE OF US ARE GONNA ATTACK THE BARGE *HEAD ON.*

HANG ON, I THOUGHT WE WEREN'T PUNCHING HOLES IN THAT THING!

WE *AREN'T.* WE'RE JUST *DRAWING* THEIR *FIRE...*

...SO *COUSIN FRANKLIN* AND *OLIVIA* CAN USE OUR ALIEN PAL'S *MAP* AND *SNEAK ON BOARD.*

WHAT ABOUT *HERO FORCE TWO?* YOU'RE GONNA *SIDELINE* OUR BEST *RESOURCE?*

ONCE YOU *FREE THE PRISONERS,* IT'S GONNA BE ALL *ABOUT* HERO FORCE TWO.

BUT YOU AND FRANKLIN ARE OUR BEST *HAND-TO-HAND COMBATANTS.*

I NEED YOU *ON THE GROUND* AND *SMALL* FOR THIS ONE.

KTHOOOM

WHAT-- WHAT IS IT, GIRL?

KLAAANG KLAAANG KLAAANK

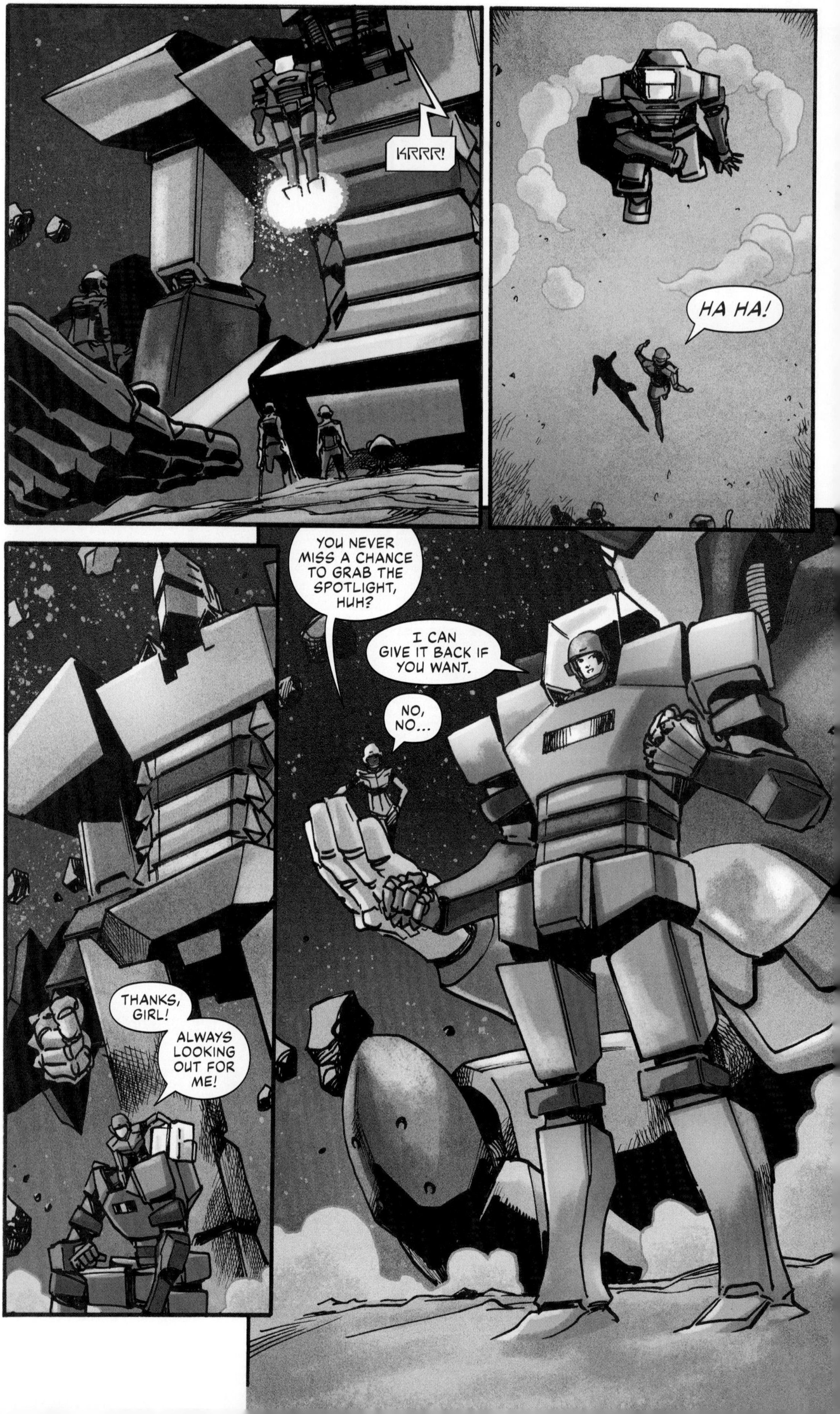
KRRRR!
HA HA!
YOU NEVER MISS A CHANCE TO GRAB THE SPOTLIGHT, HUH?
I CAN GIVE IT BACK IF YOU WANT.
NO, NO...
THANKS, GIRL!
ALWAYS LOOKING OUT FOR ME!

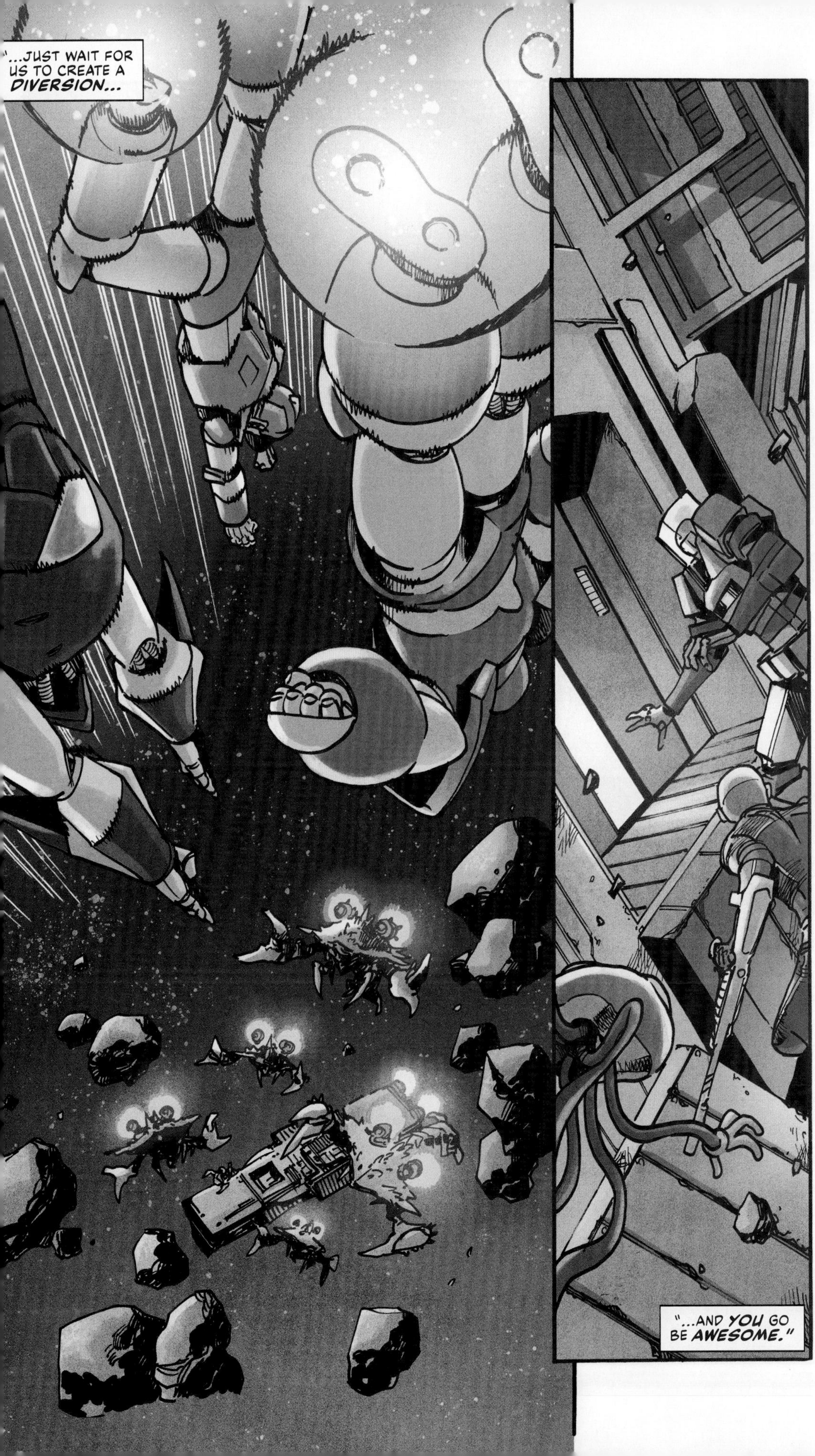
"...JUST WAIT FOR US TO CREATE A ***DIVERSION...***
"...AND ***YOU*** GO BE ***AWESOME.***"

SKRAAAKOW
SKRAAAKOW

COOL.

PTAAANG
PTAAANG
PTAAANG

SKRRAAAKTZ

COOL.

ネマザさ

YEAH, I THINK THEY'RE BEHIND THAT DOOR!

ALL RIGHT, STEP ASIDE--

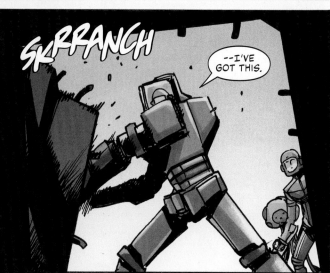

SKRRANCH

--I'VE GOT THIS.

DANG IT!
IT'S EMPTY!
WHAT THE HECK...?
HEAT SIGNATURES.
THEY WERE JUST HERE.
THE SHARG MOVED THEM.
THAT MEANS...
THEY KNEW WE WERE COMING.
RRRRMMMMMMBL
OH, MAN...
COME ON!

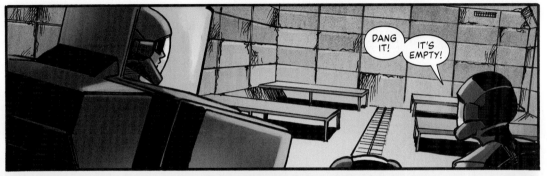

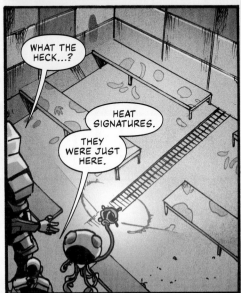

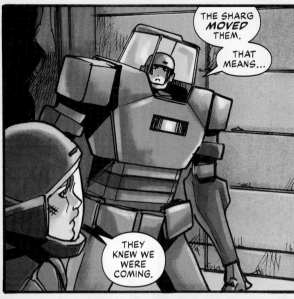

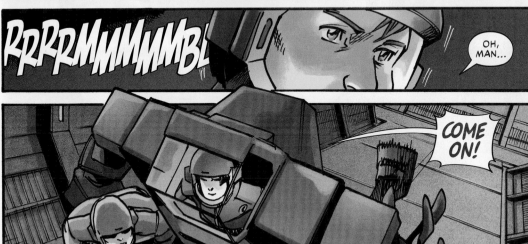

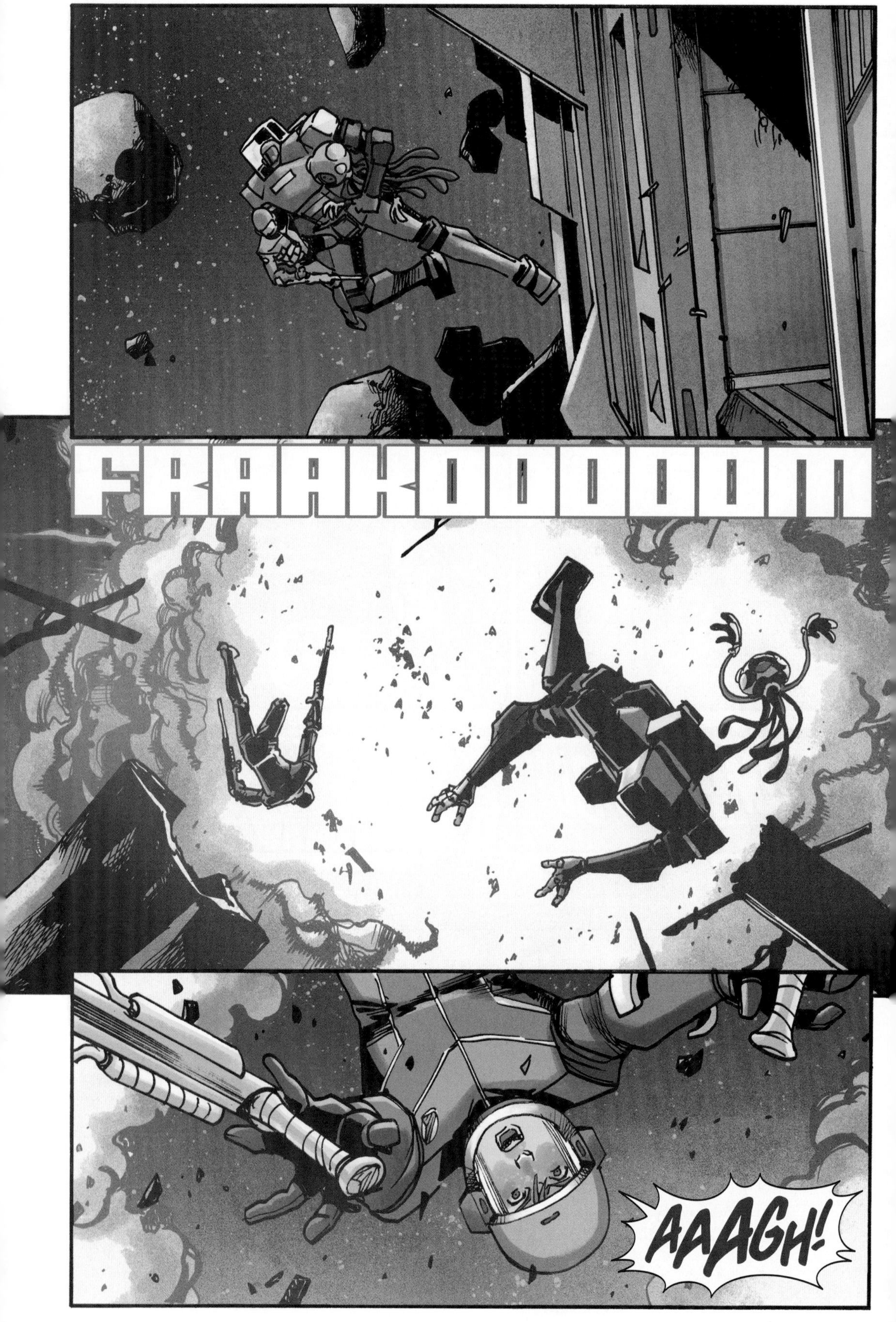
FRAAKOOOOOM
AAAGH!

GOTCHA.
THANKS.
NO PROBLEM.
I'M NOT USUALLY THE ONE WHO GETS SAVED.
GET USED TO IT.
I MIGHT.
OLIVIA!
NO--!

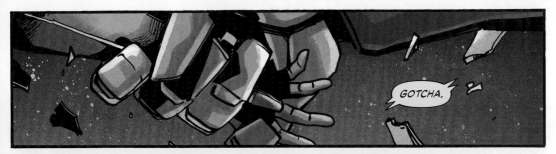

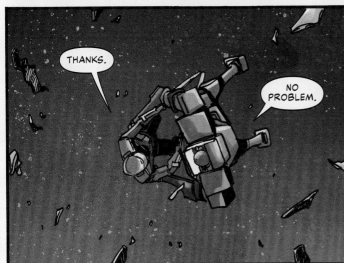

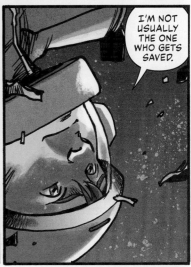

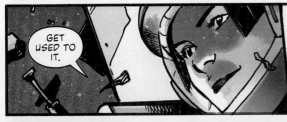

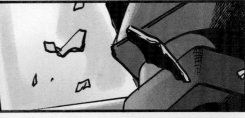

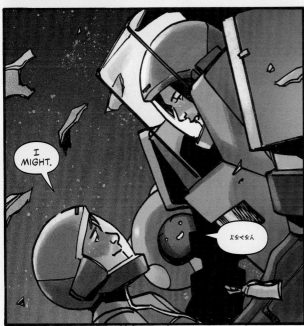

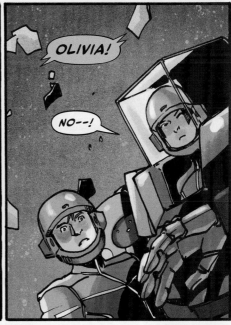

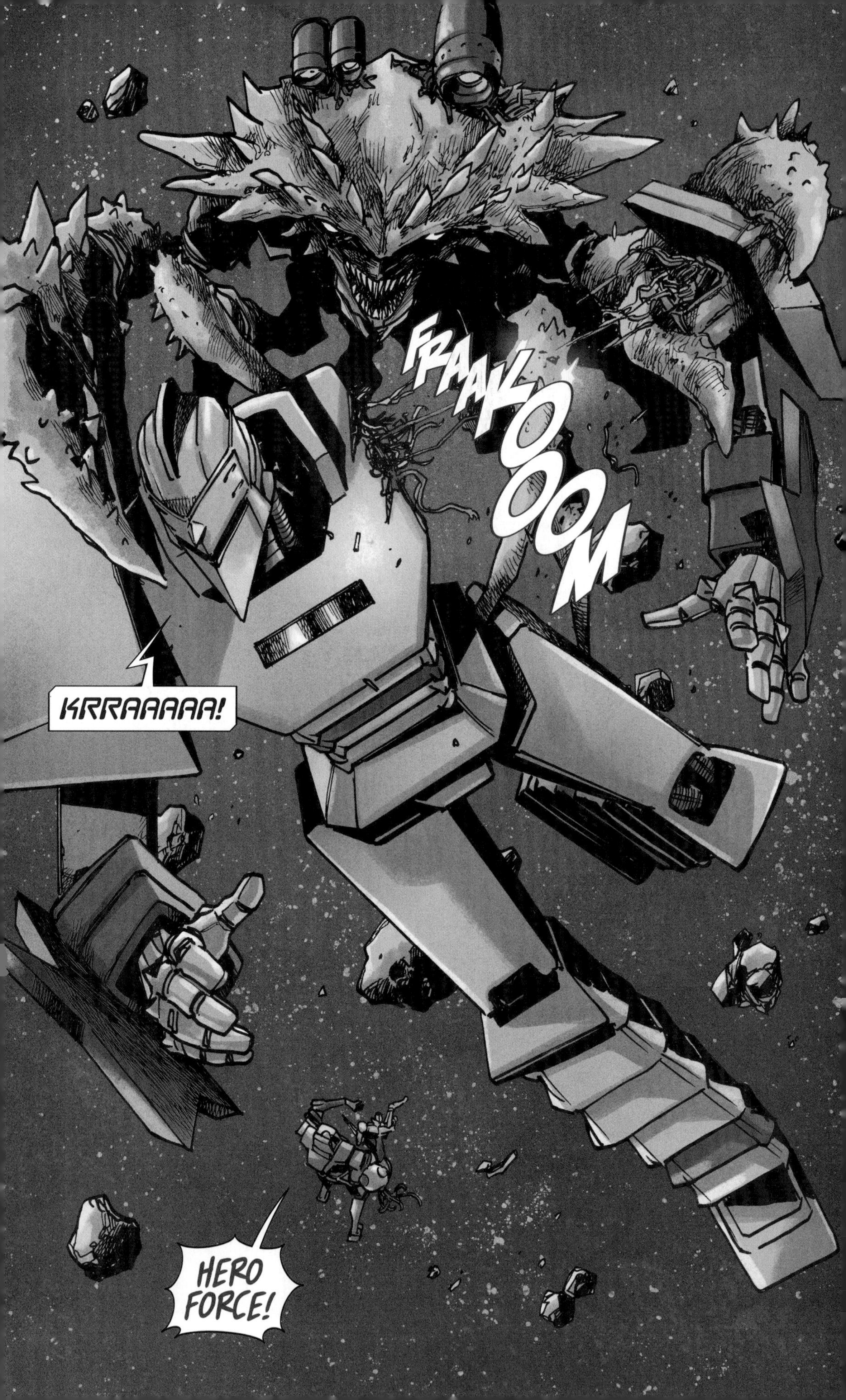
FRAAKOOOM
KRRAAAAA!
HERO FORCE!

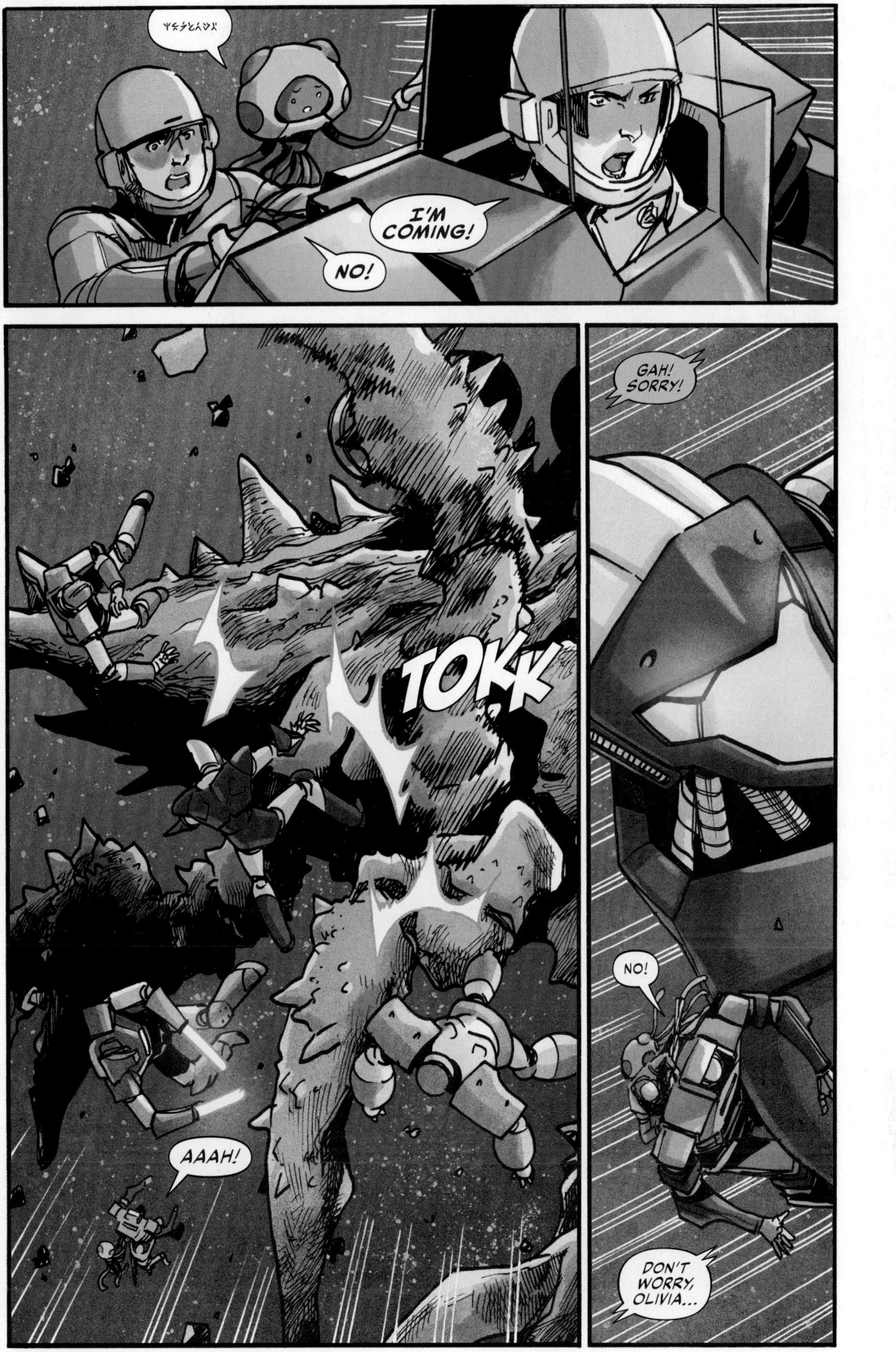
I'M COMING!
NO!
TOKK
AAAH!
GAH! SORRY!
NO!
DON'T WORRY, OLIVIA...

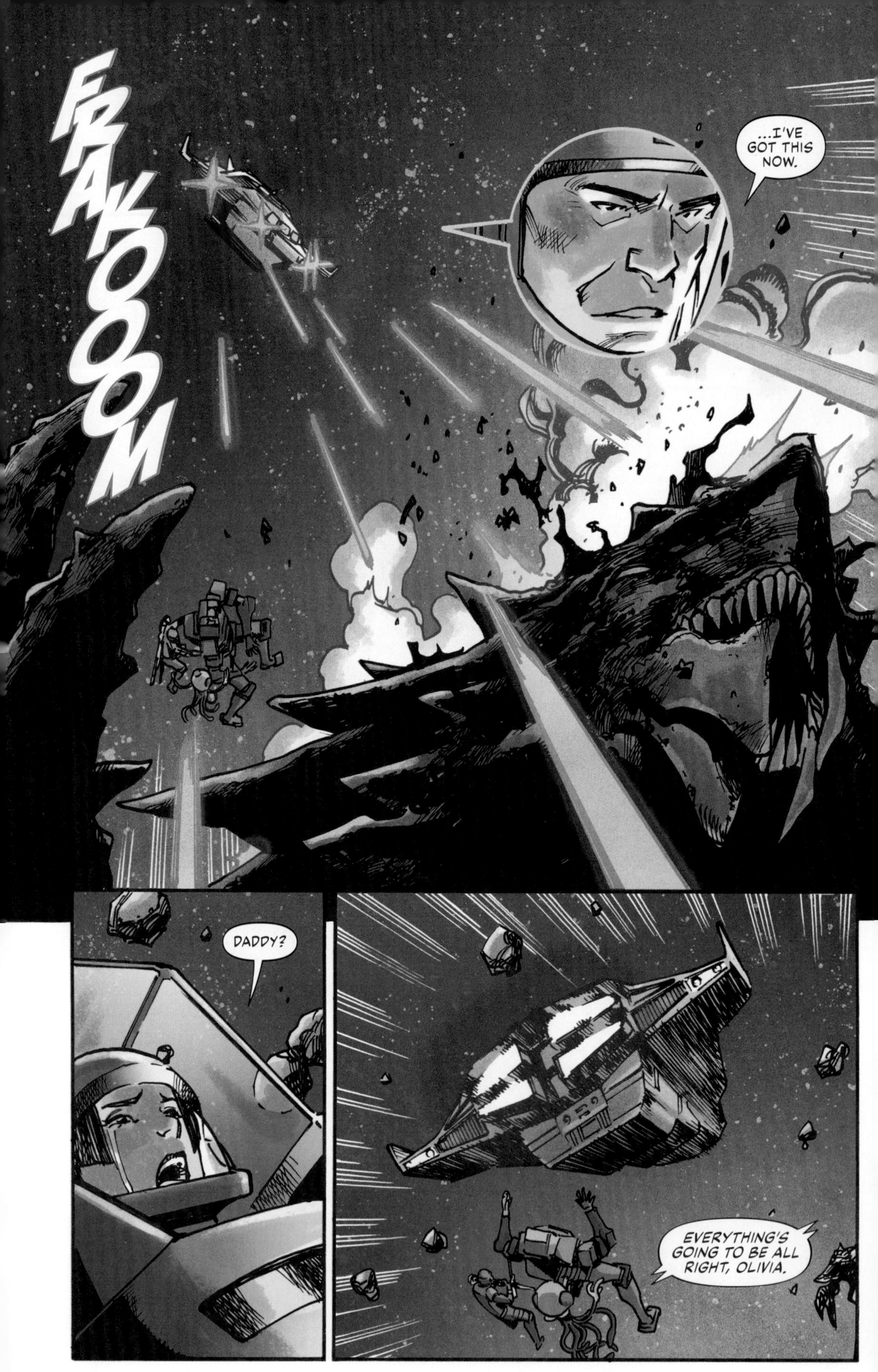
FRAKOOOOM
...I'VE GOT THIS NOW.
DADDY?
EVERYTHING'S GOING TO BE ALL RIGHT, OLIVIA.

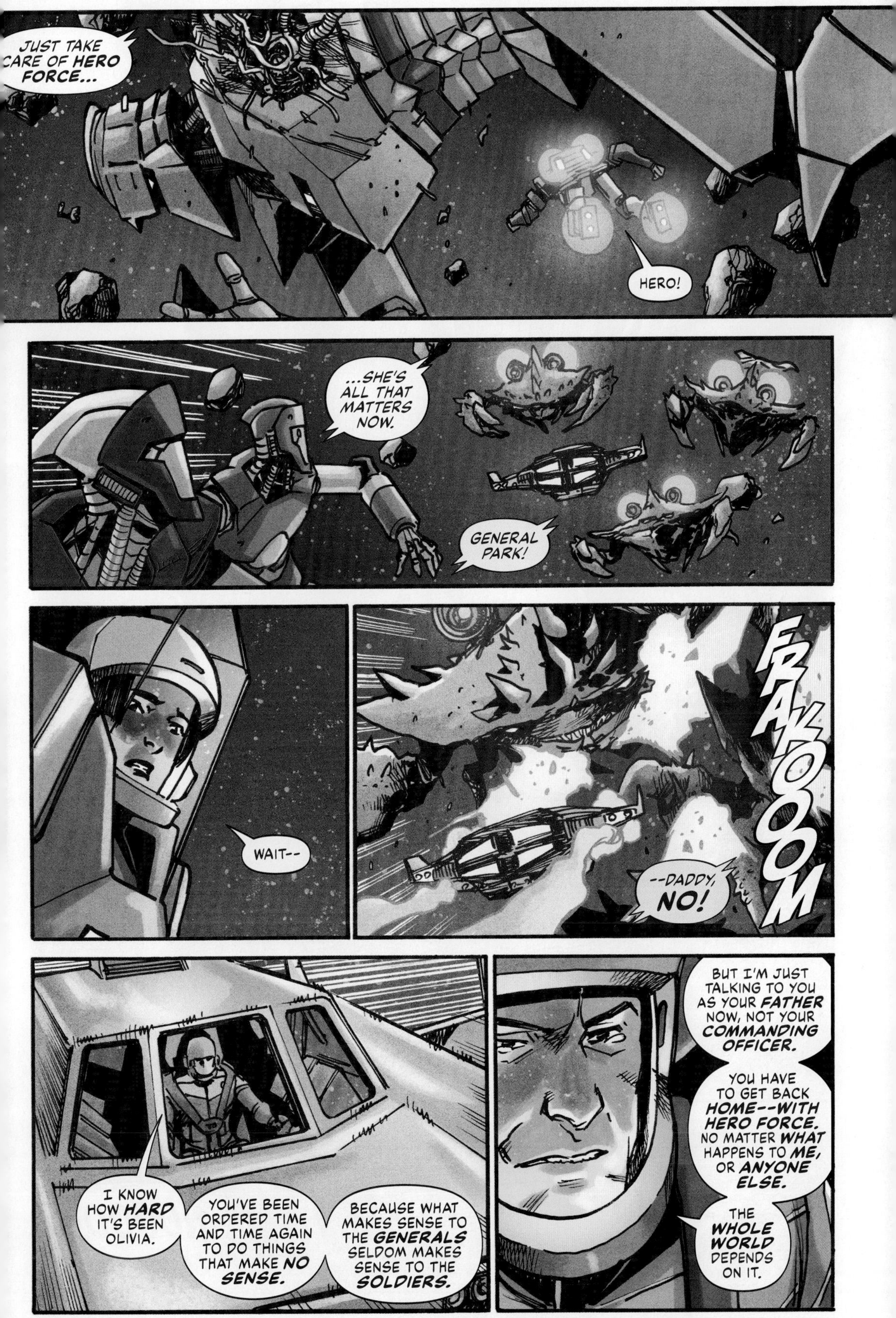
JUST TAKE CARE OF HERO FORCE...
HERO!
...SHE'S ALL THAT MATTERS NOW.
GENERAL PARK!
WAIT--
--DADDY, NO!
FRAKOOOOM
I KNOW HOW HARD IT'S BEEN OLIVIA.
YOU'VE BEEN ORDERED TIME AND TIME AGAIN TO DO THINGS THAT MAKE NO SENSE.
BECAUSE WHAT MAKES SENSE TO THE GENERALS SELDOM MAKES SENSE TO THE SOLDIERS.
BUT I'M JUST TALKING TO YOU AS YOUR FATHER NOW, NOT YOUR COMMANDING OFFICER.
YOU HAVE TO GET BACK HOME--WITH HERO FORCE. NO MATTER WHAT HAPPENS TO ME, OR ANYONE ELSE.
THE WHOLE WORLD DEPENDS ON IT.

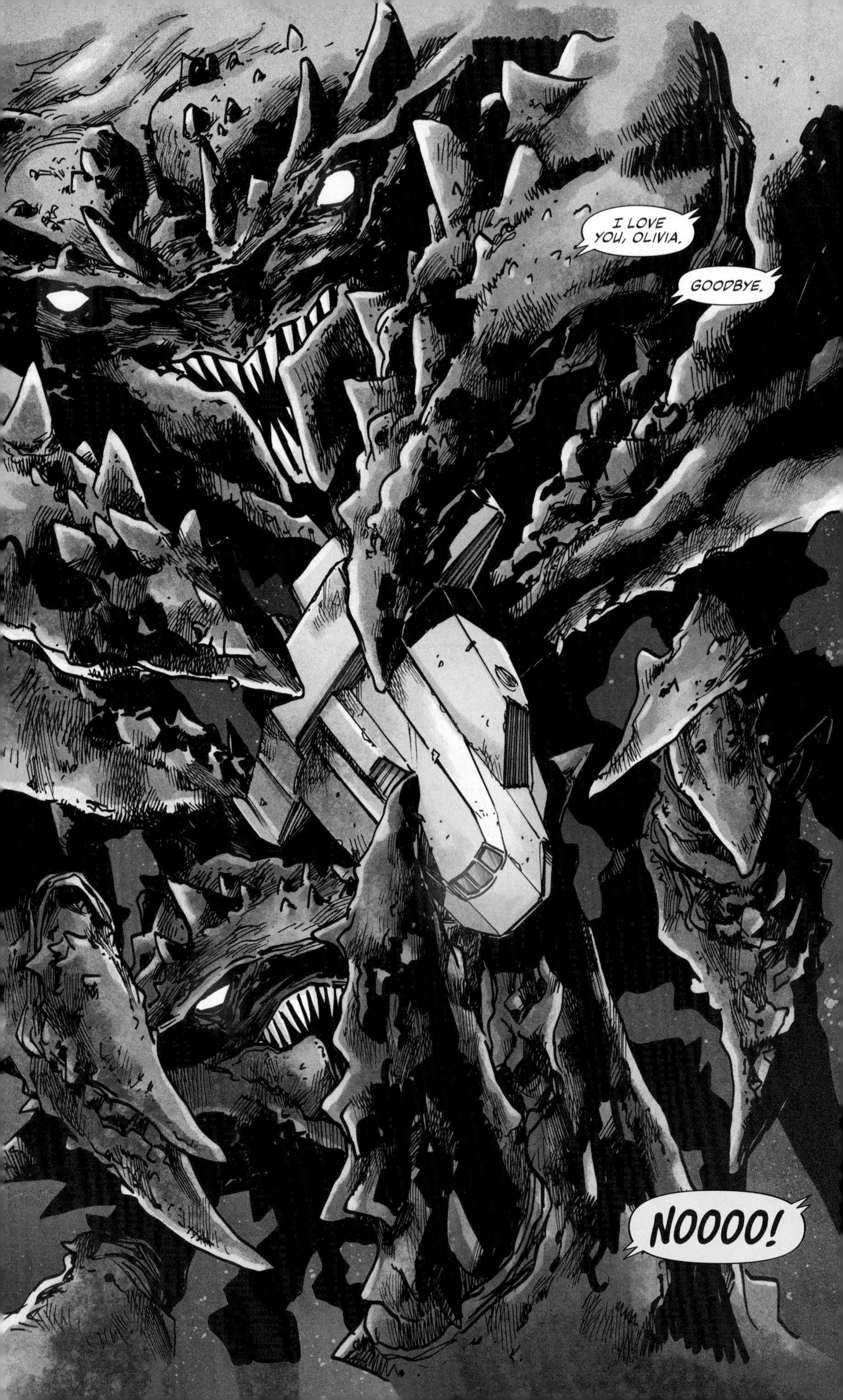
I LOVE YOU, OLIVIA.
GOODBYE.
NOOOO!

CHAPTER **THREE**

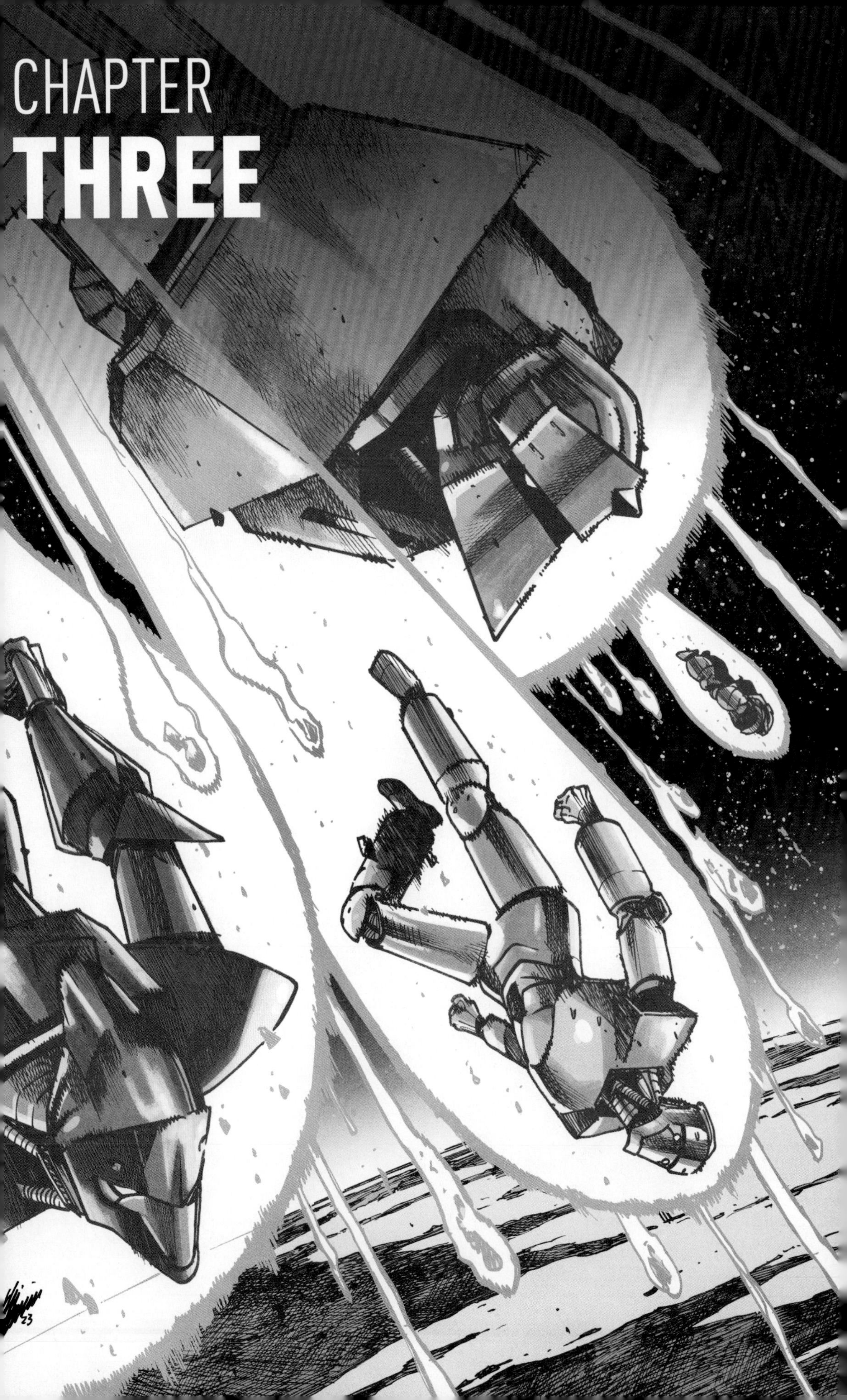

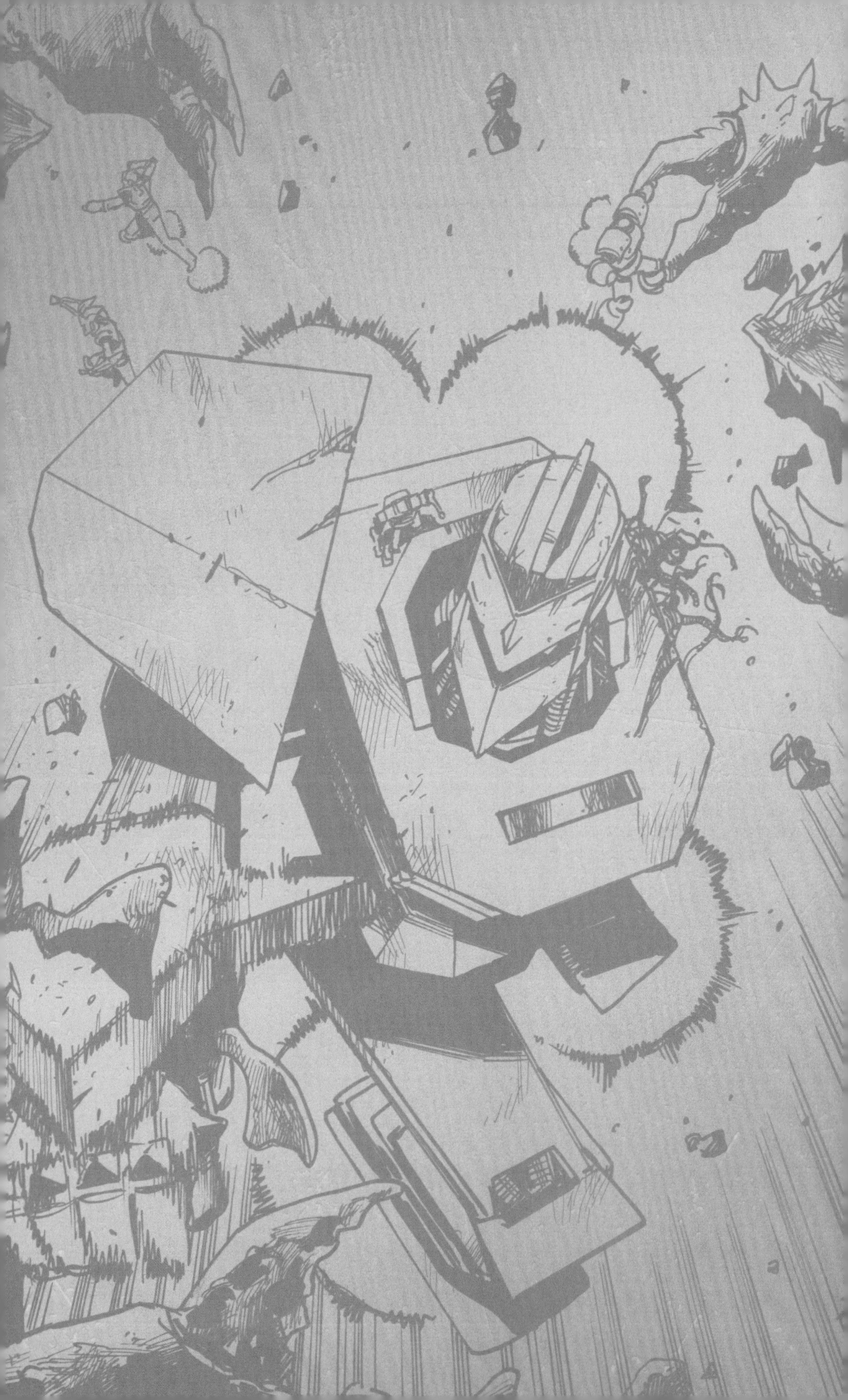

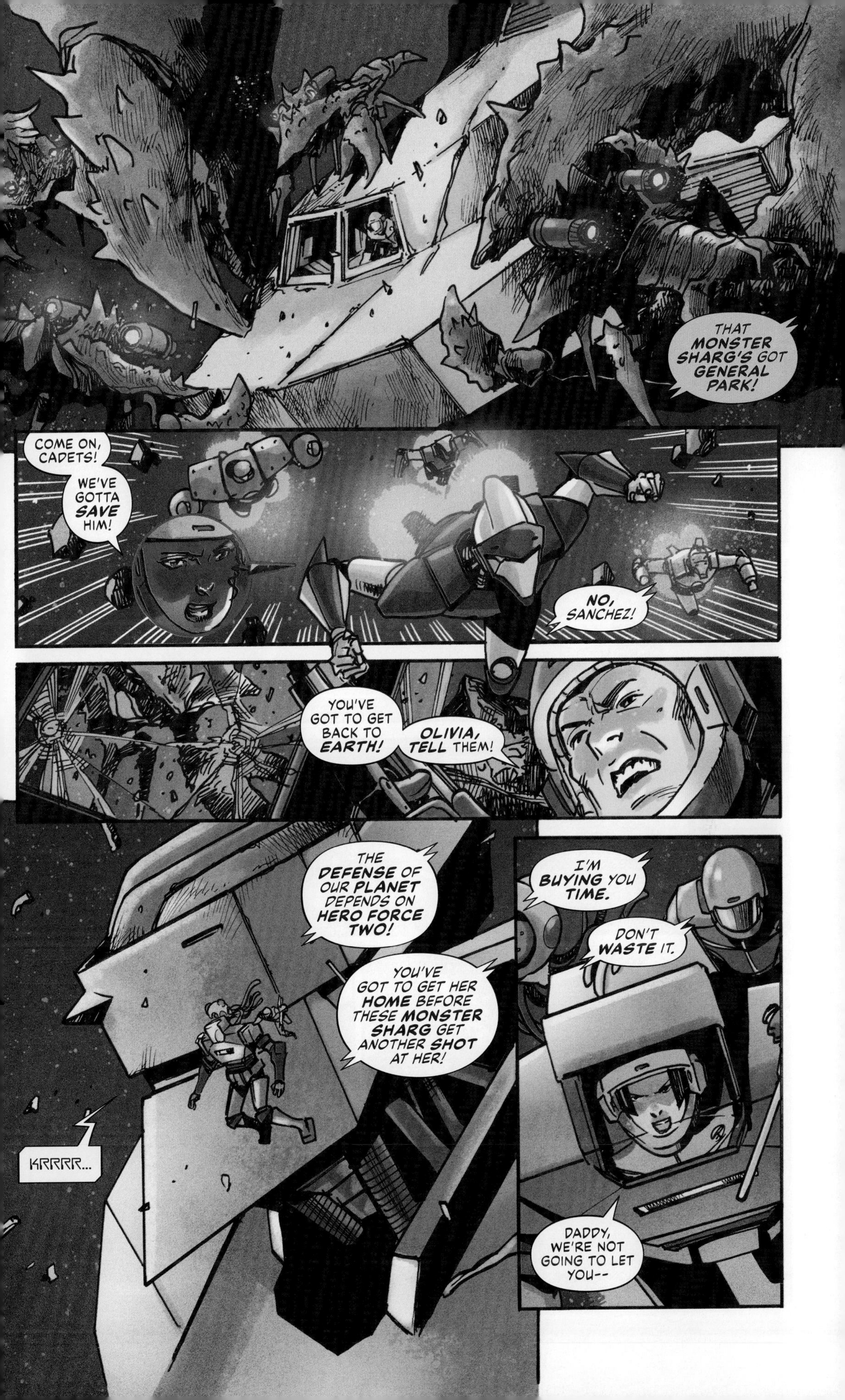
THAT MONSTER SHARG'S GOT GENERAL PARK!
COME ON, CADETS!
WE'VE GOTTA SAVE HIM!
NO, SANCHEZ!
YOU'VE GOT TO GET BACK TO EARTH!
OLIVIA, TELL THEM!
THE DEFENSE OF OUR PLANET DEPENDS ON HERO FORCE TWO!
YOU'VE GOT TO GET HER HOME BEFORE THESE MONSTER SHARG GET ANOTHER SHOT AT HER!
KRRRRR...
I'M BUYING YOU TIME.
DON'T WASTE IT.
DADDY, WE'RE NOT GOING TO LET YOU--

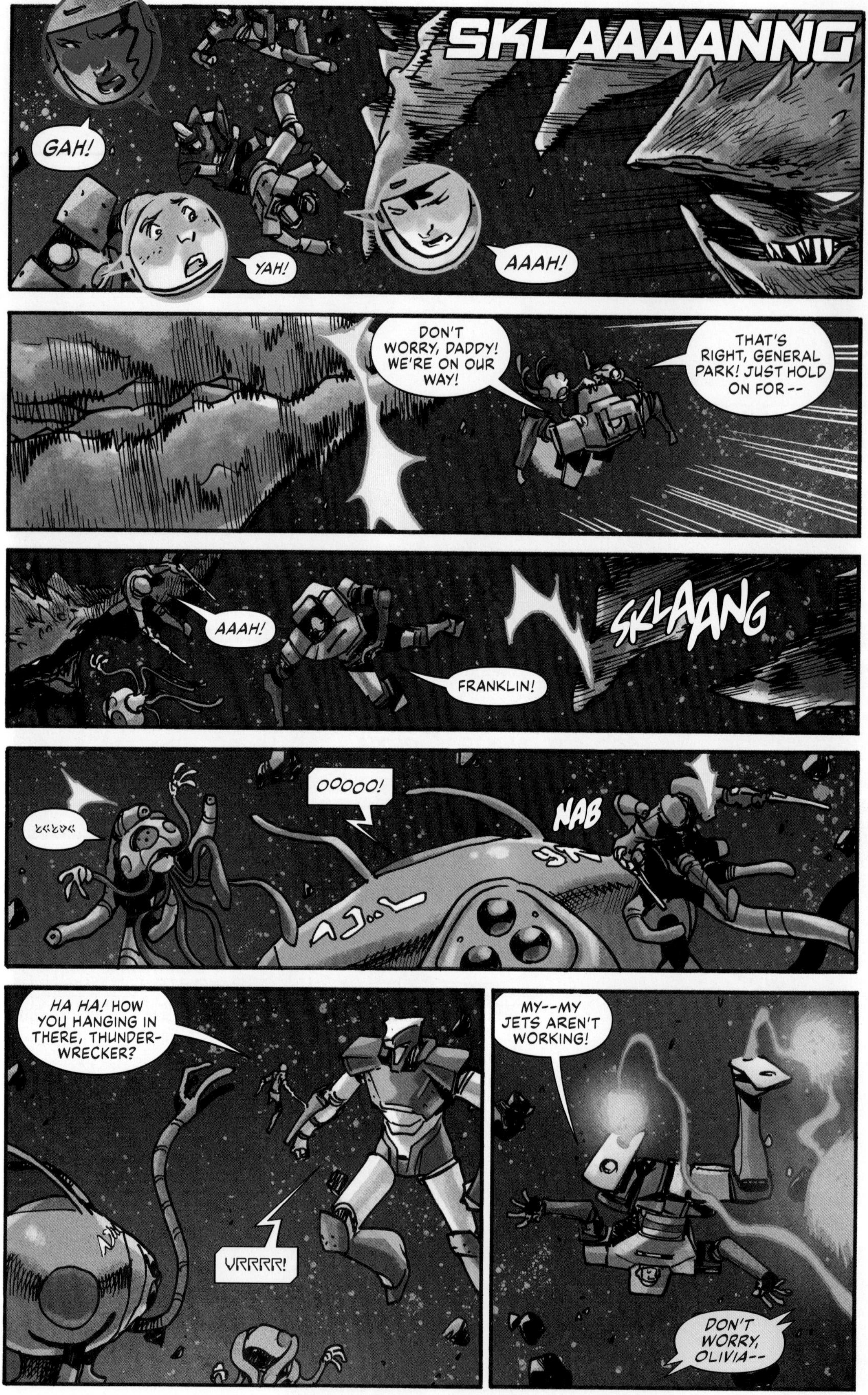
SKLAAAAANNG
GAH!
YAH!
AAAH!
DON'T WORRY, DADDY! WE'RE ON OUR WAY!
THAT'S RIGHT, GENERAL PARK! JUST HOLD ON FOR--
AAAH!
FRANKLIN!
SKLAANG
OOOOO!
NAB
HA HA! HOW YOU HANGING IN THERE, THUNDER-WRECKER?
VRRRRR!
MY--MY JETS AREN'T WORKING!
DON'T WORRY, OLIVIA--

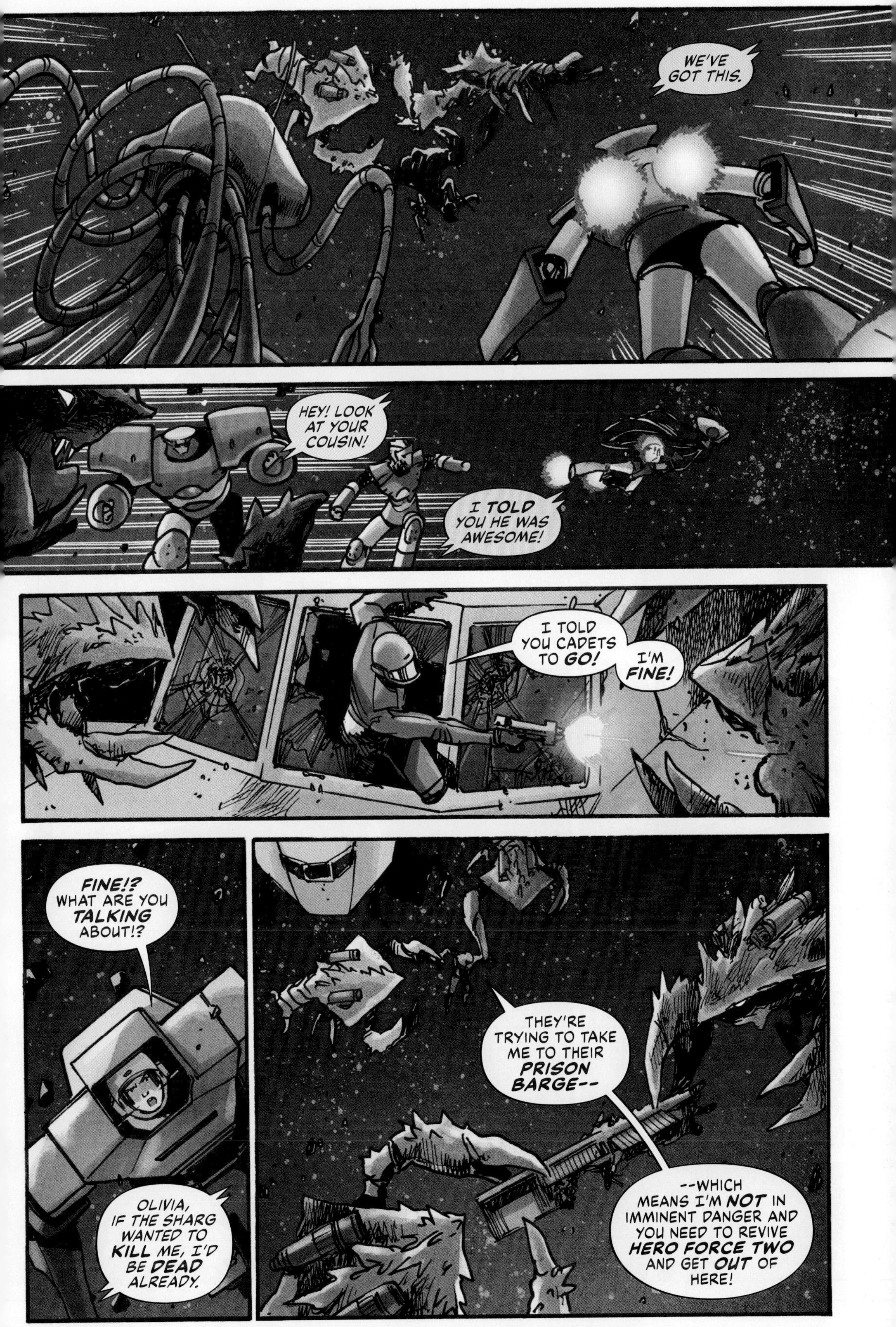
WE'VE GOT THIS.
HEY! LOOK AT YOUR COUSIN!
I TOLD YOU HE WAS AWESOME!
I TOLD YOU CADETS TO GO!
I'M FINE!
FINE!? WHAT ARE YOU TALKING ABOUT!?
OLIVIA, IF THE SHARG WANTED TO KILL ME, I'D BE DEAD ALREADY.
THEY'RE TRYING TO TAKE ME TO THEIR PRISON BARGE--
--WHICH MEANS I'M NOT IN IMMINENT DANGER AND YOU NEED TO REVIVE HERO FORCE TWO AND GET OUT OF HERE!

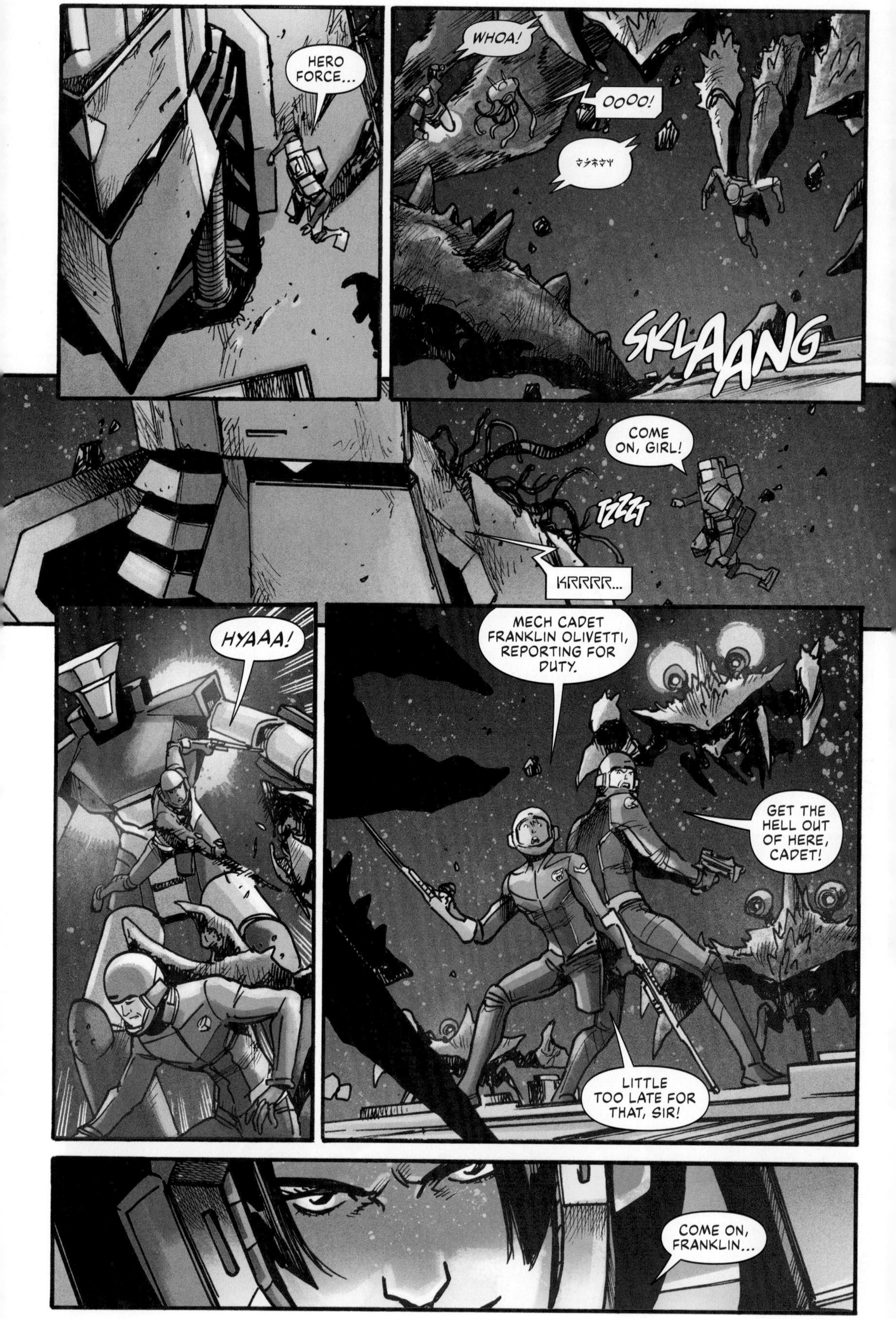
HERO FORCE...
WHOA!
OOOO!
SKLAANG
COME ON, GIRL!
TZZZT
KRRRR...
HYAAA!
MECH CADET FRANKLIN OLIVETTI, REPORTING FOR DUTY.
GET THE HELL OUT OF HERE, CADET!
LITTLE TOO LATE FOR THAT, SIR!
COME ON, FRANKLIN...

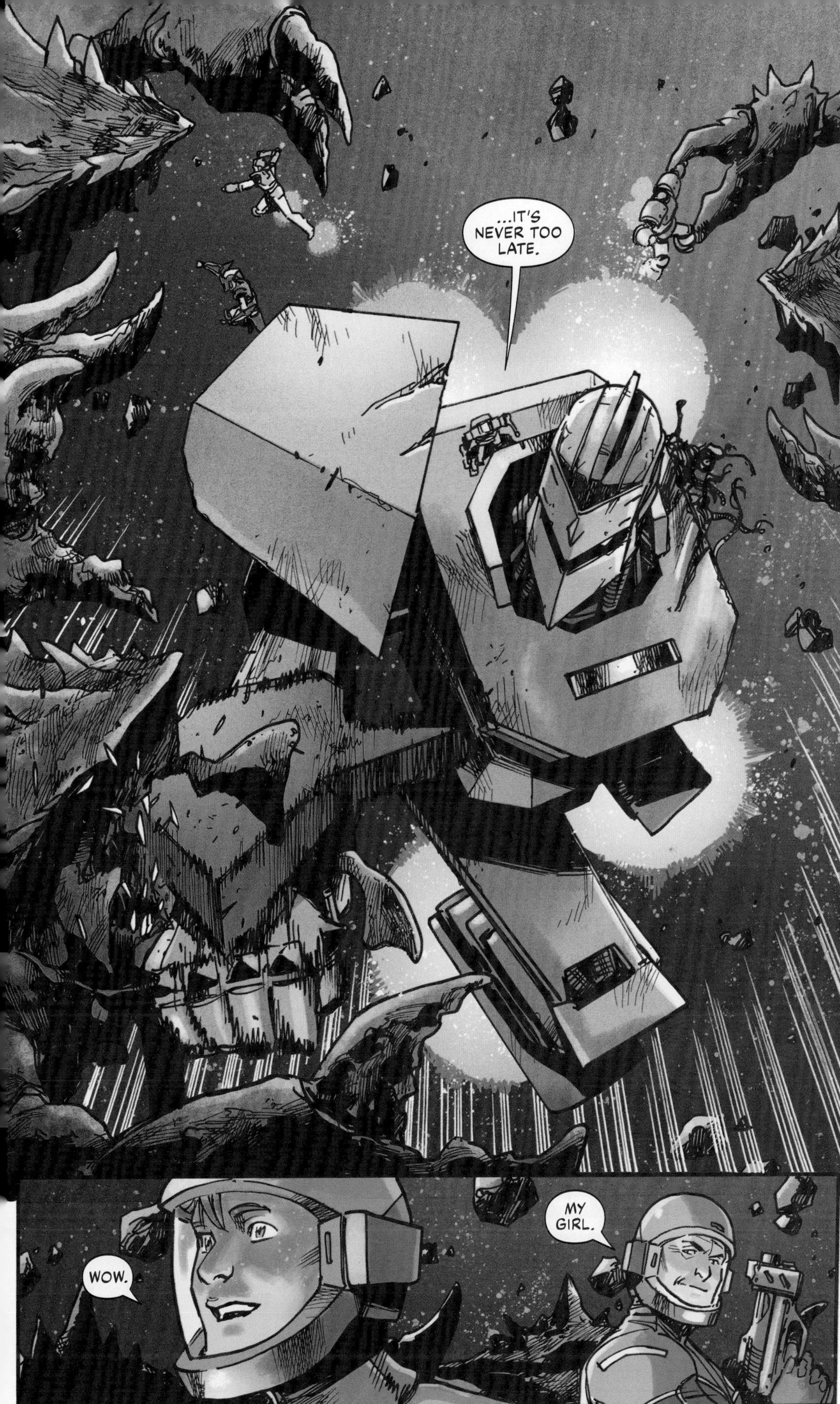
...IT'S NEVER TOO LATE.
WOW.
MY GIRL.

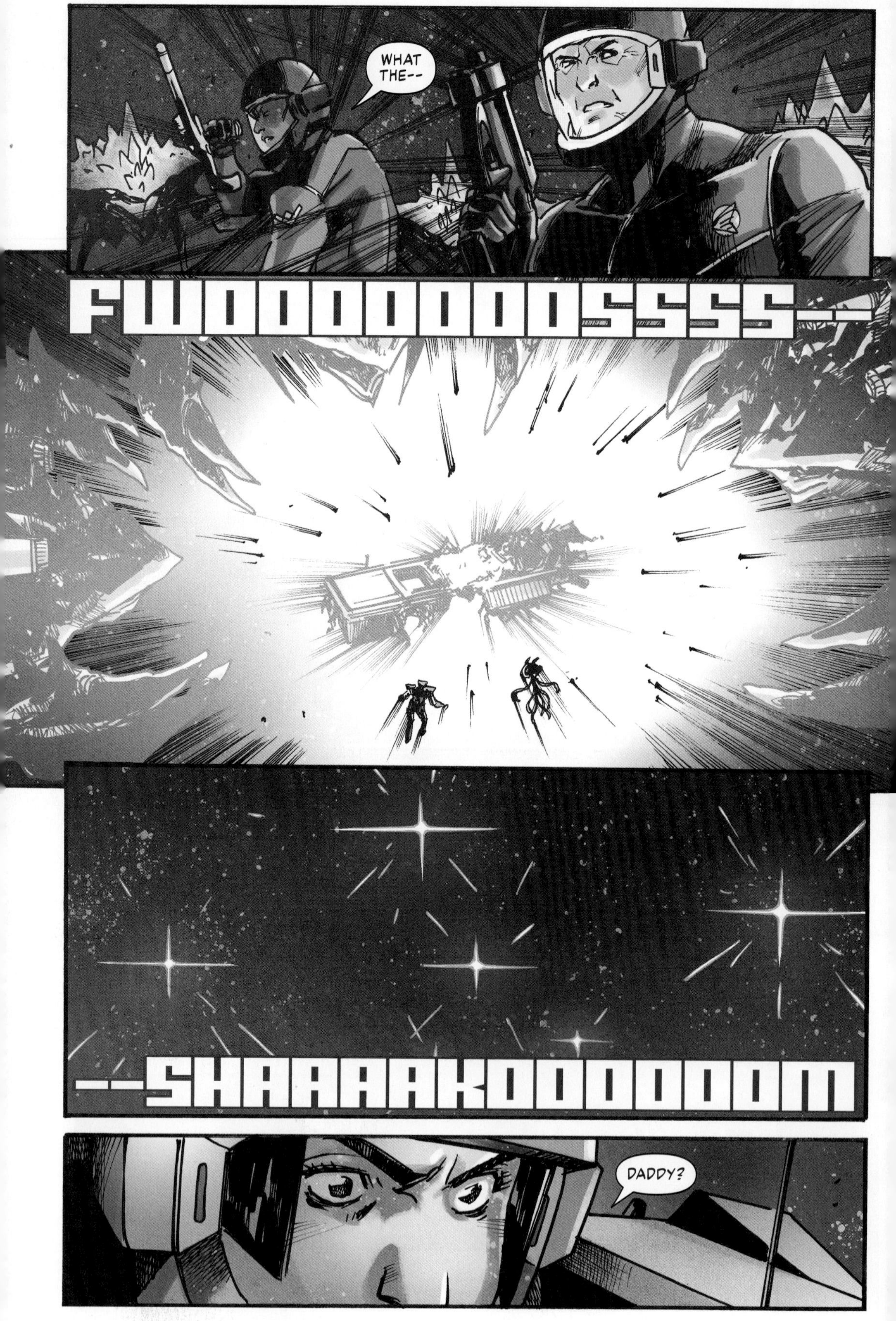
WHAT THE--
FWOOOOOOOSSSSS--
--SHAAAAKOOOOOOOM
DADDY?

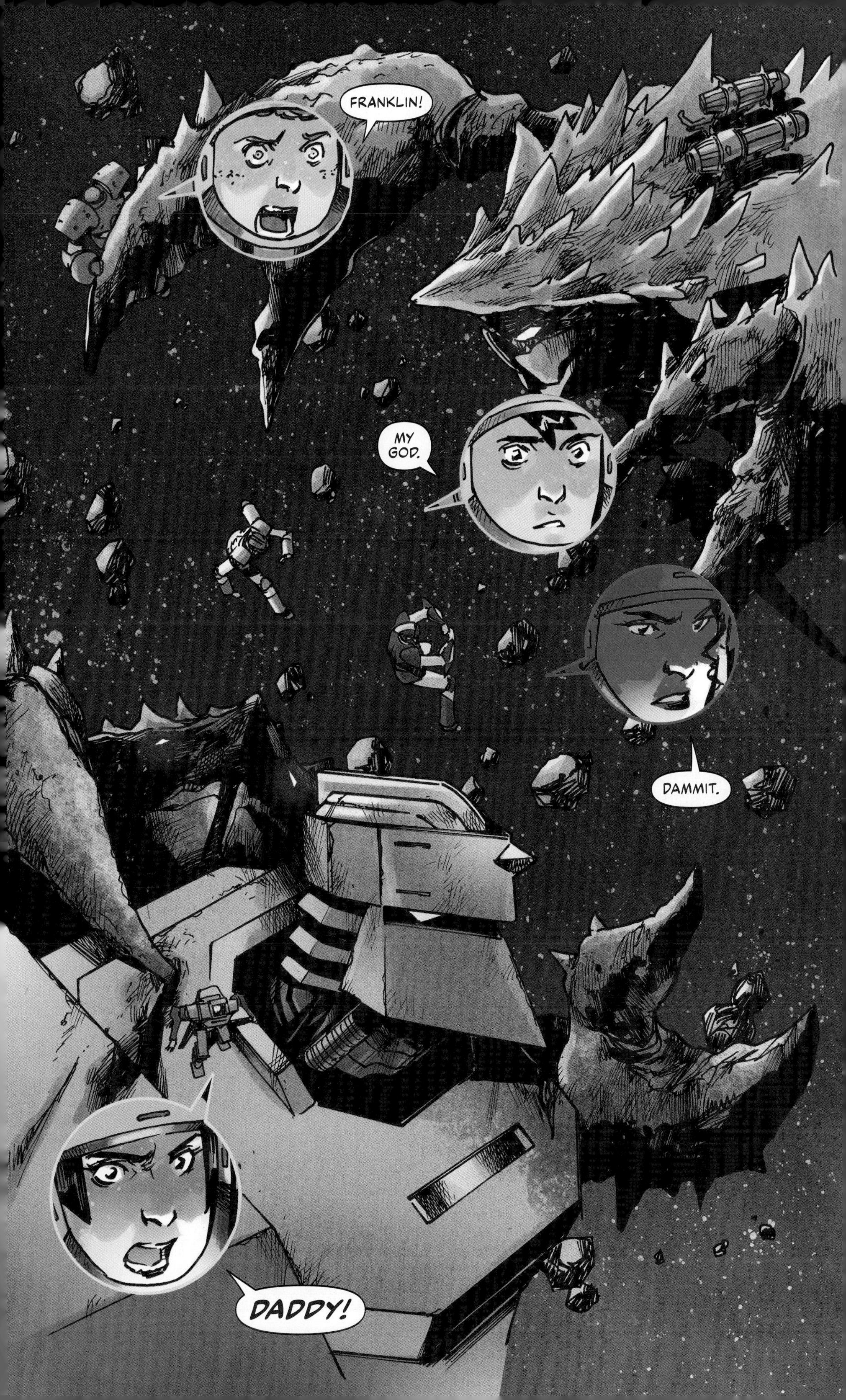
FRANKLIN!
MY GOD.
DAMMIT.
DADDY!

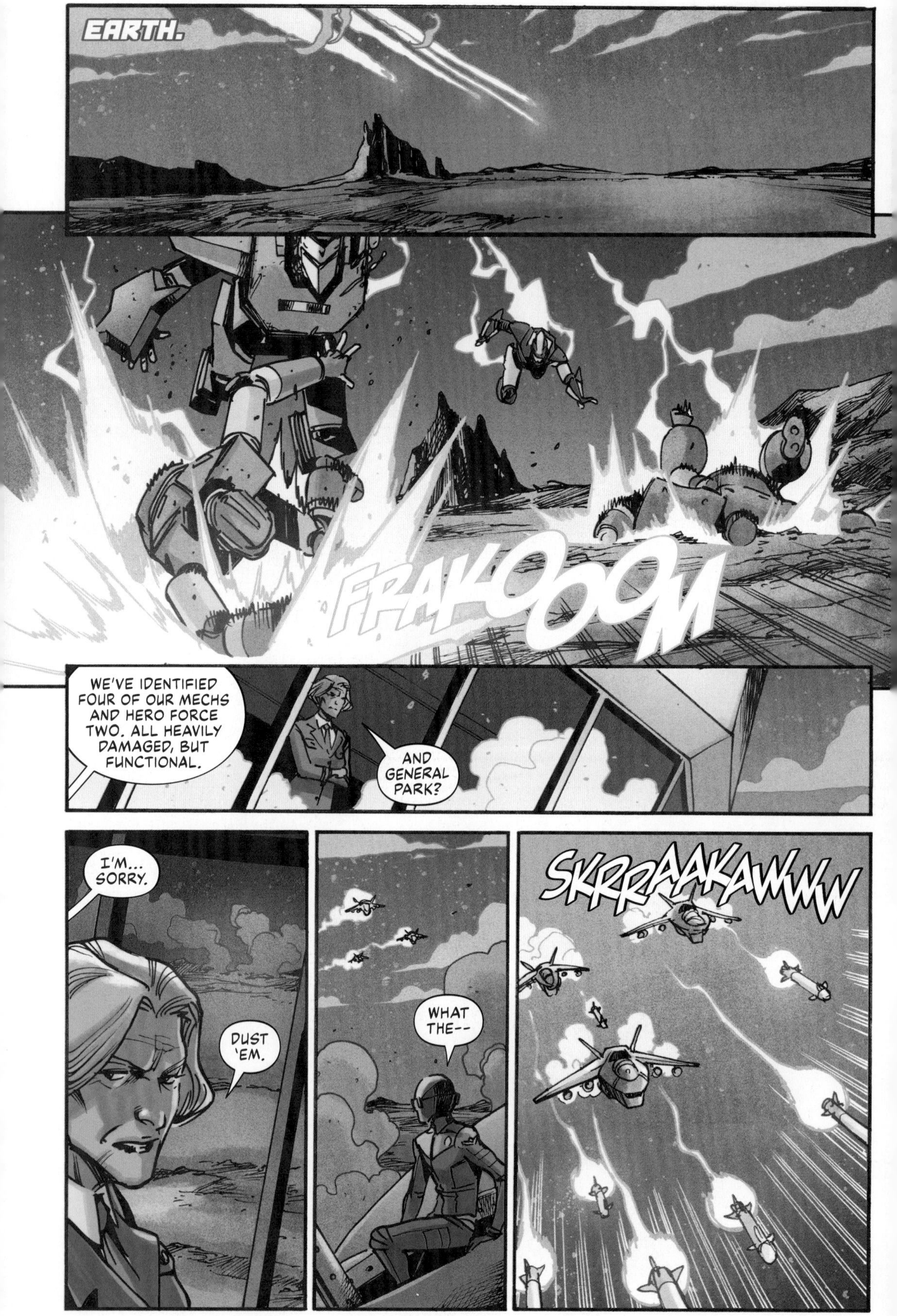
EARTH.
FRAKOOOM
WE'VE IDENTIFIED FOUR OF OUR MECHS AND HERO FORCE TWO. ALL HEAVILY DAMAGED, BUT FUNCTIONAL.
AND GENERAL PARK?
I'M... SORRY.
DUST 'EM.
WHAT THE--
SKRRAAKAWWW

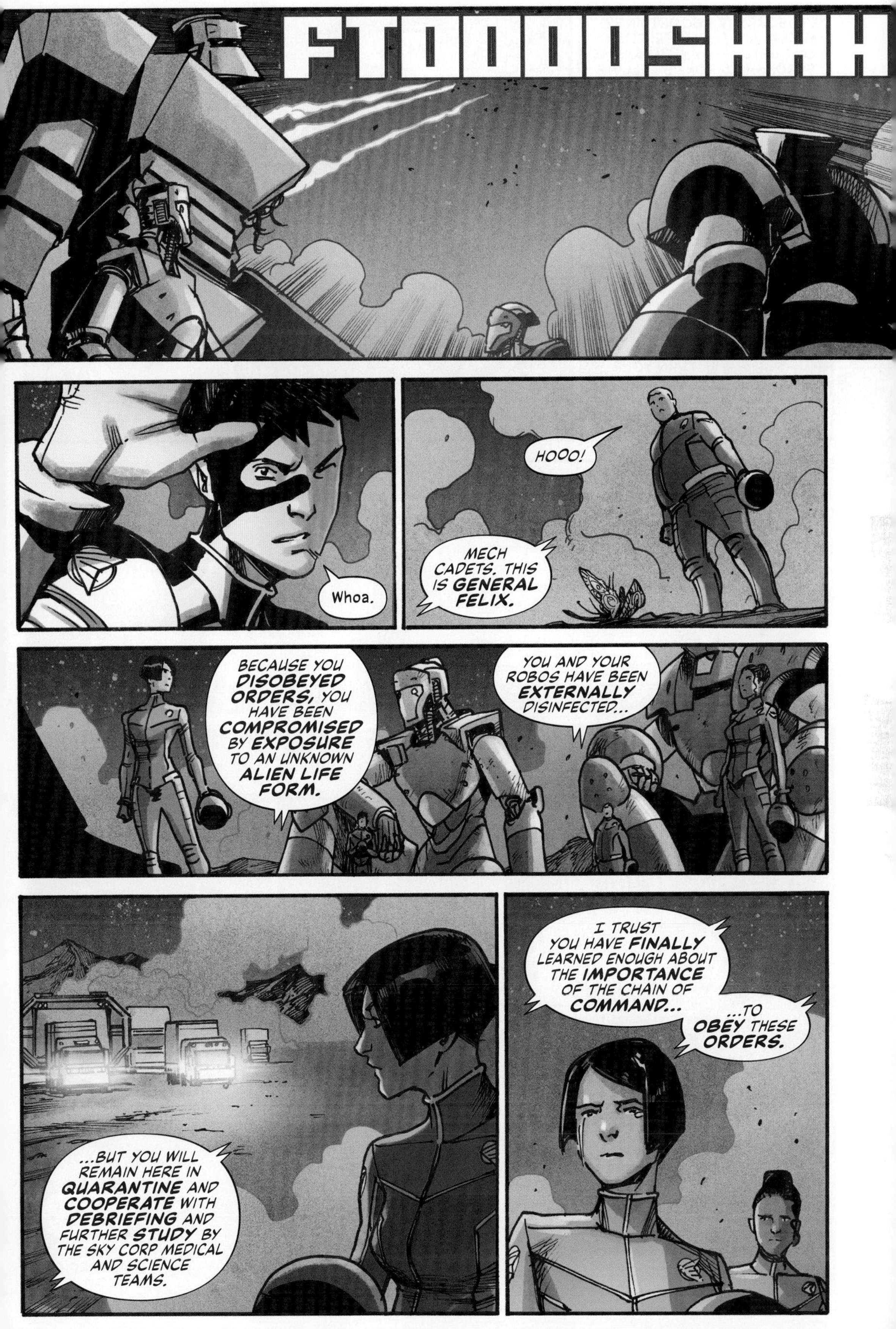
FTOOOOSHHH
Whoa.
HOOO!
MECH CADETS. THIS IS GENERAL FELIX.
BECAUSE YOU DISOBEYED ORDERS, YOU HAVE BEEN COMPROMISED BY EXPOSURE TO AN UNKNOWN ALIEN LIFE FORM.
YOU AND YOUR ROBOS HAVE BEEN EXTERNALLY DISINFECTED...
...BUT YOU WILL REMAIN HERE IN QUARANTINE AND COOPERATE WITH DEBRIEFING AND FURTHER STUDY BY THE SKY CORP MEDICAL AND SCIENCE TEAMS.
I TRUST YOU HAVE FINALLY LEARNED ENOUGH ABOUT THE IMPORTANCE OF THE CHAIN OF COMMAND...
...TO OBEY THESE ORDERS.

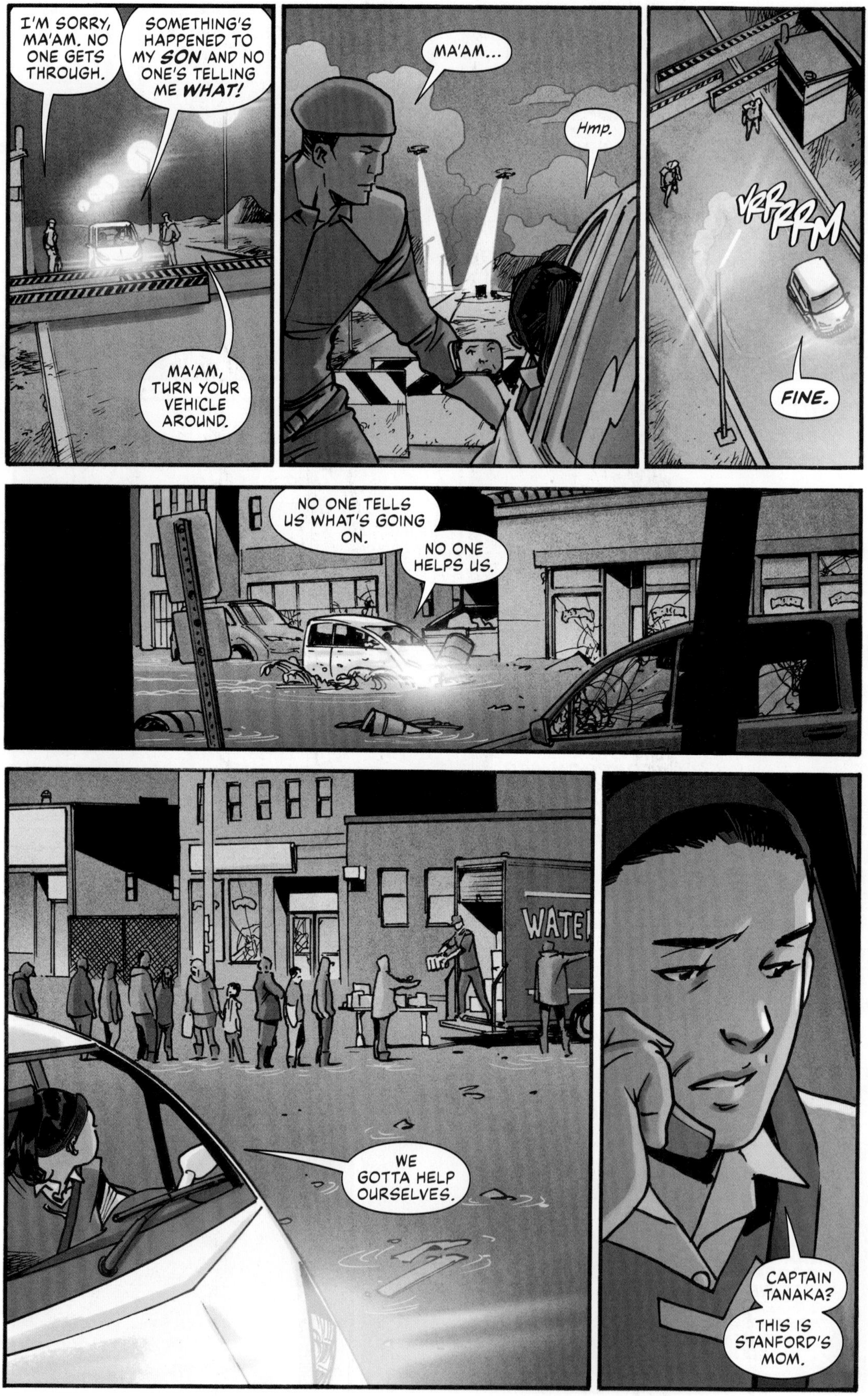
I'M SORRY, MA'AM. NO ONE GETS THROUGH.
SOMETHING'S HAPPENED TO MY **SON** AND NO ONE'S TELLING ME ***WHAT!***
MA'AM, TURN YOUR VEHICLE AROUND.
MA'AM...
Hmp.
VRRRRRM
FINE.
NO ONE TELLS US WHAT'S GOING ON.
NO ONE HELPS US.
WATER
WE GOTTA HELP OURSELVES.
CAPTAIN TANAKA?
THIS IS STANFORD'S MOM.

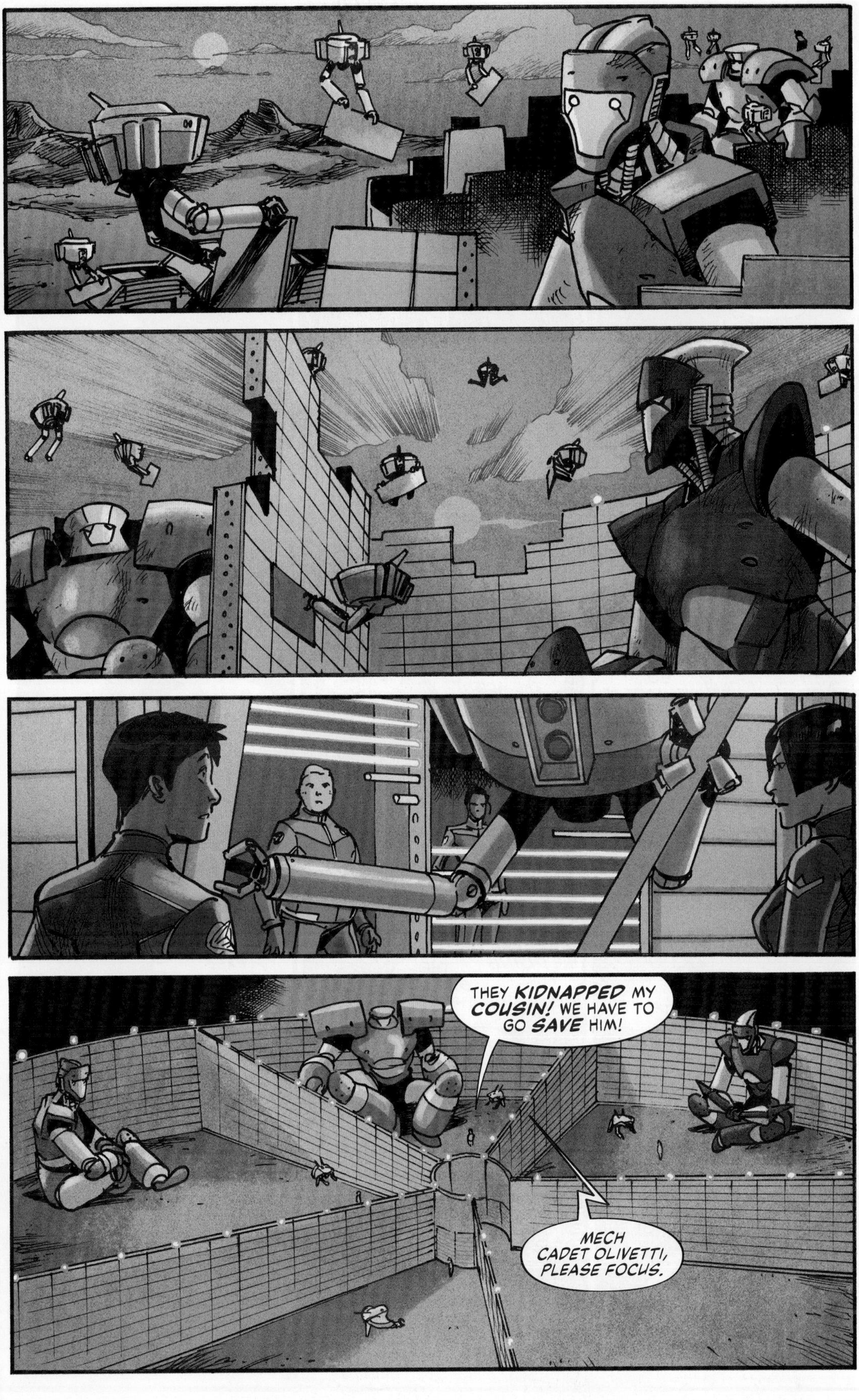
THEY KIDNAPPED MY COUSIN! WE HAVE TO GO SAVE HIM!
MECH CADET OLIVETTI, PLEASE FOCUS.

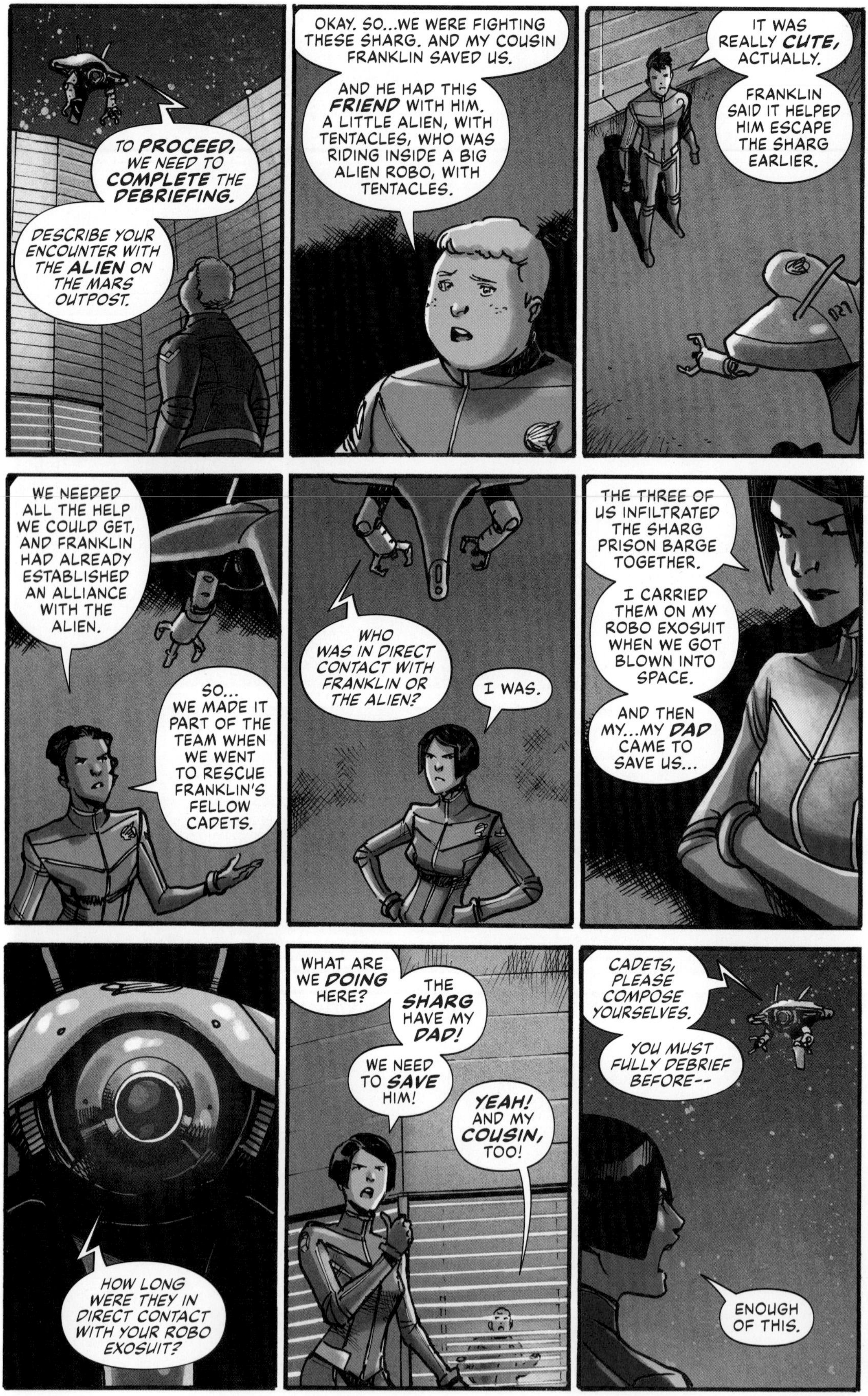
TO PROCEED, WE NEED TO COMPLETE THE DEBRIEFING.
DESCRIBE YOUR ENCOUNTER WITH THE ALIEN ON THE MARS OUTPOST.
OKAY. SO...WE WERE FIGHTING THESE SHARG. AND MY COUSIN FRANKLIN SAVED US.
AND HE HAD THIS FRIEND WITH HIM. A LITTLE ALIEN, WITH TENTACLES, WHO WAS RIDING INSIDE A BIG ALIEN ROBO, WITH TENTACLES.
IT WAS REALLY CUTE, ACTUALLY.
FRANKLIN SAID IT HELPED HIM ESCAPE THE SHARG EARLIER.
D27
WE NEEDED ALL THE HELP WE COULD GET, AND FRANKLIN HAD ALREADY ESTABLISHED AN ALLIANCE WITH THE ALIEN.
SO... WE MADE IT PART OF THE TEAM WHEN WE WENT TO RESCUE FRANKLIN'S FELLOW CADETS.
WHO WAS IN DIRECT CONTACT WITH FRANKLIN OR THE ALIEN?
I WAS.
THE THREE OF US INFILTRATED THE SHARG PRISON BARGE TOGETHER.
I CARRIED THEM ON MY ROBO EXOSUIT WHEN WE GOT BLOWN INTO SPACE.
AND THEN MY...MY DAD CAME TO SAVE US...
HOW LONG WERE THEY IN DIRECT CONTACT WITH YOUR ROBO EXOSUIT?
WHAT ARE WE DOING HERE?
THE SHARG HAVE MY DAD!
WE NEED TO SAVE HIM!
YEAH! AND MY COUSIN, TOO!
CADETS, PLEASE COMPOSE YOURSELVES.
YOU MUST FULLY DEBRIEF BEFORE--
ENOUGH OF THIS.

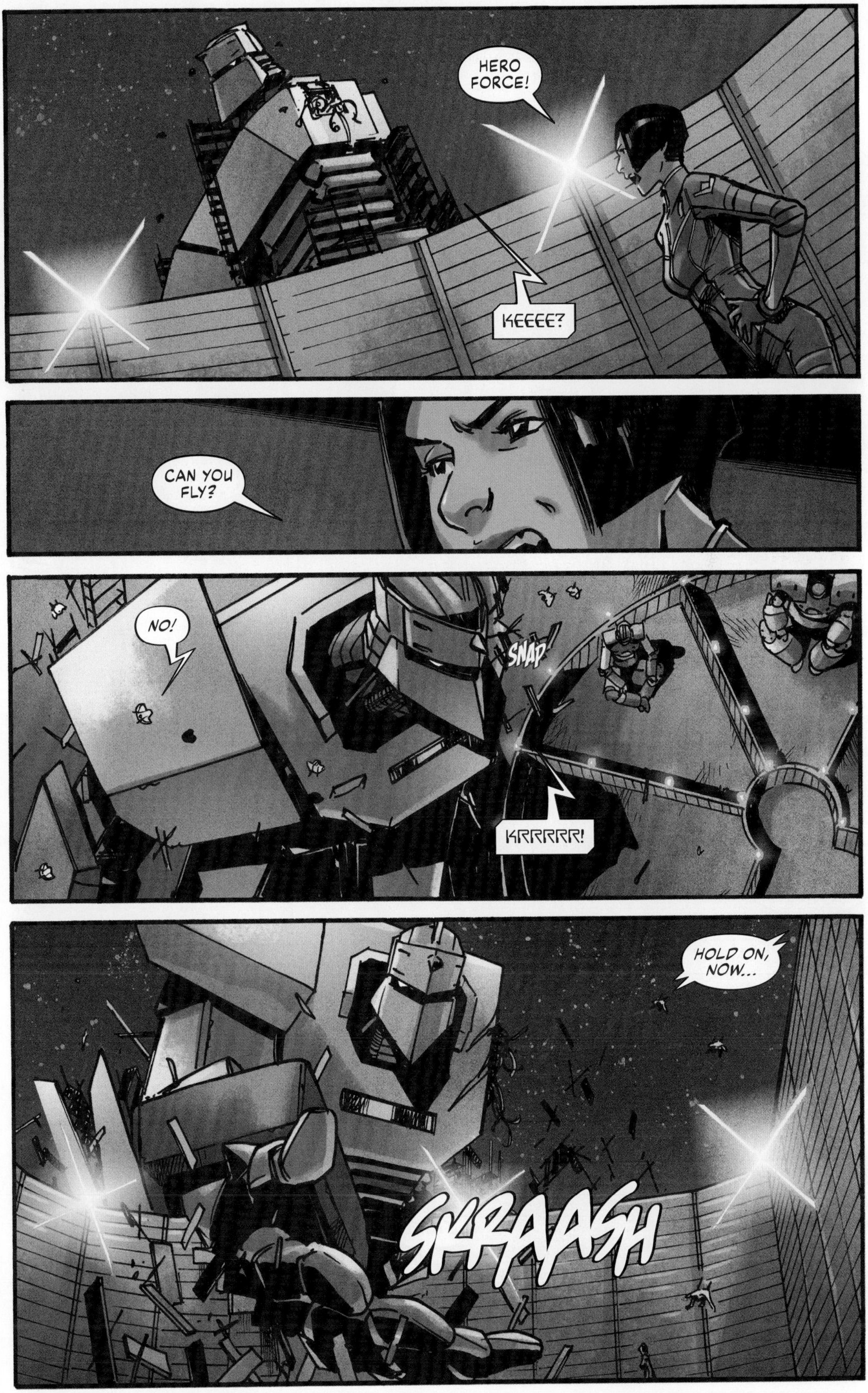
HERO FORCE!
KEEEE?
CAN YOU FLY?
NO!
SNAP
KRRRRRR!
HOLD ON, NOW...
SKRAASH

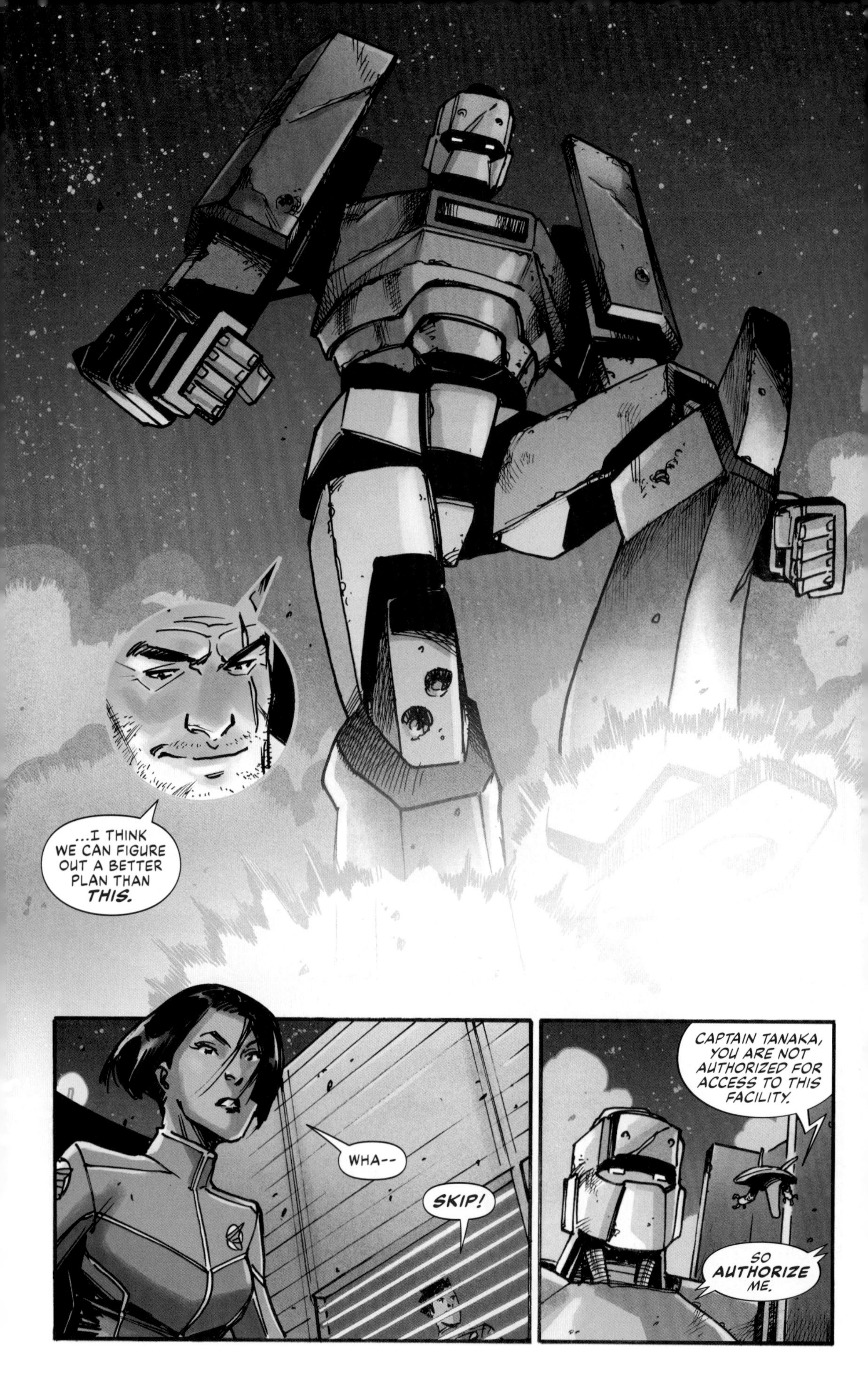
...I THINK WE CAN FIGURE OUT A BETTER PLAN THAN *THIS.*
WHA--
SKIP!
CAPTAIN TANAKA, YOU ARE NOT AUTHORIZED FOR ACCESS TO THIS FACILITY.
SO **AUTHORIZE** ME.

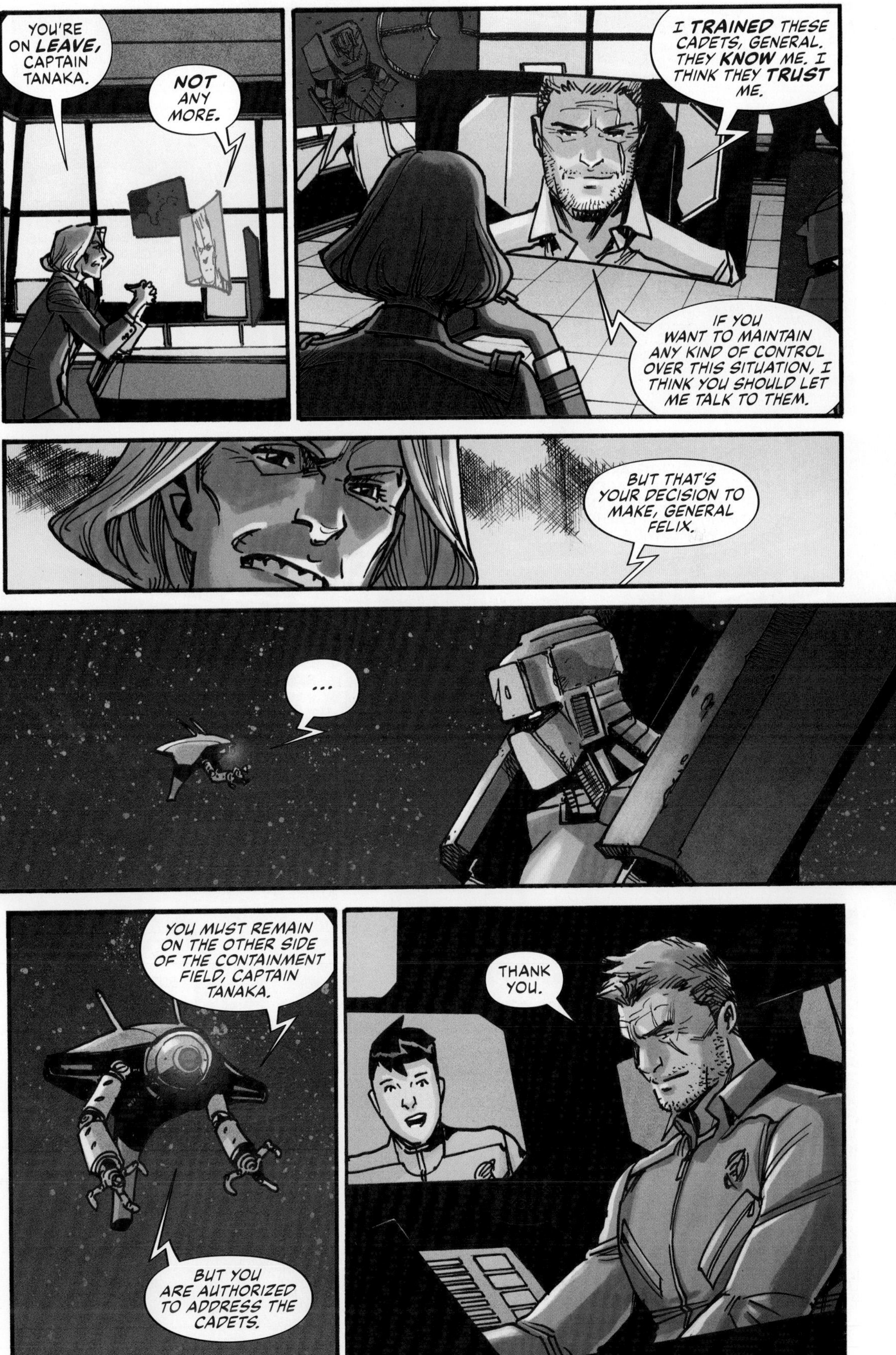
YOU'RE ON LEAVE, CAPTAIN TANAKA.
NOT ANY MORE.
I TRAINED THESE CADETS, GENERAL. THEY KNOW ME. I THINK THEY TRUST ME.
IF YOU WANT TO MAINTAIN ANY KIND OF CONTROL OVER THIS SITUATION, I THINK YOU SHOULD LET ME TALK TO THEM.
BUT THAT'S YOUR DECISION TO MAKE, GENERAL FELIX.
...
YOU MUST REMAIN ON THE OTHER SIDE OF THE CONTAINMENT FIELD, CAPTAIN TANAKA.
BUT YOU ARE AUTHORIZED TO ADDRESS THE CADETS.
THANK YOU.

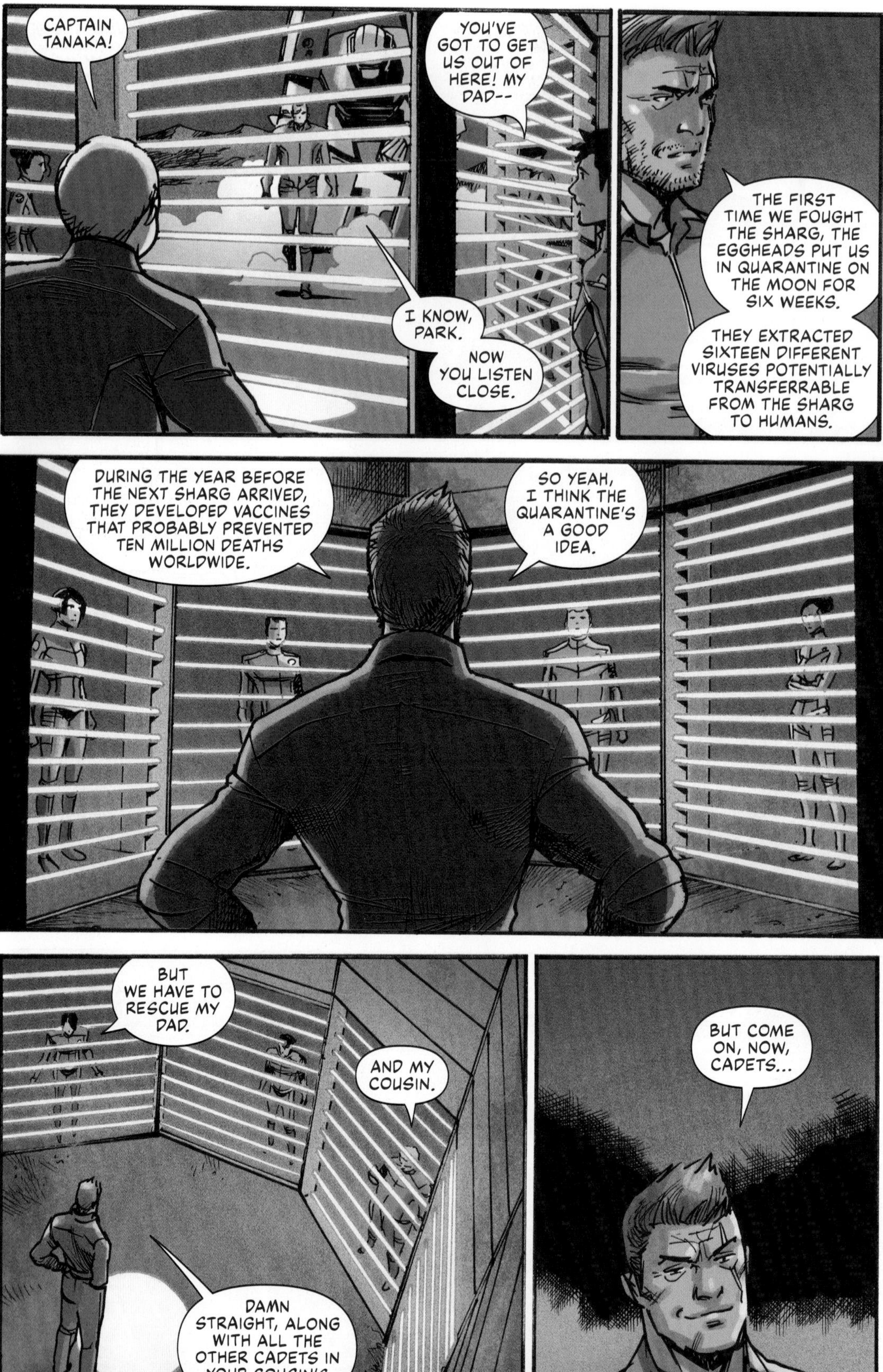
CAPTAIN TANAKA!
YOU'VE GOT TO GET US OUT OF HERE! MY DAD--
I KNOW, PARK.
NOW YOU LISTEN CLOSE.
THE FIRST TIME WE FOUGHT THE SHARG, THE EGGHEADS PUT US IN QUARANTINE ON THE MOON FOR SIX WEEKS.
THEY EXTRACTED SIXTEEN DIFFERENT VIRUSES POTENTIALLY TRANSFERRABLE FROM THE SHARG TO HUMANS.
DURING THE YEAR BEFORE THE NEXT SHARG ARRIVED, THEY DEVELOPED VACCINES THAT PROBABLY PREVENTED TEN MILLION DEATHS WORLDWIDE.
SO YEAH, I THINK THE QUARANTINE'S A GOOD IDEA.
BUT WE HAVE TO RESCUE MY DAD.
AND MY COUSIN.
DAMN STRAIGHT, ALONG WITH ALL THE OTHER CADETS IN YOUR COUSIN'S TEAM.
BUT COME ON, NOW, CADETS...

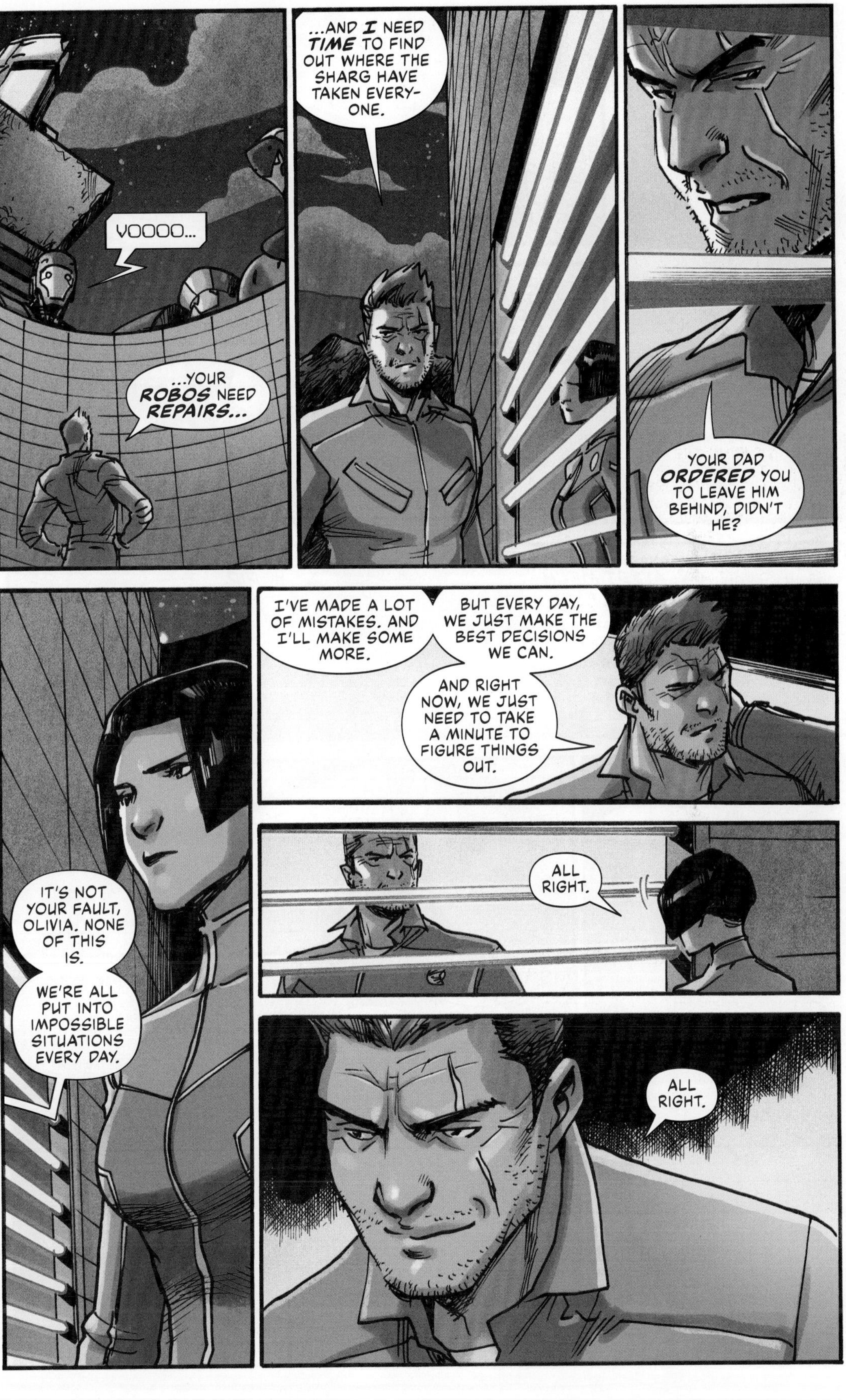
VOOOO...
...YOUR ROBOS NEED REPAIRS...
...AND I NEED TIME TO FIND OUT WHERE THE SHARG HAVE TAKEN EVERY-ONE.
YOUR DAD ORDERED YOU TO LEAVE HIM BEHIND, DIDN'T HE?
IT'S NOT YOUR FAULT, OLIVIA. NONE OF THIS IS.
WE'RE ALL PUT INTO IMPOSSIBLE SITUATIONS EVERY DAY.
I'VE MADE A LOT OF MISTAKES. AND I'LL MAKE SOME MORE.
BUT EVERY DAY, WE JUST MAKE THE BEST DECISIONS WE CAN.
AND RIGHT NOW, WE JUST NEED TO TAKE A MINUTE TO FIGURE THINGS OUT.
ALL RIGHT.
ALL RIGHT.

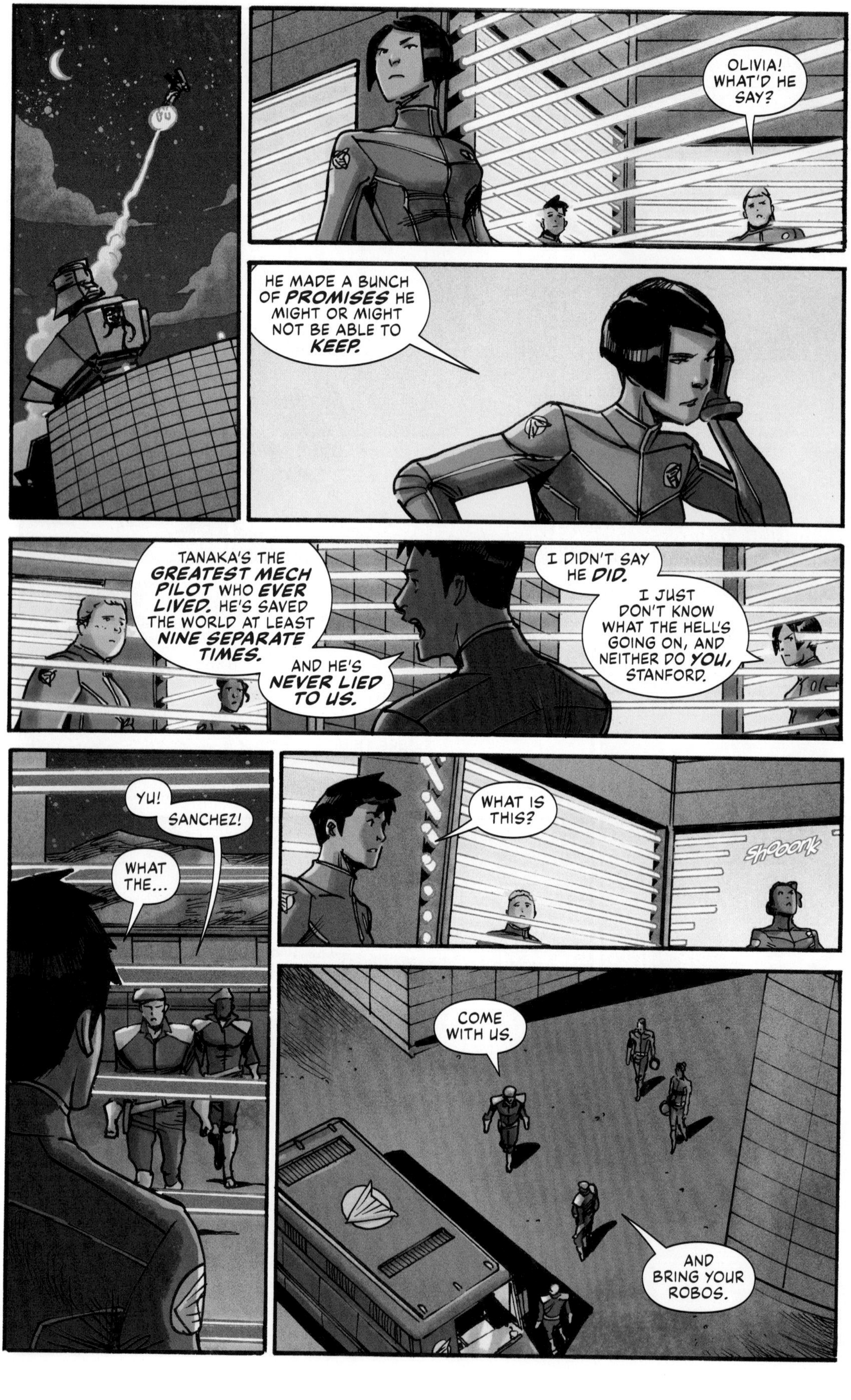

OLIVIA! WHAT'D HE SAY?
HE MADE A BUNCH OF PROMISES HE MIGHT OR MIGHT NOT BE ABLE TO KEEP.
TANAKA'S THE GREATEST MECH PILOT WHO EVER LIVED. HE'S SAVED THE WORLD AT LEAST NINE SEPARATE TIMES.
AND HE'S NEVER LIED TO US.
I DIDN'T SAY HE DID.
I JUST DON'T KNOW WHAT THE HELL'S GOING ON, AND NEITHER DO YOU, STANFORD.
YU!
SANCHEZ!
WHAT THE...
WHAT IS THIS?
Shooonk
COME WITH US.
AND BRING YOUR ROBOS.

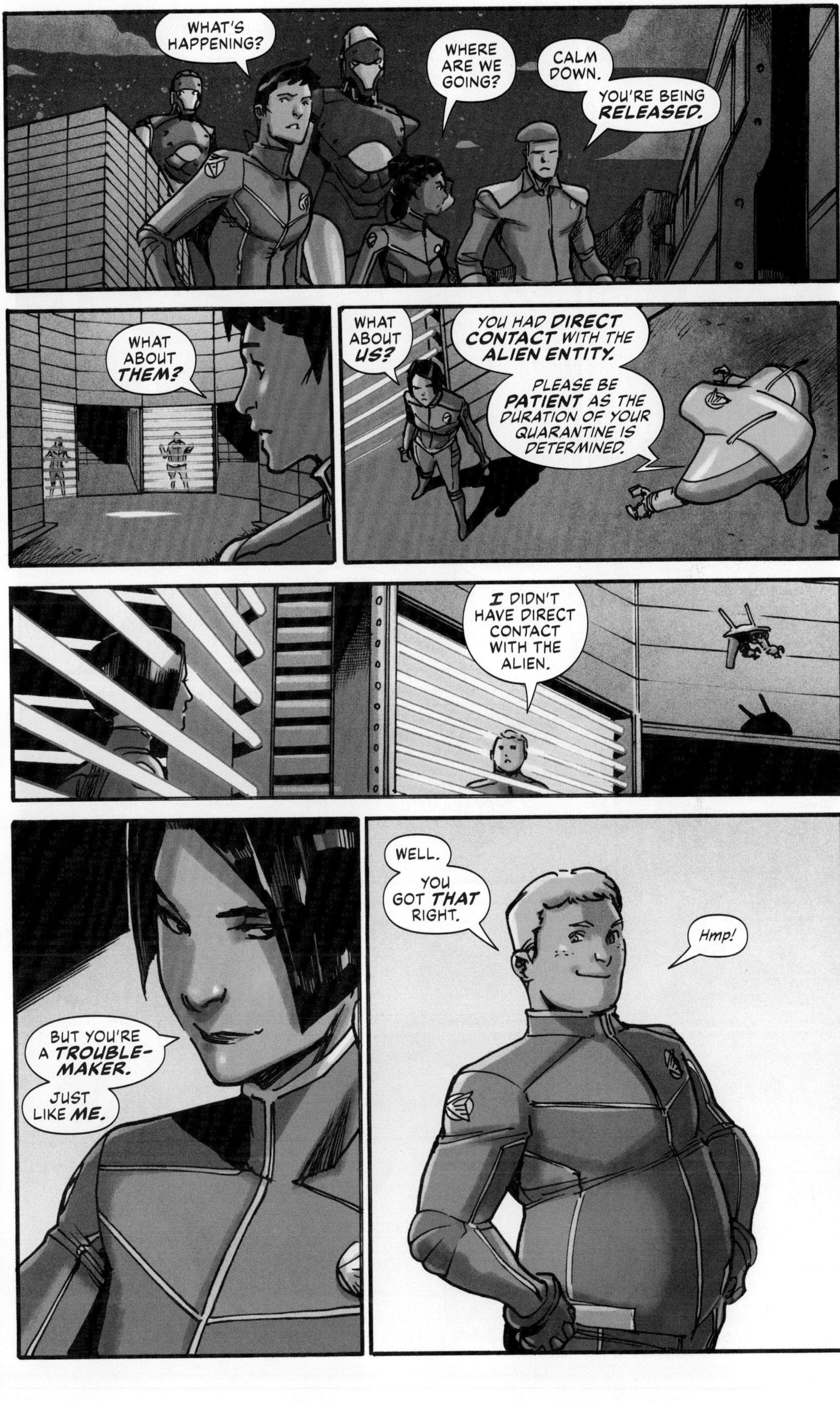
WHAT'S HAPPENING?
WHERE ARE WE GOING?
CALM DOWN.
YOU'RE BEING **RELEASED.**
WHAT ABOUT ***THEM?***
WHAT ABOUT ***US?***
YOU HAD ***DIRECT CONTACT*** *WITH THE* ***ALIEN ENTITY.***
PLEASE BE ***PATIENT*** *AS THE DURATION OF YOUR QUARANTINE IS DETERMINED.*
I DIDN'T HAVE DIRECT CONTACT WITH THE ALIEN.
BUT YOU'RE A ***TROUBLE-MAKER.***
JUST LIKE ***ME.***
WELL.
YOU GOT ***THAT*** RIGHT.
Hmp!

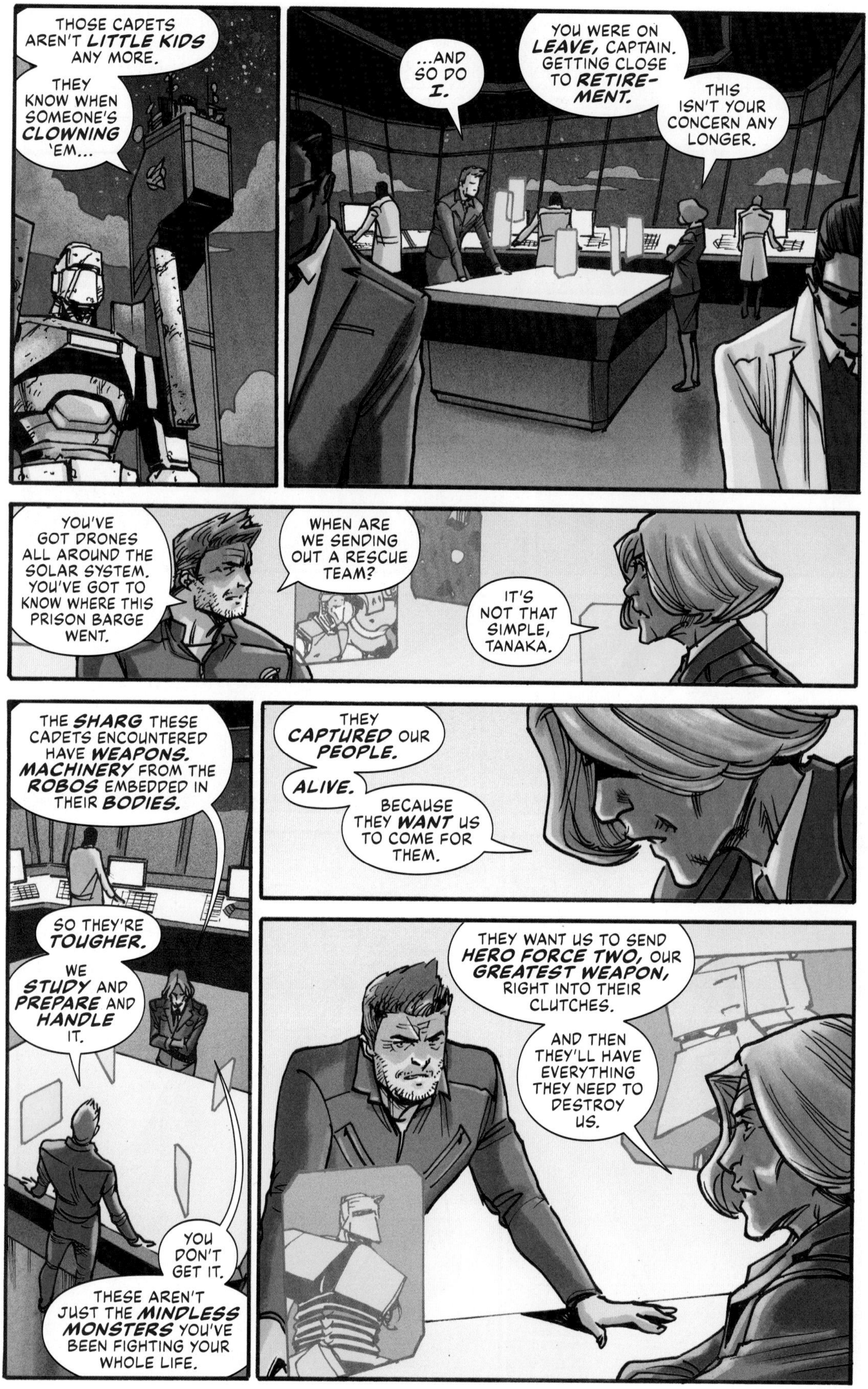
THOSE CADETS AREN'T LITTLE KIDS ANY MORE.
THEY KNOW WHEN SOMEONE'S CLOWNING 'EM...
...AND SO DO I.
YOU WERE ON LEAVE, CAPTAIN. GETTING CLOSE TO RETIRE-MENT.
THIS ISN'T YOUR CONCERN ANY LONGER.
YOU'VE GOT DRONES ALL AROUND THE SOLAR SYSTEM. YOU'VE GOT TO KNOW WHERE THIS PRISON BARGE WENT.
WHEN ARE WE SENDING OUT A RESCUE TEAM?
IT'S NOT THAT SIMPLE, TANAKA.
THE SHARG THESE CADETS ENCOUNTERED HAVE WEAPONS. MACHINERY FROM THE ROBOS EMBEDDED IN THEIR BODIES.
SO THEY'RE TOUGHER.
WE STUDY AND PREPARE AND HANDLE IT.
YOU DON'T GET IT.
THESE AREN'T JUST THE MINDLESS MONSTERS YOU'VE BEEN FIGHTING YOUR WHOLE LIFE.
THEY CAPTURED OUR PEOPLE.
ALIVE.
BECAUSE THEY WANT US TO COME FOR THEM.
THEY WANT US TO SEND HERO FORCE TWO, OUR GREATEST WEAPON, RIGHT INTO THEIR CLUTCHES.
AND THEN THEY'LL HAVE EVERYTHING THEY NEED TO DESTROY US.

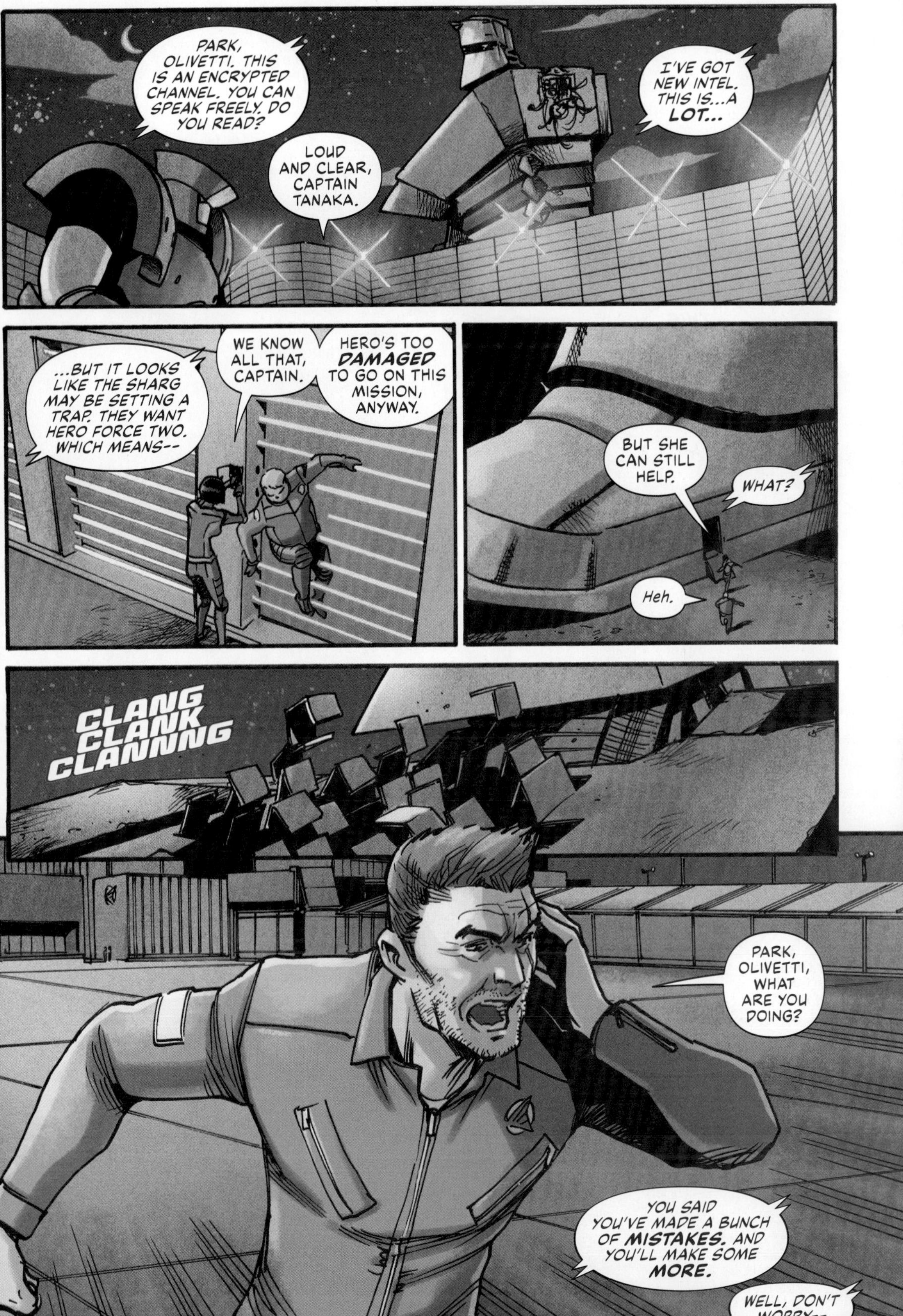
PARK, OLIVETTI. THIS IS AN ENCRYPTED CHANNEL. YOU CAN SPEAK FREELY. DO YOU READ?
LOUD AND CLEAR, CAPTAIN TANAKA.
I'VE GOT NEW INTEL. THIS IS...A **LOT...**
...BUT IT LOOKS LIKE THE SHARG MAY BE SETTING A TRAP. THEY WANT HERO FORCE TWO. WHICH MEANS--
WE KNOW ALL THAT, CAPTAIN.
HERO'S TOO ***DAMAGED*** TO GO ON THIS MISSION, ANYWAY.
BUT SHE CAN STILL HELP.
WHAT?
Heh.
CLANG CLANK CLANNNG
PARK, OLIVETTI, WHAT ARE YOU DOING?
YOU SAID YOU'VE MADE A BUNCH OF **MISTAKES.** AND YOU'LL MAKE SOME **MORE.**
WELL, DON'T WORRY--

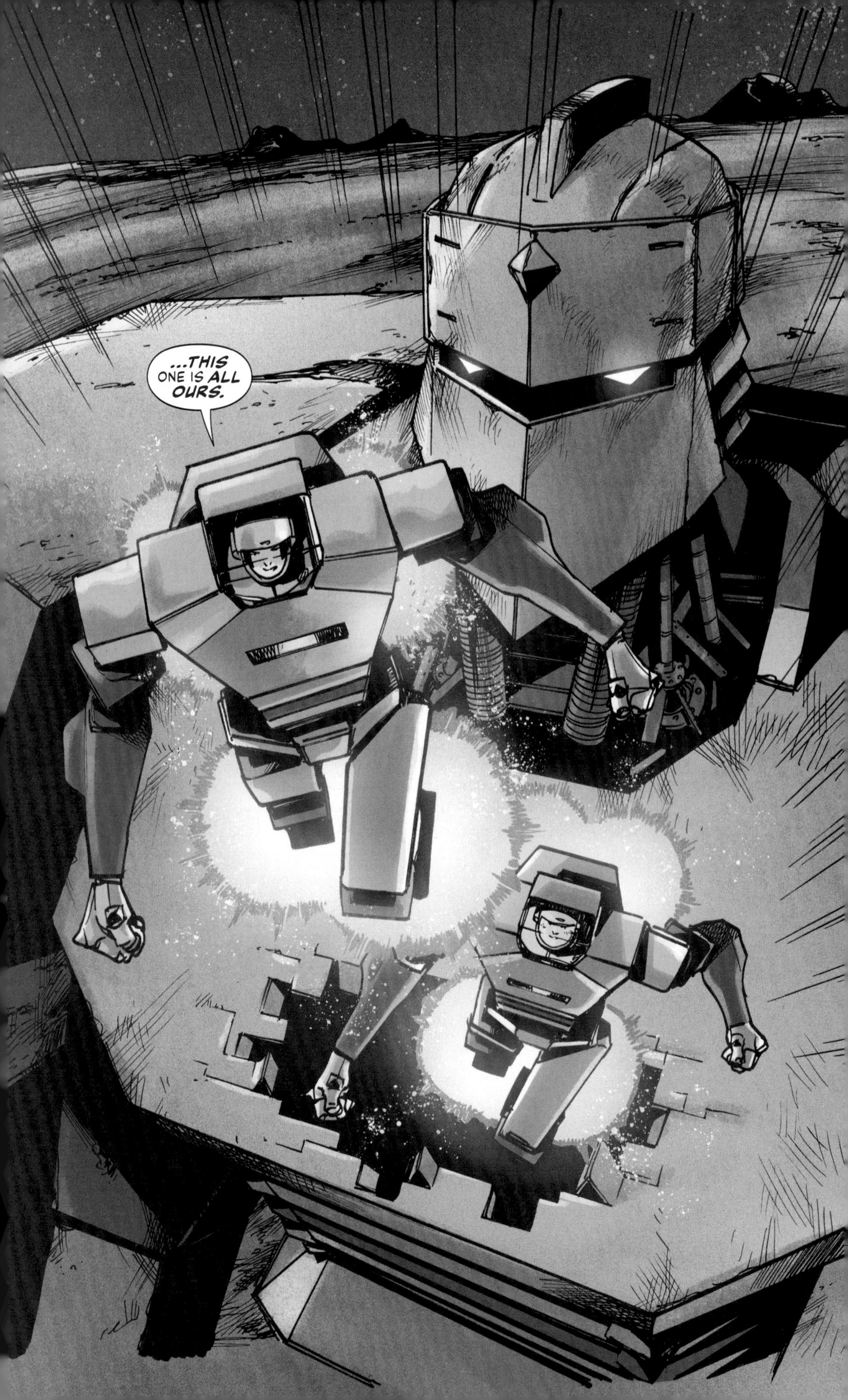
...THIS ONE IS ALL OURS.

CHAPTER FOUR

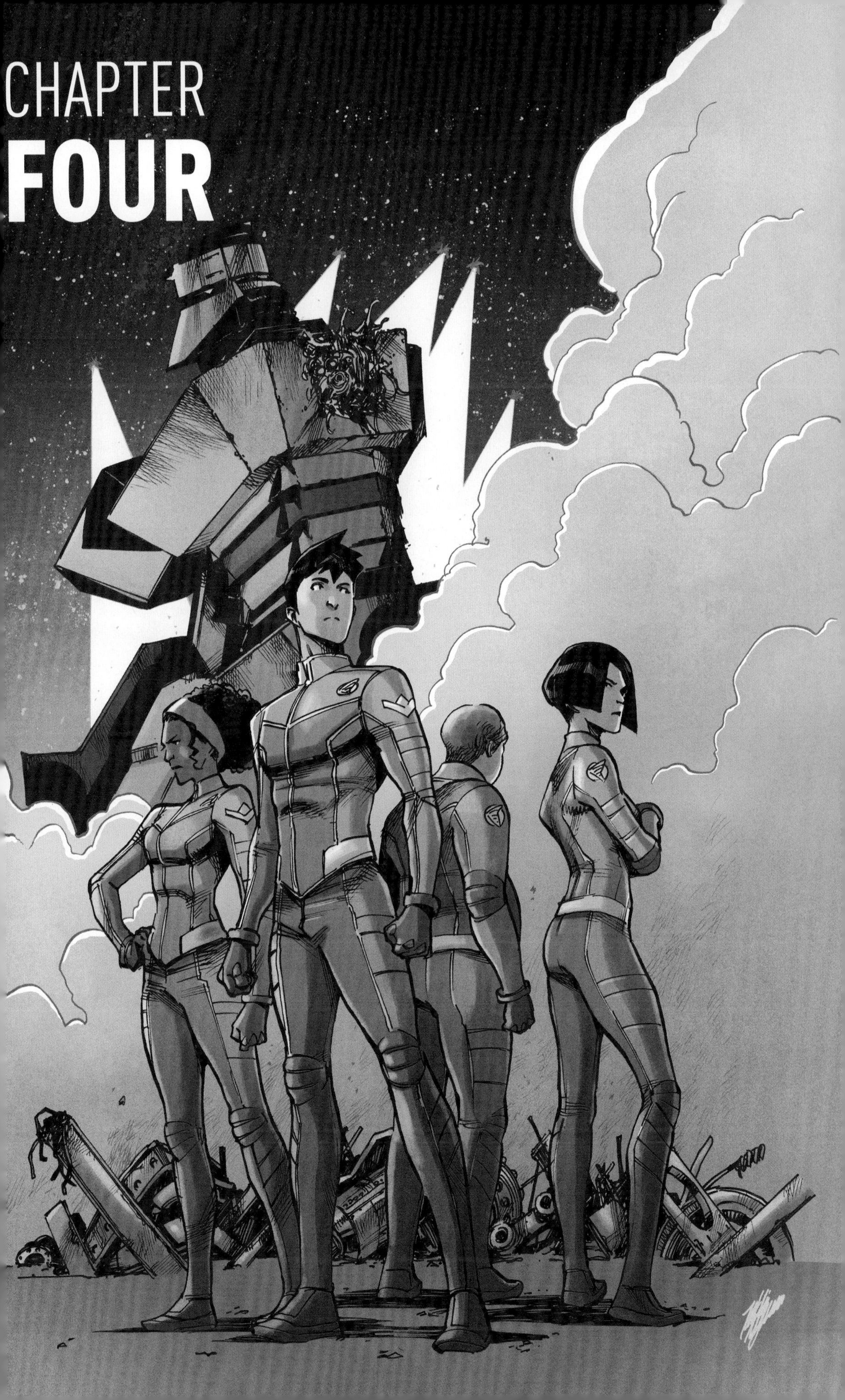

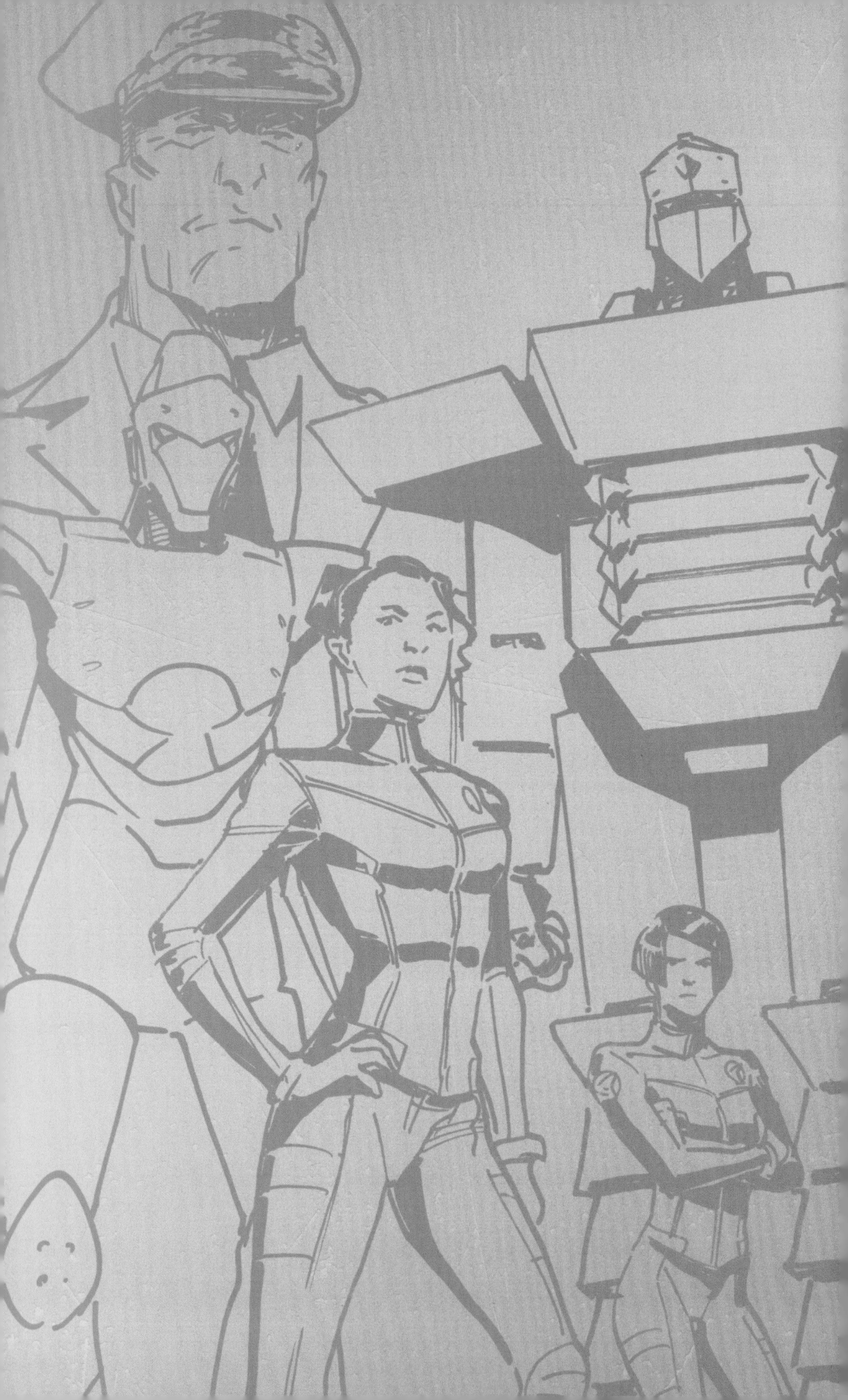

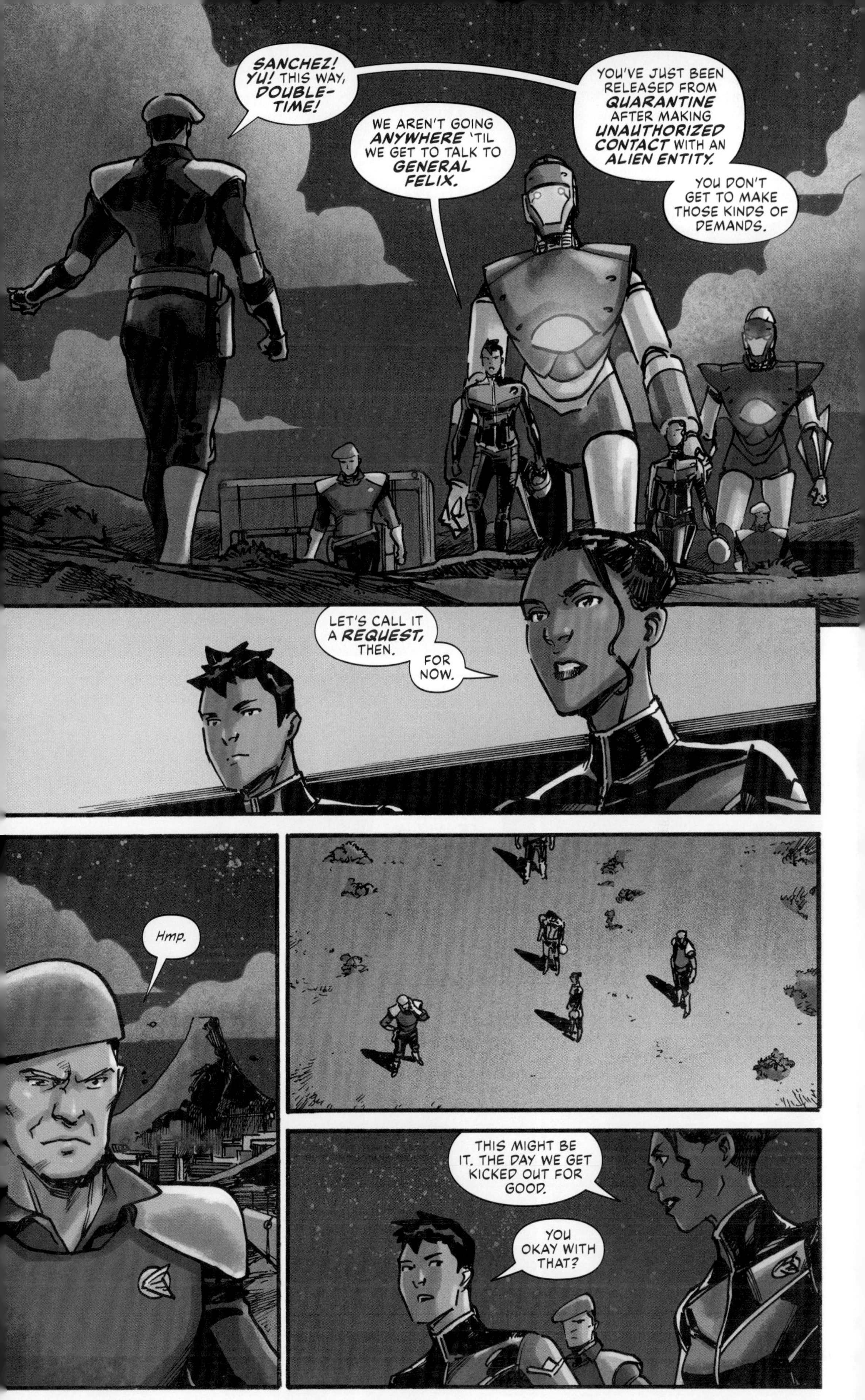
SANCHEZ! YU! THIS WAY, DOUBLE-TIME!
WE AREN'T GOING ANYWHERE 'TIL WE GET TO TALK TO GENERAL FELIX.
YOU'VE JUST BEEN RELEASED FROM QUARANTINE AFTER MAKING UNAUTHORIZED CONTACT WITH AN ALIEN ENTITY.
YOU DON'T GET TO MAKE THOSE KINDS OF DEMANDS.
LET'S CALL IT A REQUEST, THEN.
FOR NOW.
Hmp.
THIS MIGHT BE IT. THE DAY WE GET KICKED OUT FOR GOOD.
YOU OKAY WITH THAT?

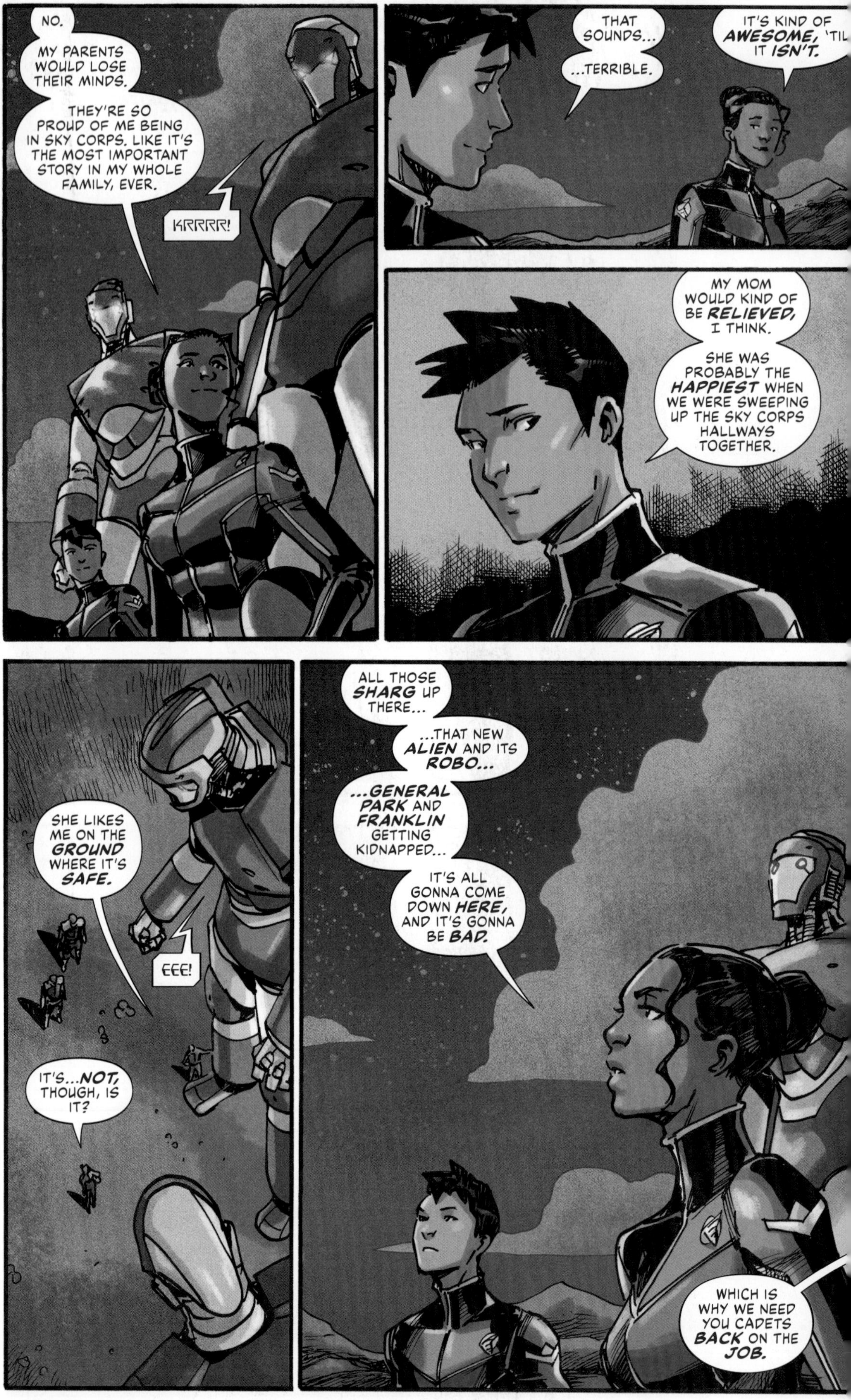
NO.
MY PARENTS WOULD LOSE THEIR MINDS.
THEY'RE SO PROUD OF ME BEING IN SKY CORPS. LIKE IT'S THE MOST IMPORTANT STORY IN MY WHOLE FAMILY, EVER.
KRRRR!
THAT SOUNDS...
...TERRIBLE.
IT'S KIND OF AWESOME, 'TIL IT ISN'T.
MY MOM WOULD KIND OF BE RELIEVED, I THINK.
SHE WAS PROBABLY THE HAPPIEST WHEN WE WERE SWEEPING UP THE SKY CORPS HALLWAYS TOGETHER.
SHE LIKES ME ON THE GROUND WHERE IT'S SAFE.
EEE!
IT'S...NOT, THOUGH, IS IT?
ALL THOSE SHARG UP THERE...
...THAT NEW ALIEN AND ITS ROBO...
...GENERAL PARK AND FRANKLIN GETTING KIDNAPPED...
IT'S ALL GONNA COME DOWN HERE, AND IT'S GONNA BE BAD.
WHICH IS WHY WE NEED YOU CADETS BACK ON THE JOB.

YOU'RE LATE FOR YOUR NEXT MISSION.

WHAT DO YOU WANT TO TALK TO ME ABOUT?

GENERAL FELIX...

ARE YOU SENDING US TO RESCUE GENERAL PARK AND FRANKLIN?

NO.

YOU CAN'T JUST LEAVE THEM OUT THERE!

WE DON'T ABANDON OUR PEOPLE, YU.

WE'RE ORGANIZING A RESCUE MISSION RIGHT NOW.

BUT WE CAN'T SEND YOUR ROBOS--ESPECIALLY NOT HERO FORCE TWO--ON THAT MISSION.

BUT HERO FORCE TWO'S OUR BEST CHANCE OF GETTING THEM BACK!

NOT WHILE IT'S DAMAGED LIKE THAT, IT ISN'T.

BUT MORE IMPORTANTLY, WE BELIEVE THE SHARG WANT US TO SEND THEM HERO FORCE TWO...

...SO THEY CAN REVERSE-ENGINEER OUR GREATEST WEAPON AND USE IT AGAINST US.

SO YOUR MISSION IS TO STAY ON THE GROUND AND DEFEND THIS FACILITY...

...WHILE WE MARSHAL ALL OUR RESOURCES TO REPAIR HERO FORCE TWO AND PREPARE FOR THE FINAL BATTLE...

...RIGHT HERE ON PLANET EARTH.

CHIEF MAX! YOU READY TO TAKE COMMAND OF THESE CADETS?

YOU GOT IT, GENERAL!

CHIEF MAX!

STANFORD!

MOM!

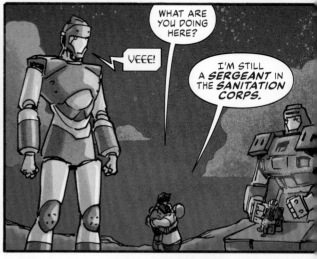

WHAT ARE YOU DOING HERE?

VEEE!

I'M STILL A SERGEANT IN THE SANITATION CORPS.

YOU'RE GONNA HELP ME CLEAN UP THE TOWN AND SET UP THE REPAIR FACILITY FOR HERO FORCE TWO.

THIS WHOLE COMMUNITY'S BEEN NEGLECTED SINCE THE LAST SHARG ATTACK. BUT WE NEED EVERYBODY NOW. IT'S TIME FOR SKY CORPS TO HELP FIX THINGS UP.

FINALLY.

BACK ON JANITOR DUTY.

I LIKE IT.

AAAOOOOOOO AAAOOOOOOO

CORPORAL! WHAT'S GOING ON?

THE OTHER CADETS-- PARK AND OLIVETTI...

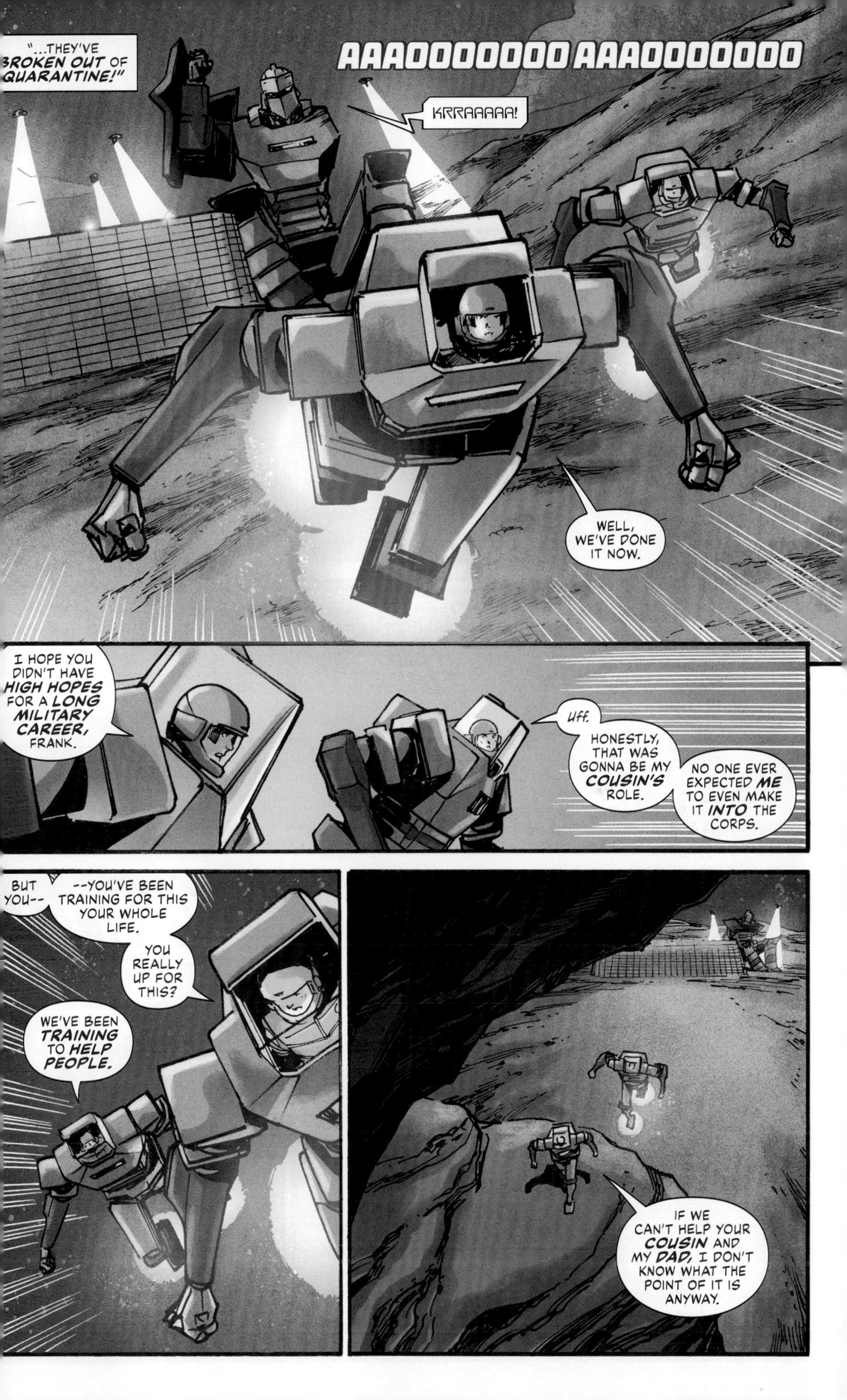
"...THEY'VE BROKEN OUT OF QUARANTINE!"
AAAOOOOOOO AAAOOOOOOO
KRRAAAAA!
WELL, WE'VE DONE IT NOW.
I HOPE YOU DIDN'T HAVE HIGH HOPES FOR A LONG MILITARY CAREER, FRANK.
UFF.
HONESTLY, THAT WAS GONNA BE MY COUSIN'S ROLE.
NO ONE EVER EXPECTED ME TO EVEN MAKE IT INTO THE CORPS.
BUT YOU--
--YOU'VE BEEN TRAINING FOR THIS YOUR WHOLE LIFE.
YOU REALLY UP FOR THIS?
WE'VE BEEN TRAINING TO HELP PEOPLE.
IF WE CAN'T HELP YOUR COUSIN AND MY DAD, I DON'T KNOW WHAT THE POINT OF IT IS ANYWAY.

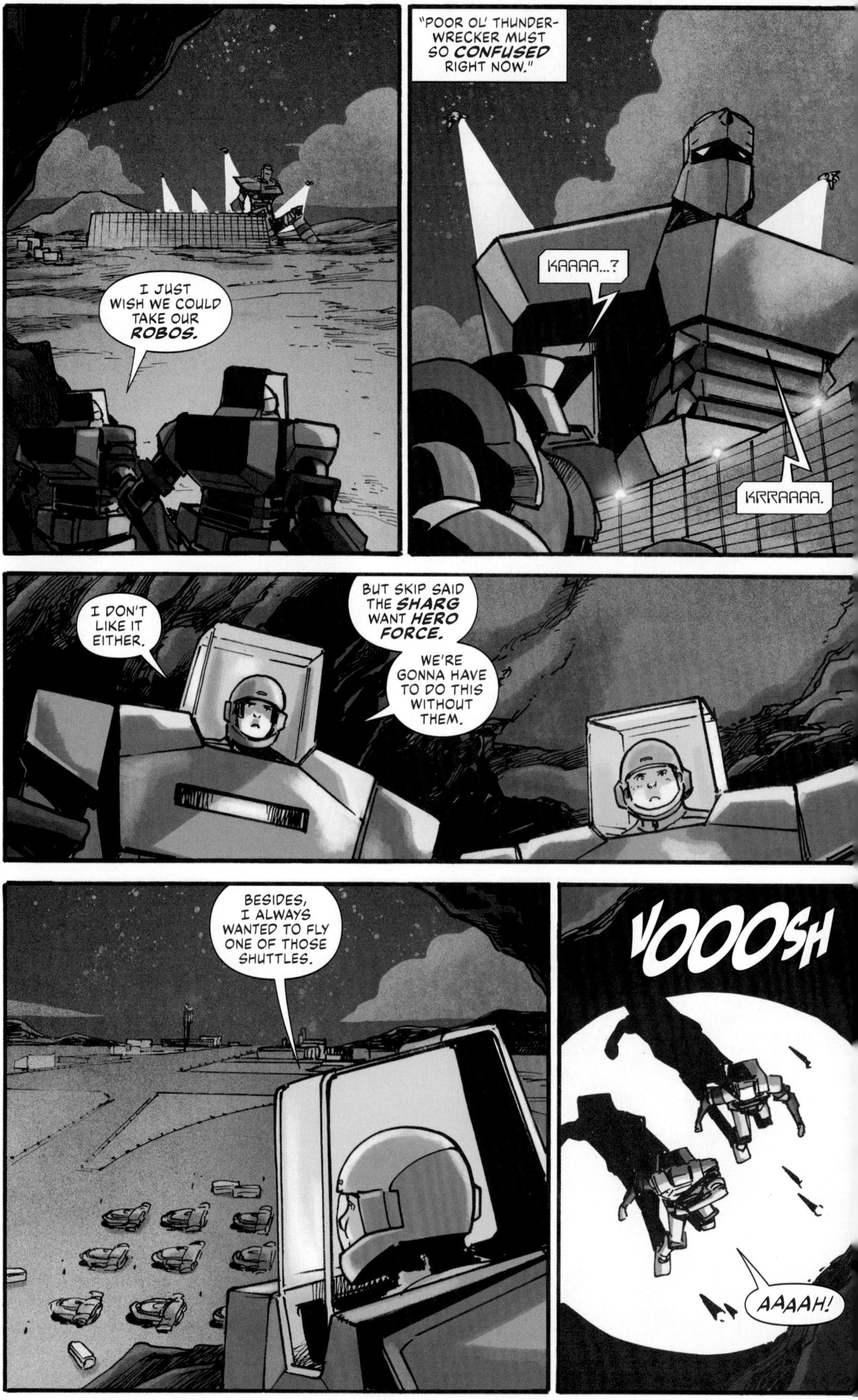
I JUST WISH WE COULD TAKE OUR ROBOS.
"POOR OL' THUNDER-WRECKER MUST SO CONFUSED RIGHT NOW."
KAAAA...?
KRRAAAA.
I DON'T LIKE IT EITHER.
BUT SKIP SAID THE SHARG WANT HERO FORCE.
WE'RE GONNA HAVE TO DO THIS WITHOUT THEM.
BESIDES, I ALWAYS WANTED TO FLY ONE OF THOSE SHUTTLES.
VOOOSH
AAAAH!

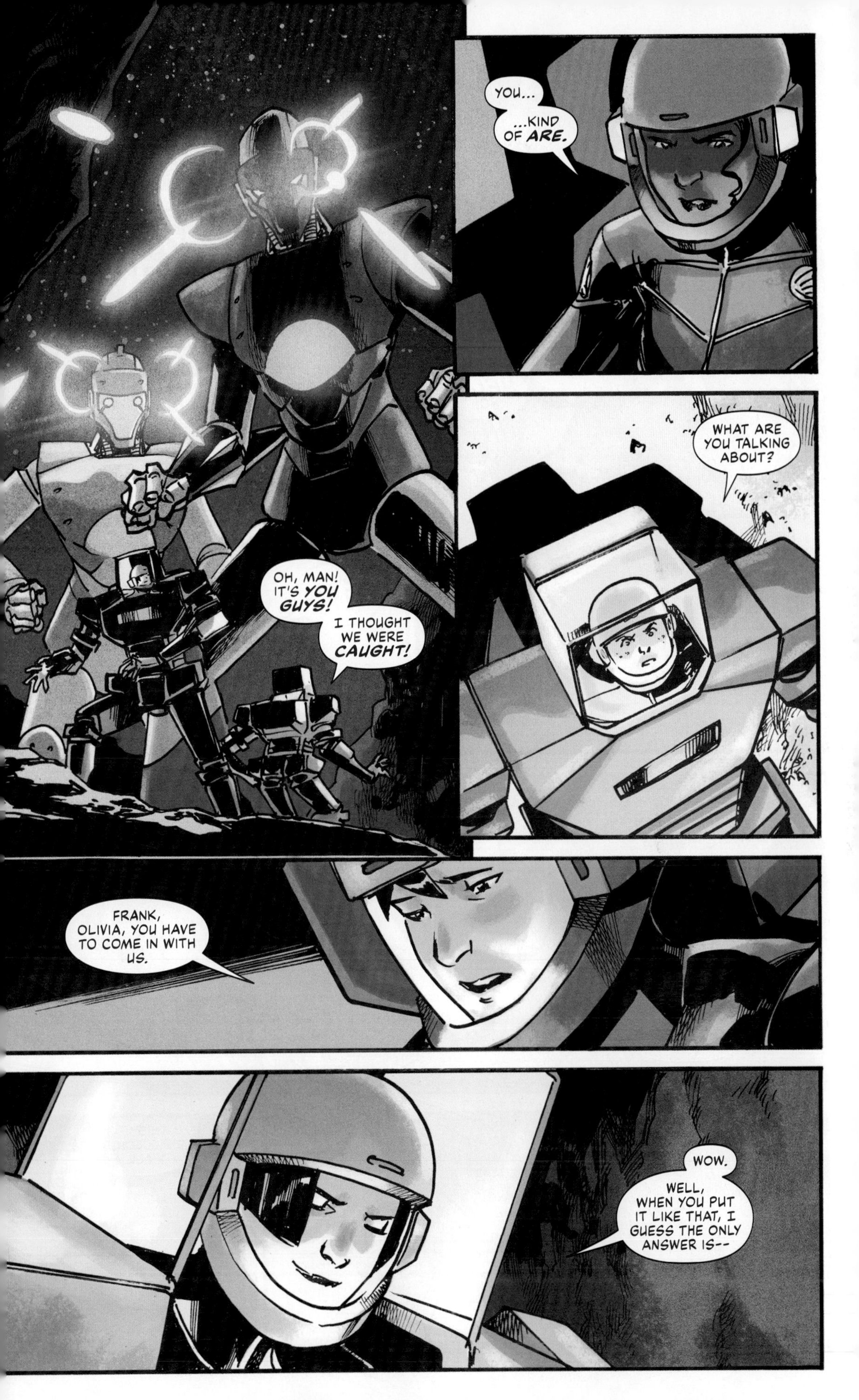
OH, MAN! IT'S YOU GUYS!
I THOUGHT WE WERE CAUGHT!
YOU...
...KIND OF ARE.
WHAT ARE YOU TALKING ABOUT?
FRANK, OLIVIA, YOU HAVE TO COME IN WITH US.
WOW.
WELL, WHEN YOU PUT IT LIKE THAT, I GUESS THE ONLY ANSWER IS--

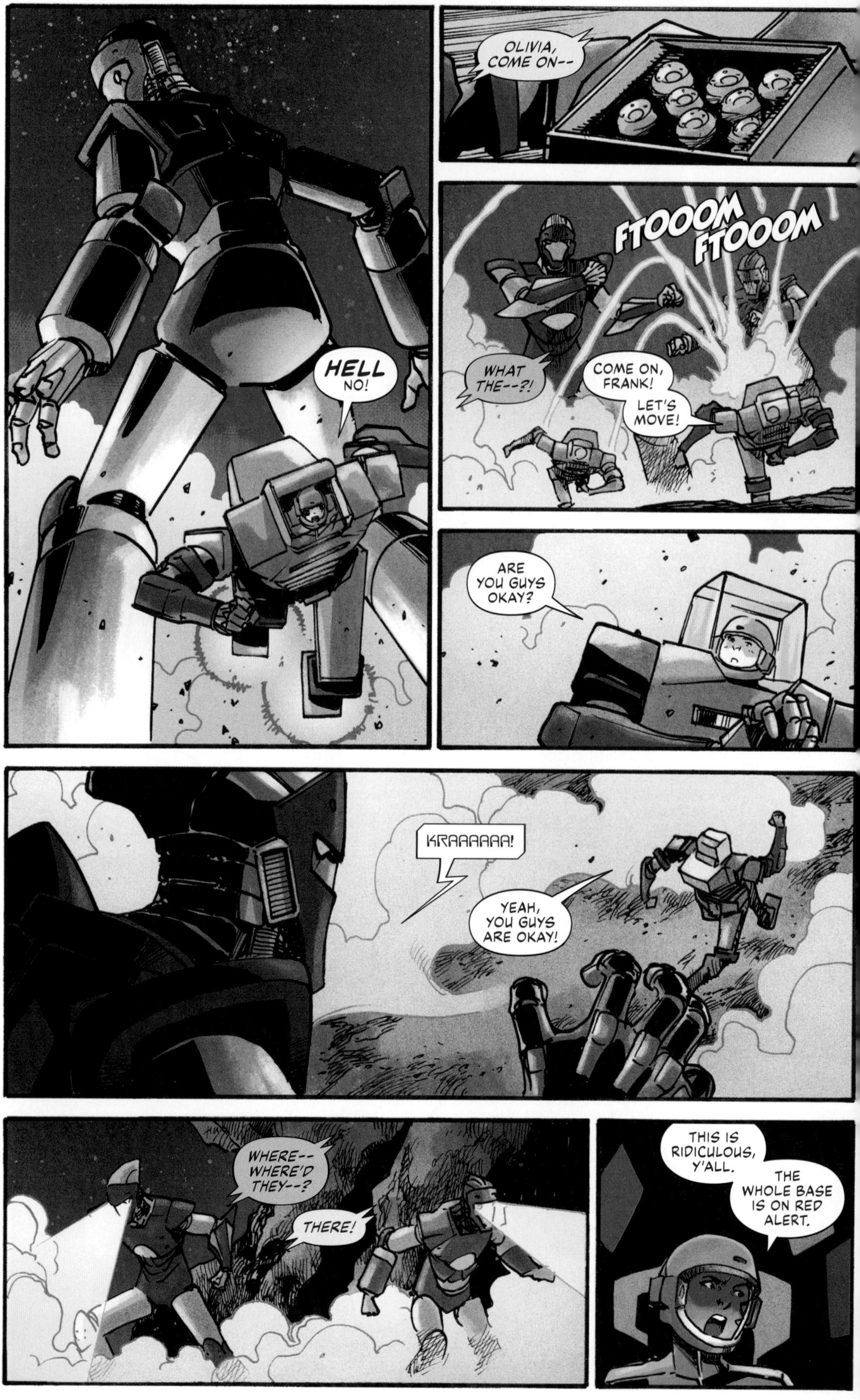
HELL NO!
OLIVIA, COME ON--
FTOOOM FTOOOM
WHAT THE--?!
COME ON, FRANK!
LET'S MOVE!
ARE YOU GUYS OKAY?
KRAAAAAA!
YEAH, YOU GUYS ARE OKAY!
WHERE-- WHERE'D THEY--?
THERE!
THIS IS RIDICULOUS, Y'ALL.
THE WHOLE BASE IS ON RED ALERT.

YOU CAN'T HIDE FOREVER.

AND EVEN IF YOU MAKE IT TO THAT STRIP...

...YOU'RE NOT GETTING A SHUTTLE INTO THE SKY.

WHAT DO THEY CARE?

WHAT DO *YOU* CARE?

WE'RE NOT EVEN TAKING OUR *ROBOS!* JUST *ONE LOUSY SHUTTLE!*

WE HAVE TO SAVE MY COUSIN AND OLIVIA'S DAD!

FELIX IS SENDING A *RESCUE TEAM* FOR THEM! IT'S *COVERED!*

WOULD YOU TRUST SOMEONE ELSE TO SAVE YOUR *MOM,* STANFORD?

I...

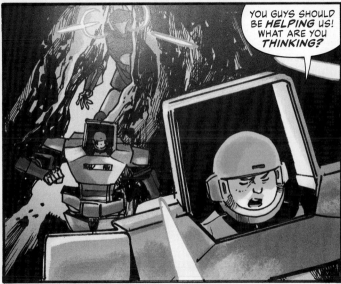

YOU GUYS SHOULD BE *HELPING* US! WHAT ARE YOU *THINKING?*

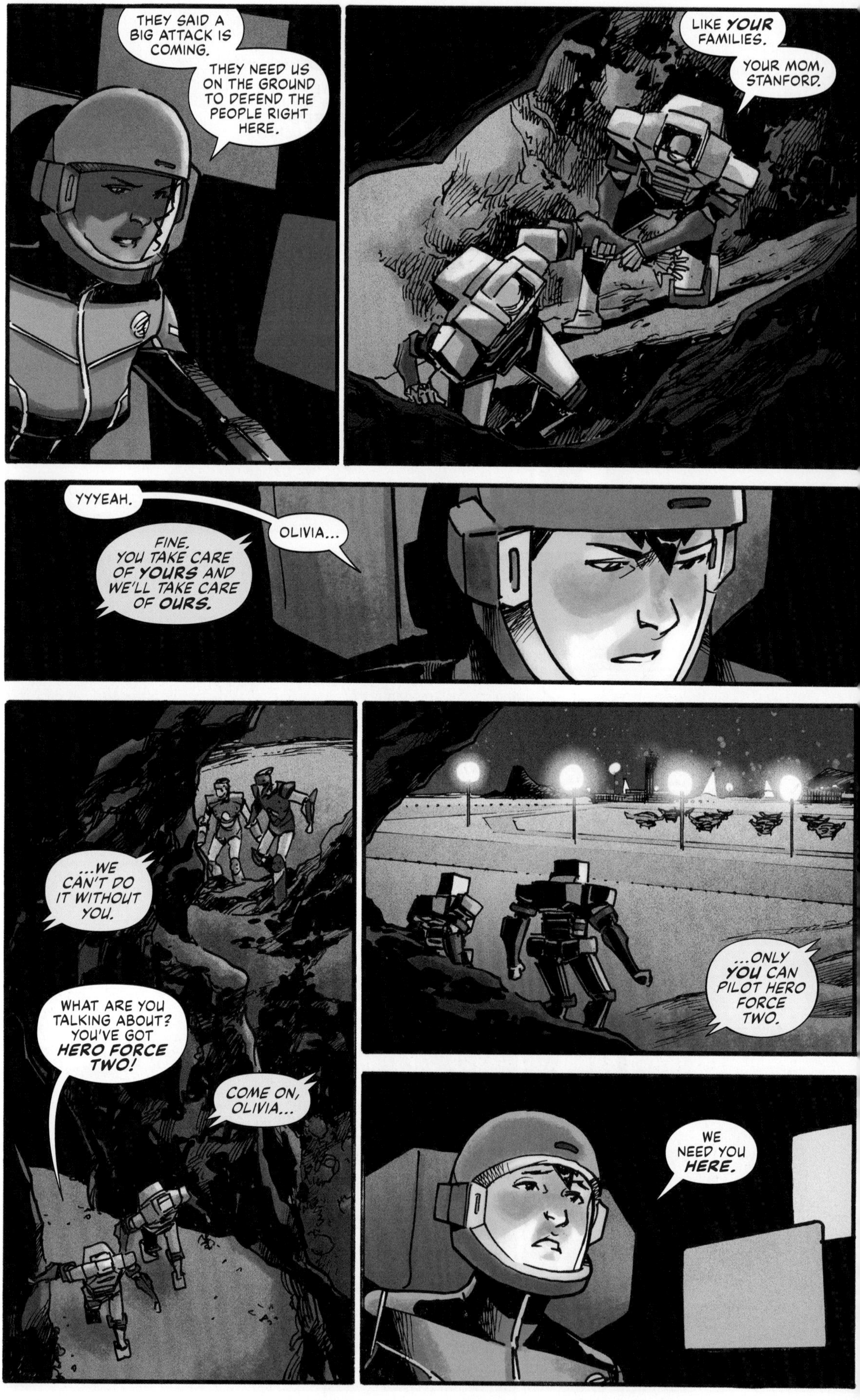
THEY SAID A BIG ATTACK IS COMING.
THEY NEED US ON THE GROUND TO DEFEND THE PEOPLE RIGHT HERE.
LIKE YOUR FAMILIES.
YOUR MOM, STANFORD.
YYYEAH.
OLIVIA...
FINE. YOU TAKE CARE OF YOURS AND WE'LL TAKE CARE OF OURS.
...WE CAN'T DO IT WITHOUT YOU.
WHAT ARE YOU TALKING ABOUT? YOU'VE GOT HERO FORCE TWO!
COME ON, OLIVIA...
...ONLY YOU CAN PILOT HERO FORCE TWO.
WE NEED YOU HERE.

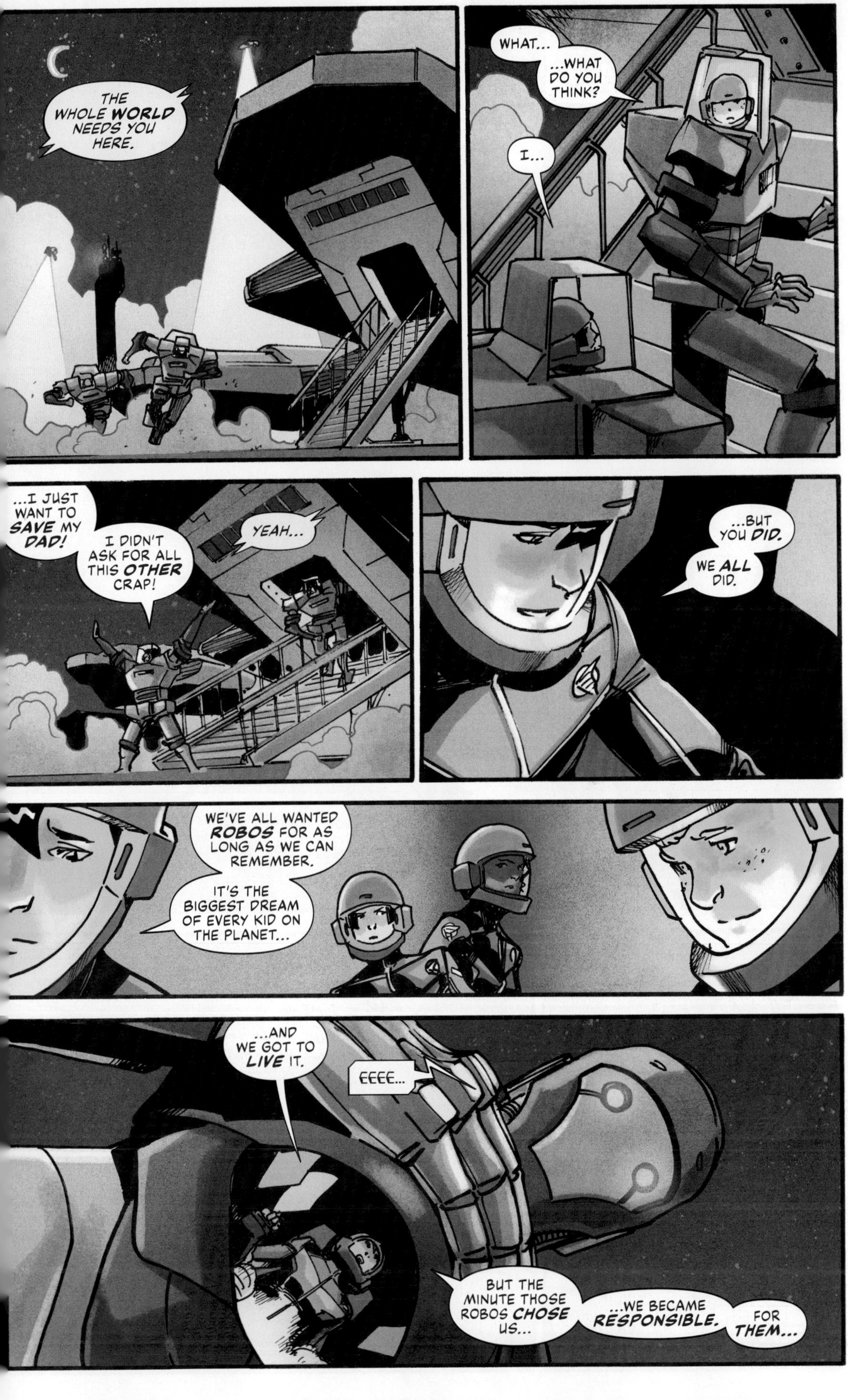
THE WHOLE WORLD NEEDS YOU HERE.
WHAT...
...WHAT DO YOU THINK?
I...
...I JUST WANT TO SAVE MY DAD!
I DIDN'T ASK FOR ALL THIS OTHER CRAP!
YEAH...
...BUT YOU DID.
WE ALL DID.
WE'VE ALL WANTED ROBOS FOR AS LONG AS WE CAN REMEMBER.
IT'S THE BIGGEST DREAM OF EVERY KID ON THE PLANET...
...AND WE GOT TO LIVE IT.
EEEE...
BUT THE MINUTE THOSE ROBOS CHOSE US...
...WE BECAME RESPONSIBLE.
FOR THEM...

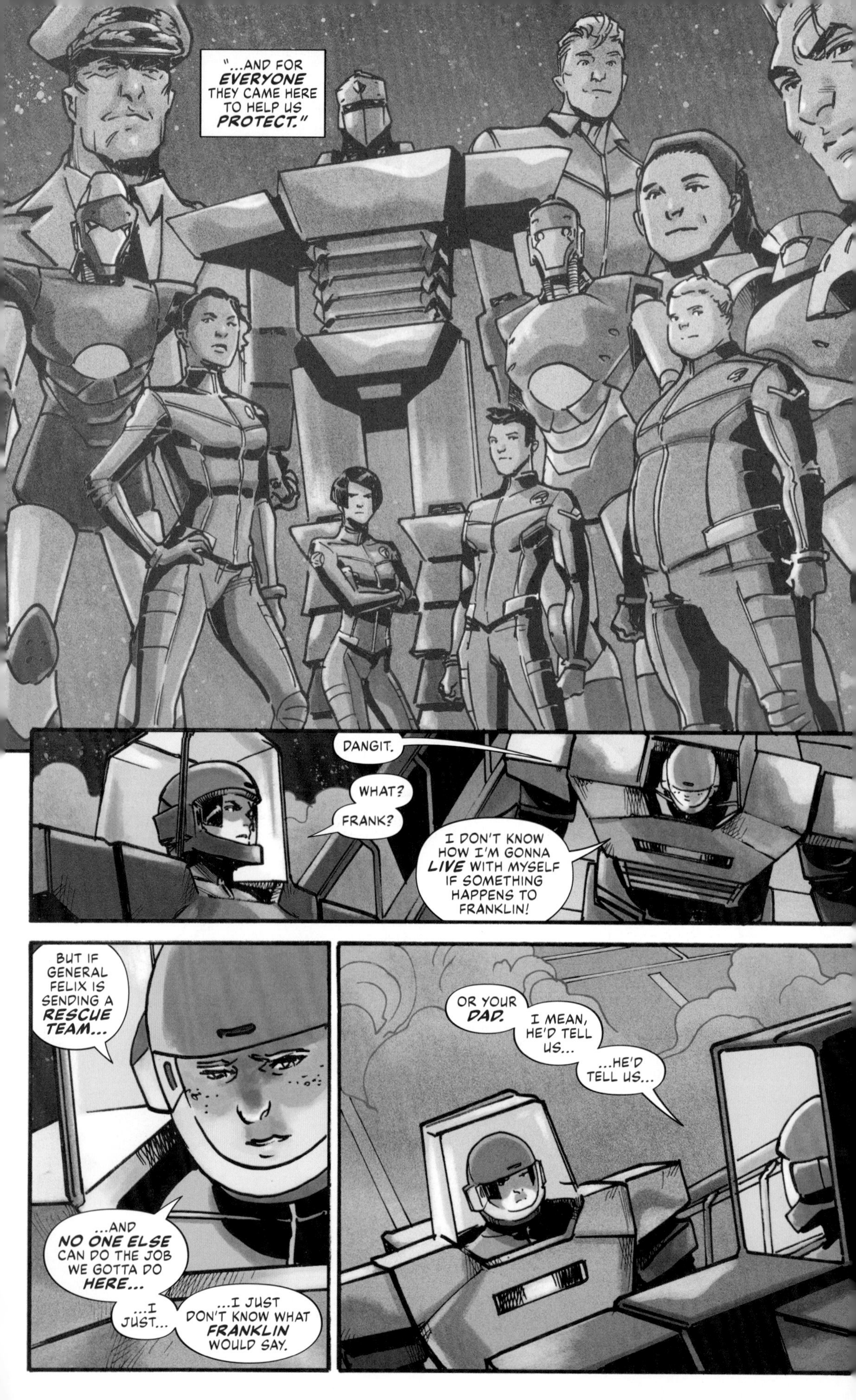
"...AND FOR EVERYONE THEY CAME HERE TO HELP US PROTECT."
DANGIT.
WHAT?
FRANK?
I DON'T KNOW HOW I'M GONNA LIVE WITH MYSELF IF SOMETHING HAPPENS TO FRANKLIN!
BUT IF GENERAL FELIX IS SENDING A RESCUE TEAM...
...AND NO ONE ELSE CAN DO THE JOB WE GOTTA DO HERE...
...I JUST...
...I JUST DON'T KNOW WHAT FRANKLIN WOULD SAY.
OR YOUR DAD.
I MEAN, HE'D TELL US...
...HE'D TELL US...

...HE'D TELL US TO STAY.

DAMMIT!

HA!

KLANG

WHA--SKIP?!

I COULDN'T BE PROUDER OF YOU CADETS.

YOU ALWAYS END UP DOING THE RIGHT THING...

...EVEN IF IT MEANS YOU ACTUALLY FOLLOW ORDERS EVERY ONCE IN A WHILE.

Psh.

BUT WHAT IF I TOLD YOU...

...FELIX ISN'T PLANNING A RESCUE MISSION?

SONOFA...

WHAT?!

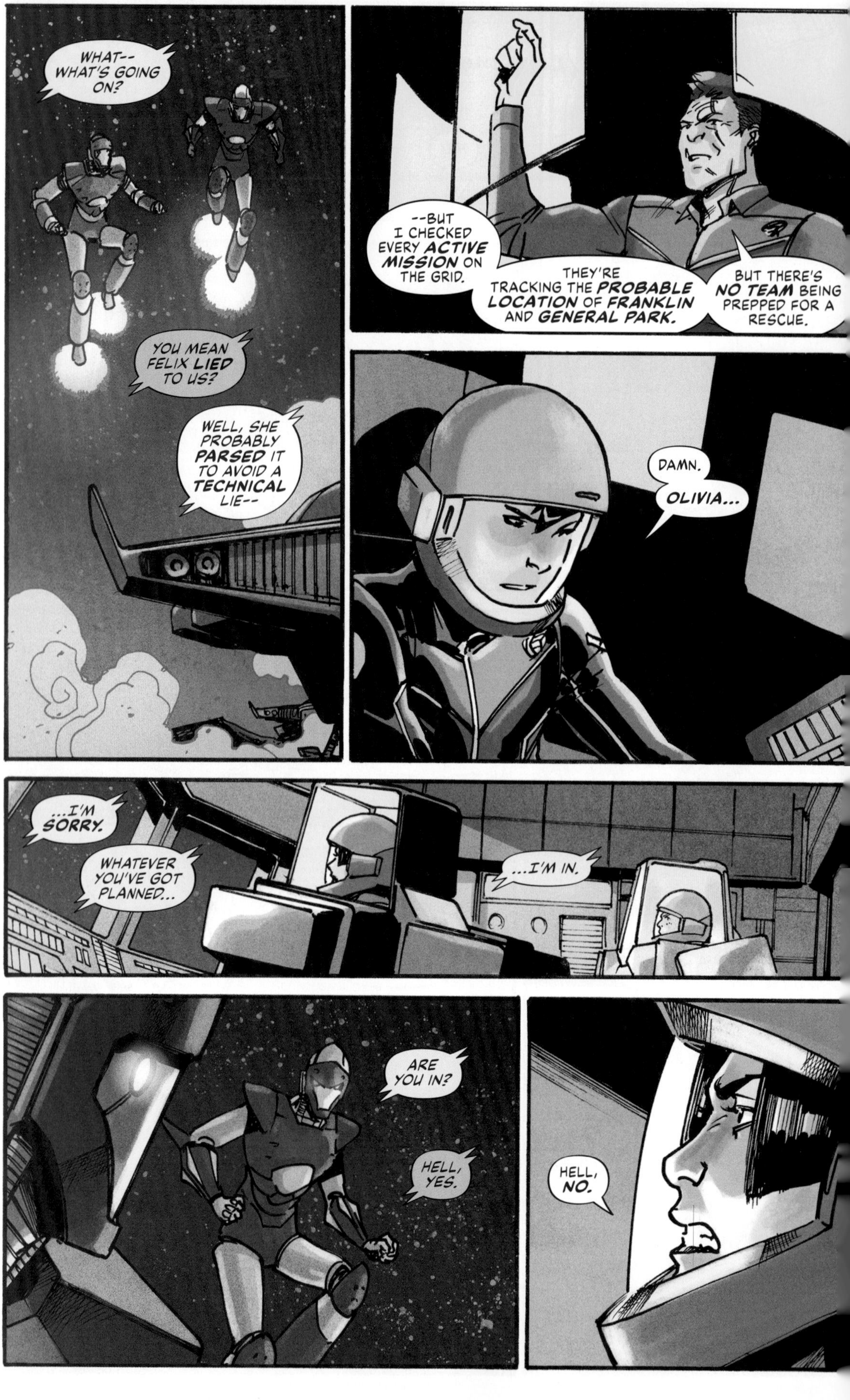
WHAT-- WHAT'S GOING ON?
YOU MEAN FELIX LIED TO US?
WELL, SHE PROBABLY PARSED IT TO AVOID A TECHNICAL LIE--
--BUT I CHECKED EVERY ACTIVE MISSION ON THE GRID.
THEY'RE TRACKING THE PROBABLE LOCATION OF FRANKLIN AND GENERAL PARK.
BUT THERE'S NO TEAM BEING PREPPED FOR A RESCUE.
DAMN.
OLIVIA...
...I'M SORRY.
WHATEVER YOU'VE GOT PLANNED...
...I'M IN.
ARE YOU IN?
HELL, YES.
HELL, NO.

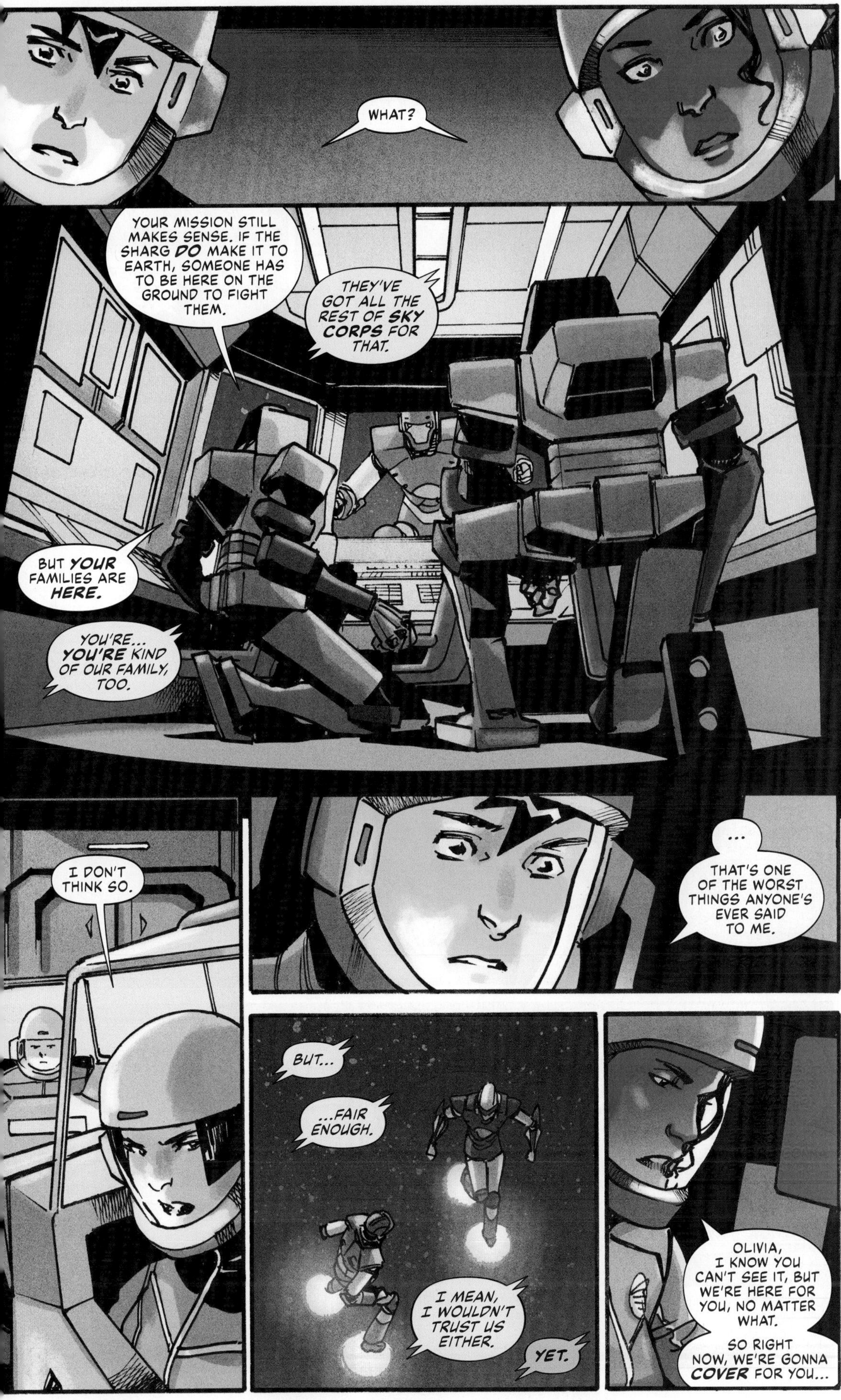
WHAT?
YOUR MISSION STILL MAKES SENSE. IF THE SHARG DO MAKE IT TO EARTH, SOMEONE HAS TO BE HERE ON THE GROUND TO FIGHT THEM.
THEY'VE GOT ALL THE REST OF SKY CORPS FOR THAT.
BUT YOUR FAMILIES ARE HERE.
YOU'RE... YOU'RE KIND OF OUR FAMILY, TOO.
I DON'T THINK SO.
...
THAT'S ONE OF THE WORST THINGS ANYONE'S EVER SAID TO ME.
BUT...
...FAIR ENOUGH.
I MEAN, I WOULDN'T TRUST US EITHER.
YET.
OLIVIA, I KNOW YOU CAN'T SEE IT, BUT WE'RE HERE FOR YOU, NO MATTER WHAT.
SO RIGHT NOW, WE'RE GONNA COVER FOR YOU...

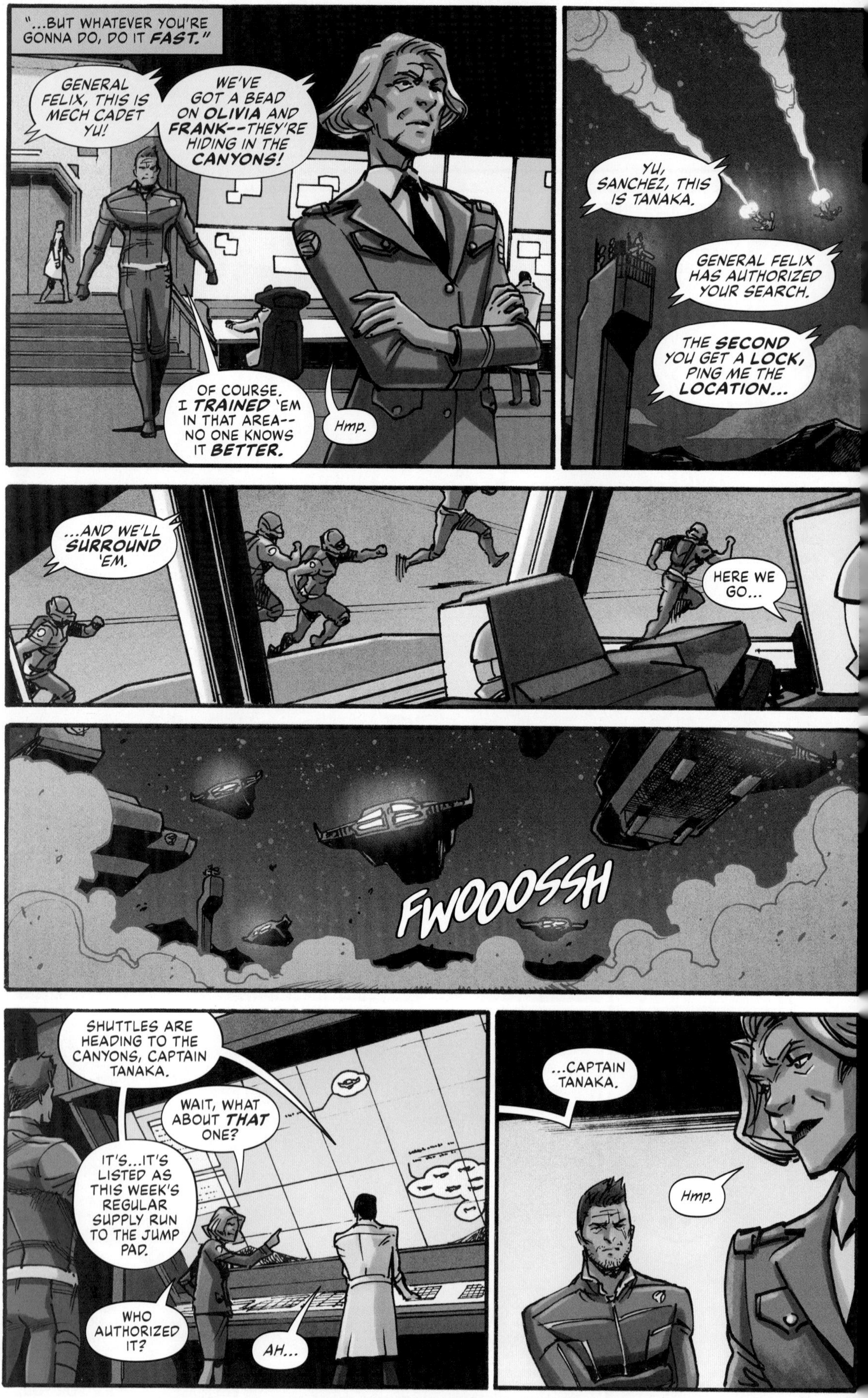
"...BUT WHATEVER YOU'RE GONNA DO, DO IT FAST."
GENERAL FELIX, THIS IS MECH CADET YU!
WE'VE GOT A BEAD ON OLIVIA AND FRANK--THEY'RE HIDING IN THE CANYONS!
OF COURSE. I TRAINED 'EM IN THAT AREA--NO ONE KNOWS IT BETTER.
Hmp.
YU, SANCHEZ, THIS IS TANAKA.
GENERAL FELIX HAS AUTHORIZED YOUR SEARCH.
THE SECOND YOU GET A LOCK, PING ME THE LOCATION...
...AND WE'LL SURROUND 'EM.
HERE WE GO...
FWOOOSSH
SHUTTLES ARE HEADING TO THE CANYONS, CAPTAIN TANAKA.
WAIT, WHAT ABOUT THAT ONE?
IT'S...IT'S LISTED AS THIS WEEK'S REGULAR SUPPLY RUN TO THE JUMP PAD.
WHO AUTHORIZED IT?
AH...
...CAPTAIN TANAKA.
Hmp.

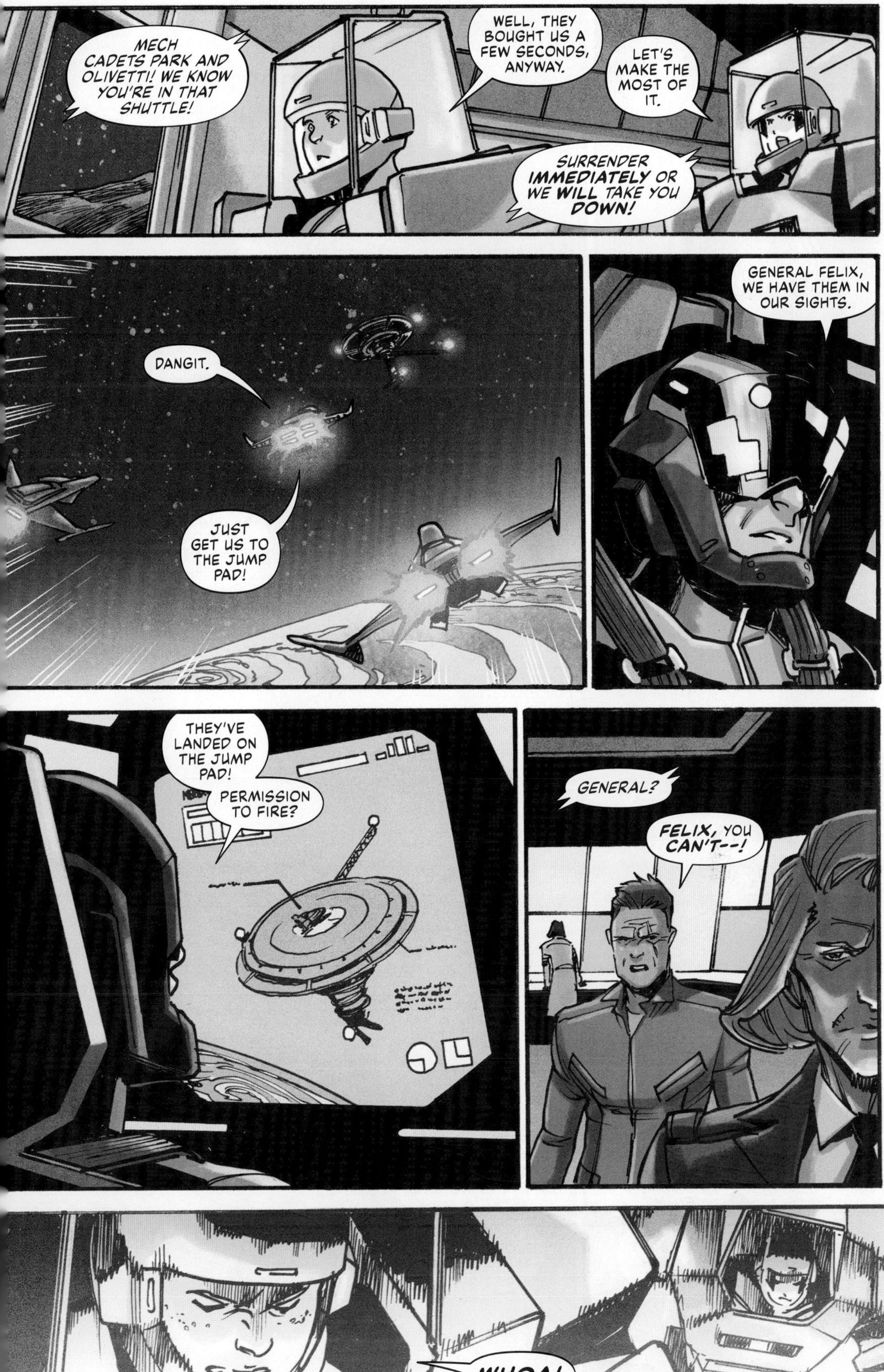
MECH CADETS PARK AND OLIVETTI! WE KNOW YOU'RE IN THAT SHUTTLE!
WELL, THEY BOUGHT US A FEW SECONDS, ANYWAY.
LET'S MAKE THE MOST OF IT.
SURRENDER IMMEDIATELY OR WE WILL TAKE YOU DOWN!
DANGIT.
JUST GET US TO THE JUMP PAD!
GENERAL FELIX, WE HAVE THEM IN OUR SIGHTS.
THEY'VE LANDED ON THE JUMP PAD!
PERMISSION TO FIRE?
GENERAL?
FELIX, YOU CAN'T--!
WHOA!

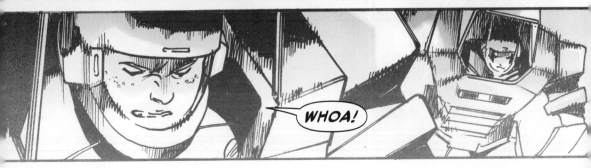

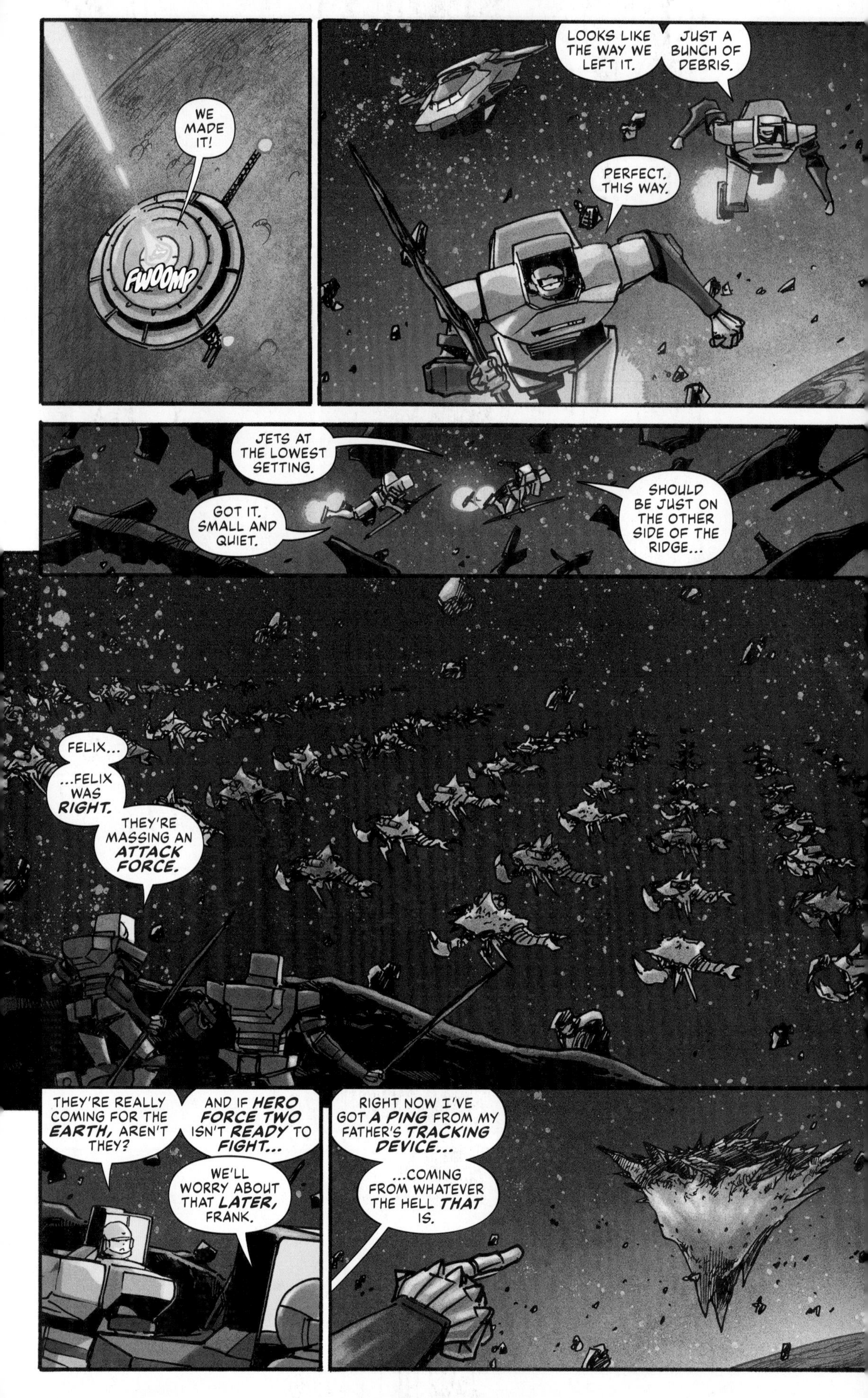
WE MADE IT!
FWOOMP
LOOKS LIKE THE WAY WE LEFT IT.
JUST A BUNCH OF DEBRIS.
PERFECT. THIS WAY.
JETS AT THE LOWEST SETTING.
GOT IT. SMALL AND QUIET.
SHOULD BE JUST ON THE OTHER SIDE OF THE RIDGE...
FELIX...
...FELIX WAS RIGHT.
THEY'RE MASSING AN ATTACK FORCE.
THEY'RE REALLY COMING FOR THE EARTH, AREN'T THEY?
AND IF HERO FORCE TWO ISN'T READY TO FIGHT...
WE'LL WORRY ABOUT THAT LATER, FRANK.
RIGHT NOW I'VE GOT A PING FROM MY FATHER'S TRACKING DEVICE...
...COMING FROM WHATEVER THE HELL THAT IS.

ALL RIGHT, THERE'S AN OPENING...

"...LET'S SEE WHAT THEY'RE *HIDING*."

KKTTT...

KRRAAA!

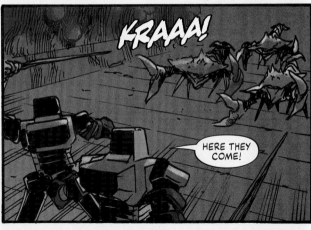

KRAAA!

HERE THEY COME!

SHUNNK

SHAAANK

LOOK OUT!

SHLAAANG

KAA?

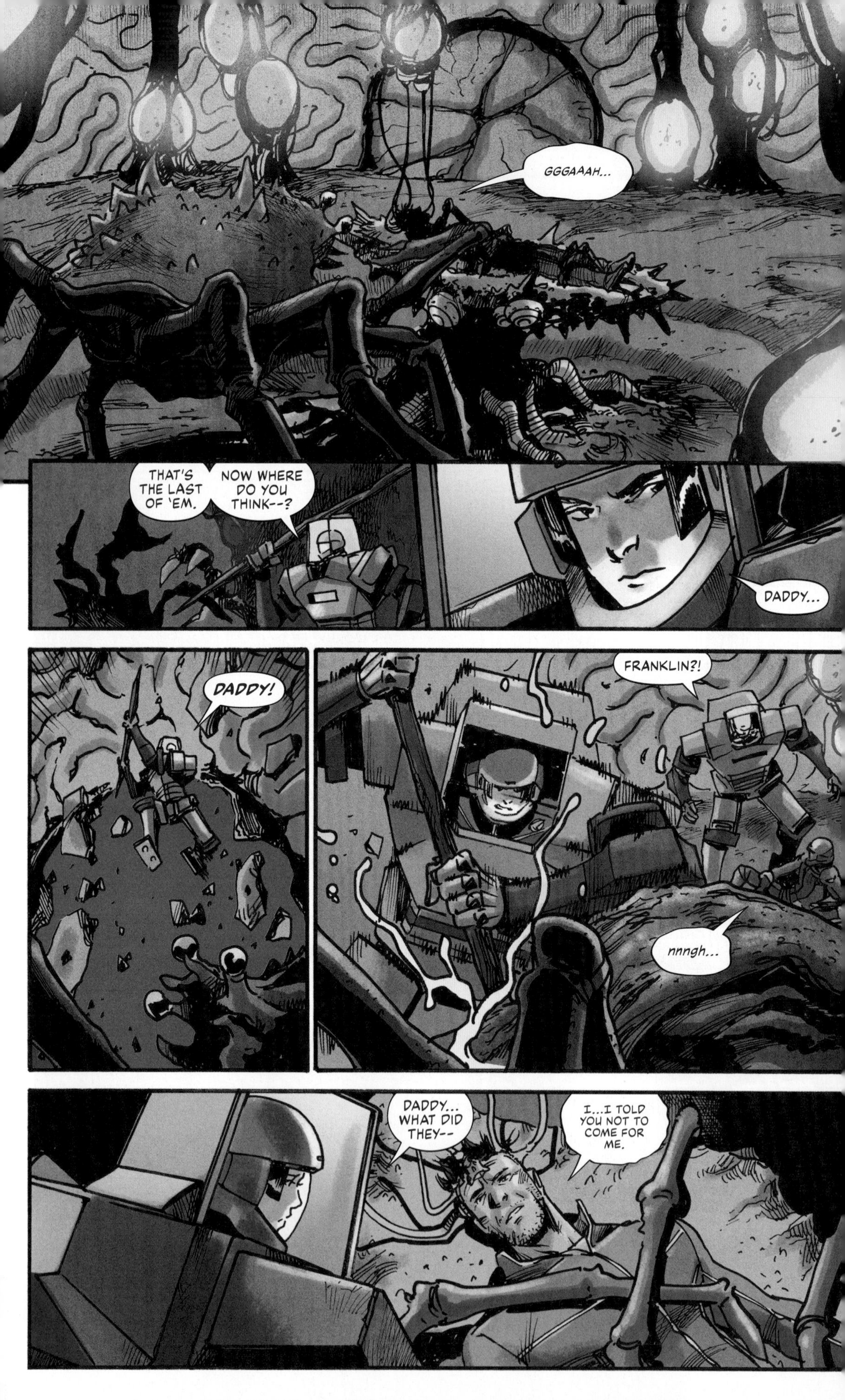

GGGAAAH...
THAT'S THE LAST OF 'EM.
NOW WHERE DO YOU THINK--?
DADDY...
DADDY!
FRANKLIN?!
nnngh...
DADDY... WHAT DID THEY--
I...I TOLD YOU NOT TO COME FOR ME.

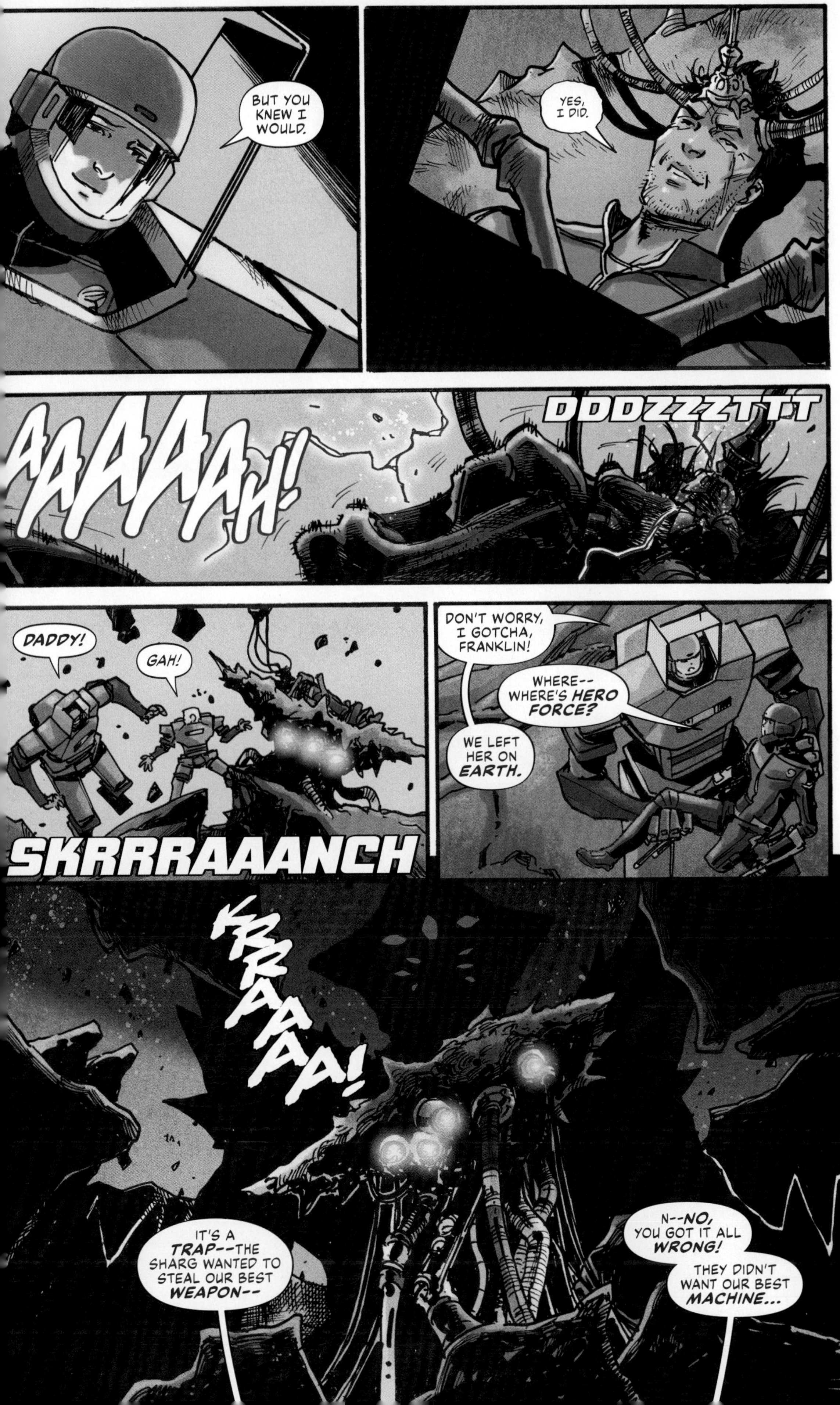
BUT YOU KNEW I WOULD.
YES, I DID.
AAAAAH!
DDDZZZTTT
DADDY!
GAH!
SKRRRAAANCH
DON'T WORRY, I GOTCHA, FRANKLIN!
WHERE-- WHERE'S HERO FORCE?
WE LEFT HER ON EARTH.
KRRAAAA!
IT'S A TRAP--THE SHARG WANTED TO STEAL OUR BEST WEAPON--
N--NO, YOU GOT IT ALL WRONG!
THEY DIDN'T WANT OUR BEST MACHINE...

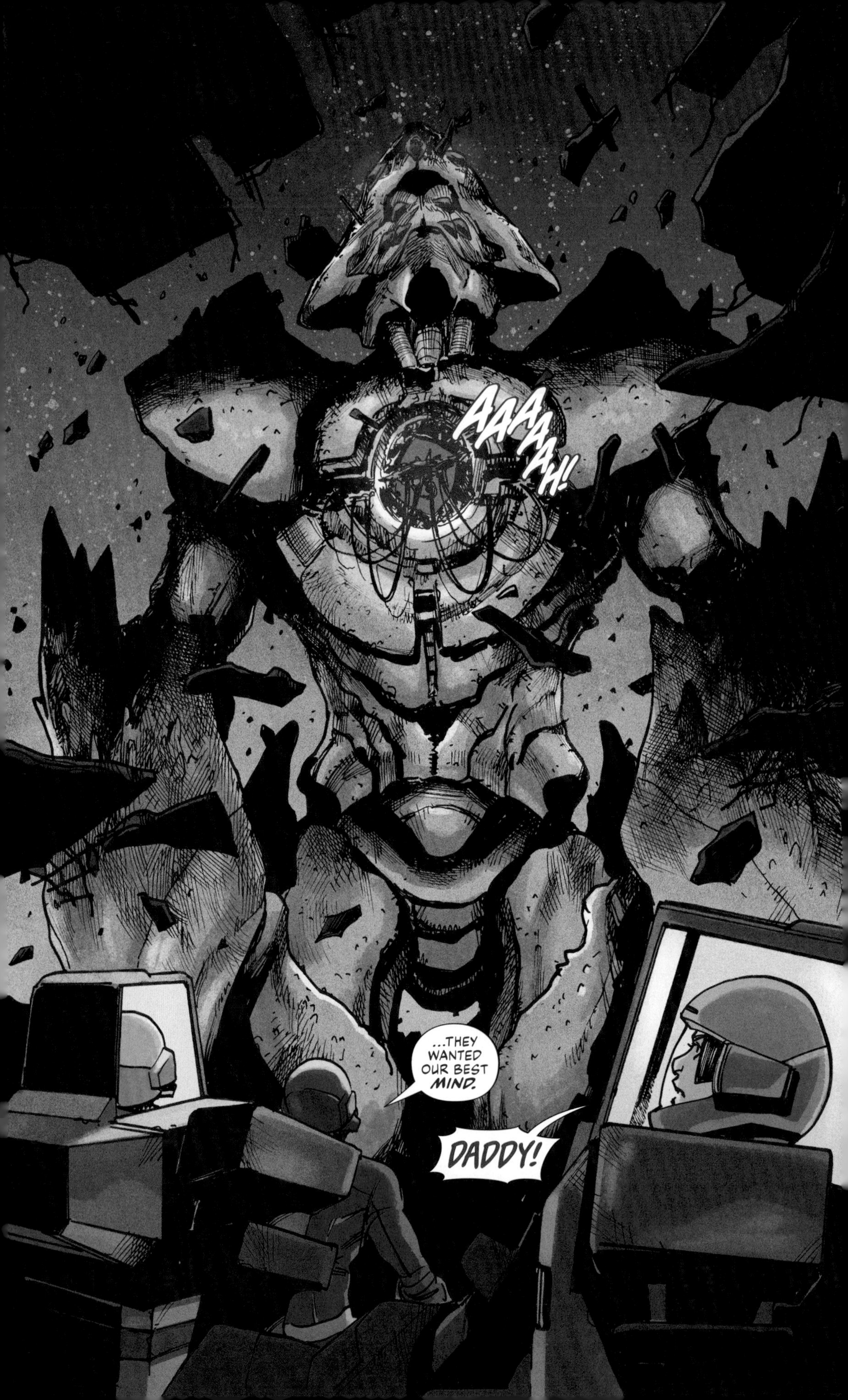
AAAAAH!
...THEY WANTED OUR BEST MIND.
DADDY!

CHAPTER FIVE

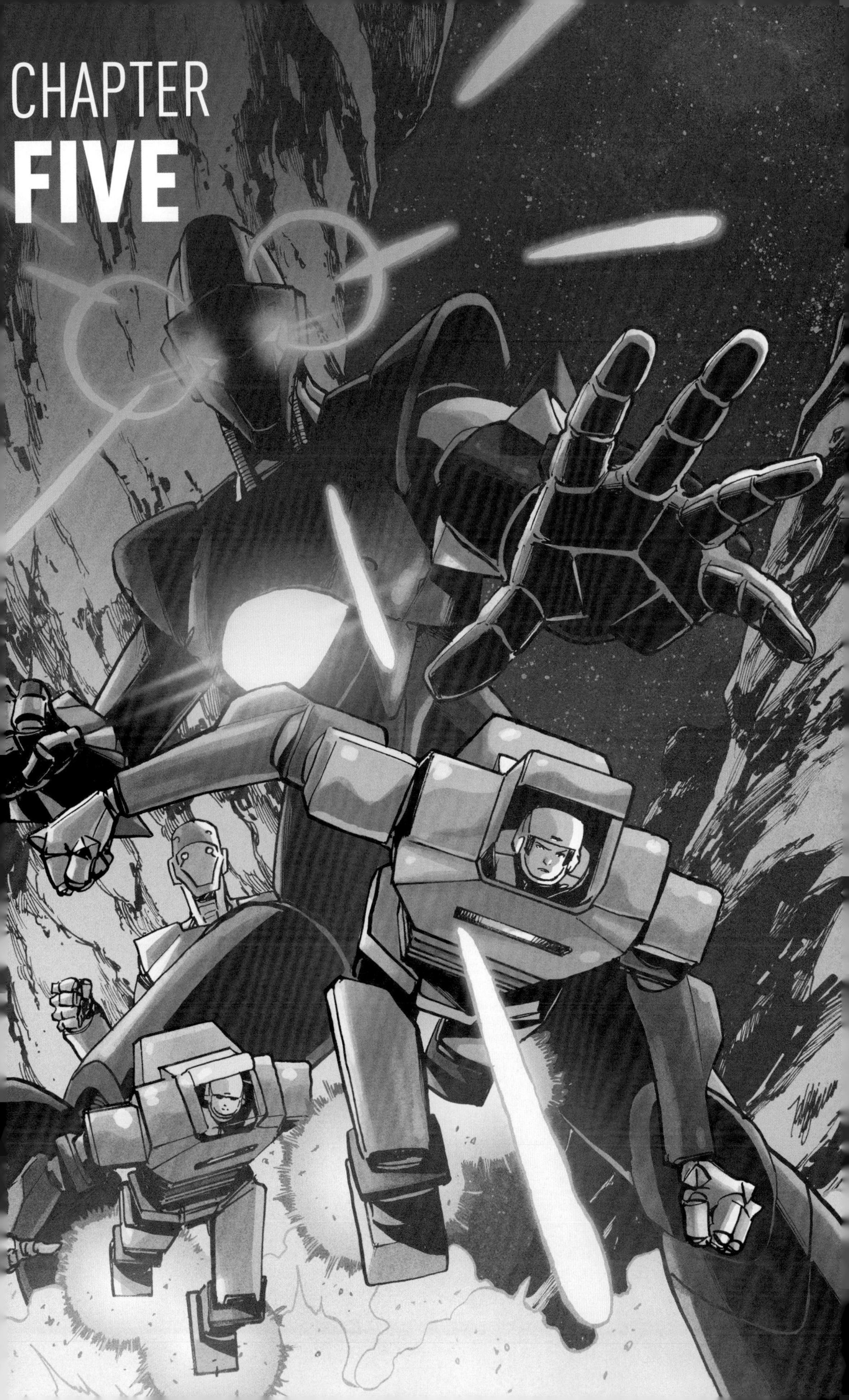

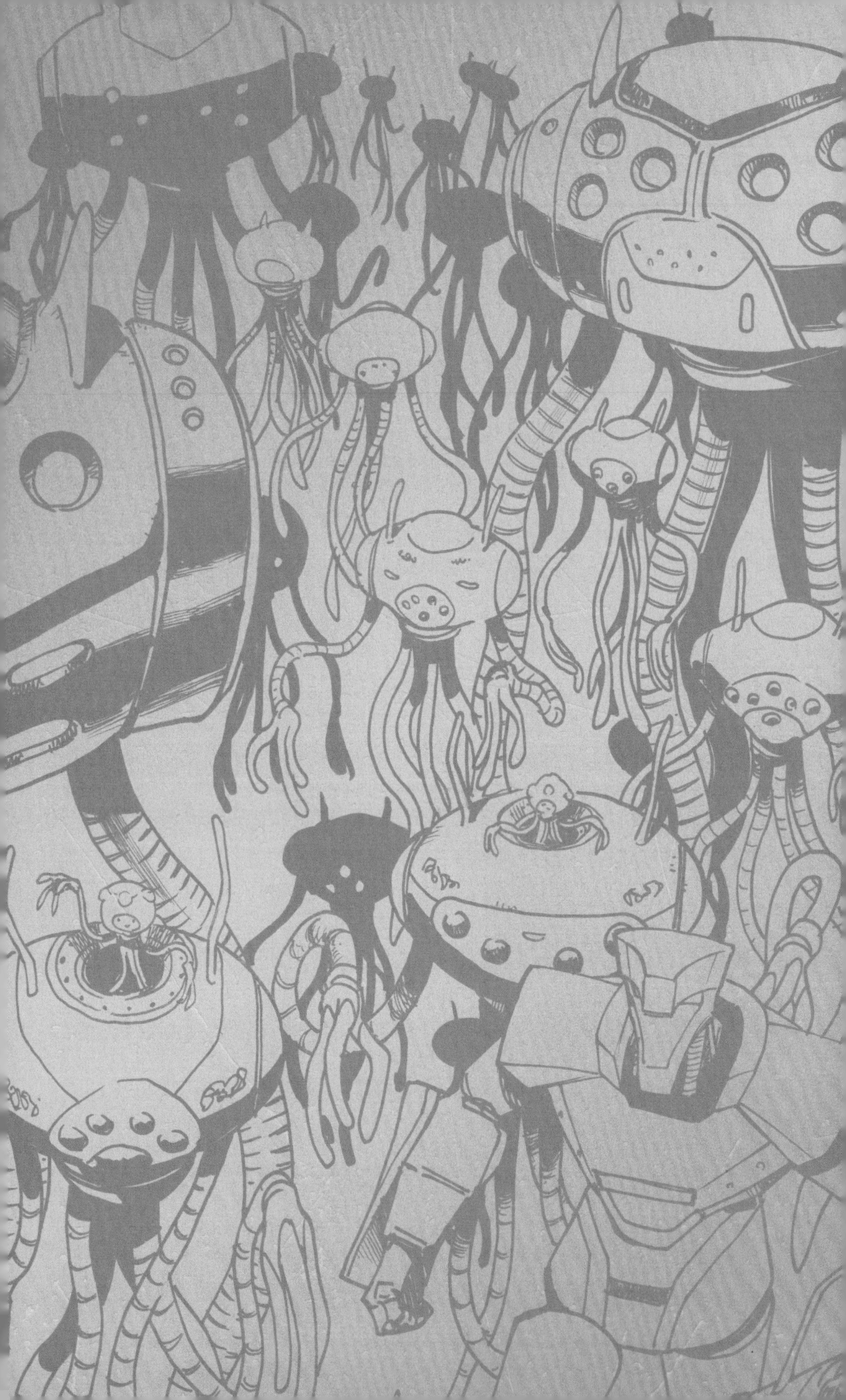

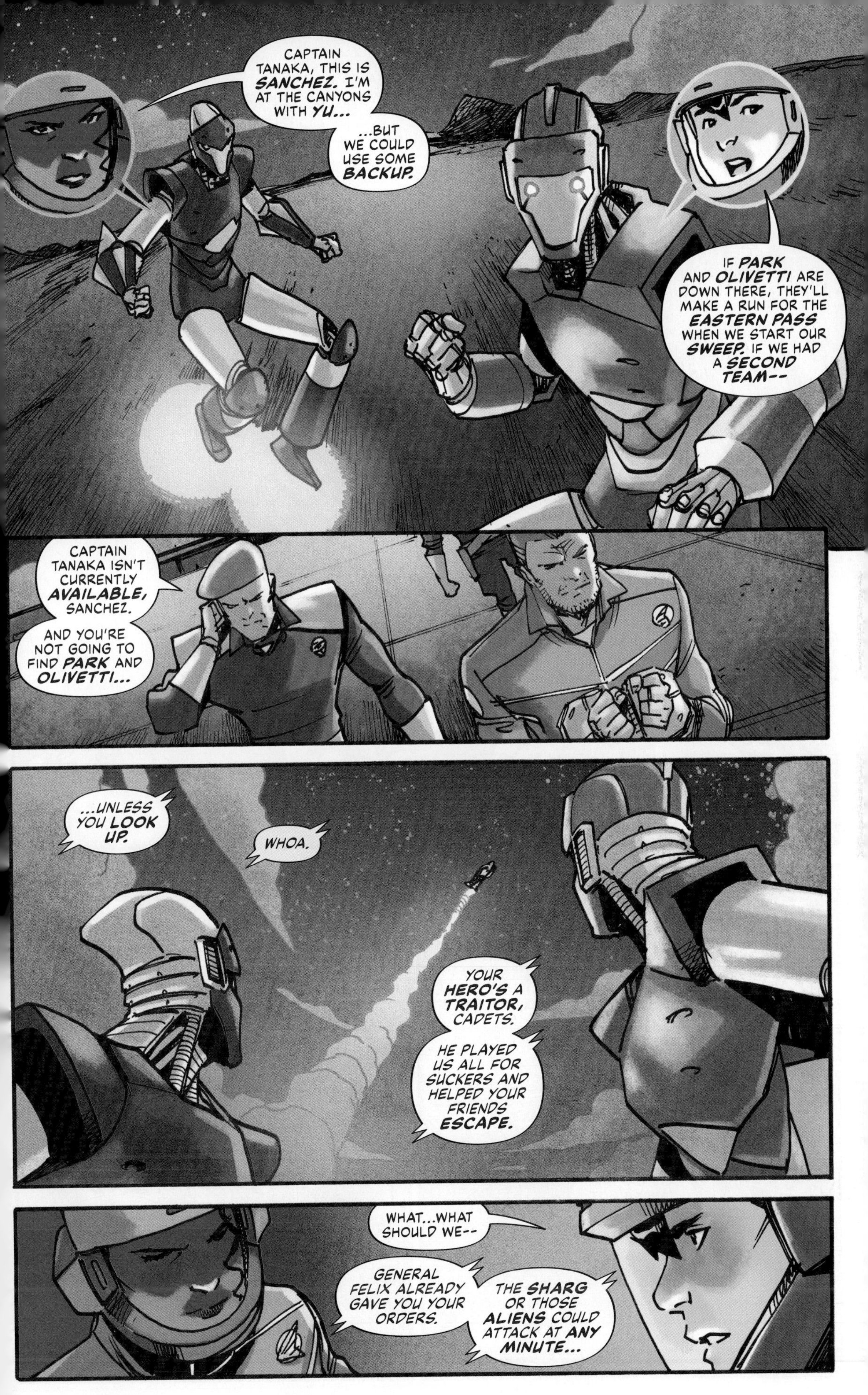
CAPTAIN TANAKA, THIS IS SANCHEZ. I'M AT THE CANYONS WITH YU...
...BUT WE COULD USE SOME BACKUP.
IF PARK AND OLIVETTI ARE DOWN THERE, THEY'LL MAKE A RUN FOR THE EASTERN PASS WHEN WE START OUR SWEEP. IF WE HAD A SECOND TEAM--
CAPTAIN TANAKA ISN'T CURRENTLY AVAILABLE, SANCHEZ.
AND YOU'RE NOT GOING TO FIND PARK AND OLIVETTI...
...UNLESS YOU LOOK UP.
WHOA.
YOUR HERO'S A TRAITOR, CADETS.
HE PLAYED US ALL FOR SUCKERS AND HELPED YOUR FRIENDS ESCAPE.
WHAT...WHAT SHOULD WE--
GENERAL FELIX ALREADY GAVE YOU YOUR ORDERS.
THE SHARG OR THOSE ALIENS COULD ATTACK AT ANY MINUTE...

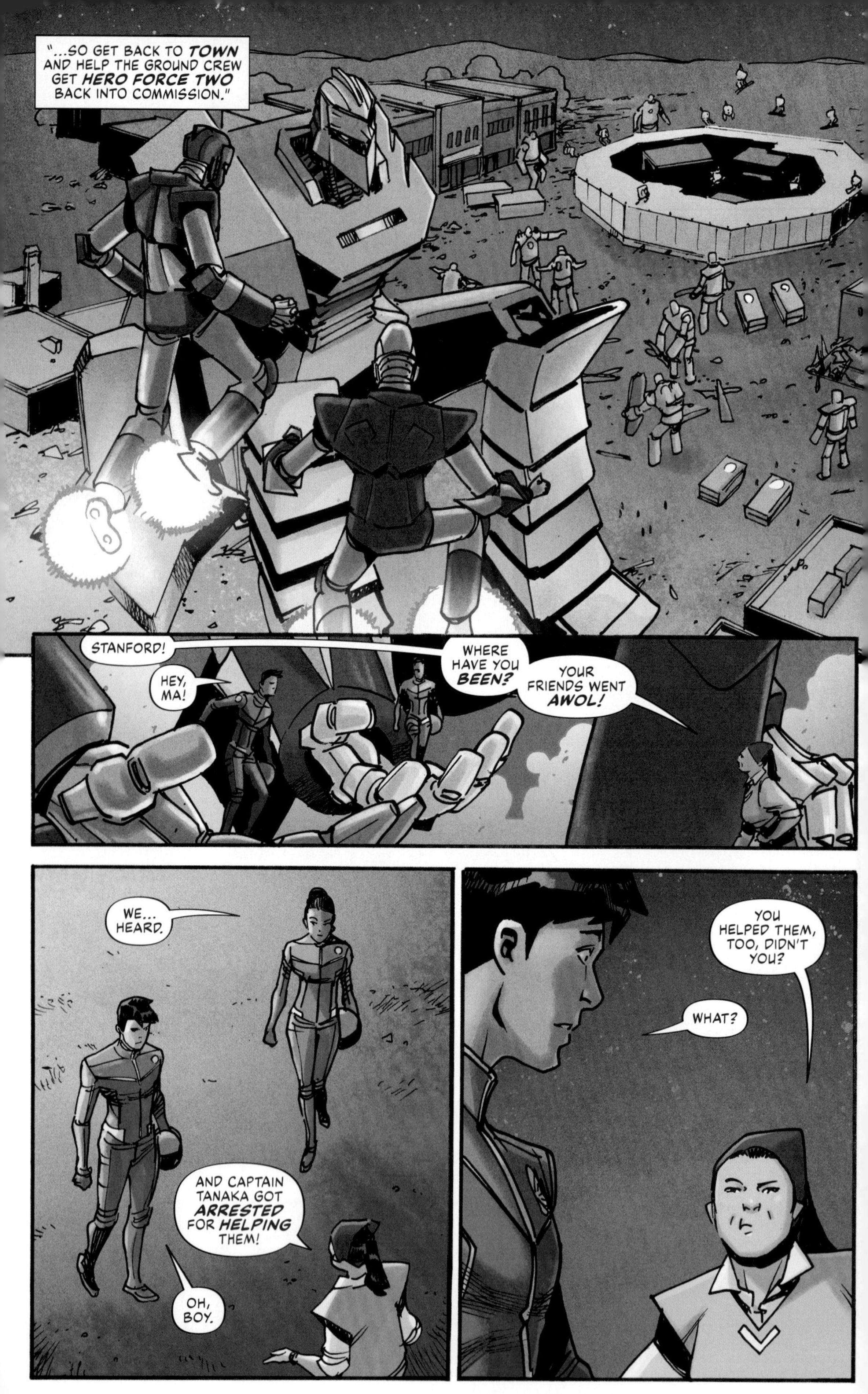
"...SO GET BACK TO TOWN AND HELP THE GROUND CREW GET HERO FORCE TWO BACK INTO COMMISSION."
STANFORD!
HEY, MA!
WHERE HAVE YOU BEEN?
YOUR FRIENDS WENT AWOL!
WE... HEARD.
AND CAPTAIN TANAKA GOT ARRESTED FOR HELPING THEM!
OH, BOY.
YOU HELPED THEM, TOO, DIDN'T YOU?
WHAT?

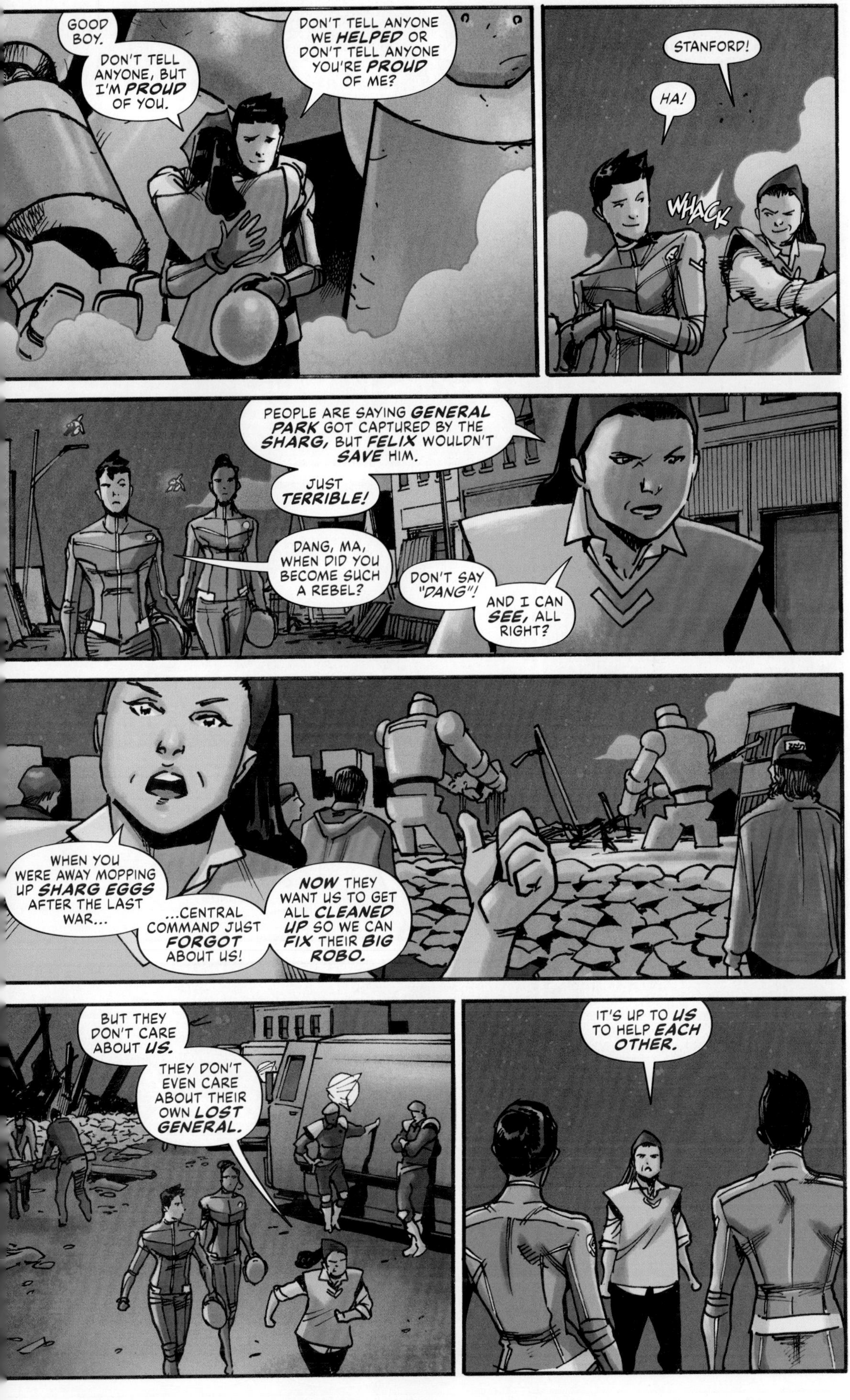
GOOD BOY.
DON'T TELL ANYONE, BUT I'M PROUD OF YOU.
DON'T TELL ANYONE WE HELPED OR DON'T TELL ANYONE YOU'RE PROUD OF ME?
STANFORD!
HA!
WHACK
PEOPLE ARE SAYING GENERAL PARK GOT CAPTURED BY THE SHARG, BUT FELIX WOULDN'T SAVE HIM.
JUST TERRIBLE!
DANG, MA, WHEN DID YOU BECOME SUCH A REBEL?
DON'T SAY "DANG"!
AND I CAN SEE, ALL RIGHT?
WHEN YOU WERE AWAY MOPPING UP SHARG EGGS AFTER THE LAST WAR...
...CENTRAL COMMAND JUST FORGOT ABOUT US!
NOW THEY WANT US TO GET ALL CLEANED UP SO WE CAN FIX THEIR BIG ROBO.
BUT THEY DON'T CARE ABOUT US.
THEY DON'T EVEN CARE ABOUT THEIR OWN LOST GENERAL.
IT'S UP TO US TO HELP EACH OTHER.

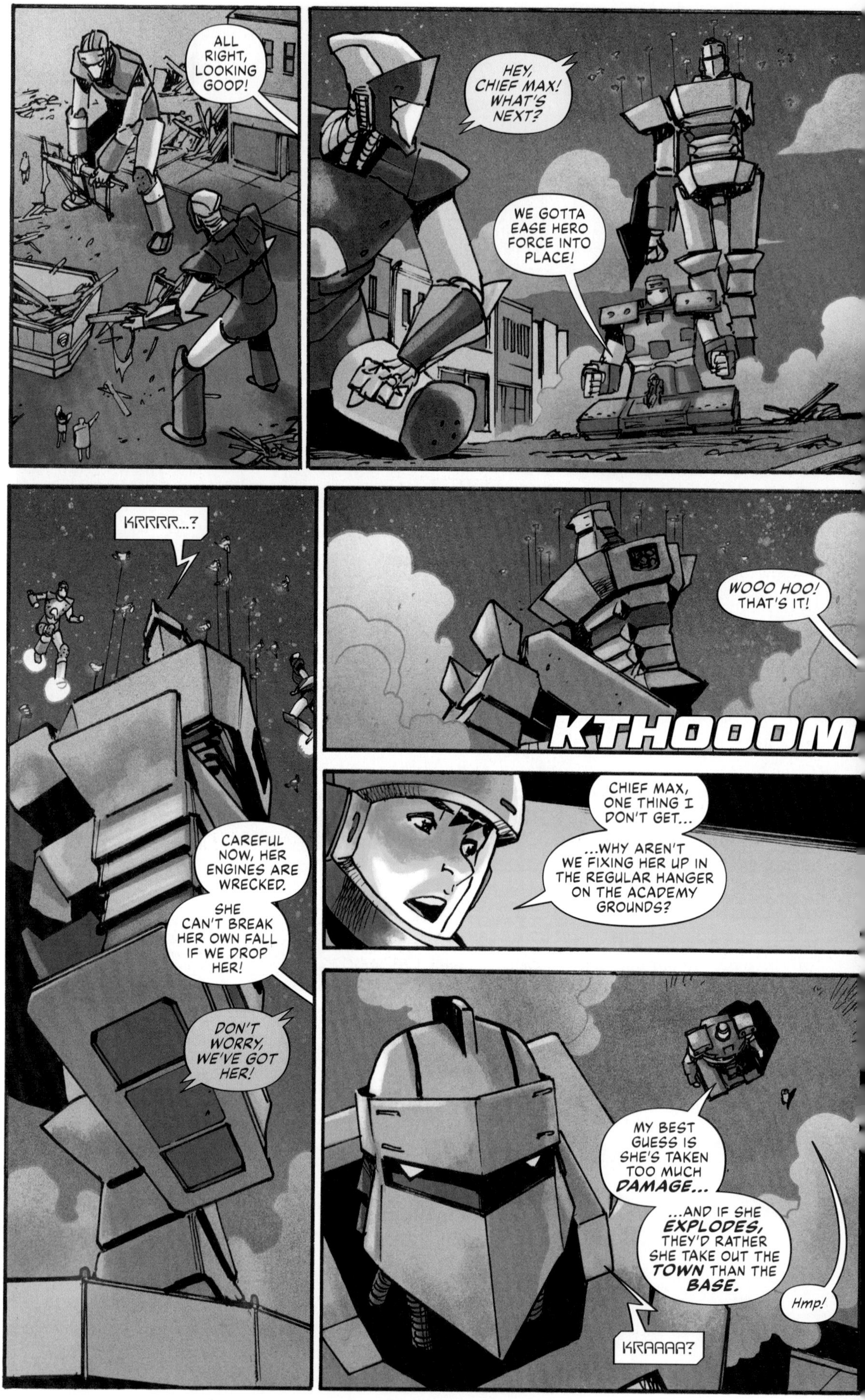
ALL RIGHT, LOOKING GOOD!
HEY, CHIEF MAX! WHAT'S NEXT?
WE GOTTA EASE HERO FORCE INTO PLACE!
KRRRR...?
CAREFUL NOW, HER ENGINES ARE WRECKED.
SHE CAN'T BREAK HER OWN FALL IF WE DROP HER!
DON'T WORRY, WE'VE GOT HER!
WOOO HOO! THAT'S IT!
KTHOOOM
CHIEF MAX, ONE THING I DON'T GET...
...WHY AREN'T WE FIXING HER UP IN THE REGULAR HANGER ON THE ACADEMY GROUNDS?
MY BEST GUESS IS SHE'S TAKEN TOO MUCH DAMAGE...
...AND IF SHE EXPLODES, THEY'D RATHER SHE TAKE OUT THE TOWN THAN THE BASE.
Hmp!
KRAAAA?

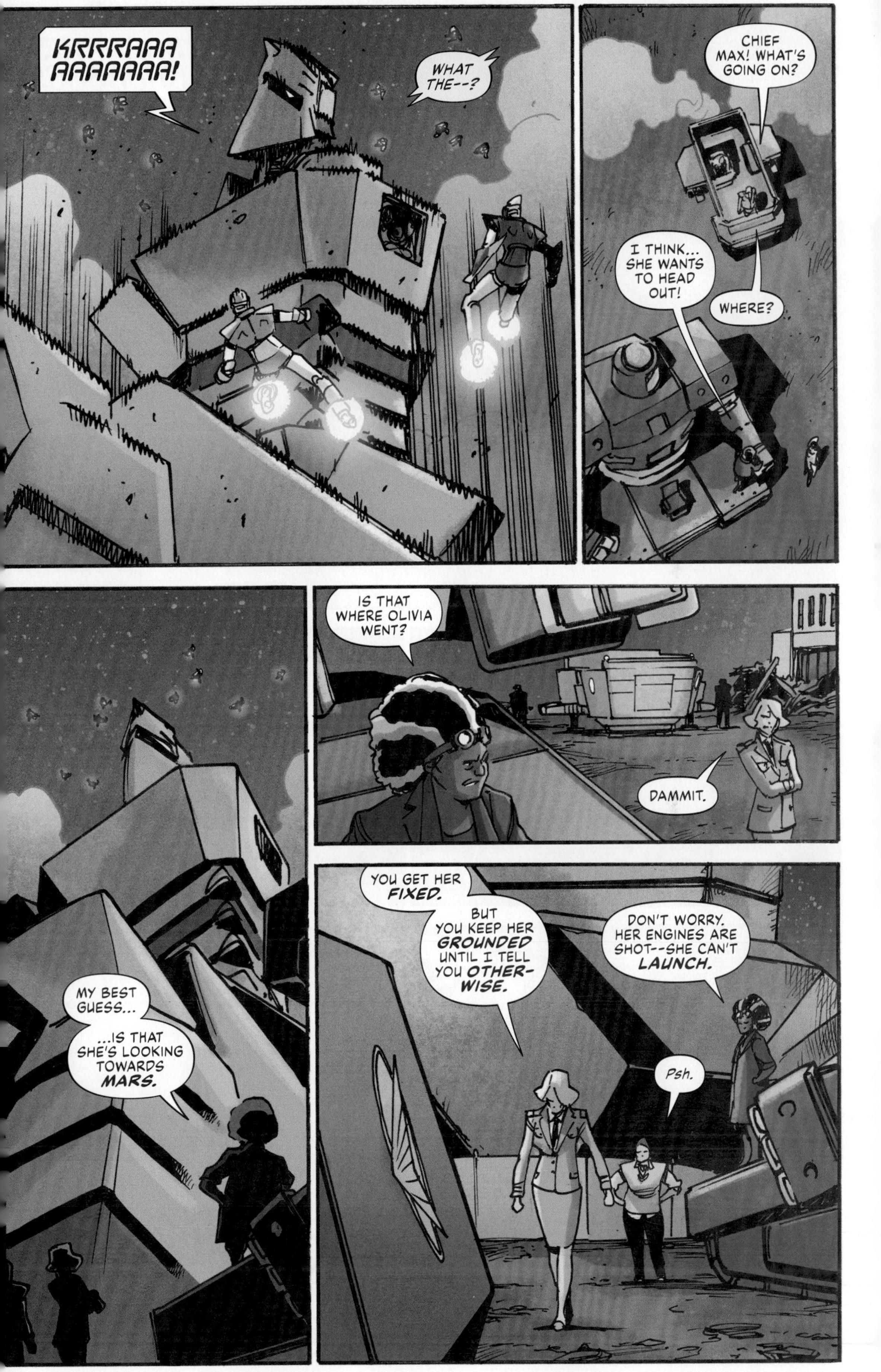
KRRRAAA AAAAAAA!
WHAT THE--?
CHIEF MAX! WHAT'S GOING ON?
I THINK... SHE WANTS TO HEAD OUT!
WHERE?
MY BEST GUESS...
...IS THAT SHE'S LOOKING TOWARDS MARS.
IS THAT WHERE OLIVIA WENT?
DAMMIT.
YOU GET HER FIXED.
BUT YOU KEEP HER GROUNDED UNTIL I TELL YOU OTHER-WISE.
DON'T WORRY. HER ENGINES ARE SHOT--SHE CAN'T LAUNCH.
Psh.

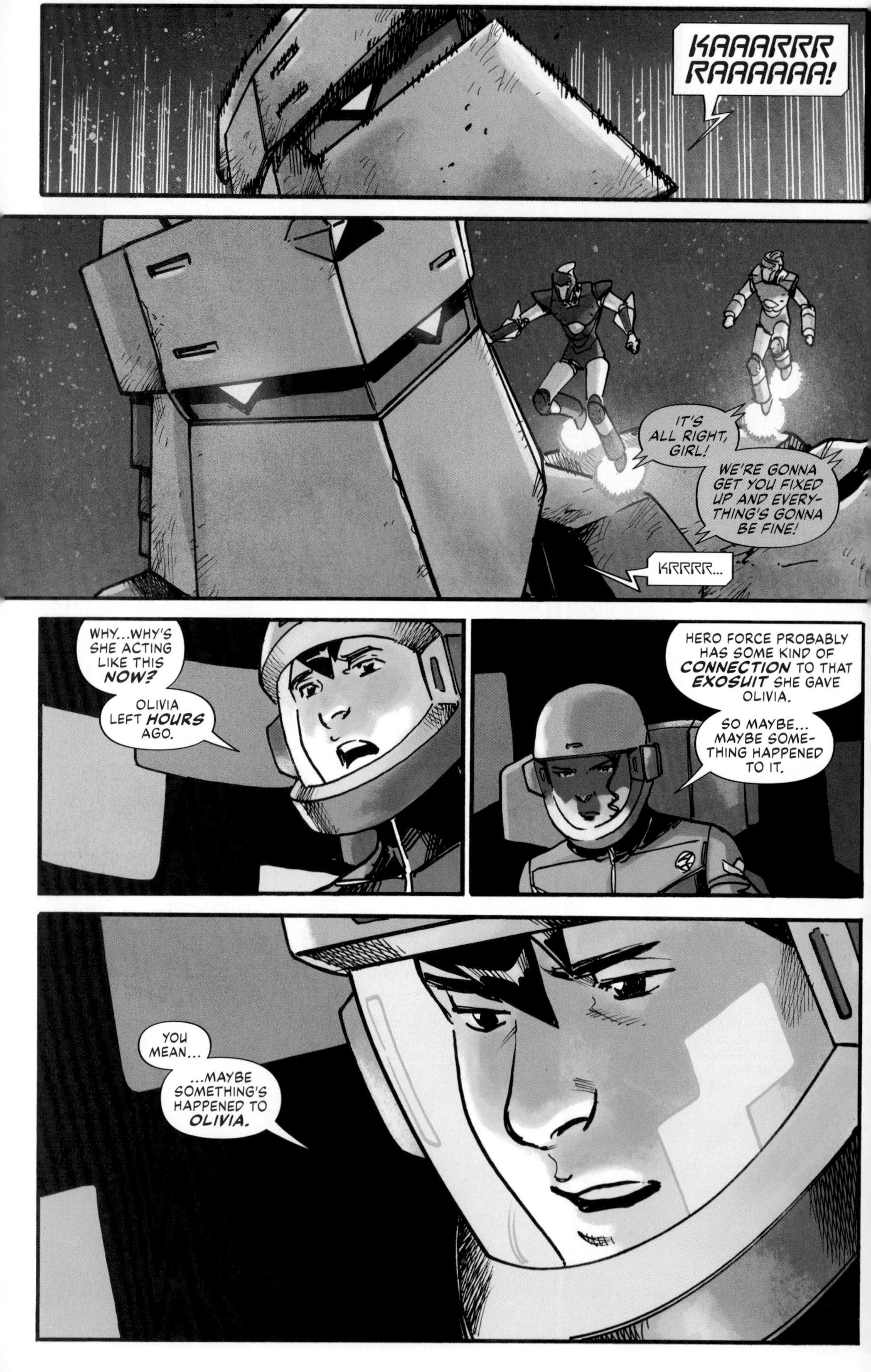
KAAARRR RAAAAAA!
IT'S ALL RIGHT, GIRL!
WE'RE GONNA GET YOU FIXED UP AND EVERY-THING'S GONNA BE FINE!
KRRRR...
WHY...WHY'S SHE ACTING LIKE THIS NOW?
OLIVIA LEFT HOURS AGO.
HERO FORCE PROBABLY HAS SOME KIND OF CONNECTION TO THAT EXOSUIT SHE GAVE OLIVIA.
SO MAYBE... MAYBE SOME-THING HAPPENED TO IT.
YOU MEAN...
...MAYBE SOMETHING'S HAPPENED TO OLIVIA.

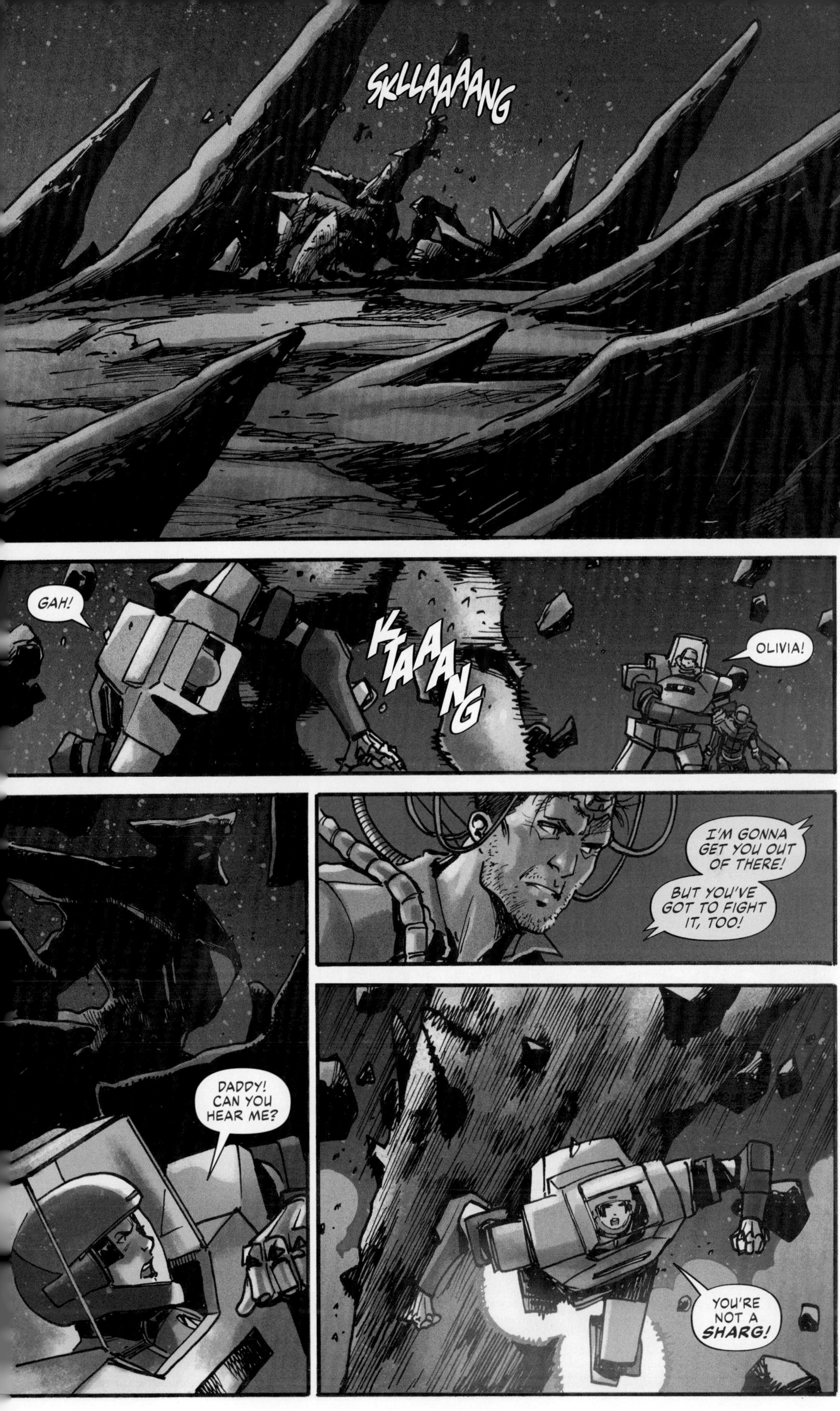
SKLLAAAANG
GAH!
KTAAANG
OLIVIA!
I'M GONNA GET YOU OUT OF THERE!
BUT YOU'VE GOT TO FIGHT IT, TOO!
DADDY! CAN YOU HEAR ME?
YOU'RE NOT A SHARG!

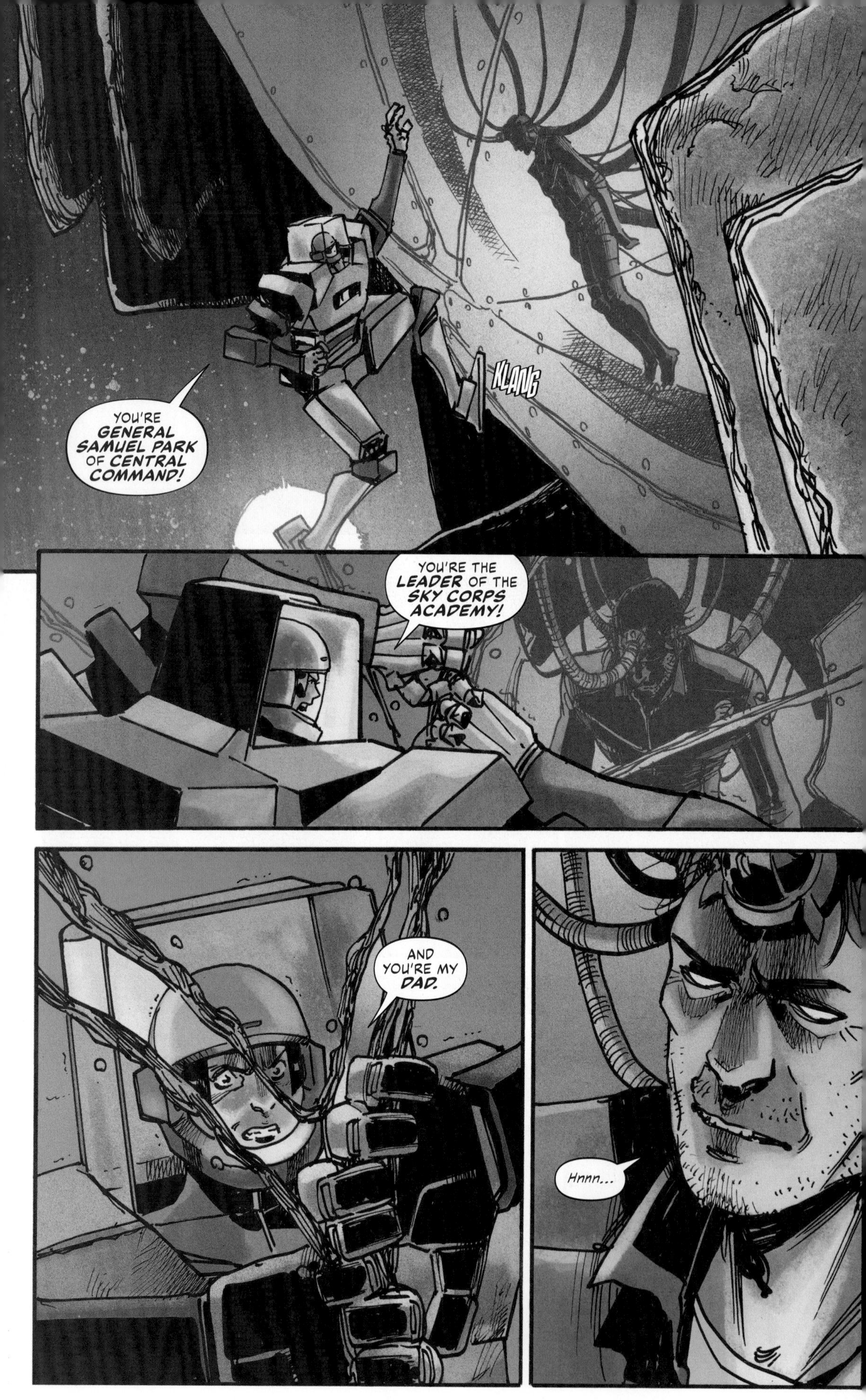
KLANG
YOU'RE GENERAL SAMUEL PARK OF CENTRAL COMMAND!
YOU'RE THE LEADER OF THE SKY CORPS ACADEMY!
AND YOU'RE MY DAD.
Hnnn...

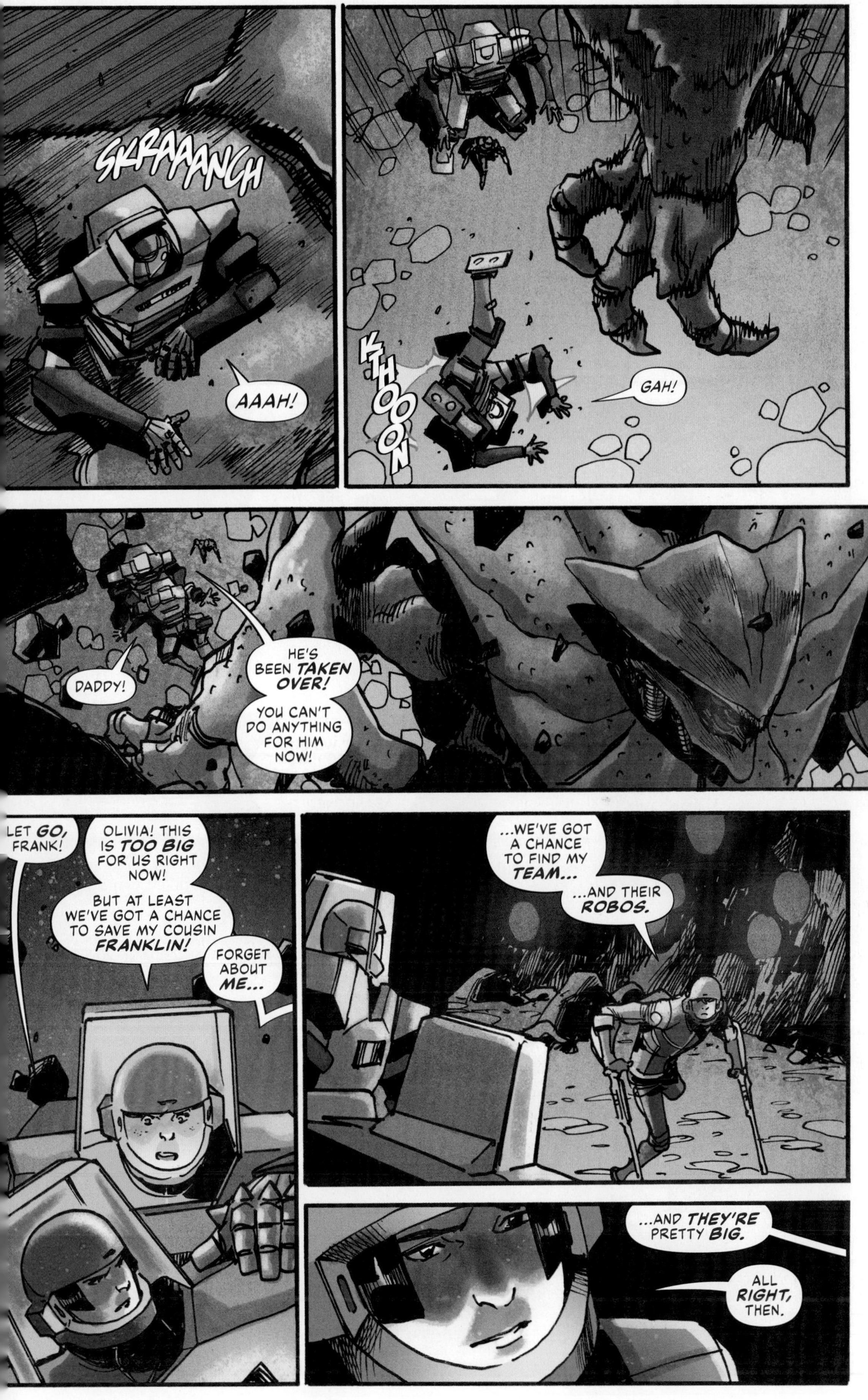

SKRAAAANCH
AAAH!
KTHOOOON
GAH!
DADDY!
HE'S BEEN TAKEN OVER!
YOU CAN'T DO ANYTHING FOR HIM NOW!
LET GO, FRANK!
OLIVIA! THIS IS TOO BIG FOR US RIGHT NOW!
BUT AT LEAST WE'VE GOT A CHANCE TO SAVE MY COUSIN FRANKLIN!
FORGET ABOUT ME...
...WE'VE GOT A CHANCE TO FIND MY TEAM...
...AND THEIR ROBOS.
...AND THEY'RE PRETTY BIG.
ALL RIGHT, THEN.

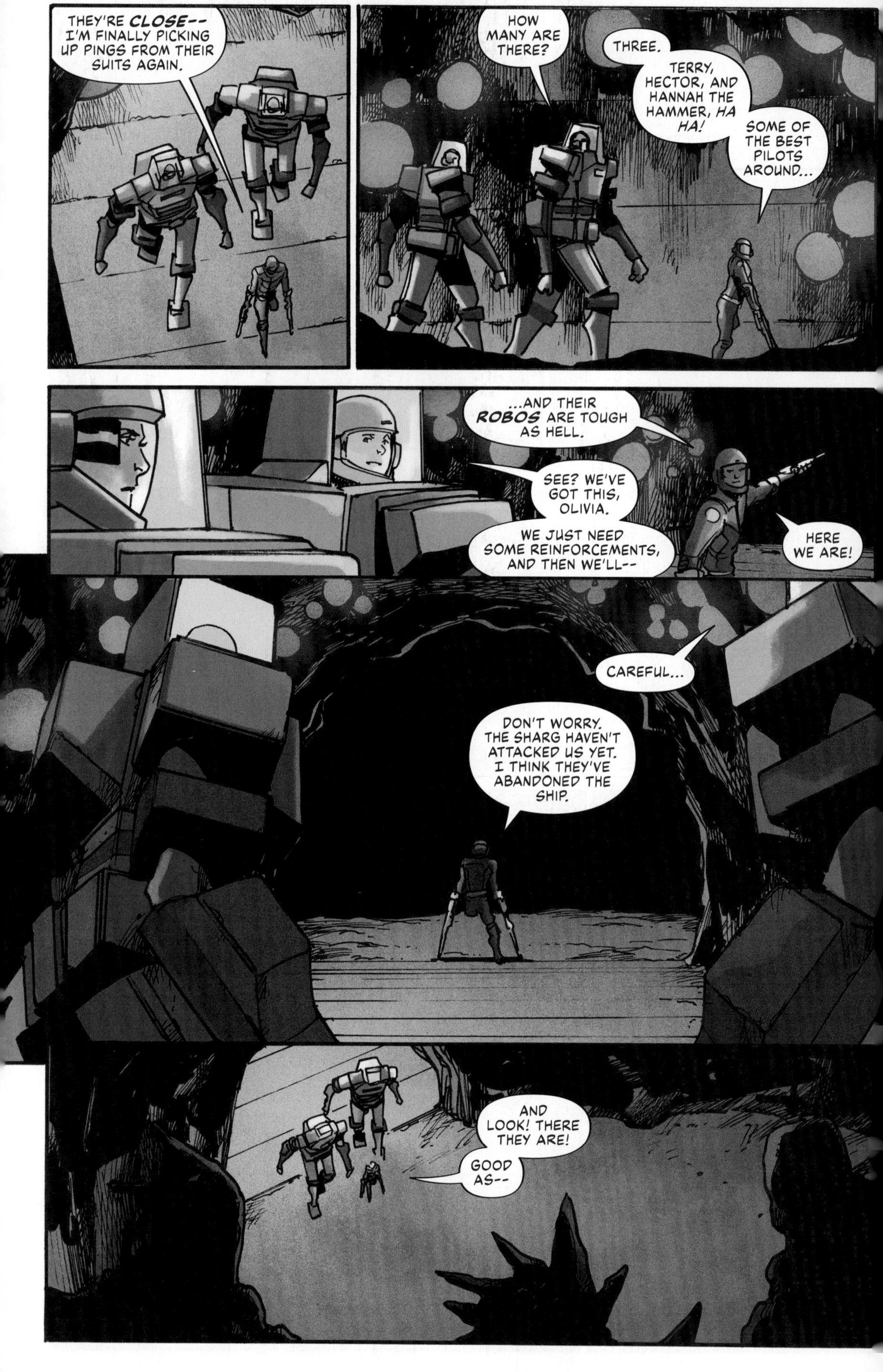
THEY'RE CLOSE-- I'M FINALLY PICKING UP PINGS FROM THEIR SUITS AGAIN.
HOW MANY ARE THERE?
THREE.
TERRY, HECTOR, AND HANNAH THE HAMMER, HA HA!
SOME OF THE BEST PILOTS AROUND...
...AND THEIR ROBOS ARE TOUGH AS HELL.
SEE? WE'VE GOT THIS, OLIVIA.
WE JUST NEED SOME REINFORCEMENTS, AND THEN WE'LL--
HERE WE ARE!
CAREFUL...
DON'T WORRY. THE SHARG HAVEN'T ATTACKED US YET. I THINK THEY'VE ABANDONED THE SHIP.
AND LOOK! THERE THEY ARE!
GOOD AS--

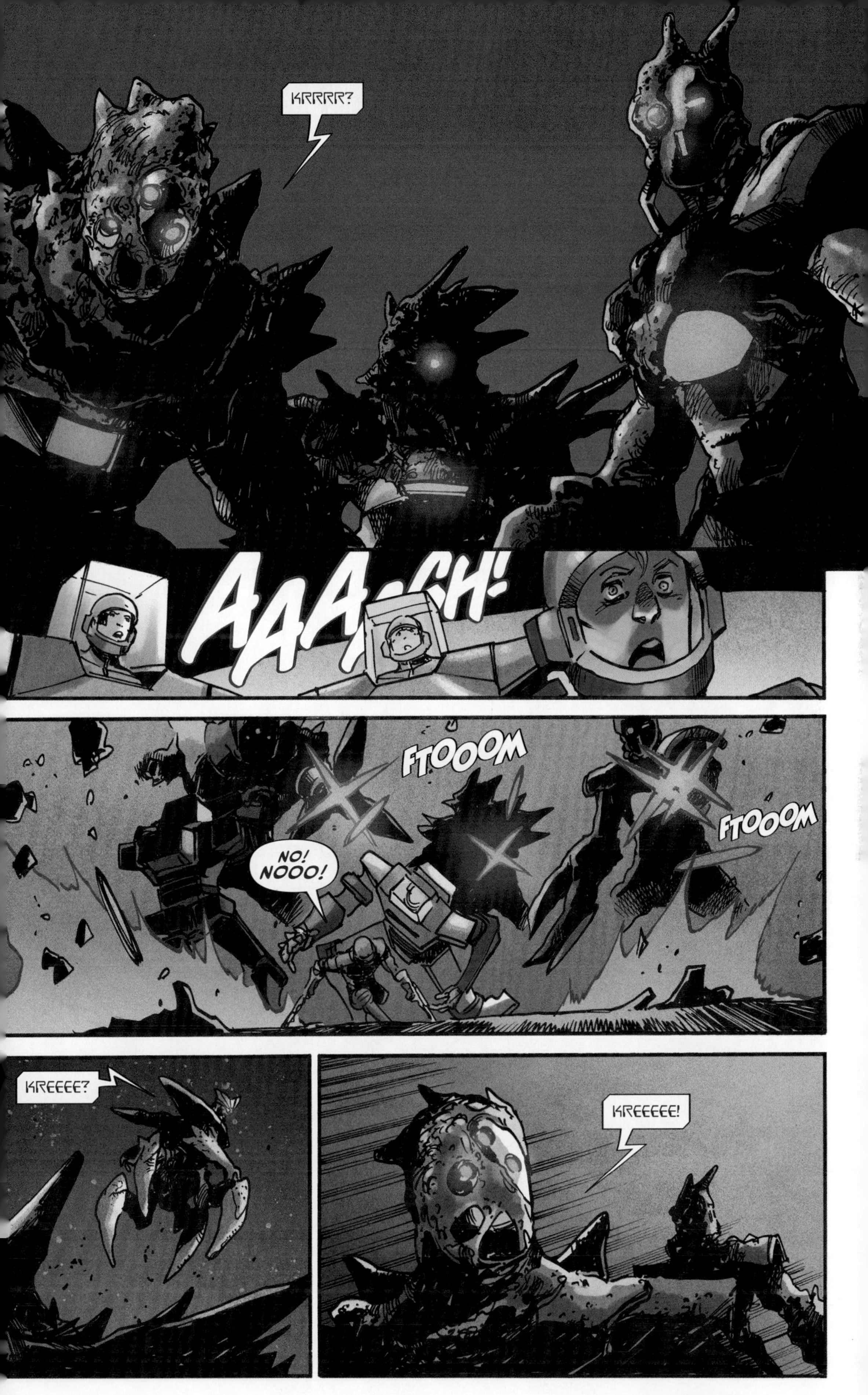
KRRRRR?
AAAAGH!
FTOOOM
FTOOOM
NO! NOOO!
KREEEEE?
KREEEEEE!

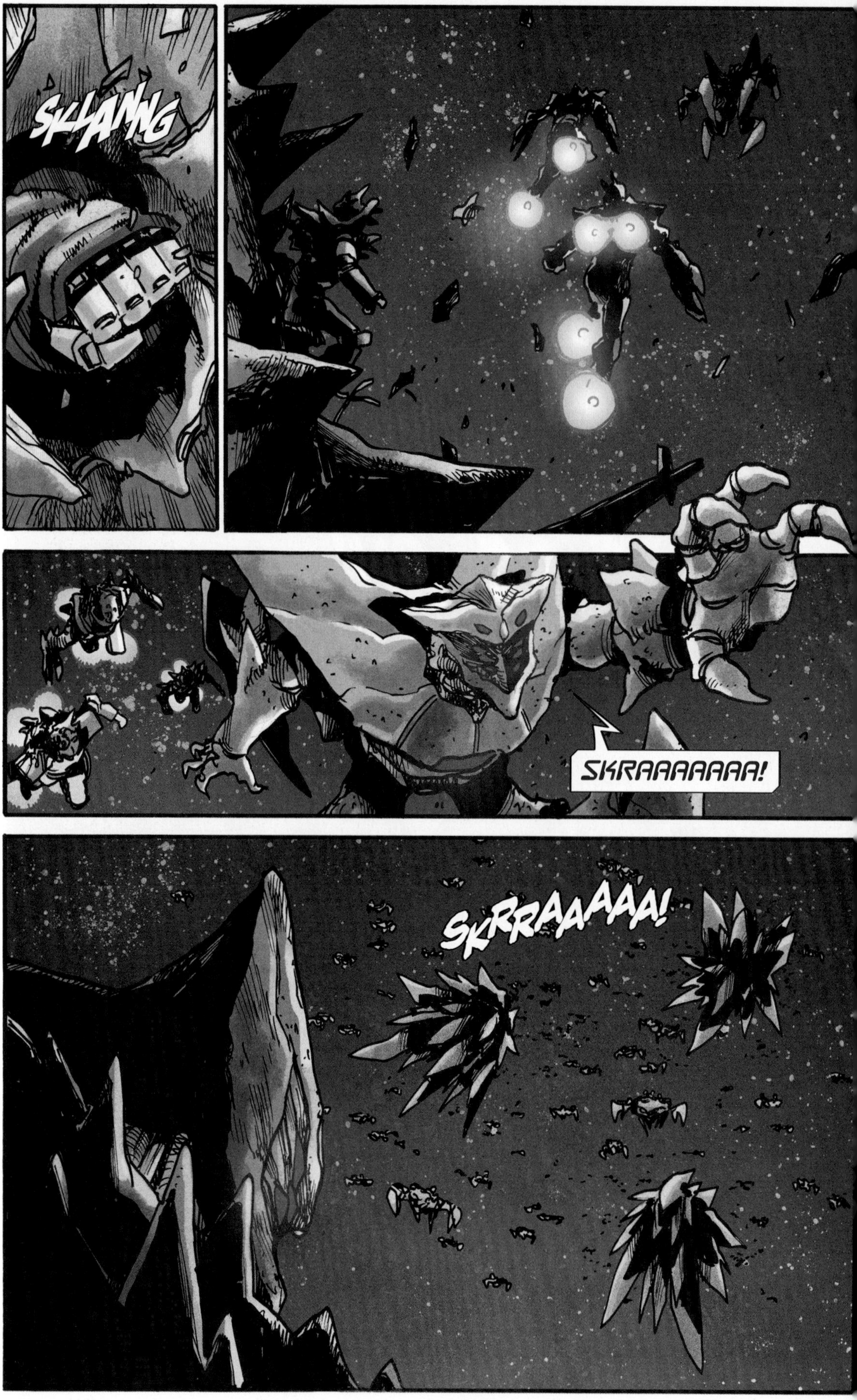
SKLANNG
SKRAAAAAAAA!
SKRRAAAAA!

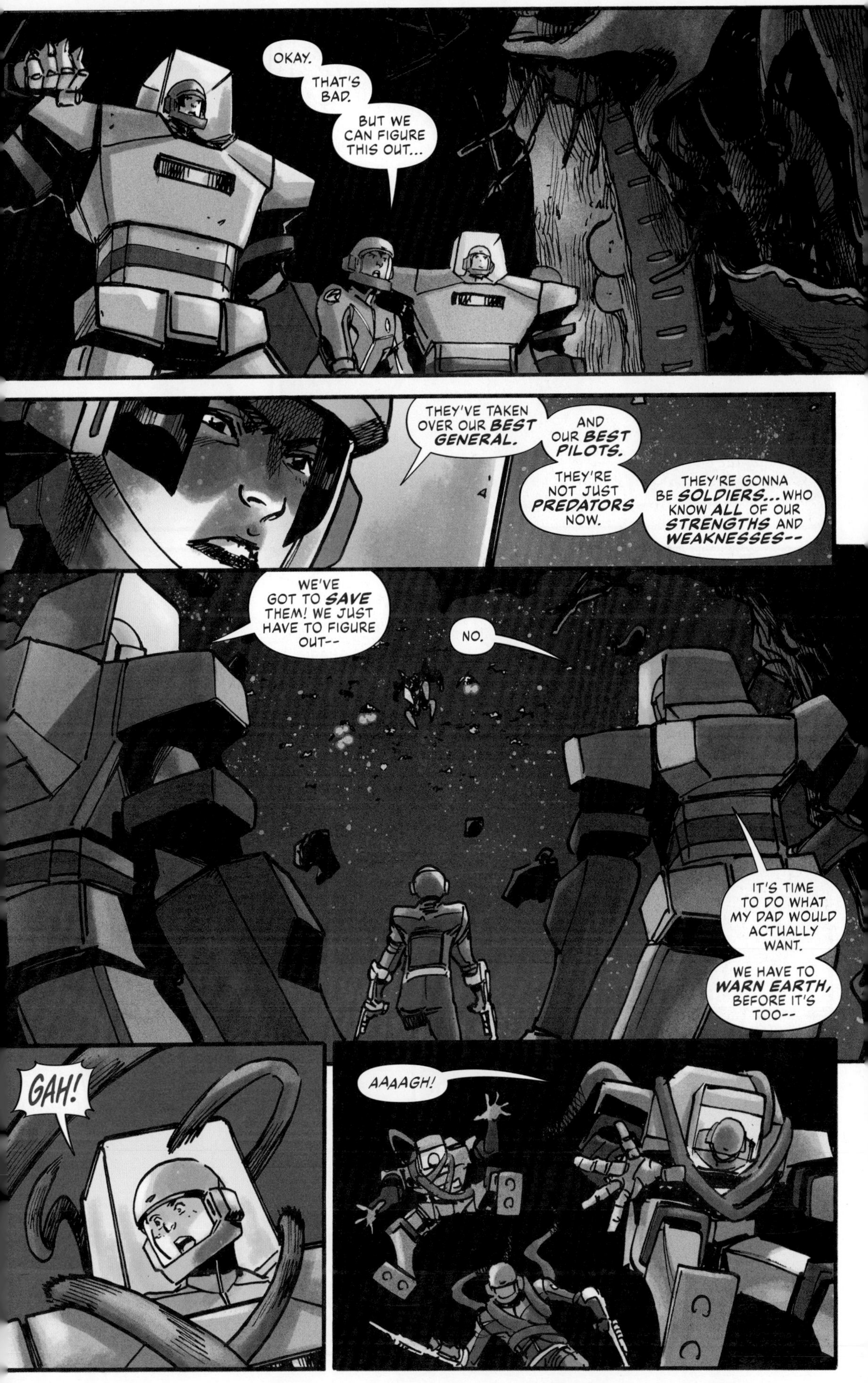
OKAY.
THAT'S BAD.
BUT WE CAN FIGURE THIS OUT...
THEY'VE TAKEN OVER OUR BEST GENERAL.
AND OUR BEST PILOTS.
THEY'RE NOT JUST PREDATORS NOW.
THEY'RE GONNA BE SOLDIERS... WHO KNOW ALL OF OUR STRENGTHS AND WEAKNESSES--
WE'VE GOT TO SAVE THEM! WE JUST HAVE TO FIGURE OUT--
NO.
IT'S TIME TO DO WHAT MY DAD WOULD ACTUALLY WANT.
WE HAVE TO WARN EARTH, BEFORE IT'S TOO--
GAH!
AAAAGH!

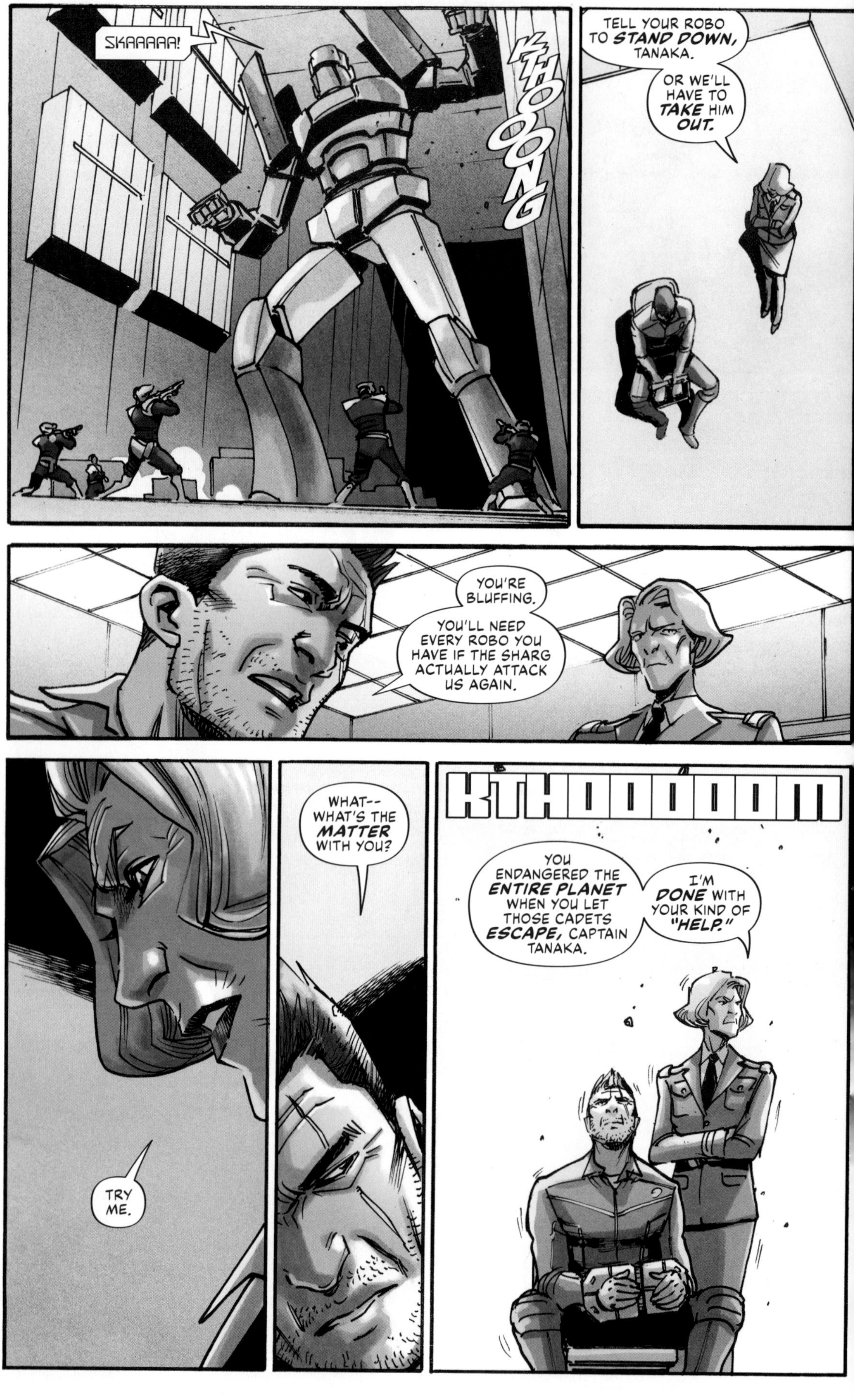
SKAAAAA!
KTHOOOONG
TELL YOUR ROBO TO STAND DOWN, TANAKA.
OR WE'LL HAVE TO TAKE HIM OUT.
YOU'RE BLUFFING.
YOU'LL NEED EVERY ROBO YOU HAVE IF THE SHARG ACTUALLY ATTACK US AGAIN.
TRY ME.
WHAT-- WHAT'S THE MATTER WITH YOU?
KTHOOOOOM
YOU ENDANGERED THE ENTIRE PLANET WHEN YOU LET THOSE CADETS ESCAPE, CAPTAIN TANAKA.
I'M DONE WITH YOUR KIND OF "HELP."

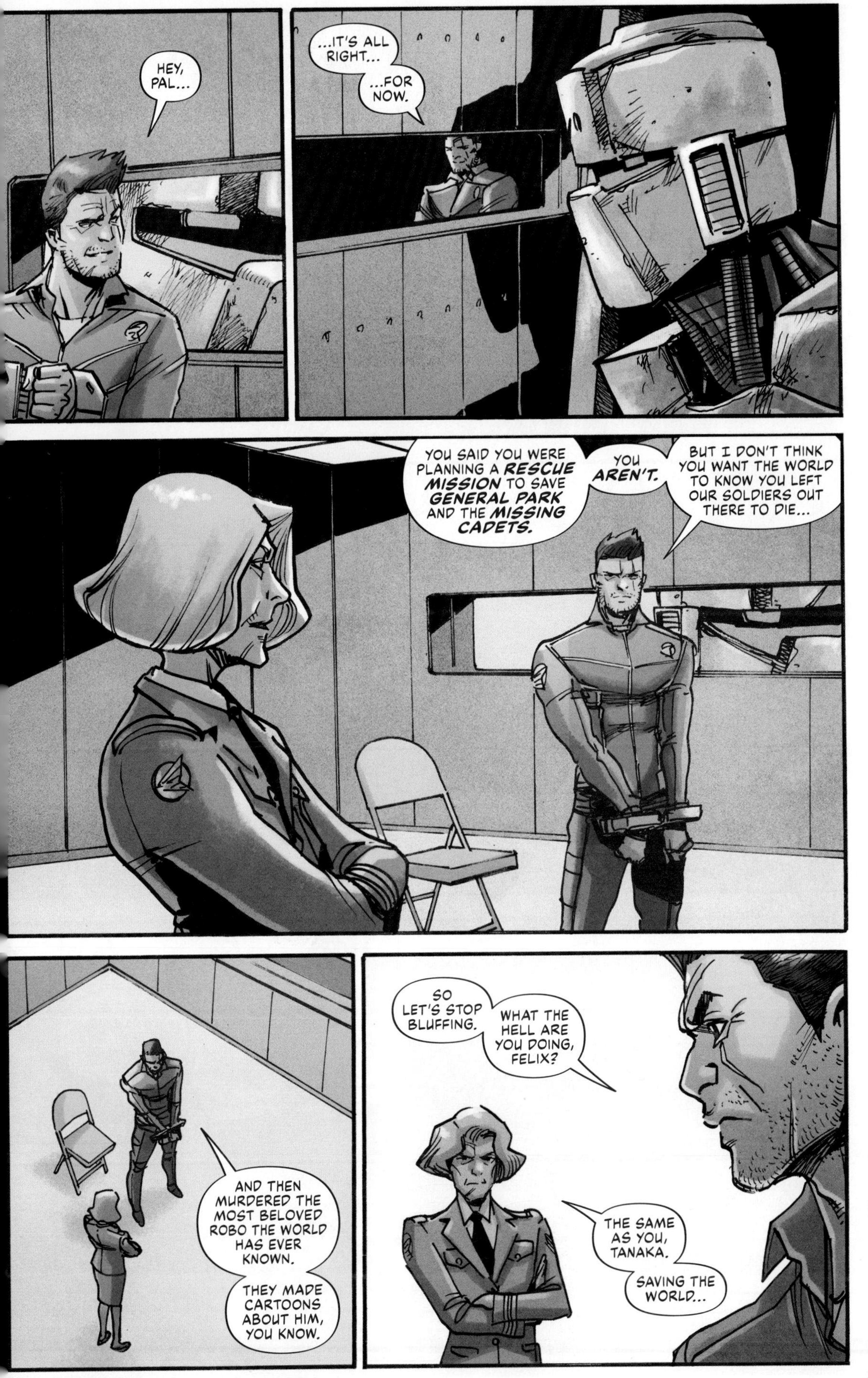
HEY, PAL...
...IT'S ALL RIGHT...
...FOR NOW.
YOU SAID YOU WERE PLANNING A RESCUE MISSION TO SAVE GENERAL PARK AND THE MISSING CADETS.
YOU AREN'T.
BUT I DON'T THINK YOU WANT THE WORLD TO KNOW YOU LEFT OUR SOLDIERS OUT THERE TO DIE...
AND THEN MURDERED THE MOST BELOVED ROBO THE WORLD HAS EVER KNOWN.
THEY MADE CARTOONS ABOUT HIM, YOU KNOW.
SO LET'S STOP BLUFFING.
WHAT THE HELL ARE YOU DOING, FELIX?
THE SAME AS YOU, TANAKA.
SAVING THE WORLD...

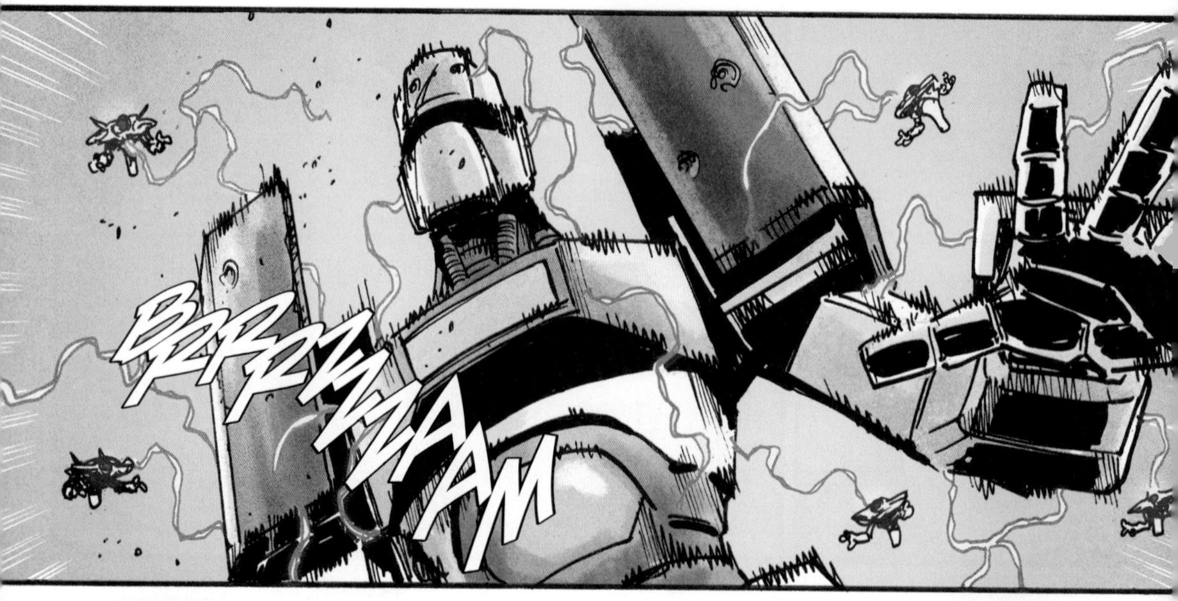
BRRRZZZAAM

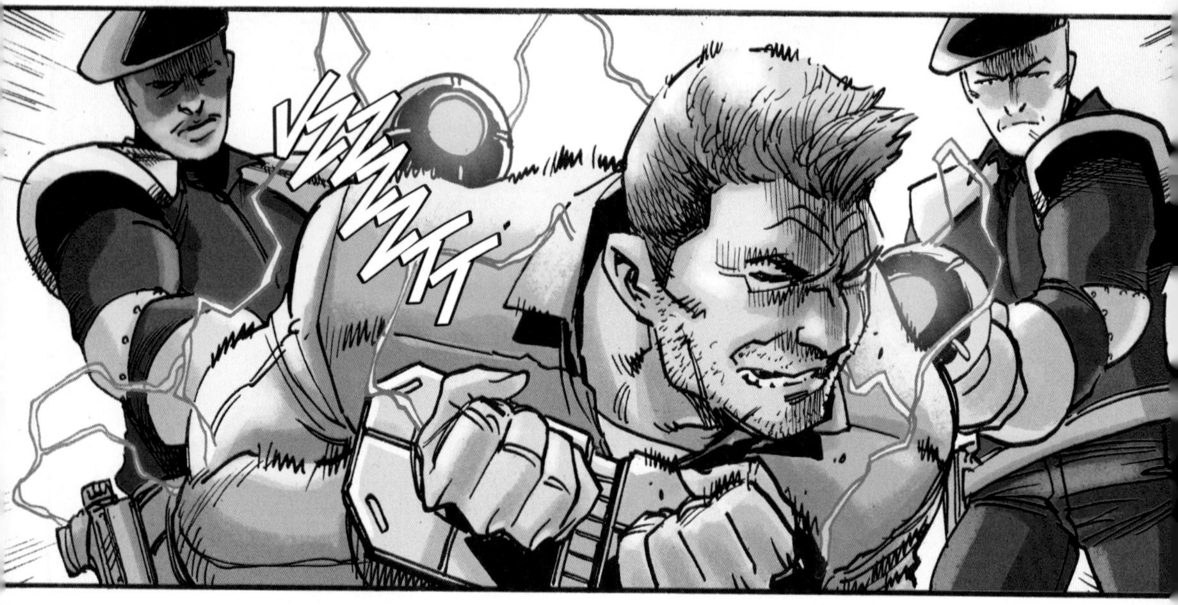
VZZZZZTT

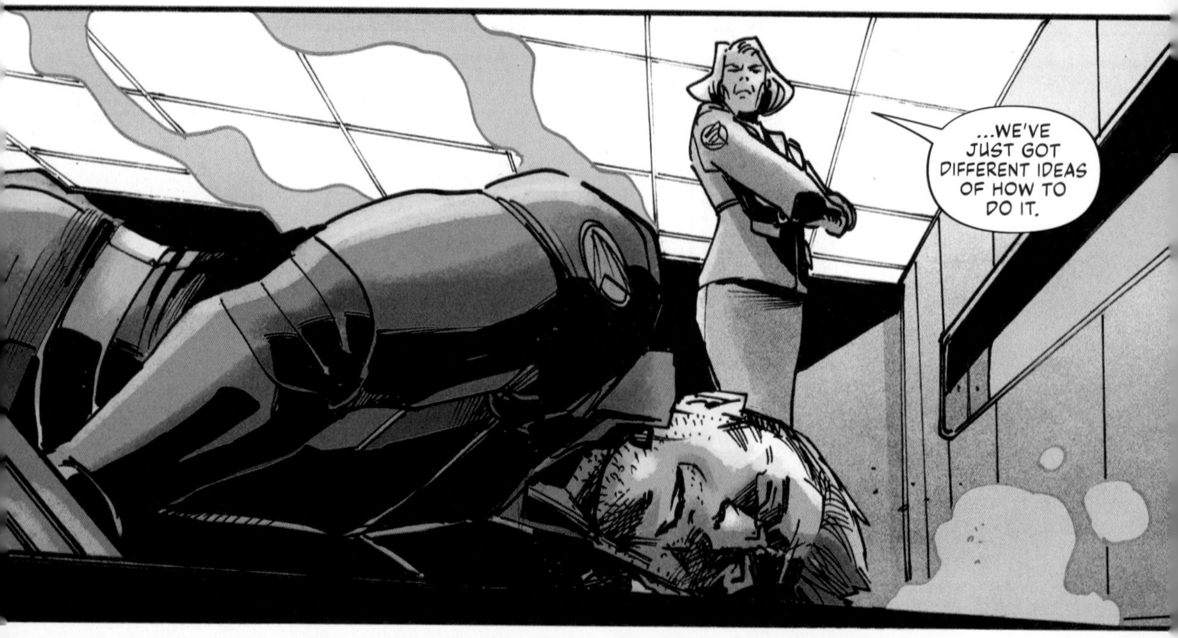
...WE'VE JUST GOT DIFFERENT IDEAS OF HOW TO DO IT.

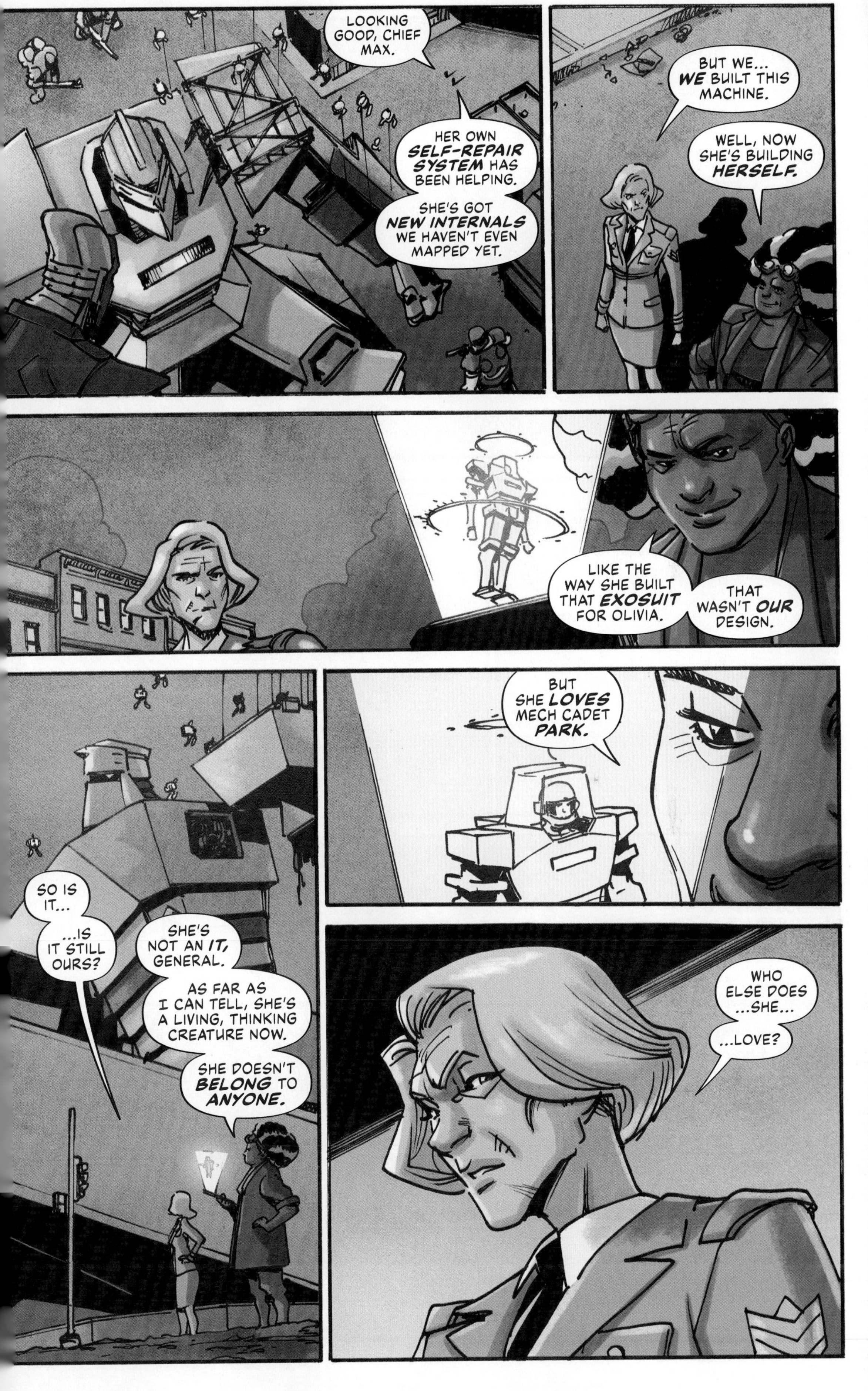
LOOKING GOOD, CHIEF MAX.
HER OWN SELF-REPAIR SYSTEM HAS BEEN HELPING.
SHE'S GOT NEW INTERNALS WE HAVEN'T EVEN MAPPED YET.
BUT WE... WE BUILT THIS MACHINE.
WELL, NOW SHE'S BUILDING HERSELF.
LIKE THE WAY SHE BUILT THAT EXOSUIT FOR OLIVIA.
THAT WASN'T OUR DESIGN.
SO IS IT...
...IS IT STILL OURS?
SHE'S NOT AN IT, GENERAL.
AS FAR AS I CAN TELL, SHE'S A LIVING, THINKING CREATURE NOW.
SHE DOESN'T BELONG TO ANYONE.
BUT SHE LOVES MECH CADET PARK.
WHO ELSE DOES ...SHE...
...LOVE?

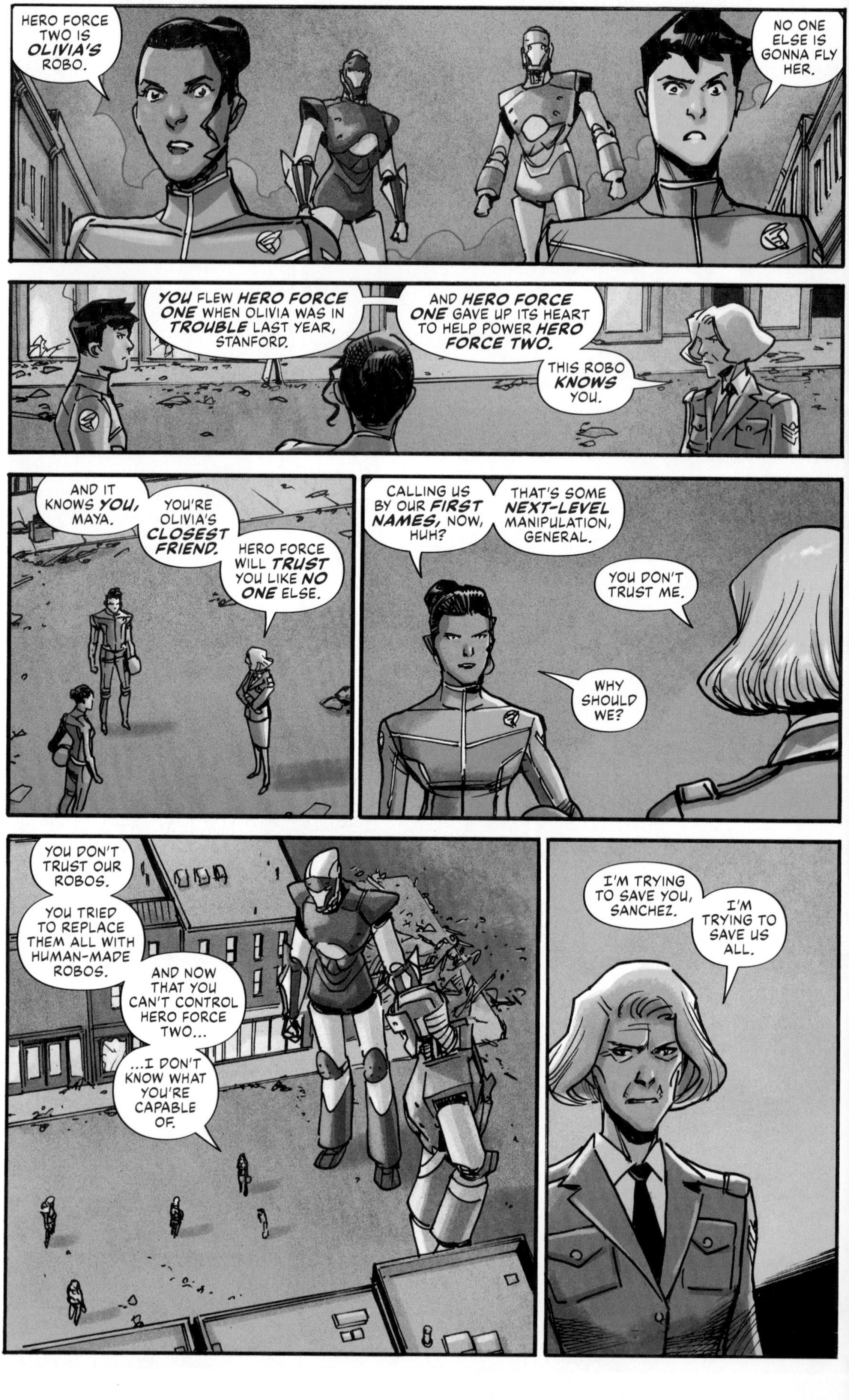
HERO FORCE TWO IS OLIVIA'S ROBO.
NO ONE ELSE IS GONNA FLY HER.
YOU FLEW HERO FORCE ONE WHEN OLIVIA WAS IN TROUBLE LAST YEAR, STANFORD.
AND HERO FORCE ONE GAVE UP ITS HEART TO HELP POWER HERO FORCE TWO.
THIS ROBO KNOWS YOU.
AND IT KNOWS YOU, MAYA.
YOU'RE OLIVIA'S CLOSEST FRIEND.
HERO FORCE WILL TRUST YOU LIKE NO ONE ELSE.
CALLING US BY OUR FIRST NAMES, NOW, HUH?
THAT'S SOME NEXT-LEVEL MANIPULATION, GENERAL.
YOU DON'T TRUST ME.
WHY SHOULD WE?
YOU DON'T TRUST OUR ROBOS.
YOU TRIED TO REPLACE THEM ALL WITH HUMAN-MADE ROBOS.
AND NOW THAT YOU CAN'T CONTROL HERO FORCE TWO...
...I DON'T KNOW WHAT YOU'RE CAPABLE OF.
I'M TRYING TO SAVE YOU, SANCHEZ.
I'M TRYING TO SAVE US ALL.

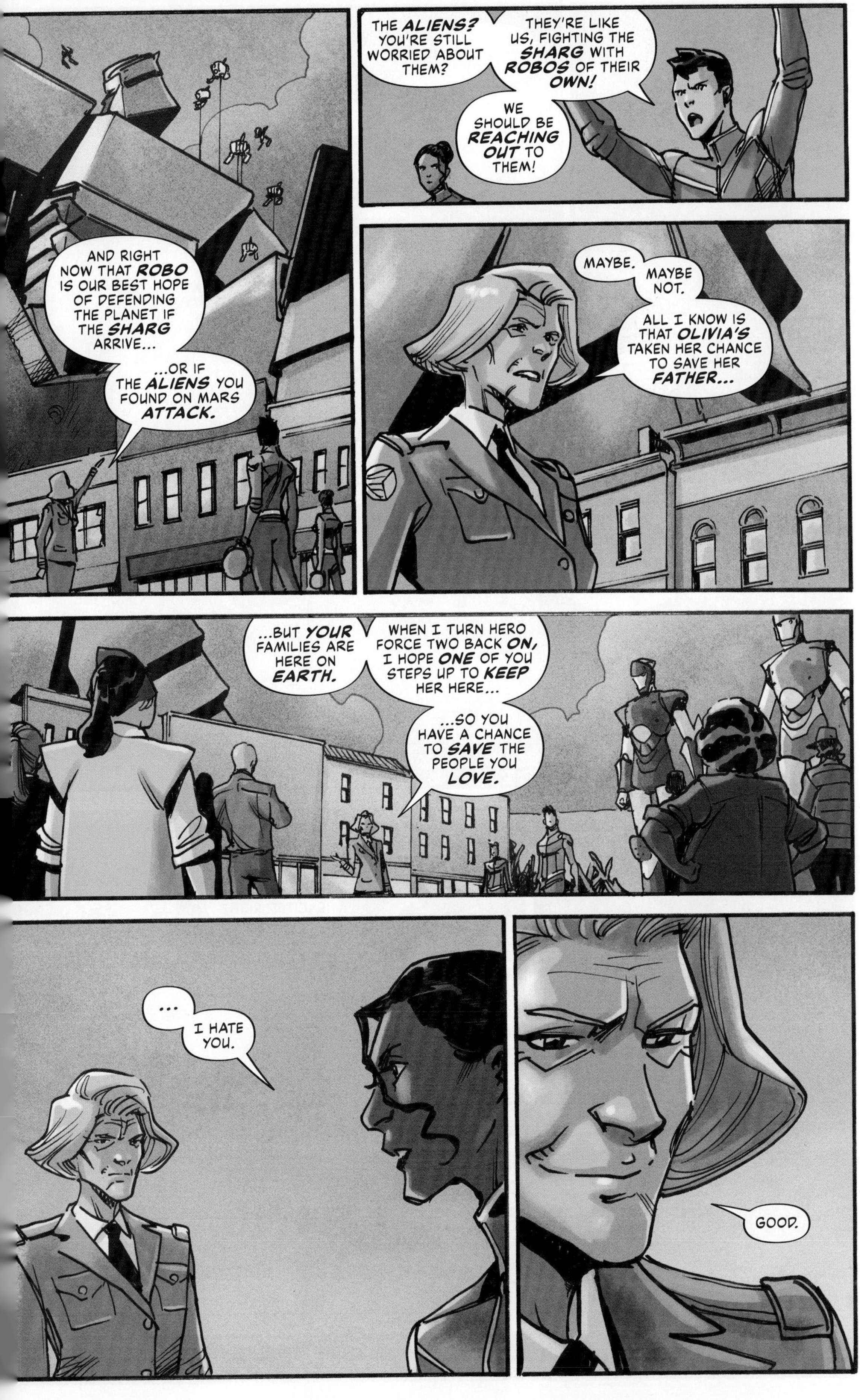
AND RIGHT NOW THAT ROBO IS OUR BEST HOPE OF DEFENDING THE PLANET IF THE SHARG ARRIVE...
...OR IF THE ALIENS YOU FOUND ON MARS ATTACK.
THE ALIENS? YOU'RE STILL WORRIED ABOUT THEM?
THEY'RE LIKE US, FIGHTING THE SHARG WITH ROBOS OF THEIR OWN!
WE SHOULD BE REACHING OUT TO THEM!
MAYBE.
MAYBE NOT.
ALL I KNOW IS THAT OLIVIA'S TAKEN HER CHANCE TO SAVE HER FATHER...
...BUT YOUR FAMILIES ARE HERE ON EARTH.
WHEN I TURN HERO FORCE TWO BACK ON, I HOPE ONE OF YOU STEPS UP TO KEEP HER HERE...
...SO YOU HAVE A CHANCE TO SAVE THE PEOPLE YOU LOVE.
...
I HATE YOU.
GOOD.

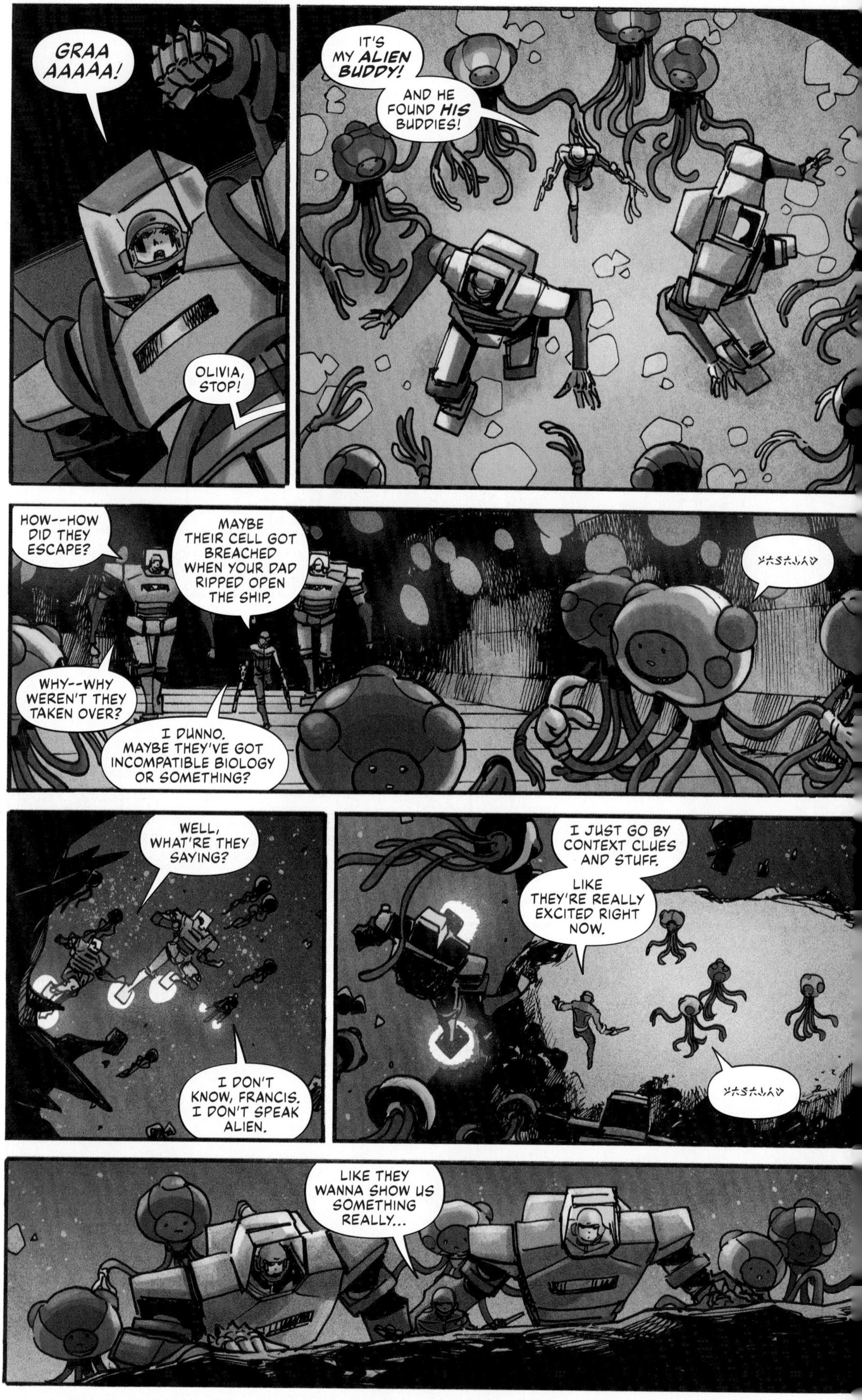
GRAA AAAAA!
OLIVIA, STOP!
IT'S MY **ALIEN BUDDY!**
AND HE FOUND **HIS** BUDDIES!
HOW--HOW DID THEY ESCAPE?
MAYBE THEIR CELL GOT BREACHED WHEN YOUR DAD RIPPED OPEN THE SHIP.
WHY--WHY WEREN'T THEY TAKEN OVER?
I DUNNO. MAYBE THEY'VE GOT INCOMPATIBLE BIOLOGY OR SOMETHING?
WELL, WHAT'RE THEY SAYING?
I DON'T KNOW, FRANCIS. I DON'T SPEAK ALIEN.
I JUST GO BY CONTEXT CLUES AND STUFF.
LIKE THEY'RE REALLY EXCITED RIGHT NOW.
LIKE THEY WANNA SHOW US SOMETHING REALLY...

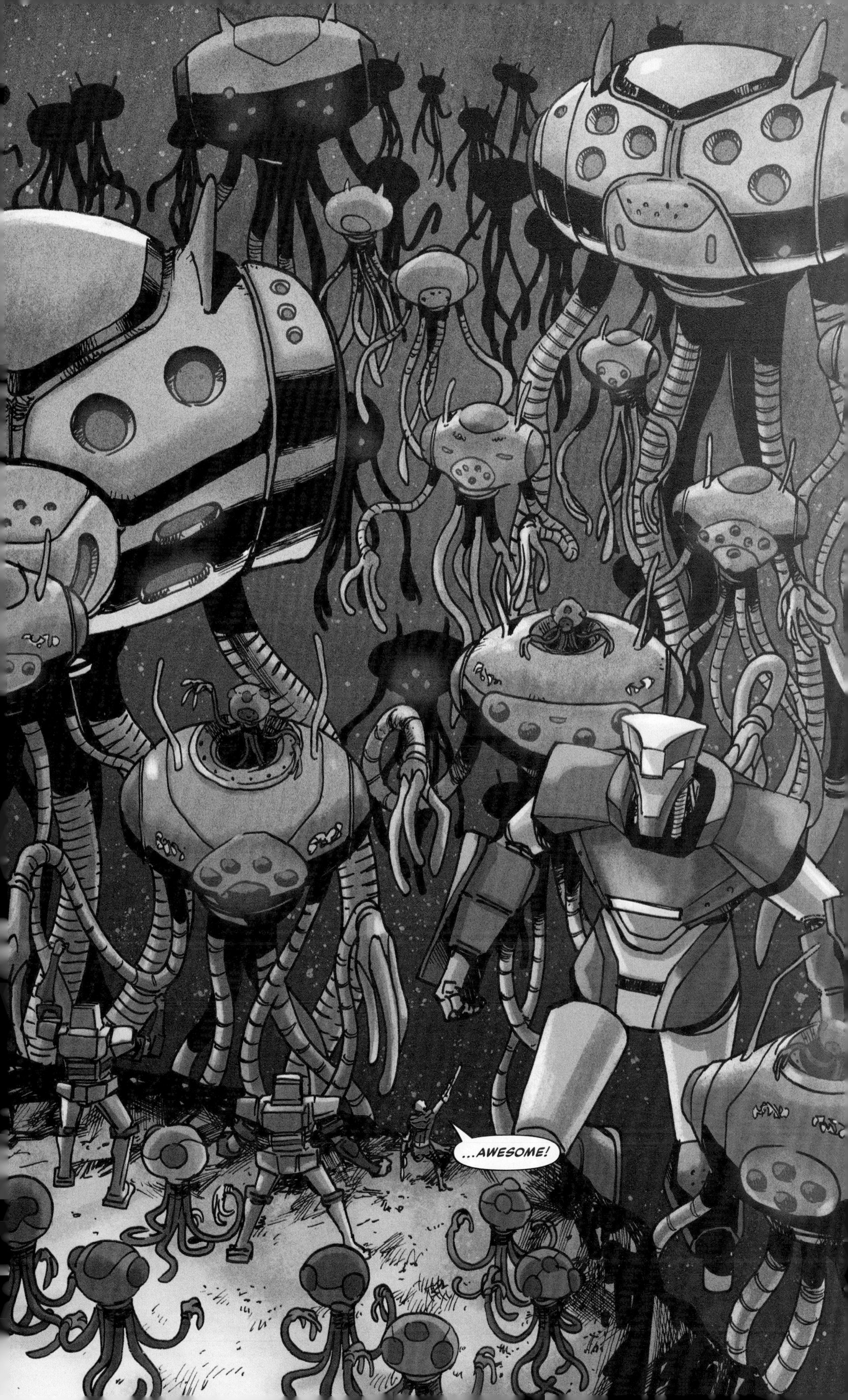
...AWESOME!

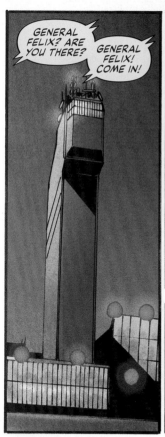

GENERAL FELIX? ARE YOU THERE? GENERAL FELIX! COME IN!

THIS IS FELIX.

OH, THANK GOD!

THIS IS MECH CADET PARK! I'M ON THE FAR SIDE OF MARS WITH BOTH OLIVETTIS...

...AND SOME NEW FRIENDS.

IT'S THE ALIENS, GENERAL FELIX.

THEY'VE GOT AN ARMY. A HUGE ARMY. AND THEY'RE READY TO TAKE ON THE SHARG.

IF WE JOIN THEM NOW, WE COULD--
click

GENERAL FELIX? GENERAL FELIX?

I'M SORRY, OLIVIA.

BUT I'M DONE LOSING SOLDIERS.

WE'RE GOING TO LET THE ALIENS AND THE SHARG...

...TAKE CARE OF EACH OTHER.

CHAPTER SIX

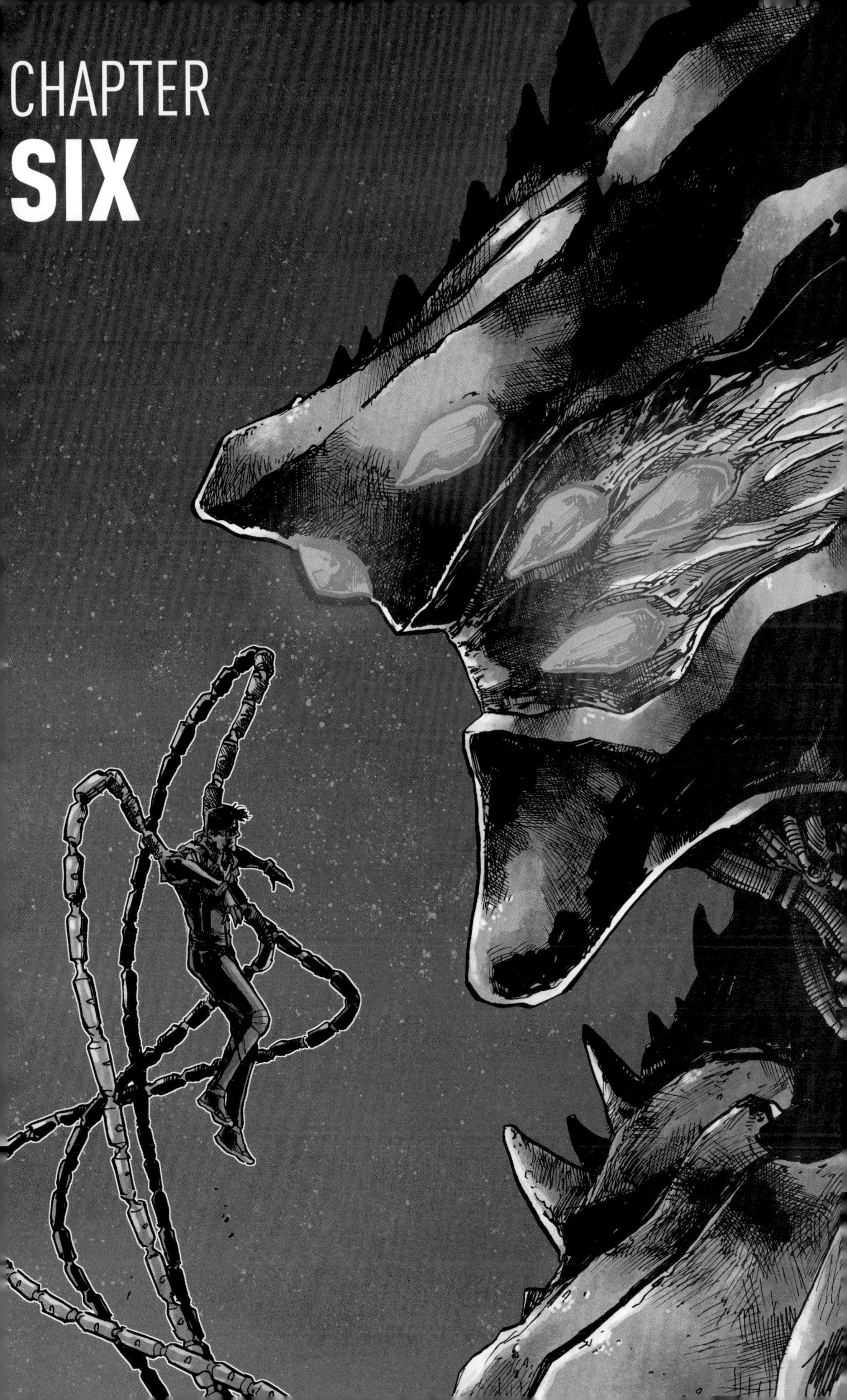

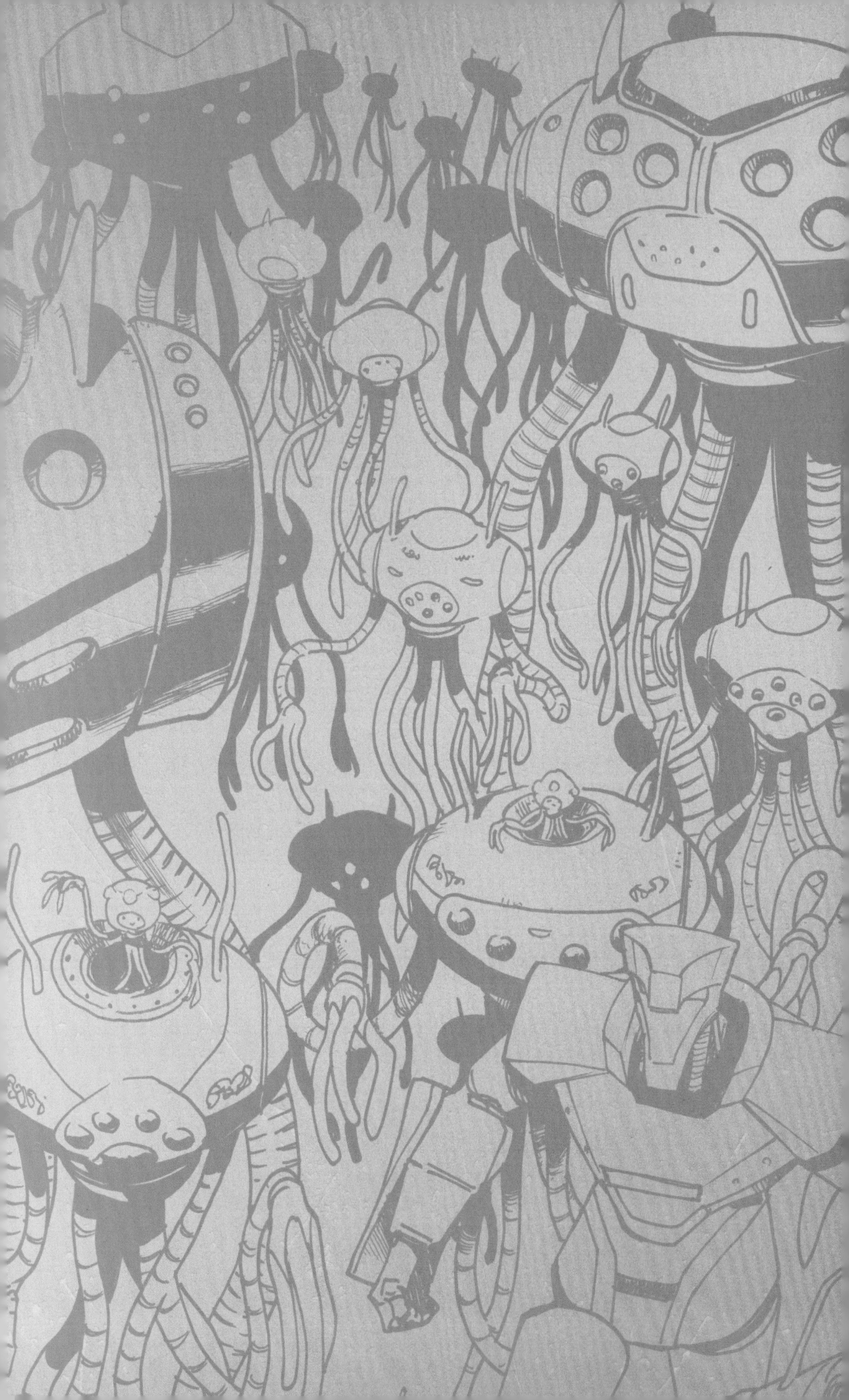

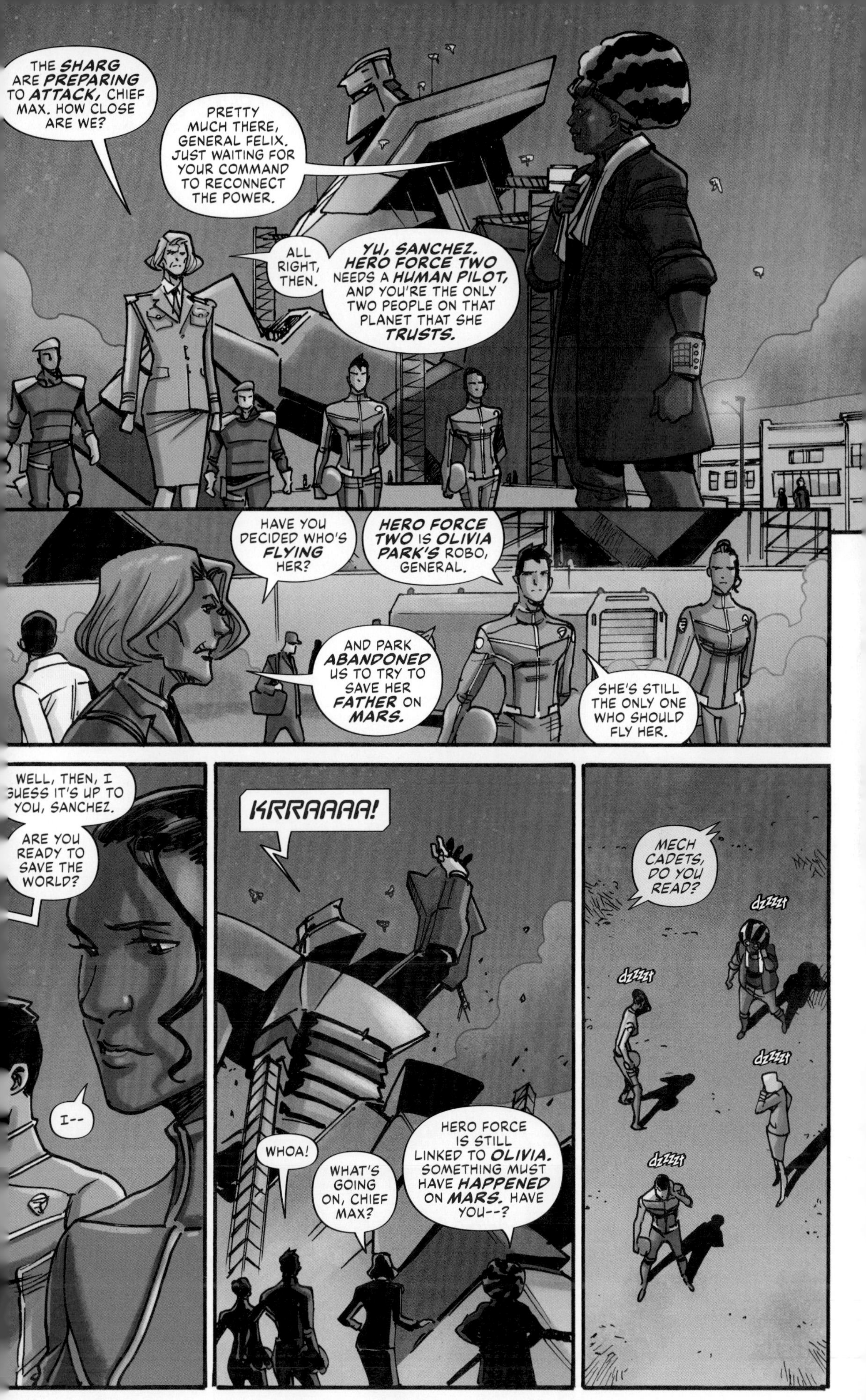
THE SHARG ARE PREPARING TO ATTACK, CHIEF MAX. HOW CLOSE ARE WE?
PRETTY MUCH THERE, GENERAL FELIX. JUST WAITING FOR YOUR COMMAND TO RECONNECT THE POWER.
ALL RIGHT, THEN.
YU, SANCHEZ. HERO FORCE TWO NEEDS A HUMAN PILOT, AND YOU'RE THE ONLY TWO PEOPLE ON THAT PLANET THAT SHE TRUSTS.
HAVE YOU DECIDED WHO'S FLYING HER?
HERO FORCE TWO IS OLIVIA PARK'S ROBO, GENERAL.
AND PARK ABANDONED US TO TRY TO SAVE HER FATHER ON MARS.
SHE'S STILL THE ONLY ONE WHO SHOULD FLY HER.
WELL, THEN, I GUESS IT'S UP TO YOU, SANCHEZ.
ARE YOU READY TO SAVE THE WORLD?
I--
KRRAAAA!
WHOA!
WHAT'S GOING ON, CHIEF MAX?
HERO FORCE IS STILL LINKED TO OLIVIA. SOMETHING MUST HAVE HAPPENED ON MARS. HAVE YOU--?
MECH CADETS, DO YOU READ?
dzzzzt
dzzzzt
dzzzzt
dzzzzt

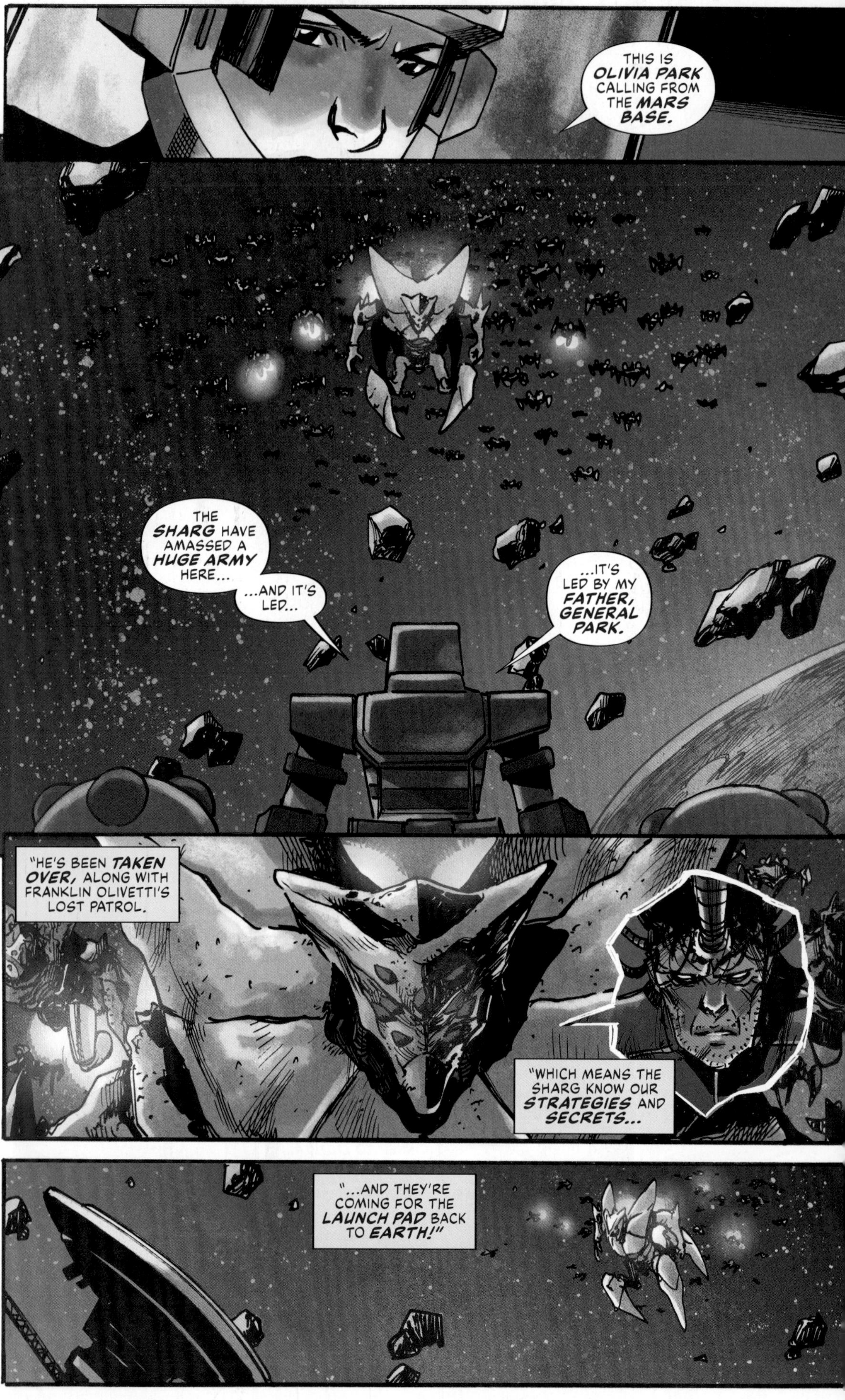
THIS IS OLIVIA PARK CALLING FROM THE MARS BASE.
THE SHARG HAVE AMASSED A HUGE ARMY HERE...
...AND IT'S LED...
...IT'S LED BY MY FATHER, GENERAL PARK.
"HE'S BEEN TAKEN OVER, ALONG WITH FRANKLIN OLIVETTI'S LOST PATROL.
"WHICH MEANS THE SHARG KNOW OUR STRATEGIES AND SECRETS...
"...AND THEY'RE COMING FOR THE LAUNCH PAD BACK TO EARTH!"

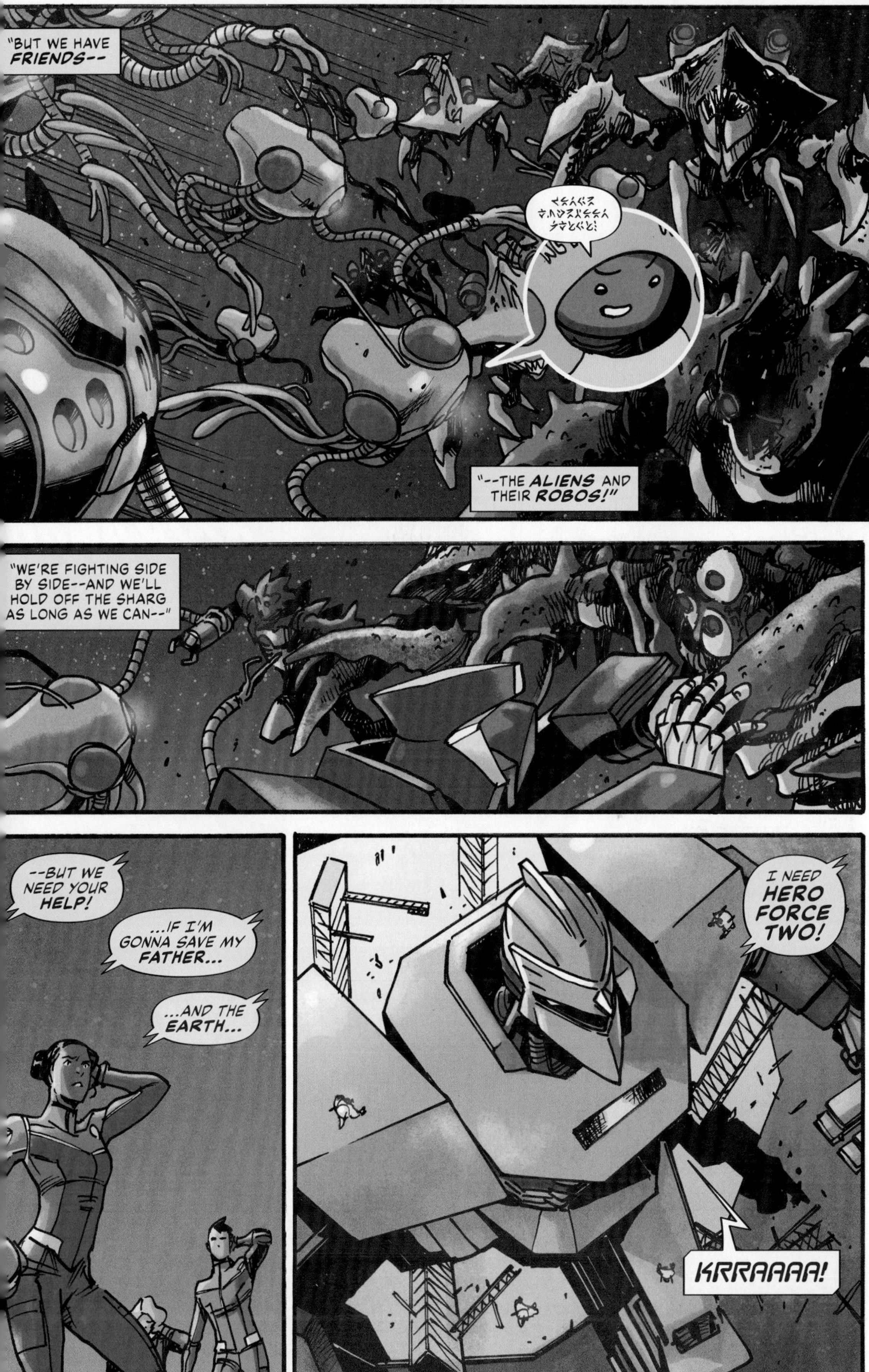
"BUT WE HAVE FRIENDS--
"--THE ALIENS AND THEIR ROBOS!"
"WE'RE FIGHTING SIDE BY SIDE--AND WE'LL HOLD OFF THE SHARG AS LONG AS WE CAN--"
--BUT WE NEED YOUR HELP!
...IF I'M GONNA SAVE MY FATHER...
...AND THE EARTH...
I NEED HERO FORCE TWO!
KRRAAAA!

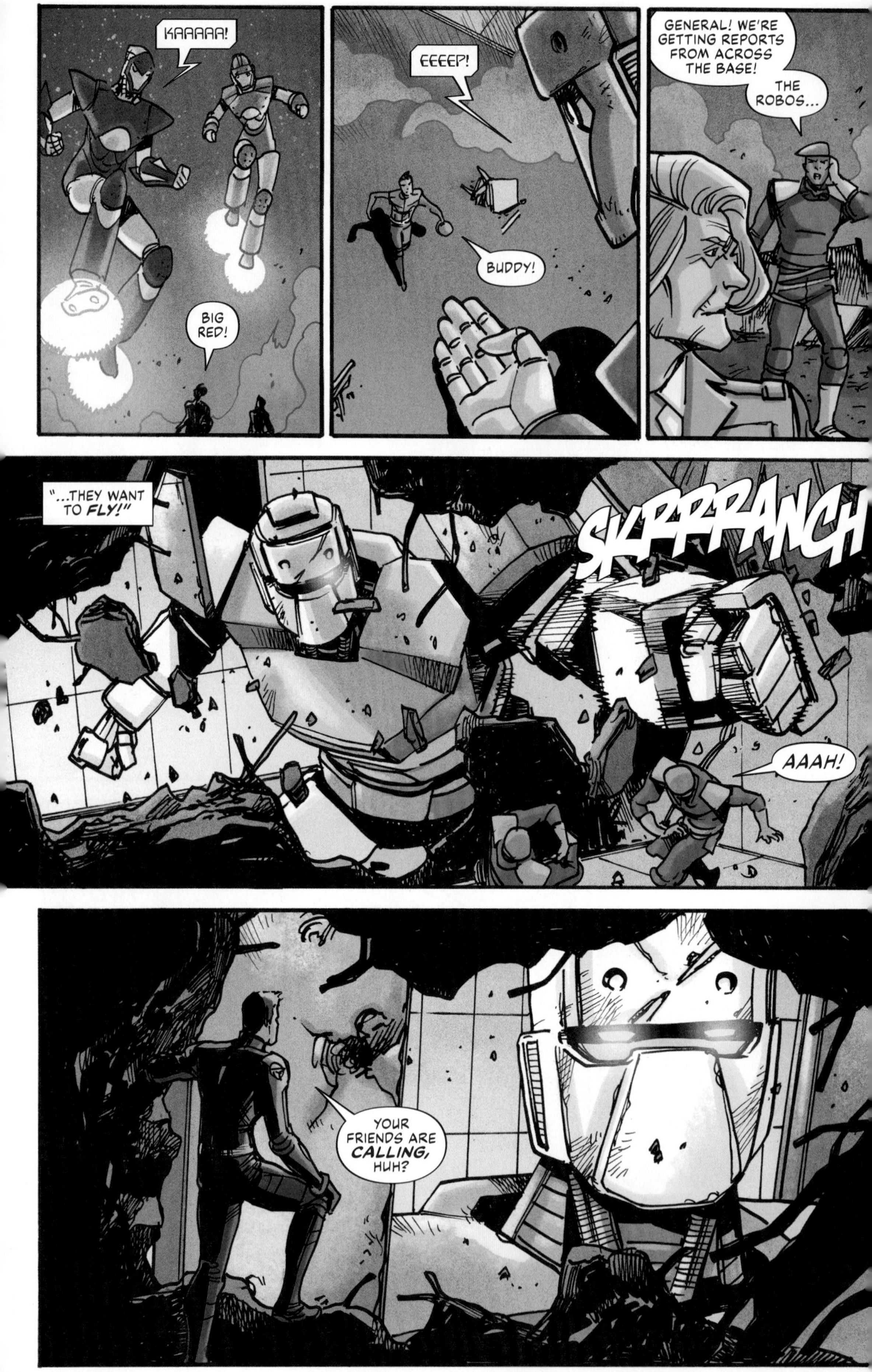
KAAAAAA!
BIG RED!
EEEEP!
BUDDY!
GENERAL! WE'RE GETTING REPORTS FROM ACROSS THE BASE!
THE ROBOS...
"...THEY WANT TO FLY!"
SKRRRANCH
AAAH!
YOUR FRIENDS ARE CALLING, HUH?

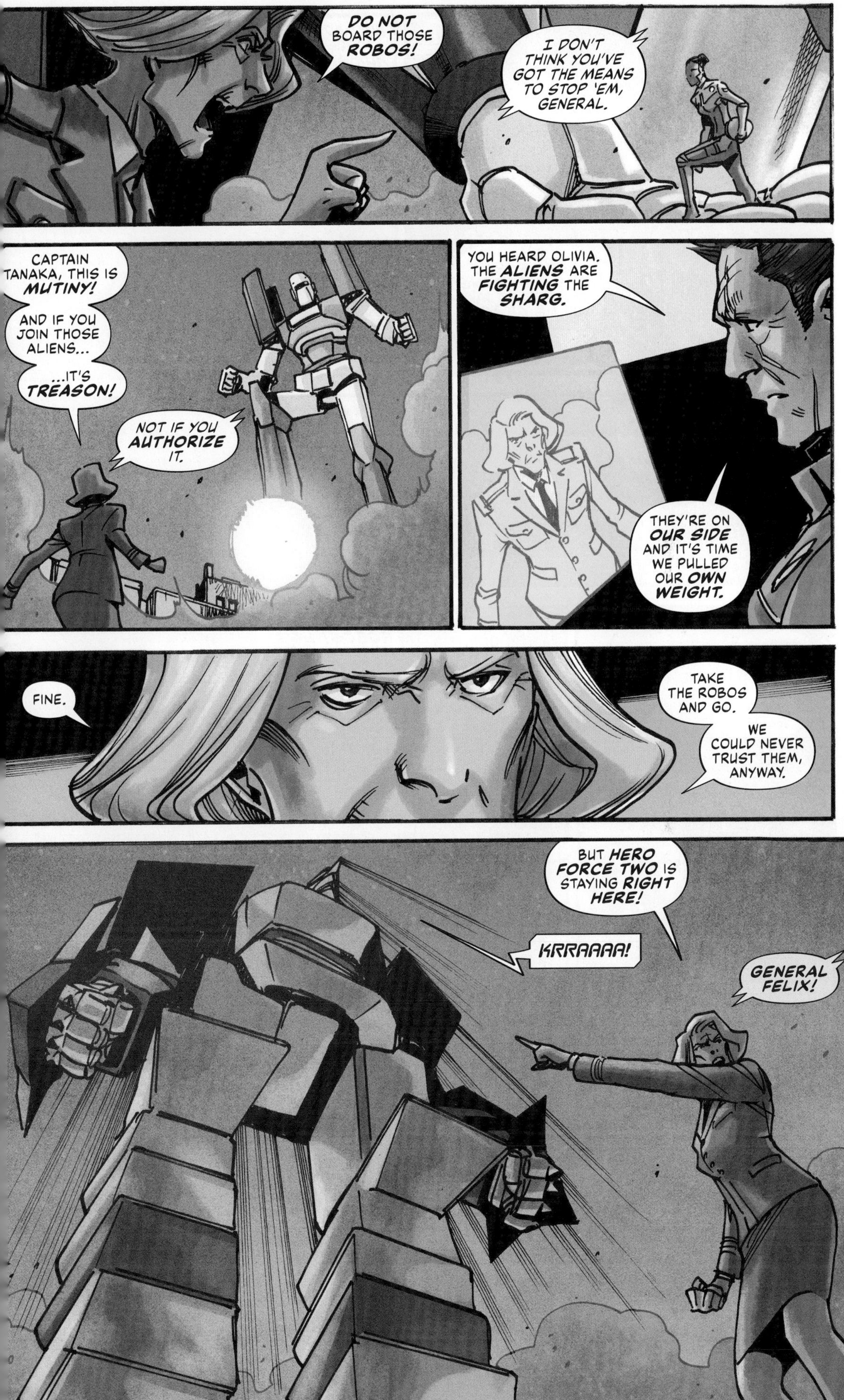
DO NOT BOARD THOSE ROBOS!
I DON'T THINK YOU'VE GOT THE MEANS TO STOP 'EM, GENERAL.
CAPTAIN TANAKA, THIS IS MUTINY!
AND IF YOU JOIN THOSE ALIENS...
...IT'S TREASON!
NOT IF YOU AUTHORIZE IT.
YOU HEARD OLIVIA. THE ALIENS ARE FIGHTING THE SHARG.
THEY'RE ON OUR SIDE AND IT'S TIME WE PULLED OUR OWN WEIGHT.
FINE.
TAKE THE ROBOS AND GO.
WE COULD NEVER TRUST THEM, ANYWAY.
BUT HERO FORCE TWO IS STAYING RIGHT HERE!
KRRAAAAA!
GENERAL FELIX!

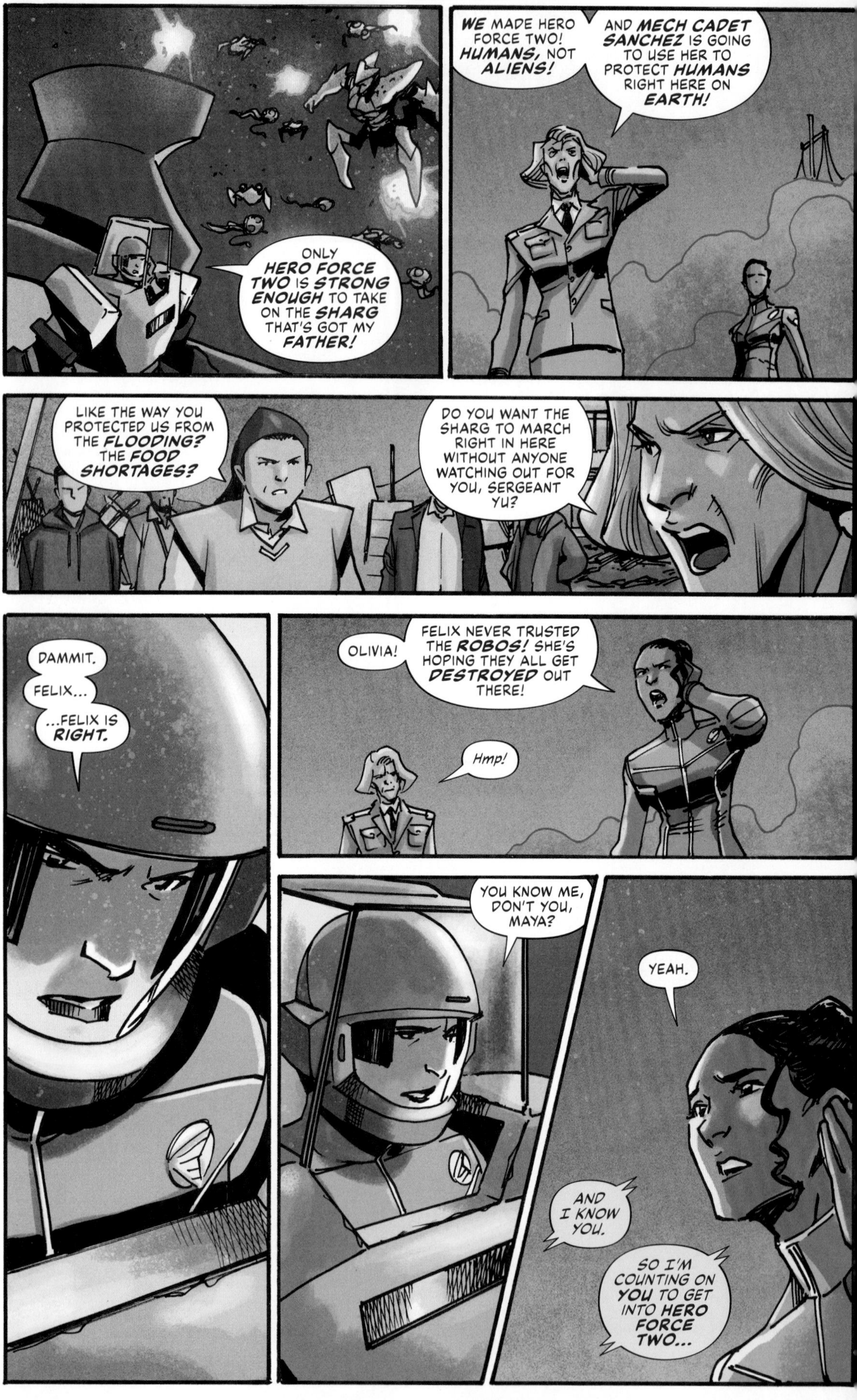
ONLY HERO FORCE TWO IS STRONG ENOUGH TO TAKE ON THE SHARG THAT'S GOT MY FATHER!
WE MADE HERO FORCE TWO! HUMANS, NOT ALIENS!
AND MECH CADET SANCHEZ IS GOING TO USE HER TO PROTECT HUMANS RIGHT HERE ON EARTH!
LIKE THE WAY YOU PROTECTED US FROM THE FLOODING? THE FOOD SHORTAGES?
DO YOU WANT THE SHARG TO MARCH RIGHT IN HERE WITHOUT ANYONE WATCHING OUT FOR YOU, SERGEANT YU?
DAMMIT.
FELIX...
...FELIX IS RIGHT.
OLIVIA!
FELIX NEVER TRUSTED THE ROBOS! SHE'S HOPING THEY ALL GET DESTROYED OUT THERE!
Hmp!
YOU KNOW ME, DON'T YOU, MAYA?
YEAH.
AND I KNOW YOU.
SO I'M COUNTING ON YOU TO GET INTO HERO FORCE TWO...

...AND DO THE RIGHT THING.

KRRAAAA...

DANGIT...

YOU'RE ABOUT TO BECOME THE MOST POWERFUL PERSON ON THE PLANET, SANCHEZ. ARE YOU PREPARED FOR THAT RESPONSIBILITY?

YES, GENERAL.

I'VE TRAINED ALL MY LIFE FOR THIS.

KRRR...

IT'S ALL RIGHT, BIG RED.

RELINK THE POWER LINES?

DO IT.

FIRE 'EM UP!

YOU GOT IT!

FWOOOSH

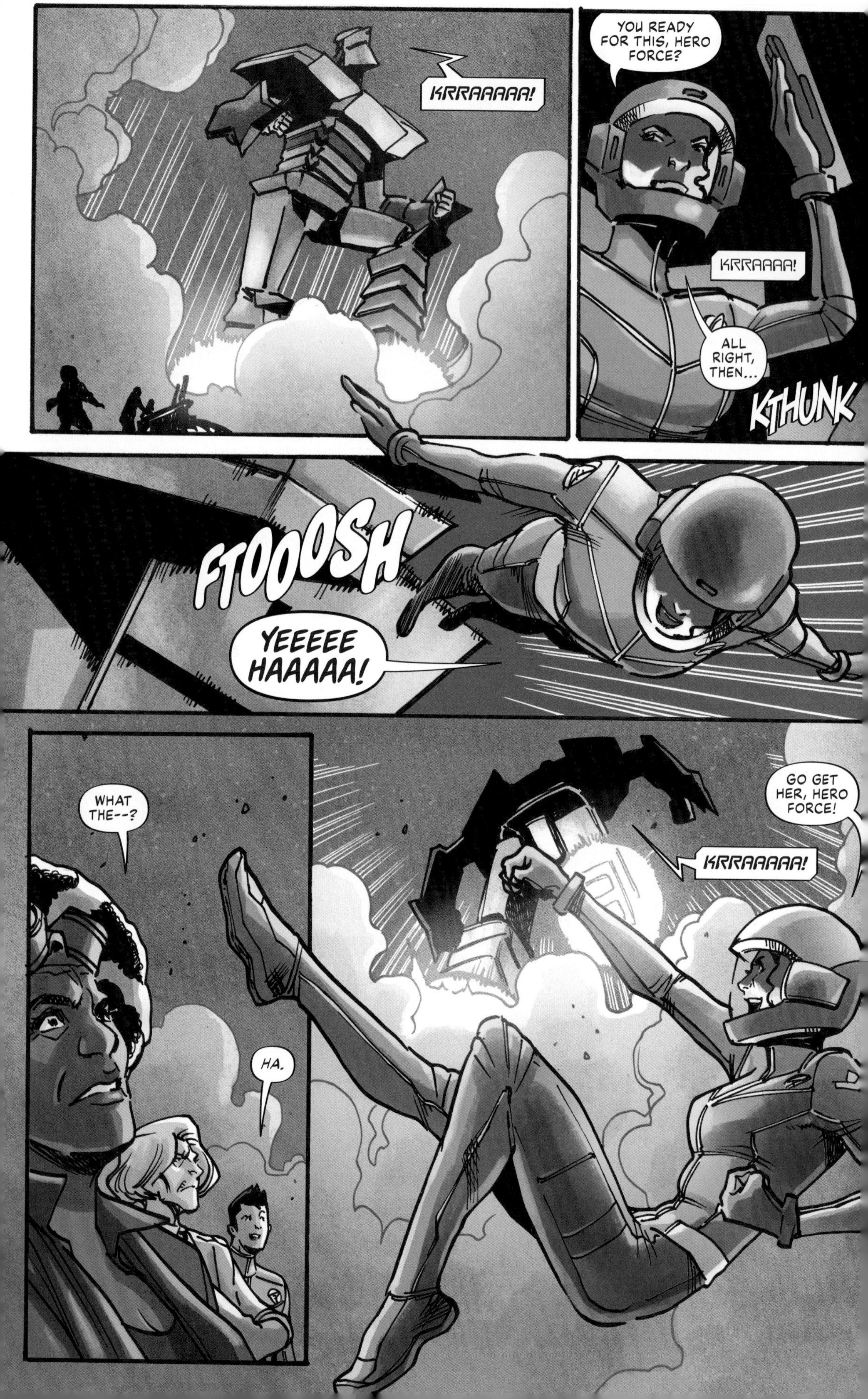
KRRAAAAAA!
YOU READY FOR THIS, HERO FORCE?
KRRAAAAA!
ALL RIGHT, THEN...
KTHUNK
FTOOOSH
YEEEEE HAAAAA!
WHAT THE--?
HA.
GO GET HER, HERO FORCE!
KRRAAAAAA!

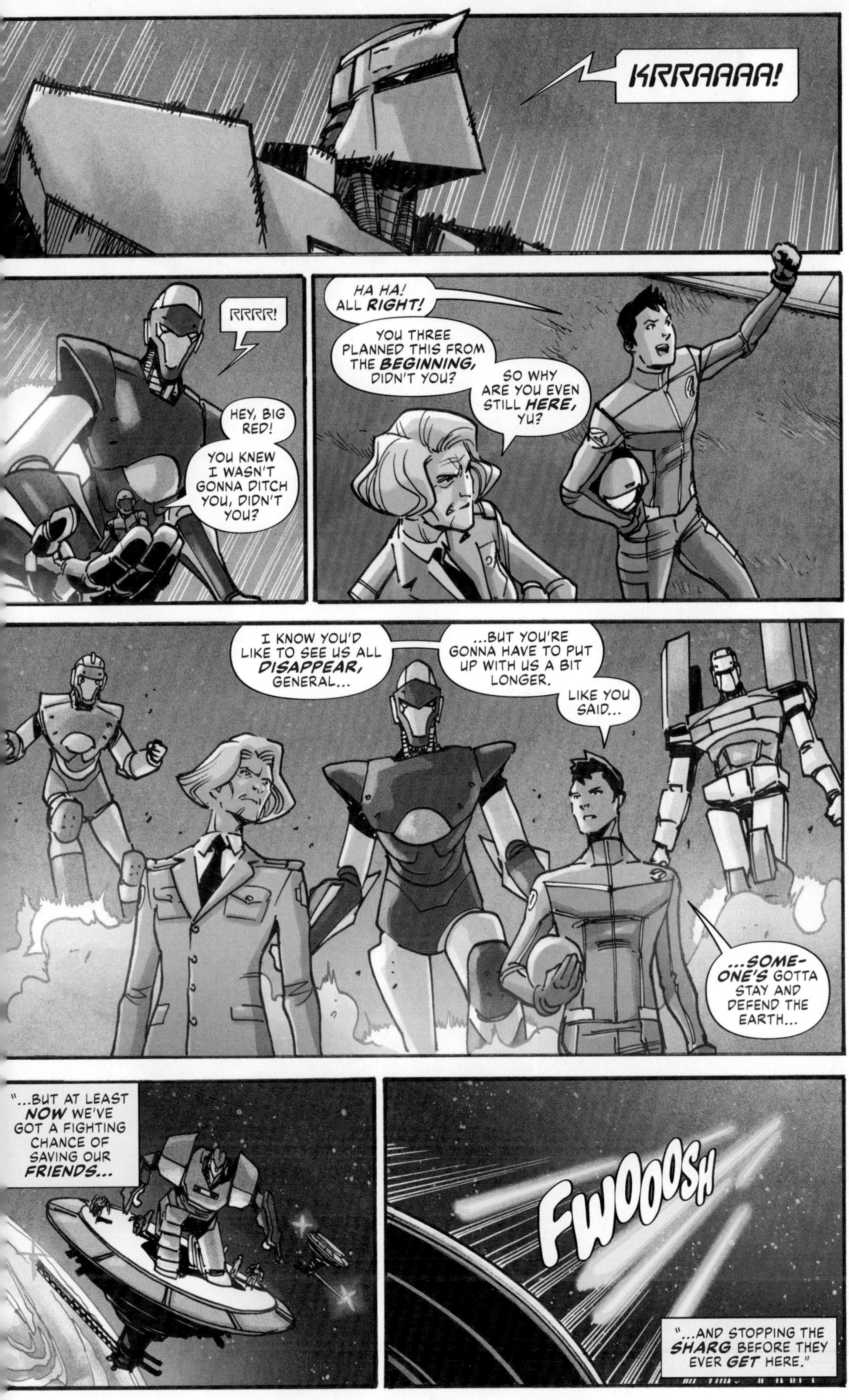
KRRAAAA!
RRRR!
HEY, BIG RED!
YOU KNEW I WASN'T GONNA DITCH YOU, DIDN'T YOU?
HA HA! ALL **RIGHT!**
YOU THREE PLANNED THIS FROM THE **BEGINNING,** DIDN'T YOU?
SO WHY ARE YOU EVEN STILL **HERE,** YU?
I KNOW YOU'D LIKE TO SEE US ALL **DISAPPEAR,** GENERAL...
...BUT YOU'RE GONNA HAVE TO PUT UP WITH US A BIT LONGER.
LIKE YOU SAID...
...SOME-ONE'S GOTTA STAY AND DEFEND THE EARTH...
"...BUT AT LEAST **NOW** WE'VE GOT A FIGHTING CHANCE OF SAVING OUR **FRIENDS...**
FWOOOSH
"...AND STOPPING THE **SHARG** BEFORE THEY EVER **GET** HERE."

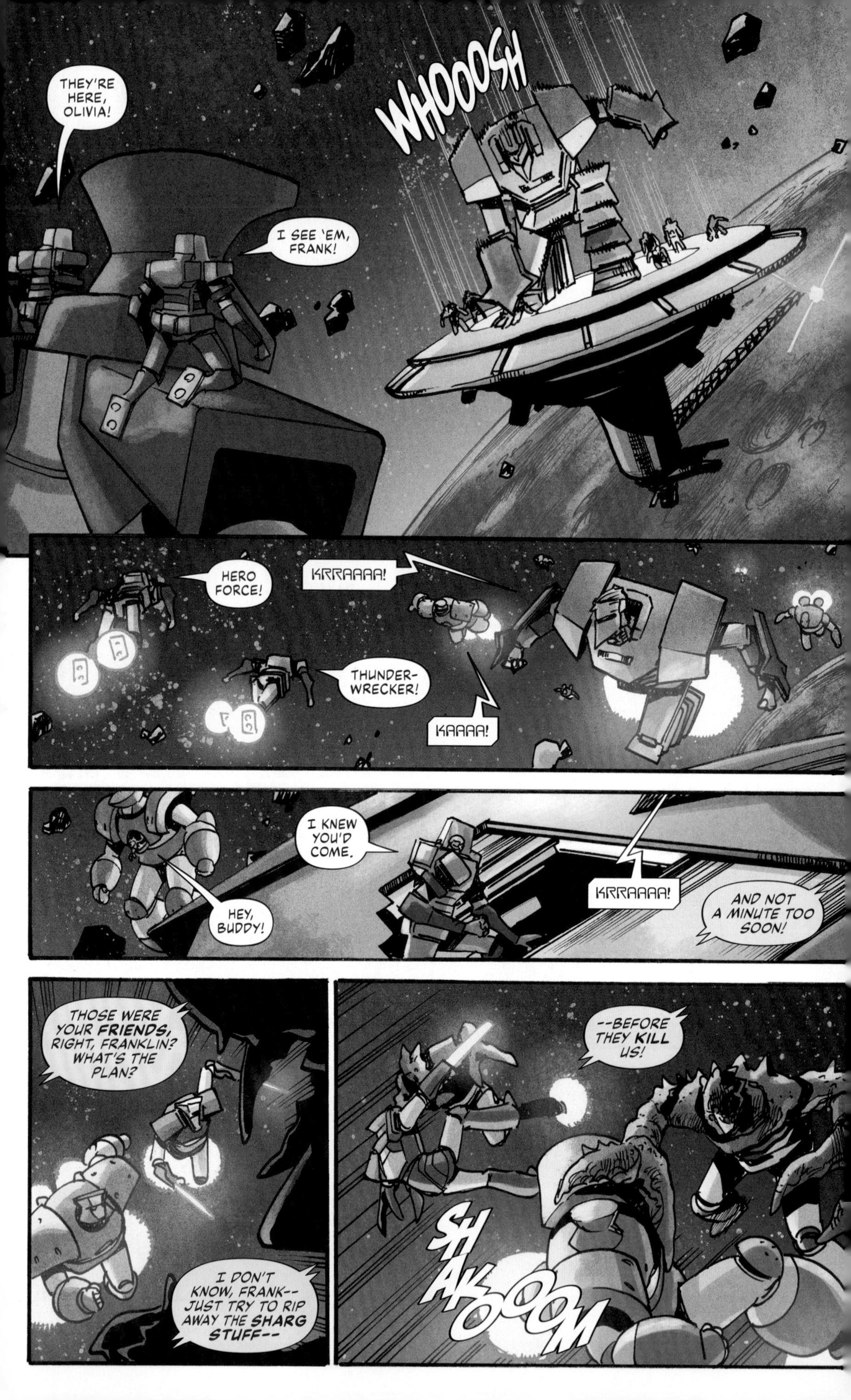
THEY'RE HERE, OLIVIA!
WHOOOSH
I SEE 'EM, FRANK!
HERO FORCE!
KRRAAAA!
THUNDER-WRECKER!
KAAAA!
I KNEW YOU'D COME.
HEY, BUDDY!
KRRAAAA!
AND NOT A MINUTE TOO SOON!
THOSE WERE YOUR **FRIENDS,** RIGHT, FRANKLIN? WHAT'S THE PLAN?
I DON'T KNOW, FRANK-- JUST TRY TO RIP AWAY THE **SHARG STUFF--**
--BEFORE THEY **KILL** US!
SHAKOOOM

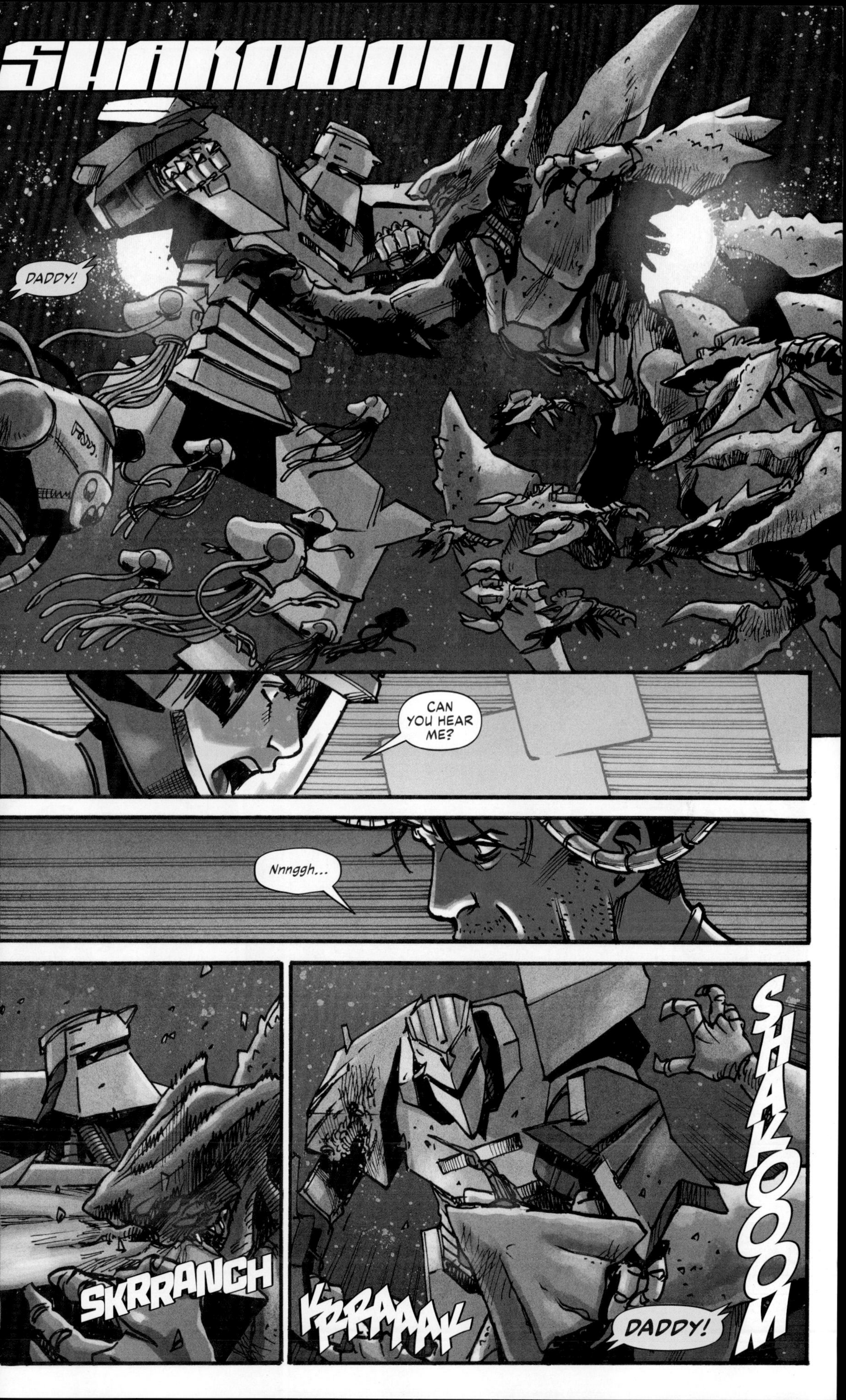
SHAKOOOM
DADDY!
CAN YOU HEAR ME?
Nnngghh...
SKRRANCH
KRRAAAAK
DADDY!
SHAKOOOOOM

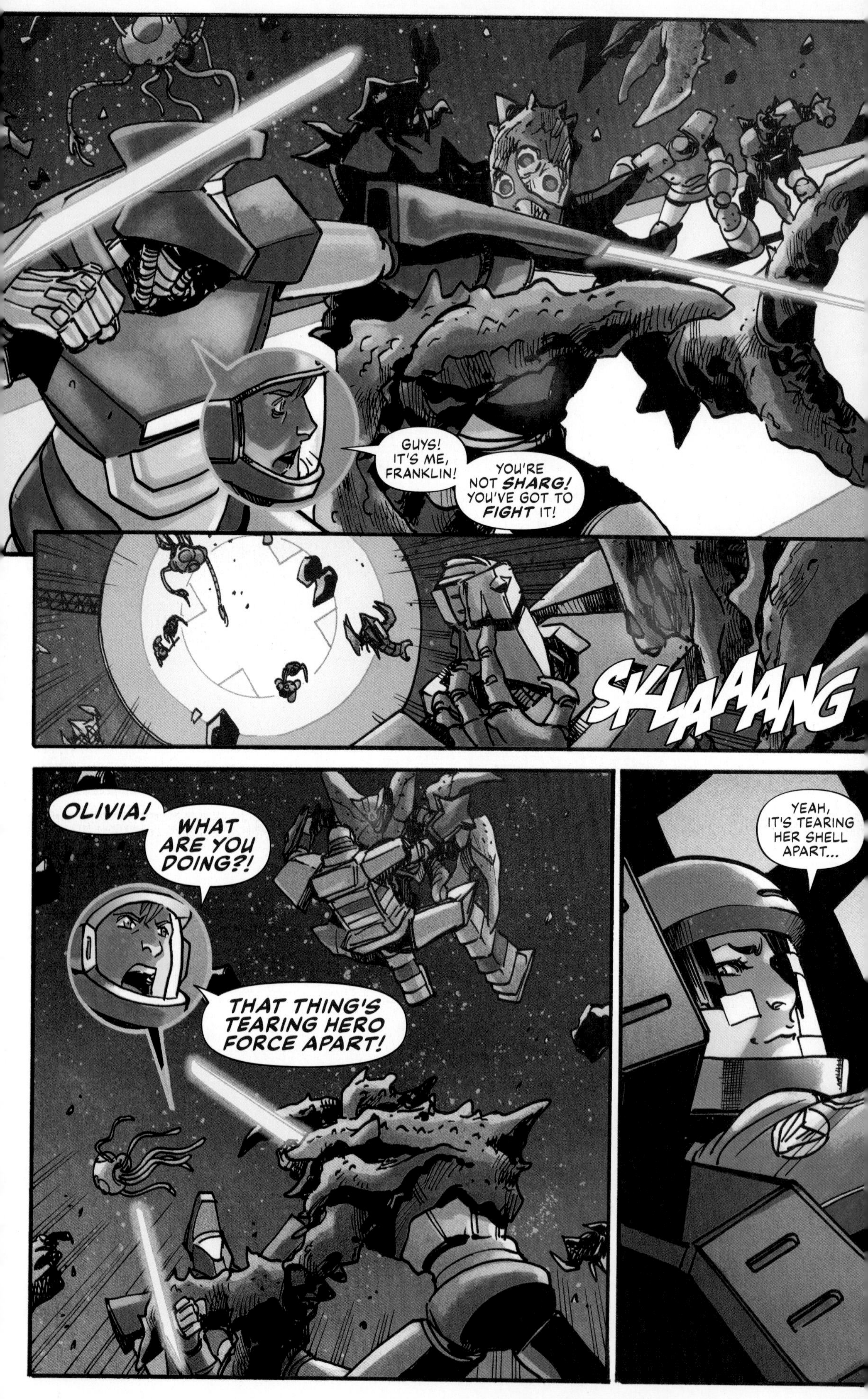
GUYS! IT'S ME, FRANKLIN!
YOU'RE NOT SHARG! YOU'VE GOT TO FIGHT IT!
SKLAAANG
OLIVIA!
WHAT ARE YOU DOING?!
THAT THING'S TEARING HERO FORCE APART!
YEAH, IT'S TEARING HER SHELL APART...

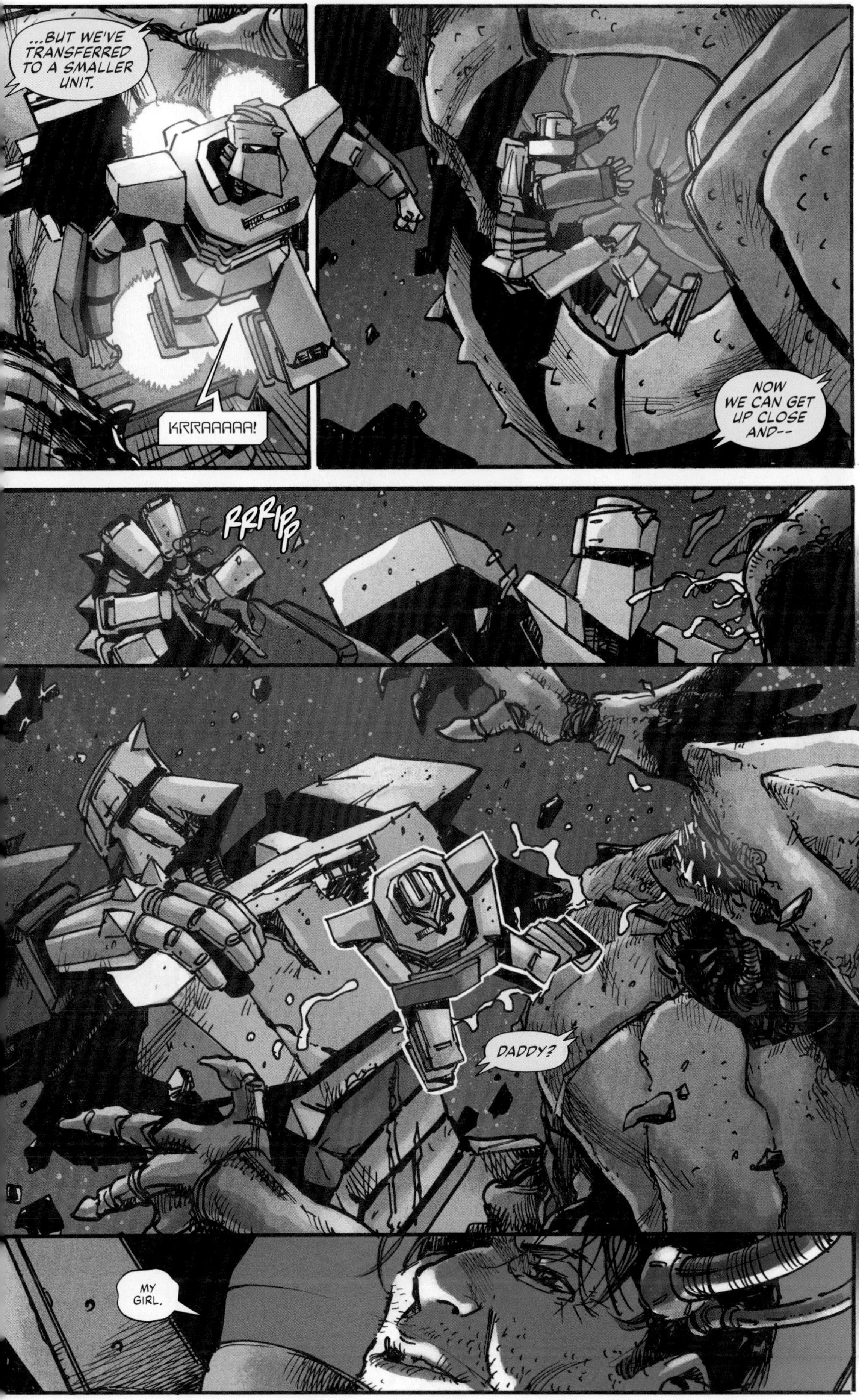
...BUT WE'VE TRANSFERRED TO A SMALLER UNIT.
KRRAAAAA!
NOW WE CAN GET UP CLOSE AND--
RRRIPP
DADDY?
MY GIRL.

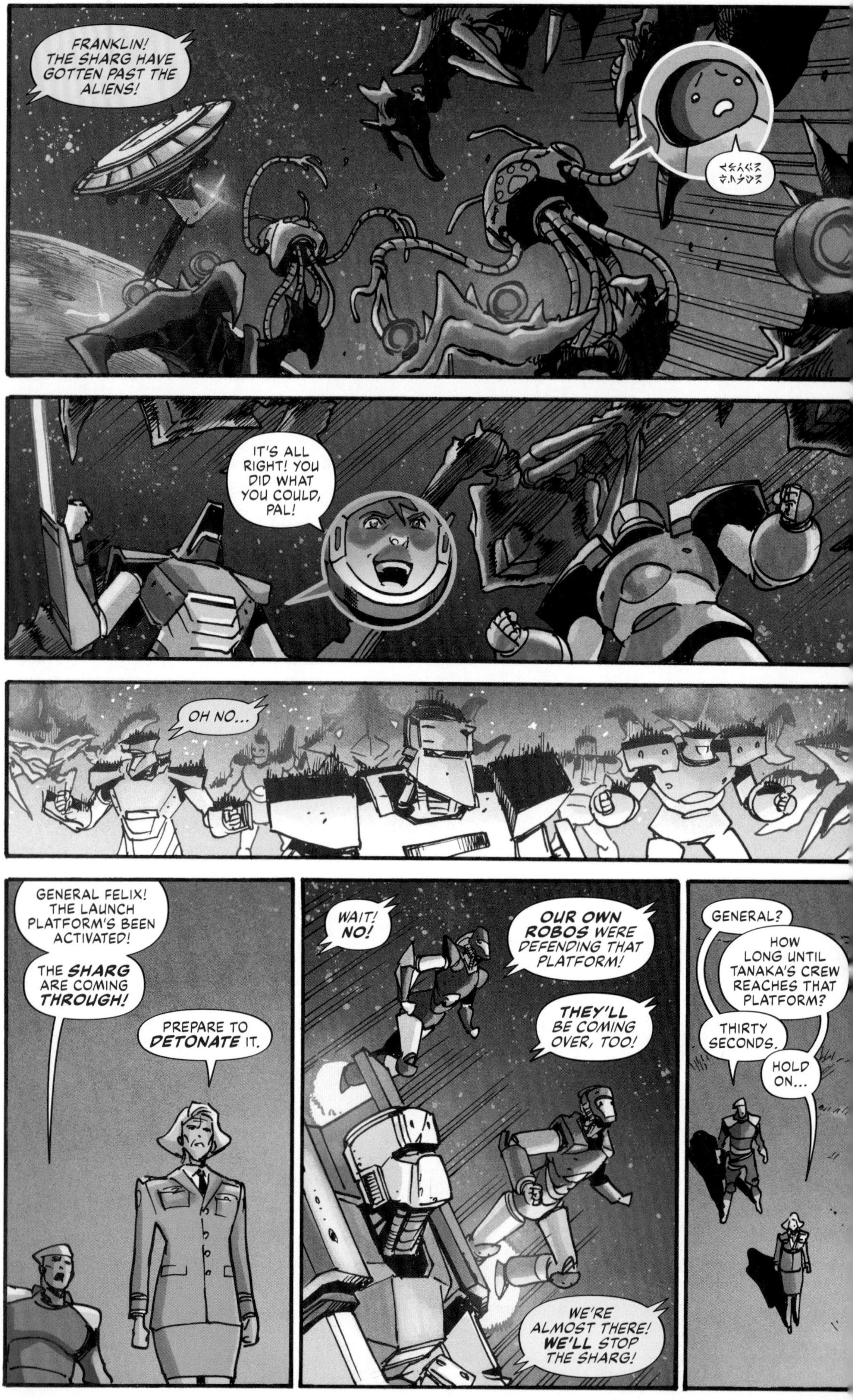

FRANKLIN! THE SHARG HAVE GOTTEN PAST THE ALIENS!
IT'S ALL RIGHT! YOU DID WHAT YOU COULD, PAL!
OH NO...
GENERAL FELIX! THE LAUNCH PLATFORM'S BEEN ACTIVATED!
THE **SHARG** ARE COMING **THROUGH!**
PREPARE TO **DETONATE** IT.
WAIT! **NO!**
OUR OWN ROBOS WERE DEFENDING THAT PLATFORM!
THEY'LL BE COMING OVER, TOO!
WE'RE ALMOST THERE! **WE'LL** STOP THE SHARG!
GENERAL?
HOW LONG UNTIL TANAKA'S CREW REACHES THAT PLATFORM?
THIRTY SECONDS.
HOLD ON...

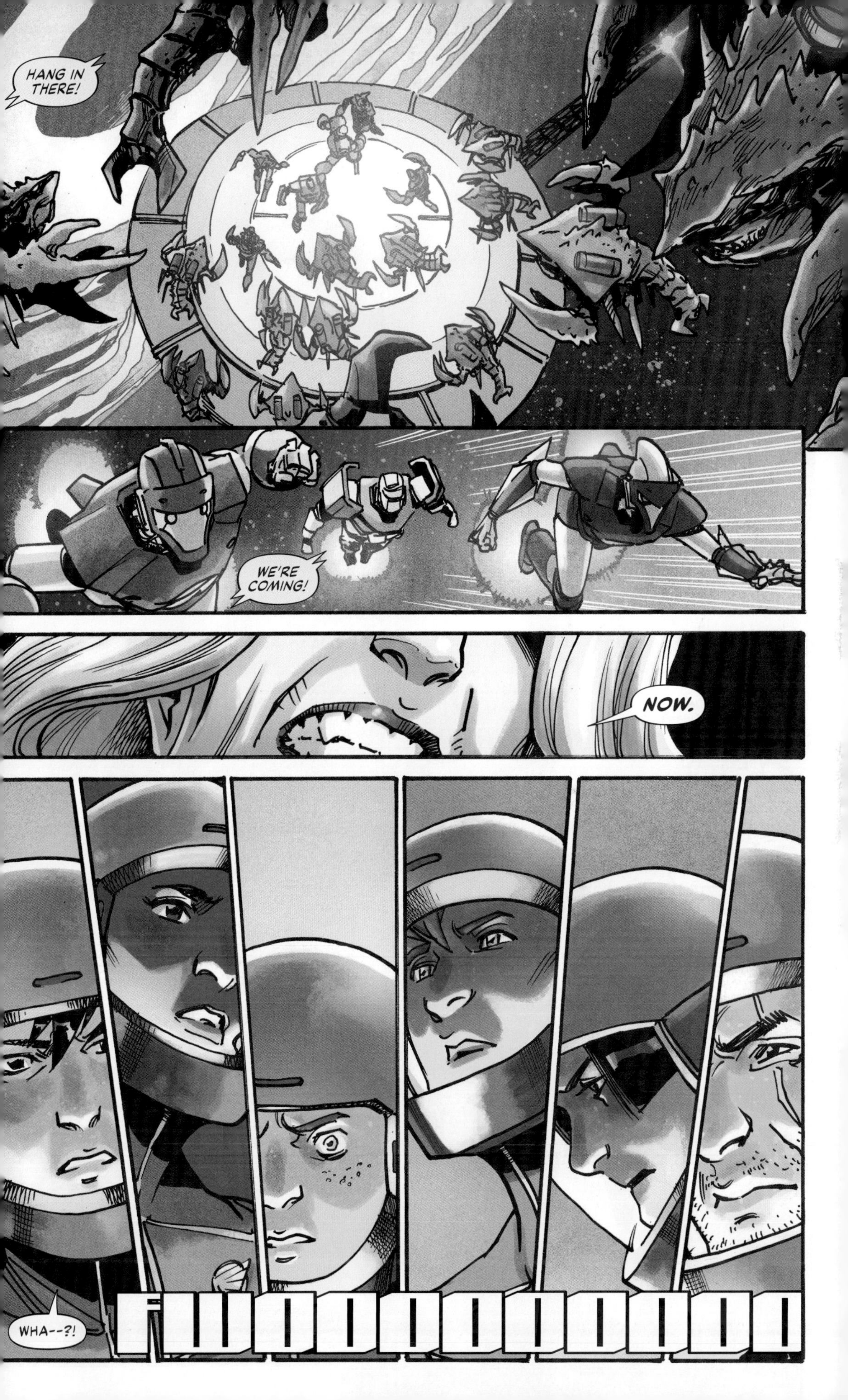
HANG IN THERE!
WE'RE COMING!
NOW.
WHA--?!
FWOOOOOOOOOOOO

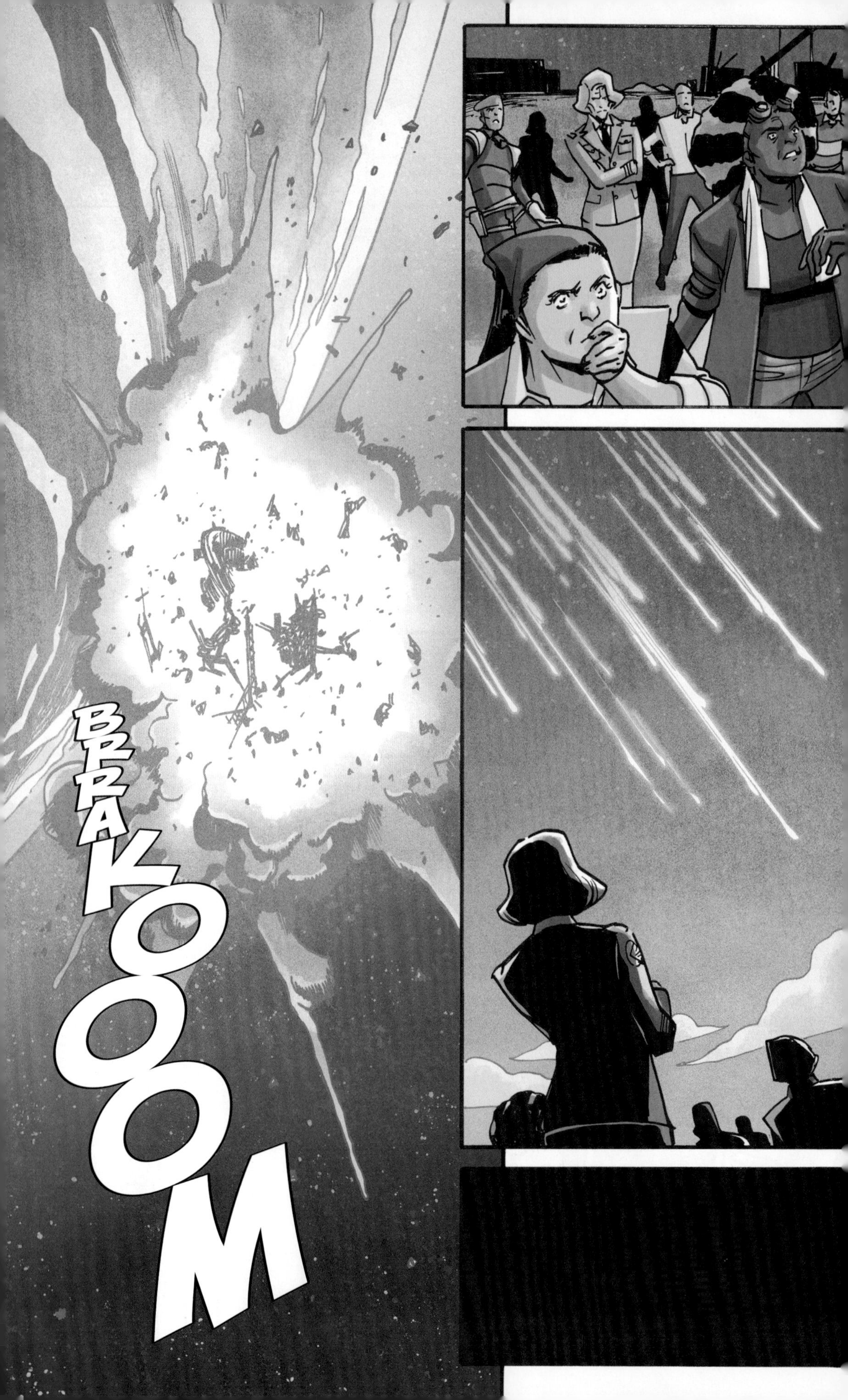
BRRAKOOOM

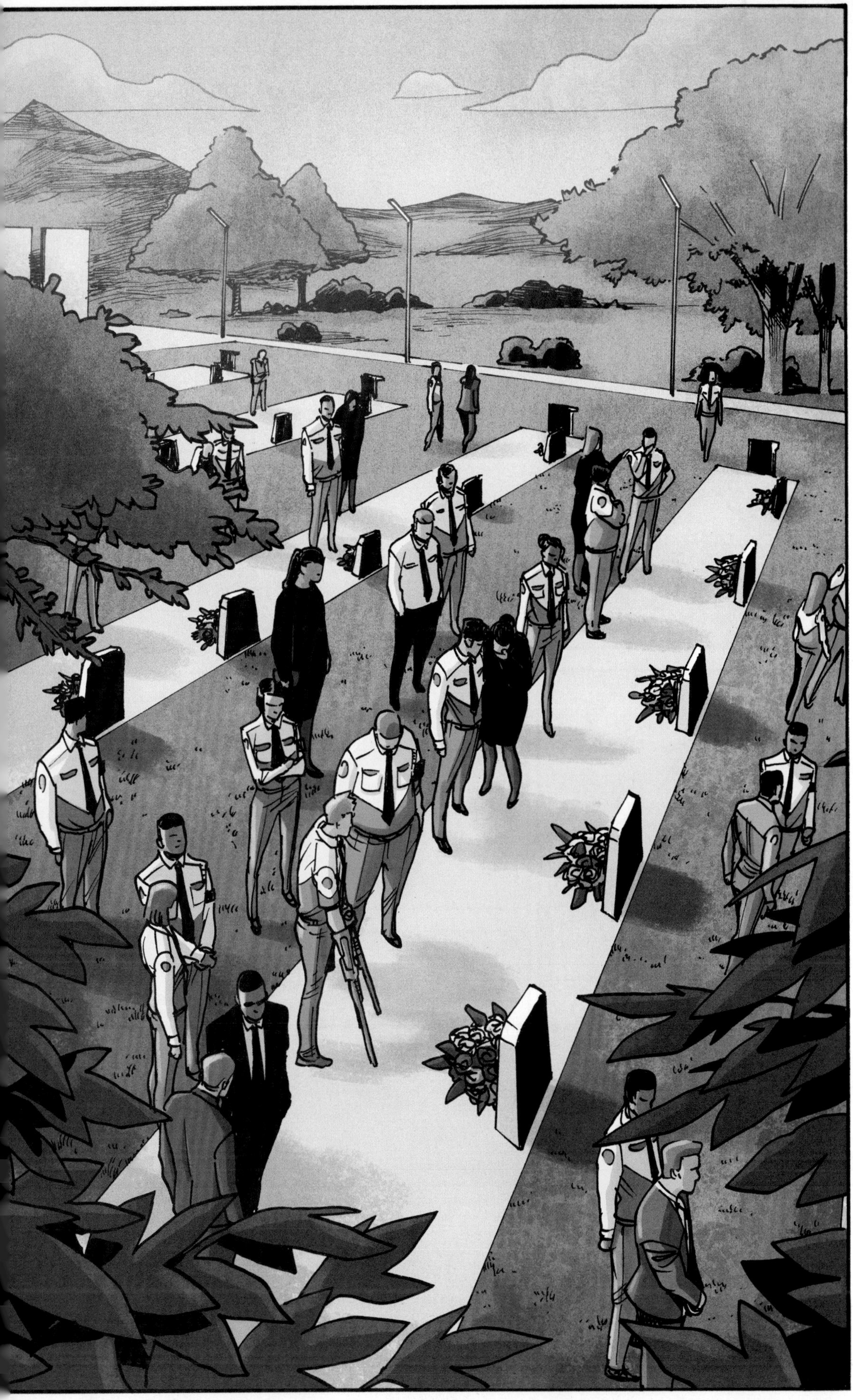

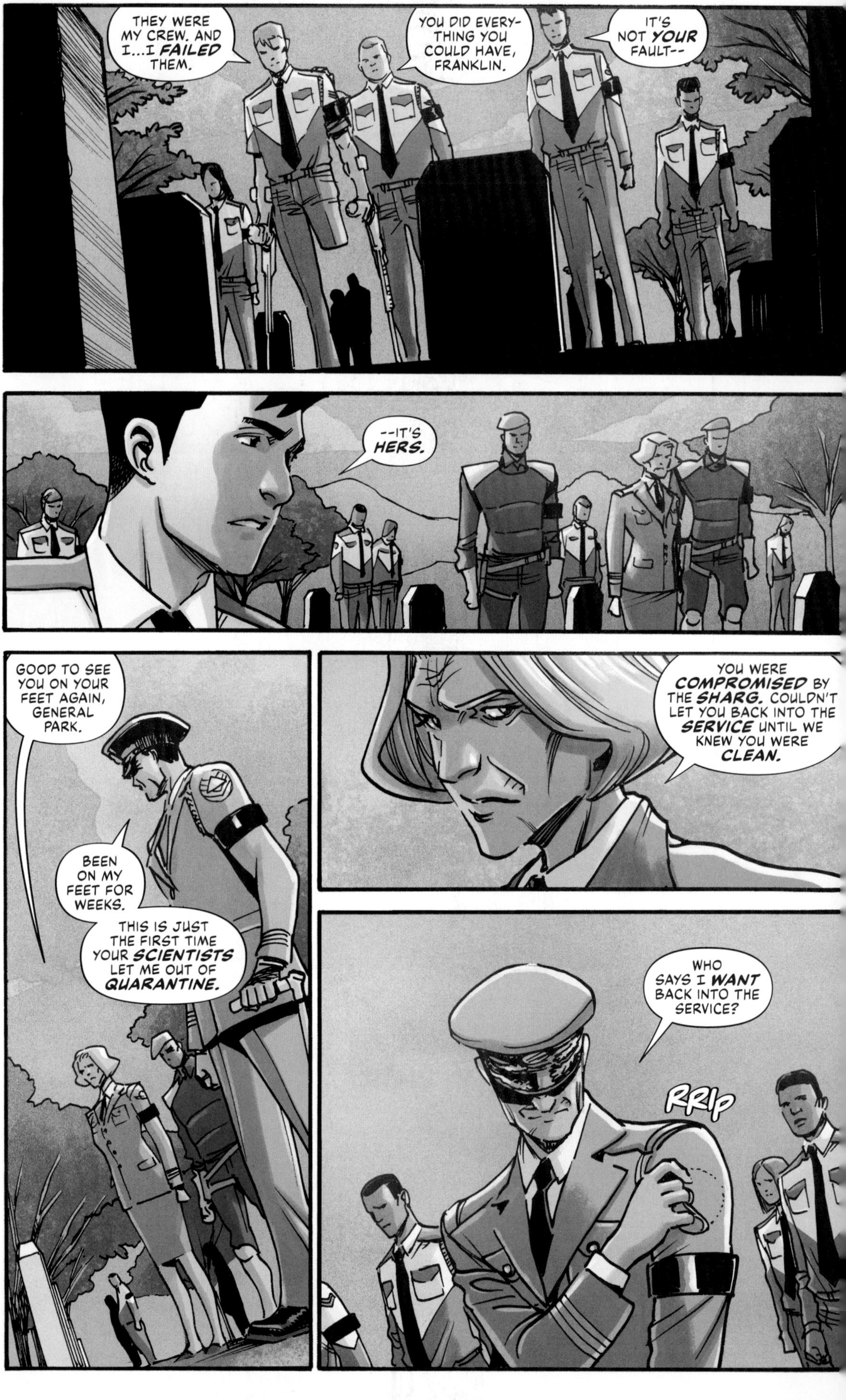
THEY WERE MY CREW. AND I...I FAILED THEM.
YOU DID EVERYTHING YOU COULD HAVE, FRANKLIN.
IT'S NOT YOUR FAULT--
--IT'S HERS.
GOOD TO SEE YOU ON YOUR FEET AGAIN, GENERAL PARK.
BEEN ON MY FEET FOR WEEKS.
THIS IS JUST THE FIRST TIME YOUR SCIENTISTS LET ME OUT OF QUARANTINE.
YOU WERE COMPROMISED BY THE SHARG. COULDN'T LET YOU BACK INTO THE SERVICE UNTIL WE KNEW YOU WERE CLEAN.
WHO SAYS I WANT BACK INTO THE SERVICE?
RRIP

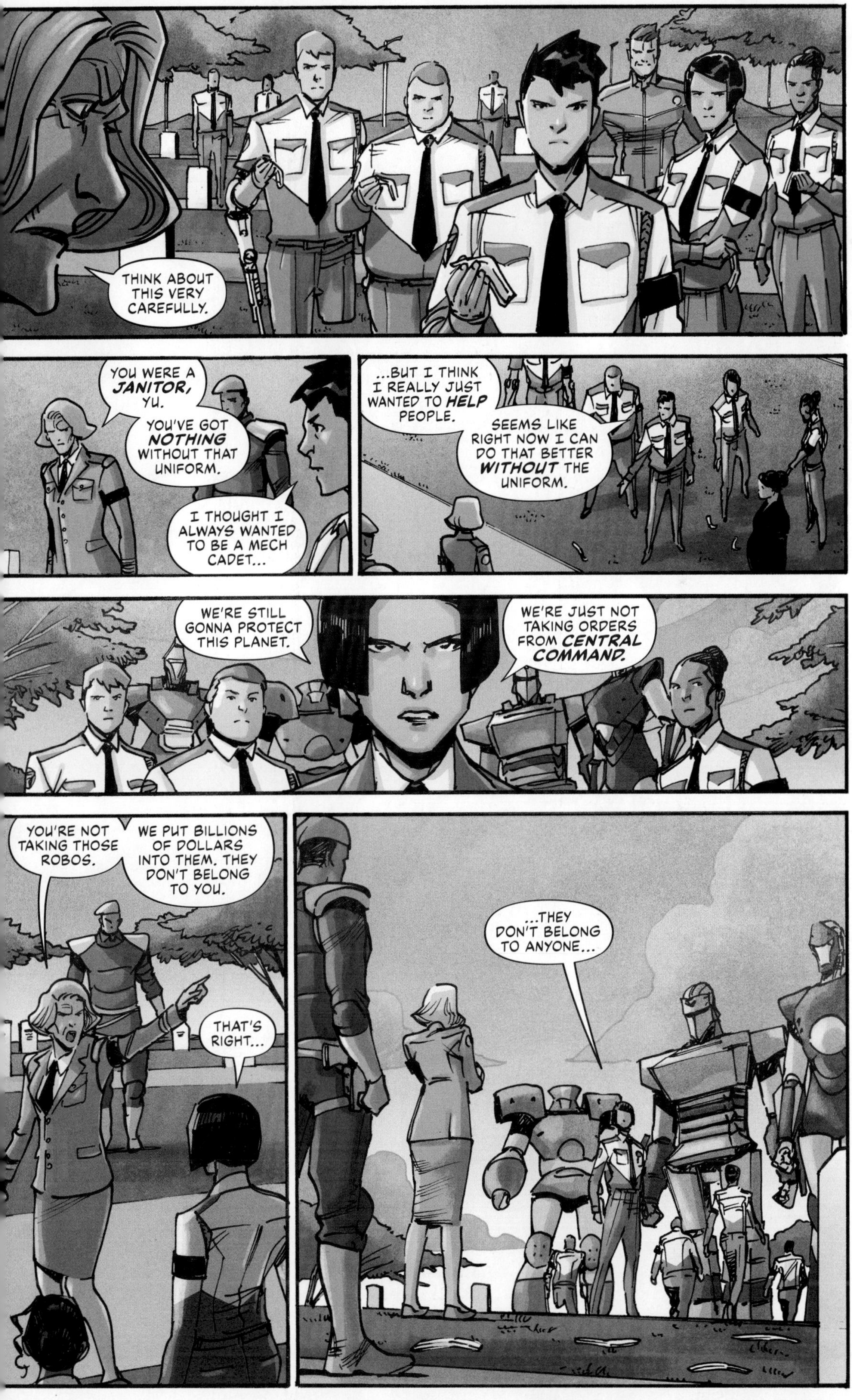
THINK ABOUT THIS VERY CAREFULLY.
YOU WERE A *JANITOR,* YU.
YOU'VE GOT *NOTHING* WITHOUT THAT UNIFORM.
I THOUGHT I ALWAYS WANTED TO BE A MECH CADET...
...BUT I THINK I REALLY JUST WANTED TO *HELP* PEOPLE.
SEEMS LIKE RIGHT NOW I CAN DO THAT BETTER *WITHOUT* THE UNIFORM.
WE'RE STILL GONNA PROTECT THIS PLANET.
WE'RE JUST NOT TAKING ORDERS FROM *CENTRAL COMMAND.*
YOU'RE NOT TAKING THOSE ROBOS.
WE PUT BILLIONS OF DOLLARS INTO THEM. THEY DON'T BELONG TO YOU.
THAT'S RIGHT...
...THEY DON'T BELONG TO ANYONE...

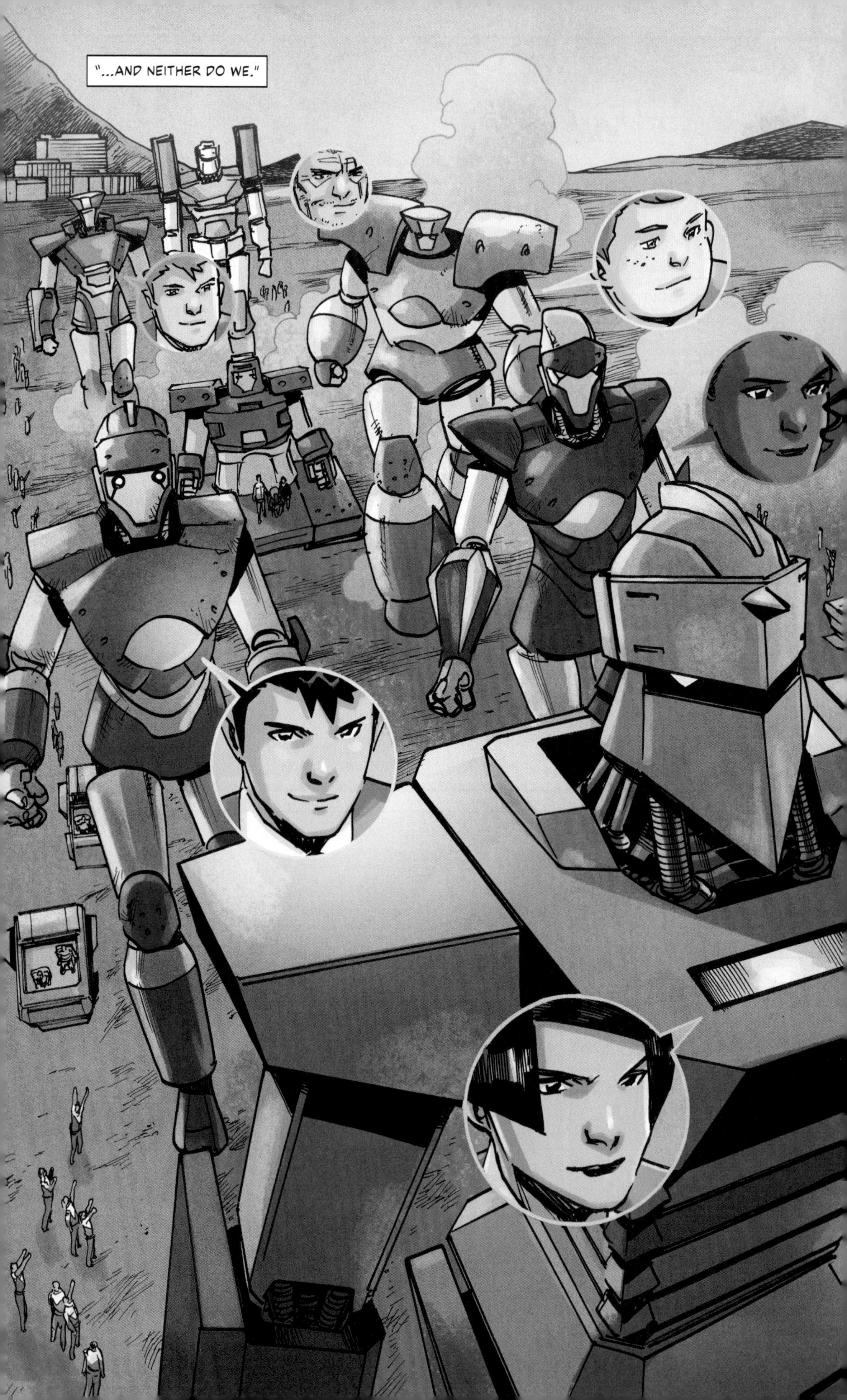
"...AND NEITHER DO WE."

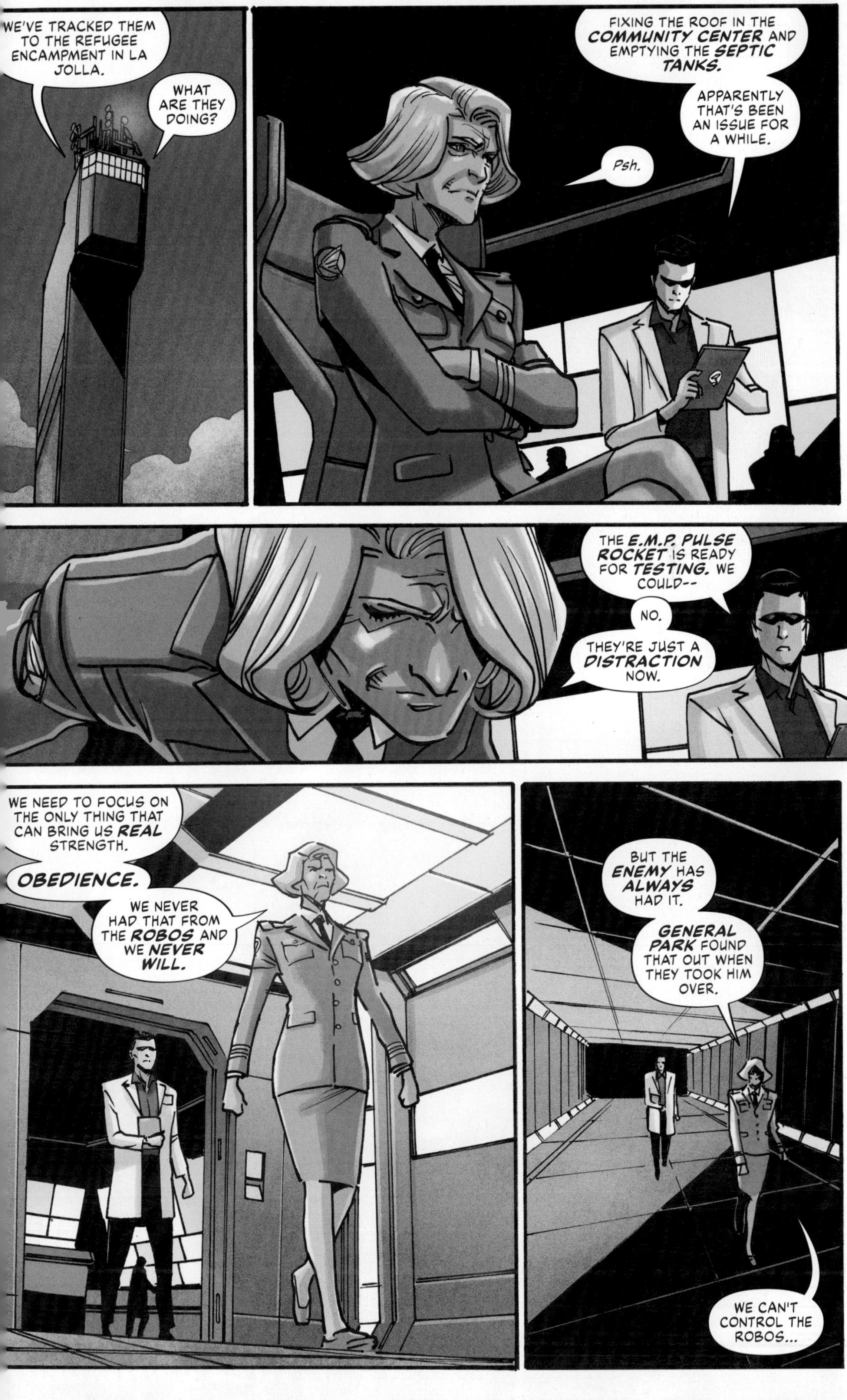
WE'VE TRACKED THEM TO THE REFUGEE ENCAMPMENT IN LA JOLLA.
WHAT ARE THEY DOING?
FIXING THE ROOF IN THE COMMUNITY CENTER AND EMPTYING THE SEPTIC TANKS.
APPARENTLY THAT'S BEEN AN ISSUE FOR A WHILE.
Psh.
THE E.M.P. PULSE ROCKET IS READY FOR TESTING. WE COULD--
NO.
THEY'RE JUST A DISTRACTION NOW.
WE NEED TO FOCUS ON THE ONLY THING THAT CAN BRING US REAL STRENGTH.
OBEDIENCE.
WE NEVER HAD THAT FROM THE ROBOS AND WE NEVER WILL.
BUT THE ENEMY HAS ALWAYS HAD IT.
GENERAL PARK FOUND THAT OUT WHEN THEY TOOK HIM OVER.
WE CAN'T CONTROL THE ROBOS...

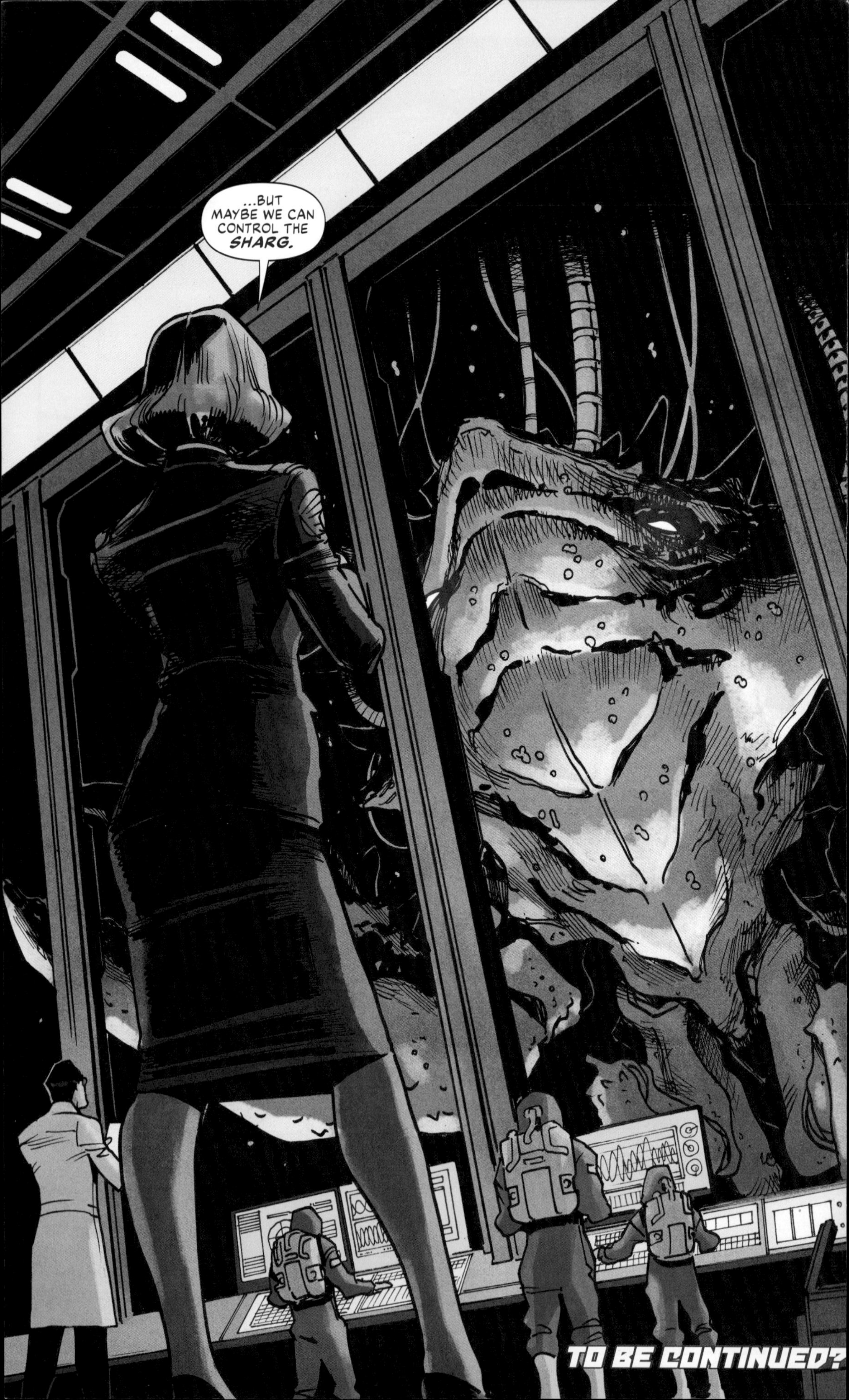
...BUT MAYBE WE CAN CONTROL THE SHARG.
TO BE CONTINUED?

COVER **GALLERY**

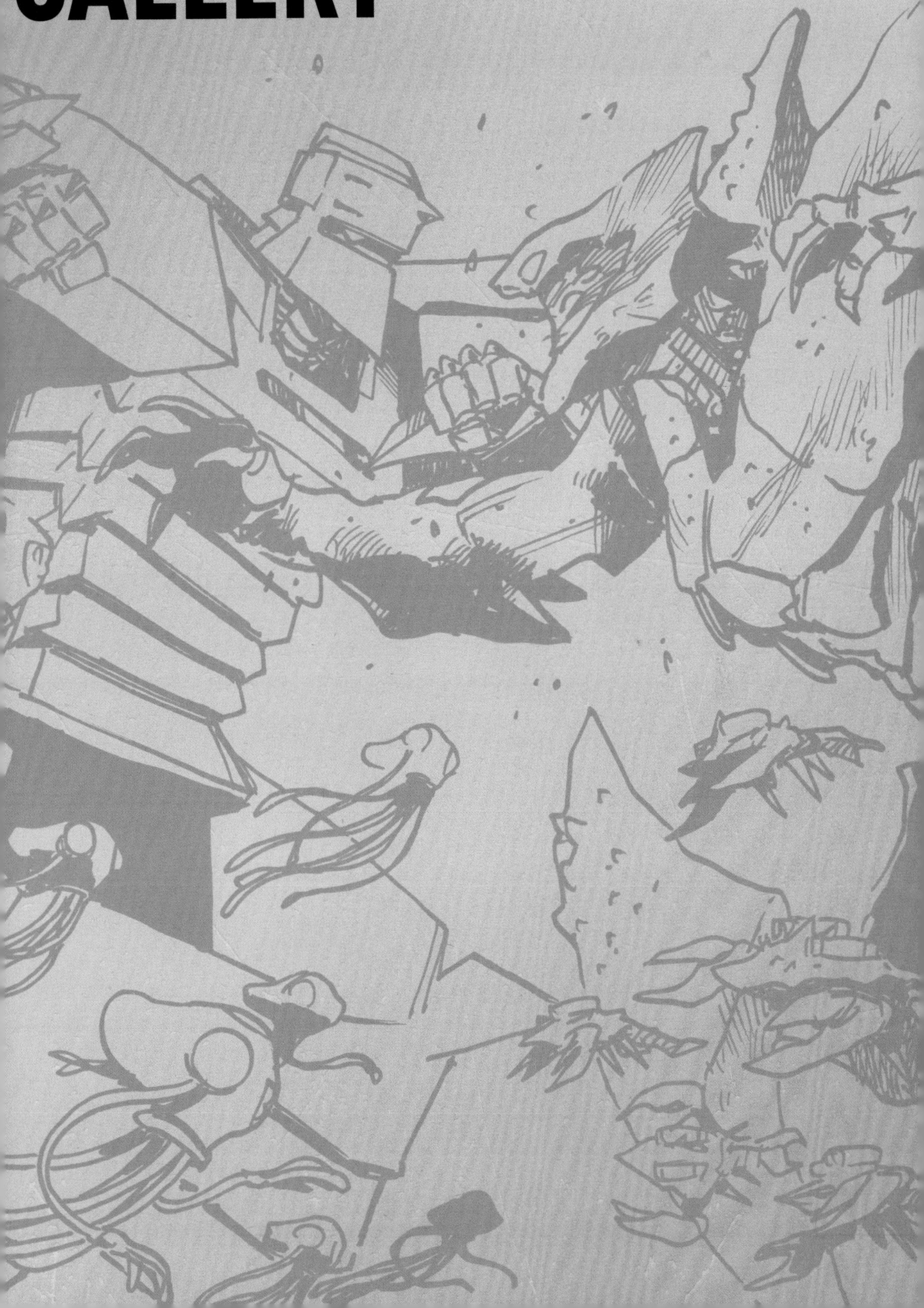

Mech Cadets #1 Variant Cover by **SONNY LIEW**

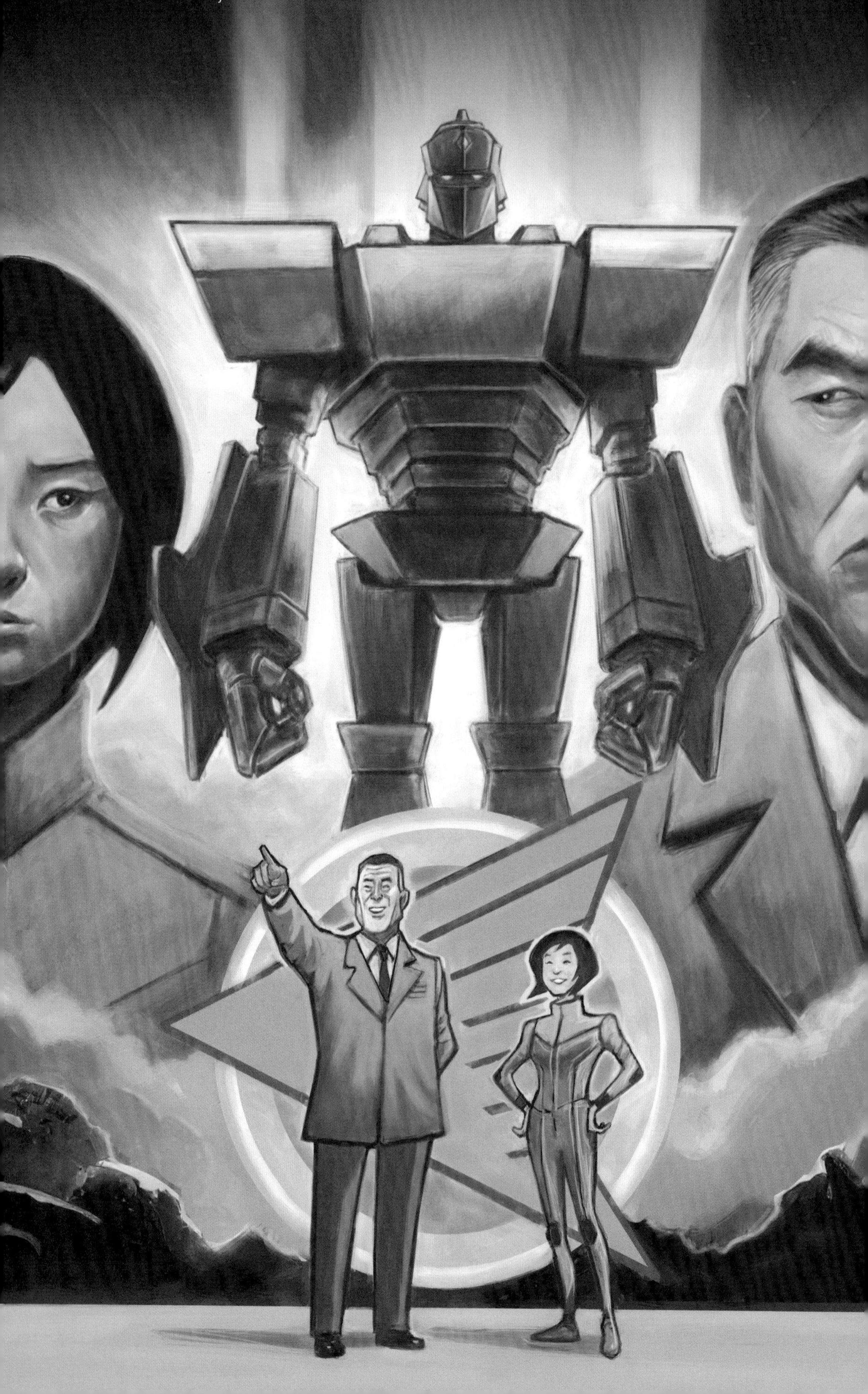

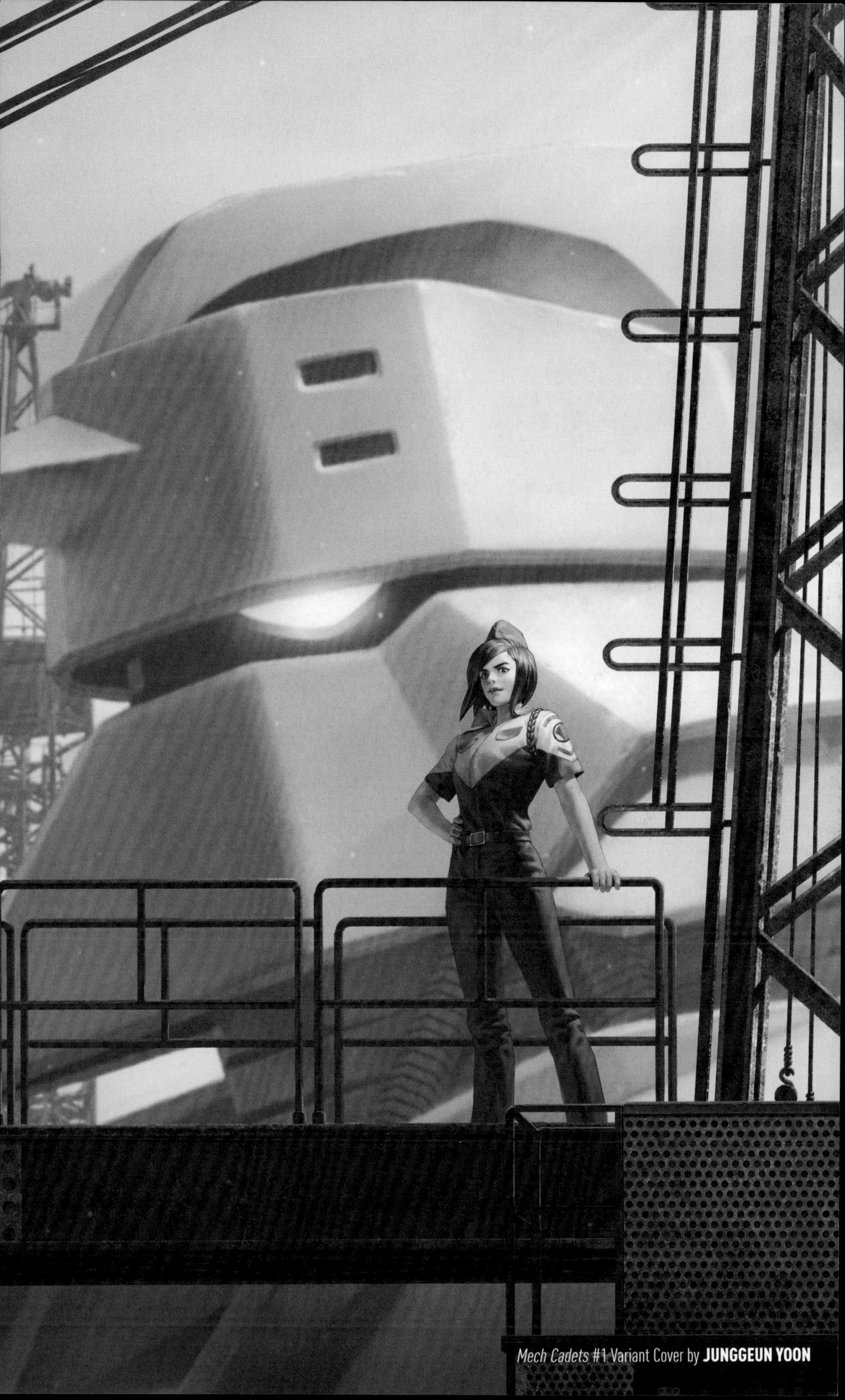

Mech Cadets #1 Variant Cover by **JUNGGEUN YOON**

Mech Cadets #2 Variant Cover by **QISTINA KHALIDAH**

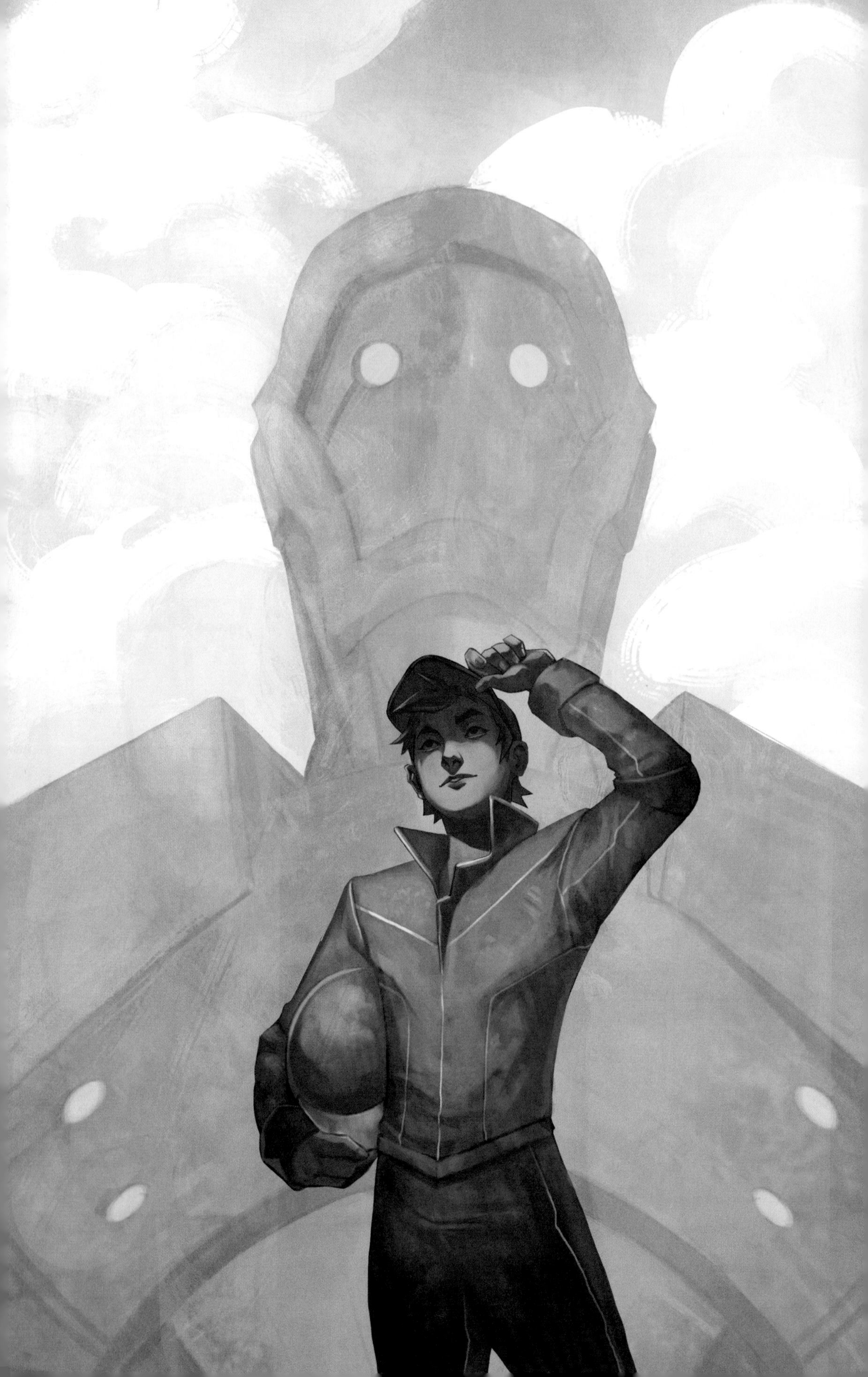

Mech Cadets #3 Variant Cover by **SONNY LIEW**

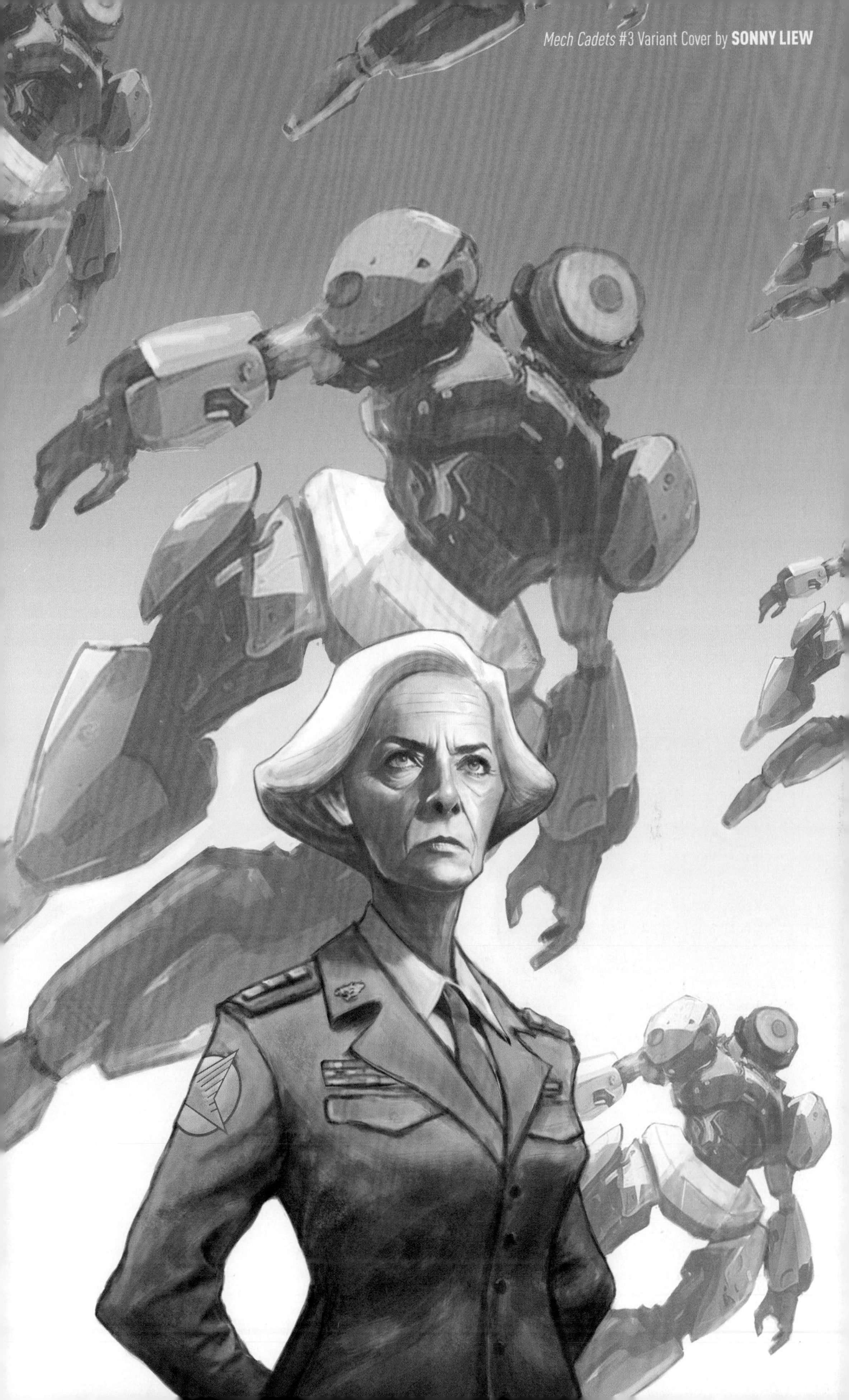

Mech Cadets #3 Variant Cover by **MIGUEL MERCADO**

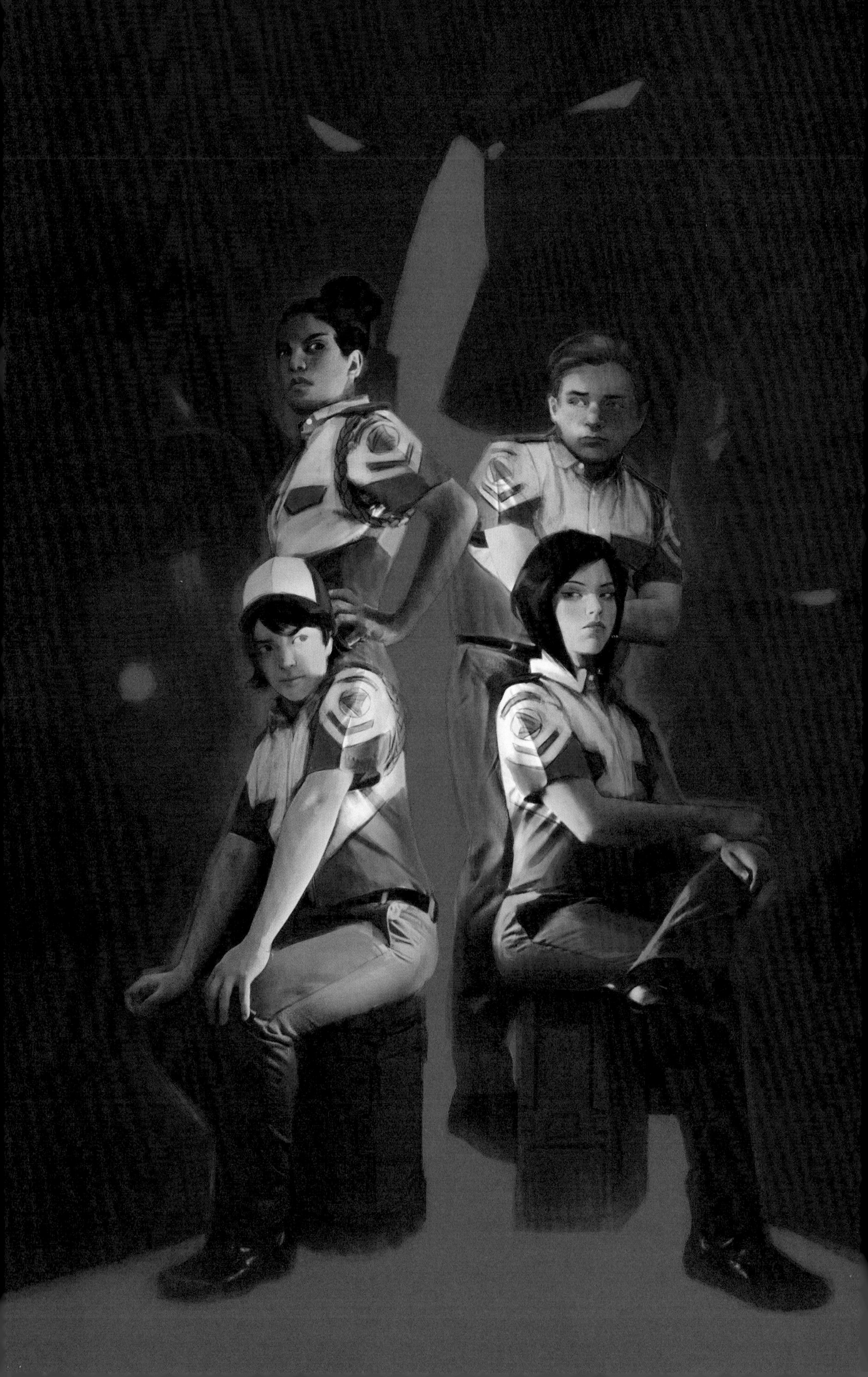

Mech Cadets #4 Variant Cover by **KEI ZAMA** with colors by **JOSH BURCHAM**

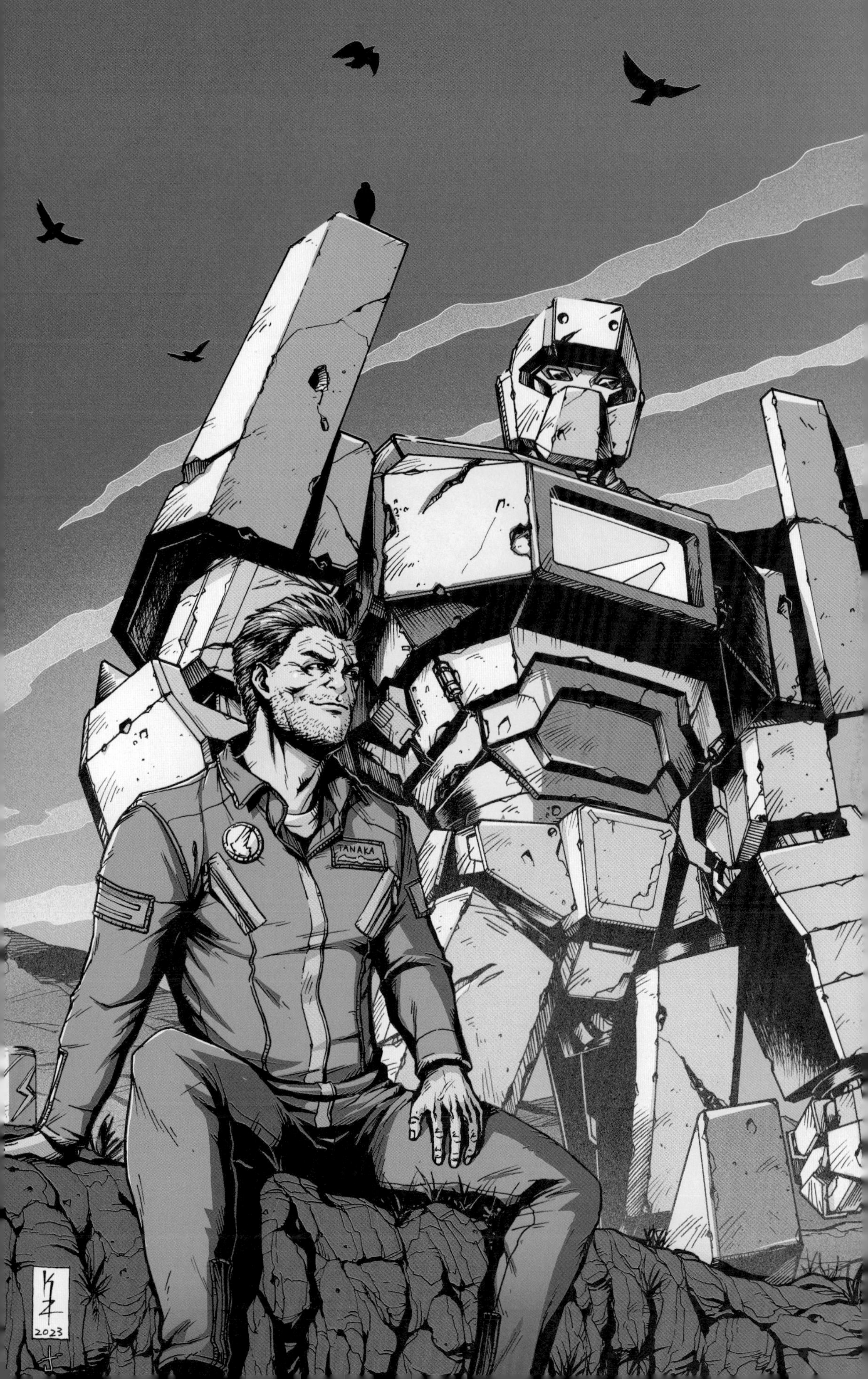

Mech Cadets #5 Variant Cover by **SONNY LIEW**

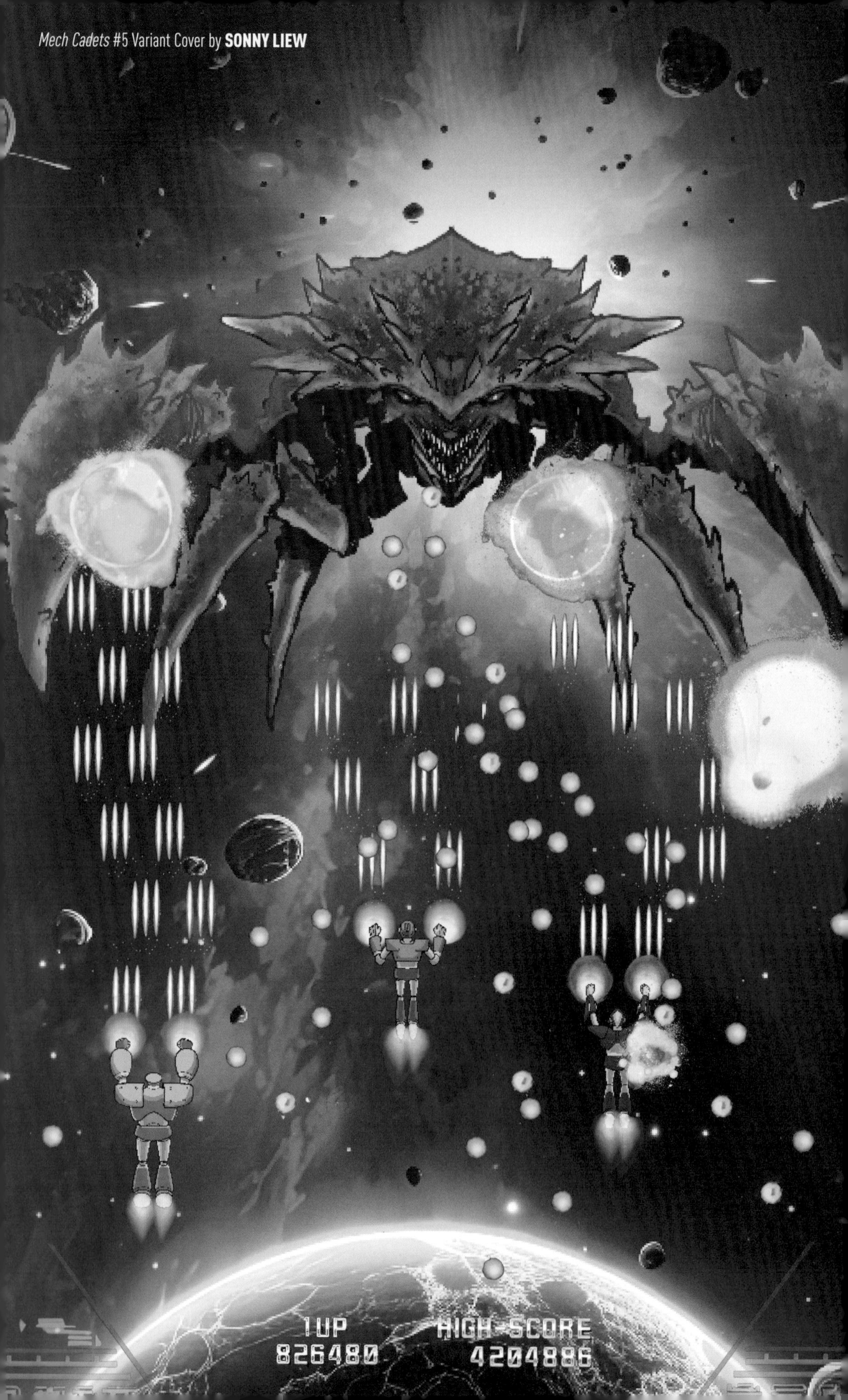
1UP
826480
HIGH-SCORE
4204886

Mech Cadets #4 Variant Cover by **TRUNG LÊ NGUYỄN**

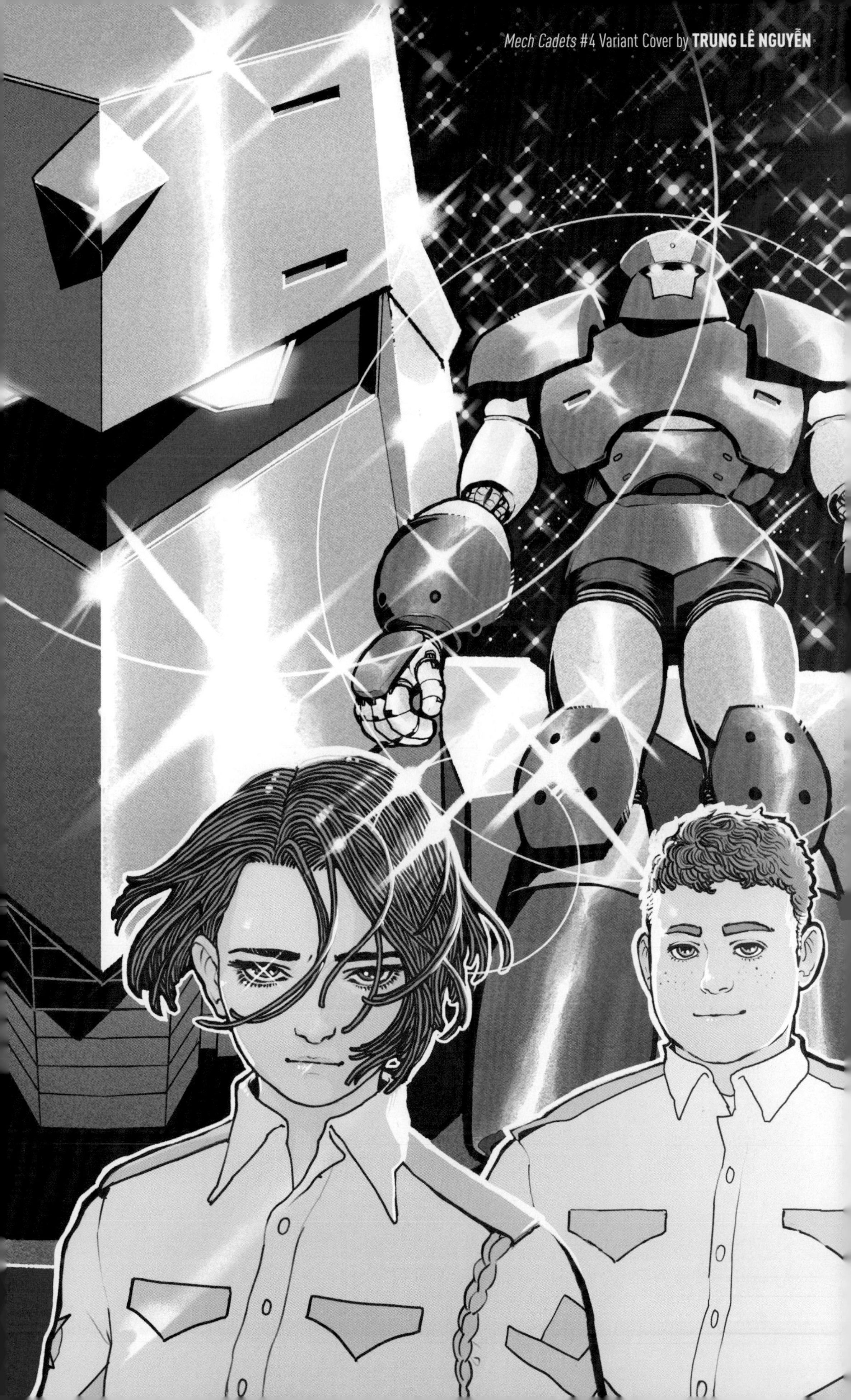

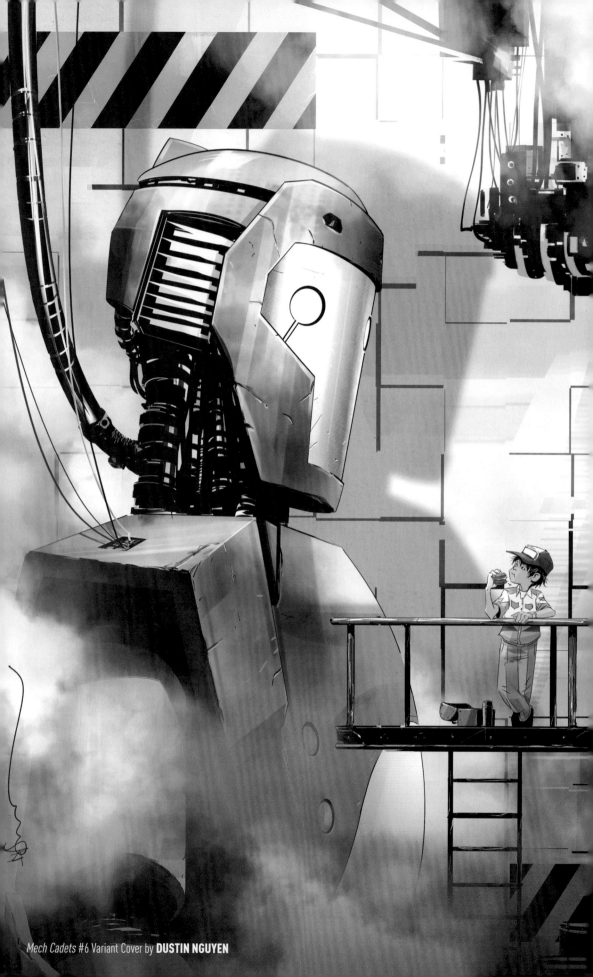

Mech Cadets #6 Variant Cover by **DUSTIN NGUYEN**

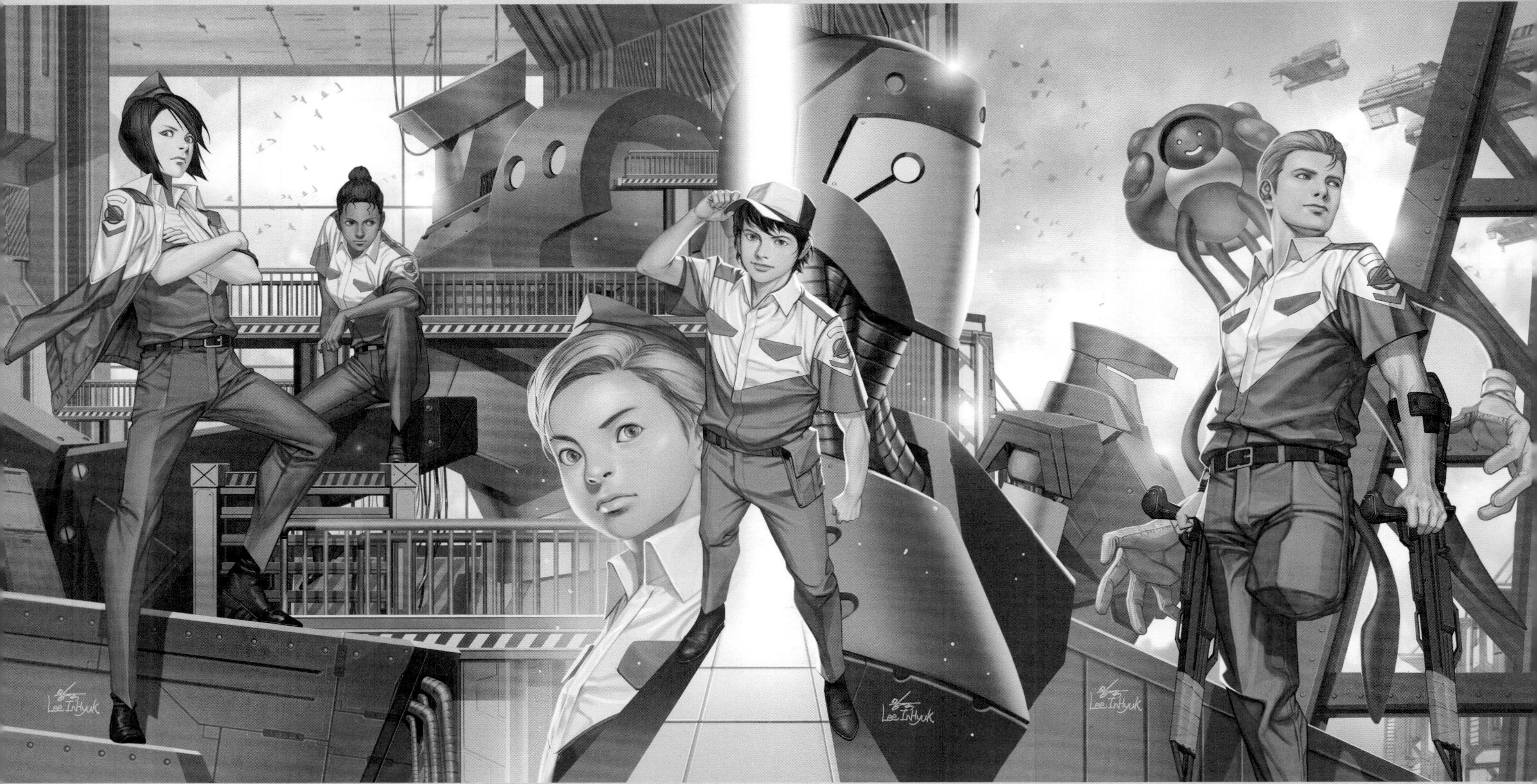
Lee InHyuk
Lee InHyuk
Lee InHyuk

Mech Cadets #2, #4, #6 Connecting Variant Covers by **InHYUK LEE**

DISCOVER NEW WORLDS WITH

KaBOOM!

PAK MIYAZAWA FARRELL KHOLINNE ANGULO
MECH CADETS
NETFLIX
A NETFLIX SERIES

LARSEN
ORCS!
THE CURSE
"ORCS!: The Curse is getting really ridiculous, but in a very good way." –ComicBook.com

Sam Davies
HexVet
Witches in Training

New York Times Bestselling Author
R.L. STINE
JUST BEYOND
IRENE FLORES & JOANA LAFUENTE
HORROR
Disney+ ORIGINAL SERIES
MONSTROSITY

nickelodeon
GARFIELD
Full Course
VOLUME ONE

Mech Cadets
Greg Pak, Takeshi Miyazawa
Book One
ISBN: 978-1-68415-917-8 | $24.99 US

ORCS!
Christine Larsen
ISBN: 978-1-68415-671-9 | $14.99 US
ORCS! The Curse
ISBN: 978-1-68415-890-4 | $16.99 US

Hex Vets
Sam Davies
Hex Vets: Witches in Training
ISBN: 978-1-68415-288-9 | $8.99 US
Hex Vet: The Flying Surgery
ISBN: 978-1-68415-478-4 | $9.99 US

Just Beyond
R.L. Stine, Kelly & Nichole Matthews
Just Beyond: The Scare School
ISBN: 978-1-68415-416-6 | $9.99 US
Just Beyond: The Horror at Happy Landings
ISBN: 978-1-68415-547-7 | $9.99 US
Just Beyond: Welcome to Beast Island
ISBN: 978-1-68415-697-9 | $10.99 US

R.L. Stine, Irene Flores
Just Beyond: Monstrosity
ISBN: 978-1-68415-697-9 | $10.99 US

Garfield: Full Course
Jim Davis, Mark Evanier, Scott Nickel
Volume 1
ISBN: 978-1-60886-128-6 | $16.99 US
Volume 1 45th Anniversary Edition
ISBN: 978-1-60886-129-3 | $16.99 US

kaboom!™

AVAILABLE AT YOUR LOCAL COMICS SHOP AND BOOKSTORE

WWW.**BOOM-STUDIOS**.COM